A MIDNIGHT MEETING

He turned into the rose garden, heavy with the scent of blossoms at their peak. And then he was at the lily pond. The flowers were closed tight, black candle flames against the still water reflecting the stars. And, on the marble bench placed where one could enjoy the most pleasing prospect, Circe come to lure him to something, though heaven alone knew what that something might be.

"I see you couldn't sleep either," he said by way of announcing his presence.

The light wrapper did indeed give her the look of a sprite out of the Greek myths as she turned and rose, backing slightly from him, eyes startled; a dryad, perhaps, or a nymph caught dreaming where she shouldn't be.

"Stephen?" she said, doubt in her tone.

"None other. Disturbed to see me here?"

"Surprised rather."

He took a step toward her. She backed two. "What's the matter—afraid of me? Because there was a time when y'wouldn't've been."

"People change."

He took another step. This time she stood her ground, a touch of defiance in the set of her shoulders and the tilt of her head. That pleased him for some unaccountable reason.

"You have nothing to fear from me," he whispered, believing he meant every word.

And then whether it was their state of undress, or the starlight, or the scent of roses—whatever the cause, he knew she couldn't trust him at all, any more than he could trust himself . . .

WATCH FOR THESE REGENCY ROMANCES

THE COLONEL'S COURTSHIP

Monique Ellis

Zebra Books
Kensington Publishing Corp.

http://www.zebrabooks.com

For Andy
With my love, admiration and congratulations:

Sometimes the longer road is the surer one.

Chapter One

"It's hardly changed at all," thirty-six-year-old Stephen Gracechurch, late of the Army of Occupation, murmured as he gazed about him, pulling his dusty bay gelding to a halt at the top of a gentle rise. "Easy, Iago, steady lad."

Home. After nine grueling, eventful, bloody years.

Before him stretched the gentle hills, the copses, the pocket-handkerchief farms of his childhood and youth, kissed by the sun of a fine late June afternoon. Bees hummed in hedgerows. Birds whose names he'd never bothered to learn made busy work of foraging for their young. Far above a hawk wheeled in a sky so clear, so blue it was almost painful, making his narrowed eyes sting with its brightness.

"No, sir," Gracechurch's former batman and current valet rasped obediently at his side. "Barely changed, it has."

"How would you know, Scully?" Gracechurch shifted in his scarred saddle, the corners of his lips twitching. "You've never seen Chipham Common."

"Why should it change, Colonel? Places don't, it's been my experience, 'less there's fighting about. There's been no fighting these parts in dunamany years. It's people as does the changing. Y'won't be seeing burned-out farms here, nor yet houses turned to rubble by a bunch of frogs."

"Right as always, Scully."

People and change. It was as if a cloud had come between sun and earth, blighting the lush countryside with the stain of winter. Yes, people changed. There were two parts to this homecoming Gracechurch dreaded. The less painful would be visiting his father's grave and offering his mother what comfort he could. Well, he'd faced the frogs at Waterloo and in the Peninsula before that and never flinched. He was damned if he'd flinch this time, either.

Strange though—how familiar haunts opened wounds one would've thought completely healed. He hadn't thought of her or the spring of '09 in years. At least he didn't believe he had. Betrayal was betrayal, whether on a battlefield or in a drawing room. The wounds were as deep and as mortal.

Head high, broad shoulders squared, back ramrod straight, craggy features schooled to neutrality, Gracechurch loosened the reins.

"Might as well get on with it," he said.

The lane curved down the hill, rutted by winter storms and gullied by spring rains, twisting past trees too venerable to fell and rocks too massive to move, just as it always had. Yes, the trees were the same, though one old hawthorn was missing and a stand of slender beech of which he'd been particularly fond had grown awkwardly thick-trunked and scarred during those nine long years, lithe youth giving way to sturdy maturity.

He passed the village church where his father had held benevolent sway for as long as he could remember. A new vicar reigned there now, a pleasant fellow according to his mother's letters, devoted to his country parish and its simple parishioners, and no more interested in toadying those from the few great houses than his father had been.

Other boys played in the vicarage garden now, fished in the stream at its base and climbed its chestnut tree. He could hear them, voices ringing in play. The kitchen garden, visible from the lane, was flourishing, but the new vicar's wife either lacked his mother's touch with flowers or else had no interest in them. A pity.

Very carefully Gracechurch kept his eyes turned from the little churchyard with its weathered stones dating from before the Conquest, a new mound backed by ancient yews scarcely softened by tender grass, its stone raw and pale. He'd come later, perhaps in the fading evening light, to pay his respects. He'd already made his despairing farewells in March, standing dry-eyed with his mother's letter crumpled in his hand, staring at the Seine's smooth reflection of the great pile that was Notre Dame. Some sorrows went too deep for tears or complaint.

Houses and cottages, scattered at first, drew together, organizing themselves in neat clumps separated by vegetable plots. The few shops had changed neither in location nor type, their signs perhaps a touch more weathered, their boards with an extra crack or two. The inn sprawled ahead, its outbuildings hunkering under a stand of ancient oaks, its yard bustling, the usual geraniums in the usual boxes flaming beneath open windows through which coarse muslin curtains flapped in the breeze.

He scowled as they waited for a pair of ragamuffins wielding willow switches to guide a flock of hissing geese across the lane to the fine feeding in the village pond. Now that he was here, he wanted the beginning over and done with.

Selling out had been an automatic decision. His special sort of services were no longer required by King or country or, more importantly, His Grace of Wellington. No more bullion to be smuggled through Pyrenean passes so ragged troops could be paid. No more murdering traitors to be caught. No more enemy encampments to be infiltrated. No more munitions shipments to be sabotaged. No more urgent messages and yet more urgent orders to be carried from one allied unit to another, most times in the garb of a peasant.

And he'd quietly made his fortune, thanks to the friendship and good offices of Nathan Rothschild. The great Waterloo coup had had a very minor and very grateful beneficiary. Impoverished vicar's son was returning wealthy former officer though no one would know it to look at him, which was just how he wanted it for now. It was time to cultivate his garden once he had one, and his nursery after he'd provided himself with a suitable wife—one who would want him for himself if that was possible, rather than his deep pockets and his friendship with those who made history as easily as they breathed, and spoke with kings and princes as equals.

No, he presented the appearance of precisely what he'd been nine long years ago: a rough military man with a fair education thanks to his father, little to recommend him beyond a talent for commanding men, a phiz that was more stern than welcoming after all those years of war, and not two shillings to rub together beyond what little he'd saved from his pay.

"Cozy place," Scully said at his side. "Sort one dreamed about at Corunna and prayed one'd see again if one survived Waterloo, but never believed one would."

Gracechurch swung around in the saddle, thought a moment, nodded. "Yes, it is that, Scully, though it has its more unpleasant types, just as France did. Wouldn't know it to glance about, but the little worlds mirror the great, human nature being what it is. There're as many here willing to fleece a neighbor or rob him of his birthright—or cut him dead—as you'd find anywhere. Only the scale differs."

"Y'don't like Chipham Common, Colonel, then why'd you come back? And speak of nothing else long as I've known you? There's a whole world out there as welcoming as it looks."

"My mother. This's always been her home."

"You could find a soft billet any place you wanted these days," Scully insisted, "including London, and cut a dash while you were at it."

"It's always been mine as well. I won't be chased off this time, though I don't doubt there'll be those who'll do their best to find a suitable rail and a pot of tar, at least at first. Later?" The former officer chuckled bitterly. "Later I shall have the pleasure of chasing them off. Pounds talk, always have, always will, with certain sorts."

"Sounds like you've chosen the roughest ground and the worst nag to take you over it. Ain't smart, to my thinking. Haven't questioned your games before, but this is different. You'd best think again, Colonel. We can be back in Town in less than—"

"Ah, but in London I shouldn't have the immense pleasure of watching those who turned up their noses at me before come courting me now—after first trying to rid themselves of my noxious presence because they don't realize my financial condition has changed a little for the better over the last nine years."

"Wondered why you wouldn't dress decent when y'left his

grace's place nor yet travel in that new carriage of yours, and left our real togs behind with Mrs. Rothschild."

"Now you know. Wasn't any need for it until we got here. You'll keep your mummer shut regarding my change in fortune or I'll turn you off, old friend, no matter what we've been through together or how many times you saved my hide in the past. I'm about to begin my most unpleasant and desperate campaign. While there's no question I'll win in the end, there're a few I want biting their knuckles and gnashing their teeth by the time I'm done."

"I don't like it," Scully grumbled. "This ain't like you—not in any way. Y'may be a hard man, but you've always been a fair one."

"Doesn't matter whether you like it or not. I'm the former colonel, you the former sergeant, I pay your wages, and you'll do as I say or suffer the consequences," Gracechurch snapped, blue-gray eyes turning to steel beneath hooded brows. "Don't worry: the justice I seek will be fine-honed and infinitely fair, but I'll have my pound of groveling before I'm done, and my bucket of tears."

"Yes sir, Colonel, sir. Whatever you say, sir, just so's it not you spills 'em. Isn't as if I've got more'n fluff in my cockloft, nor yet as if you've ever asked my advice before, Colonel, sir, when you'd a problem to solve and wanted to do it efficient-like. I'm naught but a paltry fellow, and not the least clever—we both know that, sir. A fool, sir, as you said when you took me on after Vitoria robbed me of being able to much more'n hobble about."

"Stubble it, Scully."

"Oh, yes, sir. Absolutely, sir. I'll stubble it, sir, don't you worry."

"And no more of your black looks either, you old reprobate," Gracechurch said more mildly. "I've no need of an extra conscience, my own being of sufficient vigor to see me through this without permitting me to overstep a gentleman's course."

"Nor no more looks either, sir. I promise, sir. If need be, I'll find me a sawbones to put out my daylights and sew my mummer up tight, Colonel. That should about satisfy you, temper you're in."

Gracechurch snorted. Scully would never change, which

was why he'd kept the man with him when he'd sold out. Just as well. Everyone needed one friend who never permitted one to ride a high horse, no matter how determinedly one insisted on indulging in the exercise. Most times Scully saw to it he rode a stubby Shetland pony—figuratively at least.

The geese had waddled across the lane at last, nipping the ankles of any who lingered too long in their vicinity and leaving rich white deposits in the powdery dust. Gracechurch guided his mount into the Tipsy Parson's yard at the echo of an approaching post horn.

How he'd loved to watch the stage barrel in as a boy, the coachman bellowing for a tankard of the inn's best. He grimaced as a dilapidated conveyance lumbered down the hill they'd just descended, brakes squealing against wheels, dust puffing from beneath the lathered team's hooves like smoke from a cannon's mouth. The Royal Mail came no nearer than Little Stoking, five miles to the south. Only the most unprepossessing coaches passed through Chipham Common, and yet children still turned to watch in awe just as he had in those golden days before the great world intruded, not realizing the banality of the passengers and destinations.

Yes, things changed, and not just people. Inevitably one's perceptions changed as well, jaundiced by experience. The romance of travel, the lure of exotic names held no fascination for him now. One place was, after years of learning just what lay behind all those names, much the same as another.

As for the eager young lieutenant he'd been when he departed following his last leave, that fellow'd been killed in October of 1810 just after Bussaco as surely as if he'd been felled by saber or ball, for all it was merely a few lines in a letter from his mother that'd done the job. A different man had returned, but that man had an obligation to the youth he'd been. Gracechurch was one who always met his obligations, no matter how unpleasant or onerous.

"Any news of the colonel?" fifteen-year-old Cassie Hodges demanded after giving the plump, gray-haired vicar's widow a schoolgirl's hug and receiving one equally warm, if slightly more restrained, in return. "And no, I shan't hush, Suzanne. It's only polite to ask, and as you never do it's left to me."

Cassie folded her coltish limbs into the nearest chair without waiting to be invited, removed her boot and retrieved a sharp pebble which she tossed in the fireplace. "Tiresome thing. I thought it'd cut me to ribbons, but it's only my stocking is ruined, thank goodness. Has he left France yet, Mrs. Gracechurch," she asked, glancing up as she impatiently whisked wisps of light brown hair from her eyes, "or is he still in Paris?"

"Stephen's last letter indicated we should see him within the month."

"What a deal of delay. One would think he'd be as anxious to join you as you are to have him home. Nine years, after all. I'll never believe he couldn't've found a moment to visit during all that time. It's not as if he were Wellington, after all, and even *he* managed a quick trip to England on occasion."

"Cassandra, please," Suzanne Phelps pleaded distractedly as she set a pair of heavily-laden baskets on a bench by the parlor door and gracefully extended her hands to her hostess. "One would think you'd been raised in a stable—Mrs. Gracechurch, how have you been keeping?"

"Oh, horses're far better-mannered than I," Cassie returned with a grin as the two ladies murmured greetings to which neither was paying much attention. "Have to be, or they'd be sent to the knackers. I, on the other hand, will never be sent to the knackers no matter what my faults or my lack of desirable points. As for proprieties, Suzanne, look to your own words. Running sentences together as you just did, you've offered poor Mrs. Gracechurch the most dreadful insult. Quite unmerited it was, too."

"I—what—oh, my goodness." Suzanne Phelps glanced from her younger sister to Matilda Gracechurch, her delicate features flushing as she set aside her sunshade and removed her bonnet.

"Precisely," Cassie crowed.

"I never meant—oh, dear. You know perfectly well what I meant and whom, Cassie. Do forgive my misspeaking so, Mrs. Gracechurch. I wouldn't for the world imply—"

"Of course I know you meant me, and so does Mrs. Gracechurch, but it's such fun to see you color up like that.

Then your complexion clashes with those hideous grayed lavender gowns you insist on wearing for all Sir John's been planted these five years and more. Blushing makes you look years younger, Suzanne."

"Never you mind your sister, my lady," the vicar's widow dimpled after a conspiratorial glance at Cassie. "She's a caution, but there isn't an ounce of meanness to her, and you could do with a bit of teasing on occasion, I believe. As for your wearing half-mourning, she's correct. Not in the least necessary, as both your mama-in-law and I have told you time out of mind. At your age, and for a husband so many years your senior he could've been your grandpapa? Ridiculous."

"I'm comfortable as I am," Suzanne murmured at the reopening of the old argument—a goal Cassie and Mrs. Gracechurch achieved each time they called. "I never was one to follow fashion."

"There's a deal of difference between being fashion's slave and ignoring it entirely. Far be it for me to criticize, but I often wonder what reason your stepson may have in encouraging you in the practice. Now, just you join Cassie and make yourself at home while I take these baskets to Mags, and then we'll have our tea and a comfortable coze. Were you aware Sally Parkins was brought to bed of twins last night?"

"I'm not crippled, for all it was a very sharp pebble," Cassie interrupted, bouncing to her feet, "and I know where the kitchen is almost as well as you do, Mrs. Gracechurch. Maybe Mags has some lemonade. I'll warrant she does, for we brought you ever so many lemons last time, and she knows I do love lemonade on a hot day, and I'm positively parched. Besides, I want to give her strictest orders you're not to be permitted to give away anything we brought this time.

"There's far more than just for our tea, you see: a brace of ducks and a goose, and a ham, and all sorts of fruits and vegetables—even some asparagus—and some wine, and a seed cake, and macaroons and a bottle of madeira and another of brandy, and I don't know what all."

"Mercy. And how do you expect us to consume all that? There's only Mags and me at the moment. What would we want with such things as brandy or wine?"

"The ducks and the goose're still alive—you can hear them moving in the baskets I left in the hall. They were squabbling until just before we arrived. The looks we received coming through the village! The ham'll keep. Soon or late the colonel will arrive, and you'll need more than usual."

"Cassie, please don't run on like a fiddlestick," Suzanne murmured.

"Well, that's what you said when I asked why we were bringing so much this time." Cassie whirled back to Mrs. Gracechurch. "And Suzanne's quite as put out as I am at your constantly giving most of what we bring to the first to arrive on your doorstep with a tale of woe. Why, I believe the entire village watches for us to leave in anticipation of what they can cadge from you."

"It's not quite so bad as that," Matilda Gracechurch protested, coloring in her turn, "but it always seems there's one or two in greater need than I."

"Then let them apply to Suzanne in person. Better yet, let them apply to my respected brother-in-law, or stepbrother, or whatever he is. Oren'll send them on their way quick enough if there's no truth to their tale—which I'll warrant there isn't half the time, it never being those in true need who turn to you, knowing you've problems of your own and yet would beggar yourself to assist them. It's the lazy and the greedy who come importuning you, and so Suzanne herself's said time out of mind, and Mother India too. Suzanne's fortunate in her mama-in-law, if in no one else in that family. Well, there's Emeline, of course. She's positively wonderful, but she and Mr. Dight're almost never here, living two days to the north as they do and with their own lives to lead and interests to keep them occupied."

"Cassie!" Suzanne pleaded. "Please, my love."

"Do please convince Suzanne there's no need for her to lecture after we leave," Cassie said, picking up two of the baskets and turning toward the back of the small cottage. "Otherwise she'll give me the most dreadful scold for mortifying you and embarrassing her, and I already receive a superfluity of bear-garden jaws from Suzanne's *delightful* stepdaughters on a daily basis. Prunes and prisms aren't *her* natural bent, for all they're doing their best to turn her into just such another as they. Two's enough in any household. Indeed, two is two too many."

Cassie gave Mrs. Gracechurch a minxish wink with her

offside eye and headed for the kitchen attached to the back
of the little stone cottage by a breezeway.

"I don't know what I shall do with that child," Suzanne
sighed, sinking into a chair flanking the gate-leg table beneath
parlor windows open to the warm summer breeze. "She
becomes more impossible with each passing day."

"It's merely a time she has to go through," Matilda
Gracechurch chuckled, taking her customary place across
from Suzanne and retrieving some mending from a basket at
her feet. "She'll survive, and so shall you," she said, needle
flying as she set tiny stitches to a rent in a child's dress.
"If you have doubts, ask your mama-in-law. Most girls suffer
something similar, unless they go the route of your younger
stepdaughters. Which problem would you prefer?"

"Oh, this one, naturally." Without asking, Suzanne
removed her lace mitts and retrieved a boy's shirt with a torn
sleeve along with thread and needle from the charity box
mending delivered weekly to Mrs. Gracechurch at her request.

"Even boys experience growing pains," the much older
widow said complacently, "though in them it generally takes
the form of hideous waistcoats, excessively high shirt points,
an excess of pot metal fobs and flirting with blue ruin. Yes,
even Stephen, though you wouldn't have guessed that when
you met. You were barely out of leading strings when he first
went away to school, you see, and so you escaped the worst
of it, but he was as awkward as any for a bit."

"You say Sally Parkins was brought to bed?" Suzanne asked,
desperate to hear more and even more desperate to turn the
subject.

"Yesterday evening. I'll call after you leave. I've a pair of
children's blankets set aside will be just the thing."

"Twins, you said?"

"A boy and girl. Tom Parkins was here at dawn to tell us
of it and beg an egg for the new mother's breakfast."

"Which you gave him, no doubt?" Suzanne sighed. "Please
promise me something. In the future, when they come
importuning you refer them to me. Like as not that egg went
down Tom's gullet, not his wife's.

"There're some more sets of petunias in the cart, and some
phlox, by the bye. At least I know you'll not be giving those

away. I only wish I could make the garden at Rose Cottage flourish as you do here."

No one paid Gracechurch and Scully any mind as they left the inn yard and continued through the village, an unremarkable pair of dust-stained travelers on weary mounts, invisible in their ordinariness. No eyes turned in their direction, first clouded by puzzlement, then with the light of recognition dawning warmly in their depths. No arm waved. No voice called in welcome.

"Damnable homecoming," the former colonel muttered as first one childhood playmate passed him by, then another. "Usually they pay more attention to strangers than this."

No, he hadn't expected a brass band or displays of fireworks. He wouldn't've wanted them, which was why he'd indicated a projected arrival date several weeks in the future. No more uniforms for him. No more medals. No more overblown celebrations complete with champagne flowing. No more fuss.

He'd had enough of that at Nathan's, what with the children descending on him as if he were Wellington himself and Hannah—heavily *enceinte* with the next Rothschild scion—throwing herself on his chest with tears of joy. Of course Nathan—in Aix for the deliberations regarding the floating of the next French loan, and daily suffering frustration and insult at the manner in which he and his brothers were ignored—had warned him how it would be when they met in Paris. "Hannah," he'd said, "tends to excessive emotion at times like these. She means well, and will be herself again once the little one arrives. As for the children?" Nathan had broken into a rare grin. "I could disappear from the face of the earth, and so long as you were there to dust off their hurts and applaud their triumphs, they'd barely remember to sit *shivah,* let alone say the mourner's *kaddish.* "

His strange and intimate friendship with the financially powerful but socially unacceptable British branch of the Rothschild family was perhaps the best thing that had eventuated from the long Peninsular years. Sometimes merely doing one's duty had unanticipatable and highly rewarding results, both personal and financial. Outcasts together, as Nathan often said.

"Been a while, sir," Scully murmured as Gracechurch stared after yet another childhood chum passing him by without a second glance. " 'Sides, this was how you said you wanted it, with no one the wiser until you wanted 'em to be."

"The more fool I. Never quite realized how it would feel."

"Could've told you, Colonel, having experienced it once myself." Scully shifted uncomfortably in his saddle, easing aching muscles and bones. "Course nothing changed when they realized who I was," he admitted, "which is why I've never been back, nor yet intend to darken their horizon again. It'll be different here in a bit, you'll see."

"Blast it, Scully, I'm not a self-seeking poseur demanding to be fawned over."

"Nor was I, Colonel. Could be you've changed more'n they have."

"I recognize them easily enough."

"Because they're those you're expecting to see, Colonel, begging your pardon. You they're not expecting—not yet, at any rate."

"Besides," Gracechurch snapped, ignoring reassurances he didn't want and far more comfortable with being ignored than he would've been at a warmer reception, "there'll be those whose greetings will be anything but effusive, given they devoutly wish I'd been planted in some nameless Portuguese pass years go. The cut direct is what I'll be treated to, more like."

"You're sick-livered, as the Frenchies say."

"If there's one thing I've learned from Nathan Rothschild, it's to have no illusions. The war's over, and he's as redundant as I at the moment. Dreadful thing," he grinned wryly, putting his ill-humor aside, "to find one's redundant after believing oneself to be of at least marginal use."

The bustle thinned as they approached the end of the village. Suddenly there was no one in the dusty lane but themselves, the sun beating hot on their backs, the singing of insects in the grasses along the verge soaring obligato over the muffled clop of their mounts' hooves. The countryside shimmered in the soft haze, unreal in its mirroring of every dream of home, for all the world as if it were a nasty-minded wizard's too-perfect simulation of bucolic peace. At least clouds were building over the far hills, their mushrooming tops blinding white, their leaden underbellies promising a storm come evening.

"I could've done nicely with just one smile," Gracechurch grumbled under his breath, not quite able to set the issue aside. "Even the offer of a tankard of ale in the inn yard, recognize me or not."

"They were busy changing teams and providing for the passengers, Colonel. Y'know how it is."

"I'm learning."

"Don't be blaming 'em, nor yet your mother what's waiting for you. Hasn't seen you for a long stretch either. Like as not she'll be up to her elbows with an eye to your return, and that put out when you arrive unexpected."

"No, she'll welcome us with open arms, no matter how the rest are."

They rounded a gentle bend, the last of the village scattered before them like flower-blanketed redoubts on an abandoned battlefield. Beyond lay a small wood through which the same stream burbling through the vicarage garden tumbled over moss-covered rocks on its way to the Chipple. In the distance stretched velvety fields ruffled by a breeze as playful as a fond father's hand.

Gracechurch's eyes narrowed. The lane wasn't quite as deserted as it first appeared. A cart was tied to a fence in the shade of a gnarled oak, the nose of the pony buried in a feedbag. In the back of the cart were a flat of petunias and another of phlox. Naturally visitors would be at the cottage his mother had leased from Oren Phelps when she moved out of the vicarage, spoiling his return. It was part and parcel with all the rest.

"Damn and blast," Gracechurch sighed.

"That the place?"

"It is indeed."

"Told you how it might be," Scully scolded. "Told you all the way back before Waterloo, when we were lying in the muck waiting for morning and you planning our homecoming. Callers on top of all else? And your bed not made up, nor yet anything planned for supper, or even available? This isn't the Rothschild place. Your father may've been a vicar and well-born, but y'spring from the same sort of household I do, though you've forgotten how it is when visitors arrive unexpected. We'll be as welcome as hornets in a pig wallow."

"Have done, Scully. I'm as aware of my shortcomings as anyone—especially with you to remind me of them night and day."

The lilt of feminine laughter floated through open windows, hidden by the masses of flowers his mother grew wherever she found herself. How she'd gotten such a garden to flourish in so short a time, however, Gracechurch had no idea. Determination, perhaps—a characteristic he'd inherited from her, though in him the form it took was hardly so benign, he admitted wryly to himself.

Phelps had at least had the place cleaned up—probably in deference to village opinion, for certainly the man would never've gone to such expense of his own free will. New thatch glistened through the trees, and the fence Gracechurch remembered as tumble-down had been rebuilt. A rose-covered trellis arched over the freshly painted gate. Both the track leading to the shed behind the little cottage and the path leading to the front door were freshly graveled, and someone had seen to raking the surface free of leaves and blossoms. As always with his mother, there wasn't a weed or a bramble to be seen.

"Doesn't look as ramshackle as you claimed. Not fancy, but cozy enough."

"Someone's seen to it, landlord probably. I'll have to thank him, which I don't anticipate with pleasure. Phelps was a clutch-fisted, prosy bore when we were boys, and a clutch-fisted, prosy bore when we reached manhood. Mightily impressed his father'd been knighted, though there's no title to pass on and Phelps is a simple mister. I doubt he's changed a particle since I last saw him."

Scully grunted noncommittally, swung out of the saddle, stood in the lane looking about him.

"I've seen worse billets in my time. I'm to doss in the shed yonder?"

"We'll see. Barely fit for rats and spiders in the old days." Gracechurch shook his head as Scully reached for Iago's bridle. "No, I want to know who's here before I make my grand entrance."

They followed the path to the shed—it too far sturdier and more commodious than Gracechurch remembered from roaming the area in his boyhood. Indeed, it appeared entirely rebuilt and was now more stable than shed, with adequate stalls for a pair of mounts and even space for a gig and pony. A lean-to behind housed a few chickens, two of which were pecking at a grain sack in the corner and ignoring the *pro forma* protests of a fat gray tabby. A loft held a generous supply of last year's hay, still golden and fragrant.

"I'll be damned," Gracechurch muttered. "Phelps must've been foxed when he ordered this done. Place used to be a disgrace, for all it's where he housed his superannuated nurse until her death."

He handed his mount's reins to Scully, crossed the small stable and opened the facing door. Behind it was a room clearly intended as a groom's quarters, small to be sure, but comfortably fitted-up nevertheless. He recognized the quilt covering the low cot from his childhood.

"Looks like you'll have to be reassessing your opinion of that Phelps person," Scully chuckled. "This is snug, and then a bit."

"One of my opinions, at any rate. The man's half weasel and half rat—or was. See to the horses, and then come round to the kitchen and make yourself known. Mags's still with Mother, and sure to have something to fill the spare cranny, even if it's only bread and cheese. I'll see you in a bit."

Gracechurch swiped at his dusty boots, tossed his hat on Scully's cot and ran nervous fingers through his sweat-darkened brown locks.

"Your mother won't be caring a particle what appearance you present," Scully murmured as he backed first his mount, then Gracechurch's, into their waiting stalls, ignoring the displaced chickens' incensed cluckings and angry attacks on his boots.

"Not for herself, but Lord knows who she's got with her. I'd rather not put her to the blush if I can help it."

"Should've thought of that before."

"There's a lot I should've thought of before."

With a wry twist to his lips, Gracechurch followed a narrow path past the ancient hedge separating cottage and garden from miniature stable. Lurking in the deep shade behind the screen of vegetation, swatting at mosquitoes who were finding his neck irresistible, he watched as two figures alternately appeared and disappeared in the window of the separate kitchen building, one clearly Mags, moving more slowly than in the past but unmistakable. Obviously refreshments of some sort were being prepared. The other appeared more slender and fleet of foot, and was considerably taller than either Mags or his mother. Probably younger as well. A new servant in training? Now how the devil could his mother afford that?

Then he grinned. No doubt another of the waifs she was forever housing, and eventually finding decent employment in the area. The number of cook's assistants, potboys and scullery maids his mother'd trained, the number of potential stableboys his father had housed in the buildings behind the vicarage and eventually found positions, was legion. Doubtless with his father's death the training of stableboys had ceased. He wondered how Scully would feel if pressed to take on the task.

The slender one was laughing, a gay, untrammeled sound that carried to where Gracechurch reconnoitered. He was not, he insisted, spying. The girl appeared in the breezeway toting a tray holding a pitcher of pale liquid and three glasses—a blowzy chit, capless, her hair straggling about her smudged face in wisps. No apron, either—a raw recruit if ever he'd seen one. Knowing his mother, those were infractions the girl would never repeat after the gentle reproof she'd receive once the guests departed.

"Don't worry, Mags—I shan't spill it, I promise," she called over her shoulder, then vanished into the back of the cottage. The words, "I only spill things when I want to, and then I'm clever about it so people only think I'm clumsy," floated behind her.

Minx! And a raised voice as well? His mother had her work cut out for her with this one, he chuckled. But, she'd succeed. She always did.

Once there was no chance of the would-be serving girl spotting him he entered the kitchen, placing a finger to his lips at Mags's startled glance. He gave her a quick, heartfelt hug as tears streamed silently down the elderly woman's round cheeks.

"Yes, it's really me," he whispered, "and yes, I'm whole in

body and heart, and don't plan to shake the dust of home from my boots for many a month. Scully'll be joining you in a bit. Best pull out whatever you have in the way of food, and lots of it. He's a bottomless pit. How does my mother?"

"That brave," the woman snuffled. "Not a word of complaint nor a tear out of her, and speaks of your father as if he were in the next room. I suppose to her he is."

Gracechurch nodded. "There're callers?" he asked, voice thick. Keeping this homecoming lighthearted was going to be considerably more difficult than he'd anticipated. Scully'd warned him of that, too.

"Two of 'em," Mags hissed, drying her eyes on a corner of her apron. "It's—"

"Doesn't matter who they are," he said with a forced grin. "I'll give 'em all a surprise."

"That you will," she muttered. "Mayhap there'll be one or two lurking about for yourself as well, Colonel."

"Serves 'em right. This the tea tray?" he said, turning to inspect the contents as his brows rose. "Good God—cucumber sandwiches? At this season? Seed cake *and* fairy cakes, both? And French pastries? And hothouse fruits? That's pineapple, for pity's sake. And're those ices? My mother must've beggared herself to provide such a lavish spread. Well, this sort of foolishness'll come to an end now I'm home. Couldn't you manage her any better than this?" he grumbled as he seized the tray. "No, I suppose you couldn't, but I will, by damn."

Chapter Two

Gracechurch paused in the parlor doorway, fingers tightening on the overloaded wooden tray's edges until his knuckles showed white, the entry with its narrow, crooked stairs at his back.

The gawky serving girl had joined the company as if she were their equal—a detail that troubled him not in the least. Many was the haphazard meal he'd shared with Scully, grateful for an understanding and undemanding companion with whom to share complaints of impossible food and even more impossible conditions.

The room, while small, was pleasant enough. Contrary to his initial conclusion when she wrote him of the cottage she'd taken, his mother wasn't being overcharged for accommodations a pig would've considered beneath its dignity. The walls were freshly plastered and whitewashed. The pianoforte that had formed part of his mother's dowry stood against an inner wall, gleaming from liberal applications of beeswax and determined polishing. His father's treasured engraving of Rembrandt's *Night Watch* hung above the fireplace, tall flanking bookcases holding his library. The appointments were graceful: a new circular Axminster carpet of lapis and jade and bronze in the Chinese style that glowed jewel-like where the sun struck it, modern lamps with delicate glass shades, new chairs, the few things from the vicarage which'd been theirs rather than belonging to the living refinished and recovered. An oversized wing chair upholstered in deep burgundy leather on the far side of the hearth overpowered the delicate Queen Anne sherry table at its side. Those pieces might be from his father's study, refurbished beyond recognition. Only color and style hinted at their origins. A tall chestnut dresser balanced the piano, a decanter of what had to be brandy and another of what was probably Madeira in one corner, a tray holding his mother's treasured Waterford goblets—each a gift from his father marking a significant event in their lives— in the other.

No, he had nothing to cavil at regarding his mother's surroundings. Phelps had gone to a deal of effort and expense in a very short time to make her comfortable. But her choice of company beyond the fresh-faced serving girl?

Now he understood the lavish refreshments, blast it. Suzanne Hodges, Suzanne Phelps, Lady Phelps, the great lady of the neighborhood if one discounted wives of titled absentee landlords who might deign to put in an appearance once every ten years—call the woman what you would—hadn't changed so much in nine years that he didn't recognize her. Oh, her complexion was paler than he remembered. There were unattractive smudges beneath her eyes and faint lines at their outer corners. The coppery lights had faded from her dark hair leaving it as grayed as her gown, and certainly the pleasing roundness of the girl had melted away leaving an angular, spinsterish widow garbed in half-mourning in its wake.

She faced the door, head bent over some mending from the charity box at his mother's feet, needle flying diligently. How appropriate: Suzanne the Dutiful. Suzanne the Diligent. And, many long years ago, Suzanne the Delectable. Suzanne the Diamond, at least so far as he'd been concerned—the Delight of his Heart, young fool that he'd been. Also, Suzanne the Rapacious. Suzanne the Weak. Suzanne the Traitoress.

He managed not to snarl at the sight of her in his mother's home, intruding where she wasn't wanted and didn't belong, and causing his poor mother unconscionable expense to entertain her in the style to which she apparently now felt entitled. In the old days a dish of raspberries gathered in the hedgerows had contented her well enough, or a tartlet made from windfalls.

Damn the woman to hell forever. Why couldn't she stay among those she'd chosen as her life's companions? He was amazed they'd permit her to stoop so low as to visit here. Hodges, if he learned of it, would be fuming. As for Oren Phelps, his childhood enemy and now Suzanne's no-doubt overbearing stepson? It was all Gracechurch could do to keep from snorting.

He backed into the entry, tempted to turn tail and scuttle to the kitchen as fast as his legs would carry him. It wasn't that he was a coward. It was simply that if there was one person in all of England he didn't want present at his reunion with his recently bereaved mother, Suzanne Phelps, *née* Hodges, was that person.

It was as he made his decision to absent himself from the petticoat gathering that the half-trained serving girl raised her head from the shapeless garment she was assaulting with needle and thread. Her eyes widened. His narrowed. Her brows rose. His lowered. She assayed a tentative smile. He produced a repressive scowl, backing another step into the entry. The expression on the bold hoyden's face turned at once derisive and contemptuous, for all the world as if she realized precisely who he was (which was entirely probable) and was well aware of the precise reason he desired to absent himself (which was totally impossible) and was pleased by neither.

There was nothing for it but to blunder through, damn her impertinence, or face that derision and contempt on a daily basis until he managed to have her chased from the place. That, given his mother, would probably be never. Gracechurch drew in his chin, pulled back his shoulders and threw out his chest in perfect parody of a stage butler, and opened his mouth. The chit was tossing aside the clumsily mended scrap and springing to her feet even as he intoned, "Tea is served, ladies," doing his best to keep his voice light and humorous, and refusing to give in to the ludicrous character of the moment.

"Cawker! You've even less sense than a peahen," the girl hissed, darting to his side and struggling to relieve him of the tray.

Suzanne—no, Lady Phelps—raised her eyes. He must remember to think of her that way, blast it. He'd believed her pale before? She was chalk-faced now, hazel eyes huge above their unattractive smudges, cheeks turning an unpleasant red, the round stains in the awkward style of a clown's paint, hands with their burden of mending twisting the fabric as they sank to her lap. The expression in those muddy eyes was as unreadable as her actions were clear.

"Damn," he muttered, wrenching his gaze from her with the sensation the earth had whirled wildly from its course, lurching like a carousing grenadier. It was even worse than he'd imagined it would be, and his imagination where Suzanne Hodges was concerned had been both active and fertile over the years when he'd permitted himself to think of her, which'd been rarely, or couldn't help himself, which had been uncomfortably often.

The serving girl wrestled the tray from him as his grip unconsciously loosened. His mother had stilled in the middle of some inconsequential comment, was laying the mending in the work basket at her feet, was rising. And then she was in his arms with a glad cry, an anchor of certainty and security to which he clung almost like a child who wanted its hurts fussed over and bandaged.

She said nothing at first, merely raising a work-roughened hand to touch his cheek as if in wonder, her eyes overly bright with tears she refused to shed. Then her hand rose, touching the hair at his temple.

"Winter's given you its first touch of frost, Stevie," she said with a shaky laugh. "I hadn't considered that might happen, though certainly your father's temples turned silver at just your age. It's not unattractive, but you've aged so. Where has my bonnie boy gone?"

And then she lost the battle with her tears. The sobs were stifled against his chest, soul-shattering things that shook him to the foundation of his being as she gave way to years of terror for him hidden perhaps even from herself, and to the despair at his father's senseless death from an inflammation of the lungs contracted when he'd been caught in his gig in a freakish ice storm halfway between the village and an outlying farm where he'd been attending a deathbed.

His arms tightened about her. A brown linnet—one of the few birds he recognized on sight—clung to the ivy surrounding one of the open windows, its joyful warble rising over his mother's sobs. He turned so his back sheltered them from prying eyes. And then his mother gave herself a shake and stood straight, pulling slightly away from him, erect as ever even if her hands did cling to his shoulders.

"Look at me," she chuckled, "acting as if your homecoming required a baptismal ceremony when your father did a perfectly good job of it right after you were born. How he'd scold me were he here. I do apologize, Stephen, and promise it won't happen again. You know I'm not generally a watering-pot, but it was the unexpectedness of it, for you'd written it would be another month before we could look to see you, and I received your latest letter only days ago. You do *not* resemble Mags in any particular, and it was she should've been carrying the tray."

"I plead guilty to all sorts of nefarious plots," he said, the slightest of tremors in his voice, "but I didn't want you to go to any fuss."

" 'Fuss,' as you call it, is a mother's greatest joy. But there, I shan't complain, and I promise not to call you Stevie again. It just slipped out in the surprise of the moment, don't you see?"

"I rather liked it," he said with a forced grin. "It had the sound of home, coming from you. Besides, I'm not as puffed up with my own consequence as I was as a lad. A name's a name, after all. I'm the same person either way."

"You *have* changed."

"For the better, I hope."

"Now then, I'm not so sure of that." She gave a watery chuckle, making good use of the square of yellowed lawn he gave her. "You never fished for compliments before."

"And am hardly wielding the fly rod now," he countered, reddening about the ears. Amazing, that his mother could make him feel the callow youth now as easily as she had when he was a schoolboy. And it was unconscious, that was the funniest part.

"We must be leaving," a soft voice said behind them.

Suzanne. Her voice hadn't changed a particle, even if she had.

"With this glorious spread? Why, half of it'll go to waste if there's only Mother, Mags and I to consume it," he said coldly, turning to face her. "No, you must certainly linger long enough to partake of that seed cake at the least, my lady. One of your favorites, as I recall."

She'd risen from her chair, was pulling lace mitts over slender fingers, her eyes lowered.

"You will want to be private," she said, ignoring his taunting words.

"We're not private, however."

Her eyes lifted then, seeming to study him. He flushed beneath the gentle, almost impersonal scrutiny.

"But would much prefer to be so." She turned to his mother, who was bustling forward. "I'll take the sewing with me, Mrs. Gracechurch," she said, "for you'll hardly want to be troubling with it now and I know the vicar was hoping to have the things ready for delivery by this Saturday."

"Excellent notion," Gracechurch snarled, turning to the wide-eyed little serving girl. "Here, you, whatever your name is, make yourself useful by carrying that box to Lady Phelps's cart, and remove the flowers. I presume those're intended for my mother," he said, turning back to Suzanne.

"Who do you think you are, ordering me about?" the hoyden snapped from by the table where she'd deposited the tray, further demonstrating her ill-breeding and lamentable lack of training. "This isn't the army, sir, and I'm not your servant."

"You're my mother's, and will soon learn you'll accept instructions from me or be sent packing," he growled, ignoring his mother's attempt at whispered protest. "Someone should've taken a birch to you years ago. I will not suffer impertinence in my home, and I won't permit my mother to tolerate it, either."

"Hoity-toity! And high in the instep into the bargain? No one ever mentioned that," the girl retorted.

"Colonel Gracechurch, permit me to present my sister, Miss Cassandra Hodges," Suzanne Phelps said in the leaden silence following the girl's words. "I don't believe you've ever been introduced as she was barely out of the nursery the last time you were here. Cassie, this is Colonel Stephen Gracechurch, Mrs. Gracechurch's son. Make your curtsy, please. Then carry the charity box to the cart as he requested, and wait for me there. And not a word from you, Cassie— not one. Perhaps now you understand why I don't consider that gown suitable for paying calls."

"Wasn't a request. It was an order from lofty superior to lowly inferior."

"I, ah, please do forgi—" Gracechurch said on a strangled note.

"There's no need for you to say a word, Colonel, anymore than there is for me. Your *servant*, sir." Cassie stared back at Gracechurch, her head insolently high, and barely dipped her knee in obeisance to his superior years and intellect. Then she crossed the room with a schoolgirl's stride, bundled the mending back in the box, picked it up, and stalked to the parlor door. "I'm sorry we didn't have a chance to have tea, Mrs. Gracechurch," she said with an impish grin. "It appeared uncommonly good, and I'm uncommonly hungry."

Then she was out the door and on the path leading to the front gate, first her suppressed giggles and then full-throated laughter floating back to them.

"I do apologize for Stephen's misconstruction of the situation," Matilda Gracechurch said, eyes dancing, "but Cassie's grown so in nine years. Why, she could barely have been out of leading strings the last time he saw her. Now she's almost a young lady."

"And there are times when I truly believe it would be better were she still in them," Suzanne Phelps said, an answering twinkle at the back of troubled eyes. "I do know assessing a situation rapidly was essential when you were in the Peninsula, Colonel," she continued, turning to Gracechurch—who devoutly wished there were a breastworks behind which he could dive, no matter how greatly at fault the woman was regarding the tea his mother'd provided. "However, here in England one does have a bit more time in which to make an assessment. It's often wise to take that time. As Cassie said, however rudely, you're no longer in the military."

"Yes, well, so unexpected, and—" he babbled, for all the world as if he were a half-fledged youth.

"Certainly," the woman said.

And woman she was, complete with an innate dignity that surprised him. The girl he'd once loved had vanished as surely as his love had, replaced by this calm, quiet stranger whose voice was so low he had to strain to catch the words. Was this how she would have been had she had the courage to go against her father's orders and wait for him? He doubted it.

"Do accept my best wishes on your return, and my sympathies regarding your father's death," she was continuing, eyes not quite meeting his. "Mr. Gracechurch was greatly loved and is sadly missed, for all the new vicar is everything that is kind-hearted and his wife and sons are a delight to all. I hope you'll find the neighborhood congenial, though I doubt not it will prove sadly flat after your Continental years.

"And now," she said, putting on her bonnet and swiftly tying its thin lavender ribbons beneath her chin, then retrieving her reticule and sunshade, "I must be on my way." She turned to his mother, giving her a swift hug he found distasteful in its familiarity. "If there's anything we didn't think of, Mrs. Gracechurch, please do send a message. Don't worry about the charity sewing. Between Cassie and I, we'll have it done in a trice."

"I'll see you to your cart," Gracechurch snapped, "as I want a word with you before you leave."

"Certainly, Colonel."

"I'll be back in a moment, Mother," he said more evenly, seizing Suzanne Phelps's elbow in a determined grip.

"Stephen, dear, please—"

"Not to worry," he said on a tight smile, "I won't disgrace any of us. Wellington was rather clever in training his staff in the use of smooth words—though he generally eschewed them himself, not being of a diplomatic bent."

Then they were in the entry and through the front door, descending the series of cracked half-millstones that served as steps, and on the gravel path.

He glanced at the slight figure garbed in depressingly grayed lavender beside him, then at their idyllic surroundings. Flowers bloomed in profusion. Sunlight dappled the path, striking through the leaves of shrubs and trees. Butterflies flitted about like so many petals given leave to take wing by a benevolent fairy.

What a bitter joke—that this should be the setting for this most uncomfortable and unpleasant reunion. He'd imagined something far more formal: the churchyard following services perhaps, or even some crowded social event, she relegated to a corner with the other widows, he lionizing it with the cream of that year's débutantes and able to ignore her except for a glance of pity lacking recognition, even a question to some new acquaintance regarding the identity of the faded widow—in her hearing, of course. Then the look of disbelief, almost but not quite insolent in its casual scrutiny, followed by a comment within which lurked barbs only she would recognize.

"It's not your fault you were here," he said by way of a beginning, annoyed that the deep brim of her straw bonnet made her face invisible. He'd earned the right to watch her writhe.

"No, it's not," she agreed.

"I do understand you would have avoided this meeting as determinedly as I, had you known I was to arrive today."

"Naturally, Colonel."

"Dammit, stop throwing my rank in my face," he snapped under his breath, wanting none but her to hear him. "I've sold out, as well you know, Suzanne."

"Yes, you've sold out, though you appear to've retained your military manners."

Then they were around a slight bend in the path, hidden

both from the lane and the cottage. That was a bit better, though not much. No matter how sympathetic a witness his mother might be, there were certain things she had no right to see with her brightly observant eyes. A man deserved a certain amount of privacy in his dealings with the opposite sex, after all.

"Please thank your stepson for the kindness he's shown my mother in having the place fixed up for her," he said with considerable reluctance and even more discomfort. "I'm all stunned appreciation, and shall tell Oren so myself at the first opportunity. However, I'd like to know what the devil you thought you were about, causing her the unconscionable expense of that tea she'd set out to honor you with," he snarled, getting to the point. He slung her around to face him, seized her chin in his other hand and tilted her head so she couldn't avoid his eyes. "She could ill afford it, and unfortunately I'm currently unable to frank such luxuries for her."

She gazed at him, features expressionless except for a slight puckering of her brows.

"Well, dammit, what d'you have to say for yourself?" he ground on, unable to stop himself no matter how much he wished he could, her very silence and air of incomprehension an irresistible goad. "There must've been a month's supply of sugar in those cakes, let alone the waste of eggs and butter and cream. As for the pineapple and hothouse fruits, you may be accustomed to them at Placidia, but we common mortals rarely see such things, let alone taste them."

"I live at Rose Cottage, the dower house on the other side of the village, with my mother-in-law, two of my stepdaughters and Cassie," was all the answer she gave him, apparently startled he might believe her otherwise domiciled and ignoring the far more important issue of her beggaring his mother. "My stepson, his wife and their four daughters are in residence at Placidia."

"Oren chased you from the place, did he? Typical. How long did you queen it there? Three years? Four? Was the game worth the candle, *Lady* Phelps?"

"Sir John died in 1813," she said after a moment's consideration. "My father was disappointed, naturally. It was rather a short run, as marriages go. As soon as the will was read Cassie and I were packing our bags, as were my stepdaughters. My stepson wished a more peaceful household in which to raise his children, which is understandable. That his grandmother also preferred a more peaceful household, and that Rose Cottage of a sudden became filled with girls at the most awkward age mattered not in the least to him. And now, if you'll excuse me, my sister is waiting for me."

He wanted to say he couldn't excuse her—not then, and not now. Not for forgetting him so quickly and easily. Not for marrying Sir John Phelps on her father's orders. Not for causing his mother all that expense. Not for breaking his heart. Not for any of it. Not ever. And that he intended she pay for every second's agony she'd caused him over the years, though what the exact nature of the penalty might be he had no notion at the moment.

Instead he dropped his hands and bowed so deeply as to offer intentional and deep insult.

"Naturally, my lady," he said, voice reeking sarcasm. "Your wish, as always, is my command. Amazing your father didn't order you home though, and marry you off again to the highest bidder he could then unearth. Excellent source of income for him, especially if he chose equally well and your second expired as quickly as your first." He straightened, eyes boring into hers. "However, given my mother cannot afford to entertain you in the style to which you obviously feel you are entitled, I must request that you refrain from calling here in the future. I can't afford you, either."

"Don't worry, Colonel," she said, "you shall never be asked to do so."

Then she was turning her back, head high, continuing along the path to the lane.

"Nor shall I come calling at Rose Cottage merely because that's where you've informed me you live now, nor shall my mother."

"That is your choice, Colonel."

"Dammit, Suzanne," he called after her, "can you not even give me my name?"

"I don't believe that would be wise," she said, the slightest tremor in her voice, back still turned, "as you appear determined we shall be perpetually at daggers drawn."

She disappeared around the last bend in the path, hidden

by the profusion of flowers. The gate opened and closed. The chit, Cassie, said something. Suzanne responded, her words indecipherable. Moments later came the clop of the pony's hooves and the creak of a cart that wasn't in its first youth. They were gone.

He stood there, cursing himself and fate, and a homecoming that couldn't've been worse if Squire Hodges had planned it that way. Then he sighed, shoulders sagging.

The confrontation had left him unbearably wearied and even more unbearably discouraged. Returning to Chipham Common had obviously been the second worst mistake of his life. He'd simply have to make the best of it, at least for a while, just as he had of the other. Perhaps eventually he'd be able to convince his mother to move to a different part of the country, one with a milder climate in deference to the aches with which she was beginning to be afflicted in the depth of winter. Certainly it was a good enough excuse, one she'd accept while blessing him for his consideration.

After his highly changed circumstances were discovered in the neighborhood, however. After he'd looked about for a residence compatible with his current affluence, and let it be known there was nothing of sufficient quality to meet his requirements in the environs of Chipham Common. No, not even Placidia or the squire's place would suffice, even if they were available.

And after he'd had the opportunity of publicly turning his back on Squire Hodges when the lout came courting him in hopes of puffing up the used goods that was now Suzanne, offering the squire the identical insult the squire had offered him in front of his father's church on the Sunday before he departed for London and then Portugal nine years ago.

Those moments would be sweet.

He shrugged, striding back to the cottage. Sweet as they might be, they might never come. He wasn't certain he could pull it off, no matter what he pretended to himself. Old habits of respect and deference died hard. Not habits of deference to Hodges or Oren Phelps. They were inconsequential nonentities, if truth were told, and in many ways hardly worth bothering with had he not been promising himself the pleasure if he survived the Peninsular campaigns, and later Waterloo. No, the one person who might stop him, should she have an inkling of what he planned, was his mother. She, and the memory of his gentle father.

Scully and Mags, clearly already on the best of terms, had joined his mother in the parlor. The trio raised glasses containing thimble-fulls of wine high as he entered the room.

"Welcome home, my dear," his mother said. "May you never feel impelled to wander again. And you too, Mr. Bates, for you must consider this cottage your home from now on." Then, with an impish grin totally out of keeping with her position as staid vicar's widow, she said in perfectly accented French, "A bas les français! Qu'ils restent chez eux d'aujourd'hui à jamais."

"The frogs weren't so bad once they were disembarrassed of their glorious Little Colonel and their illusions." Gracechurch chuckled as they drained their glasses. "What began in Moscow we finished at Waterloo, but yes, let them stay forever in their own country—I agree with you there, and let Nappy stay forever on Saint Helena under strictest guard. Strange to think a man whose rank was no higher than my own when he began to make trouble could cause so much turmoil for so many years. Best take a stick to me if I show an inclination to declare myself Emperor of Chipham Common, Mother, and cast my eye longingly toward the fat farms near Timsborough."

They joined in his laughter as they set their glasses back on the dresser.

"I'll have a care. See you do as well, Stephen. Now, you must be positively famished, and you too, Mr. Bates."

"Please, ma'am," Scully broke in, "it's Scully to the colonel, and I'd be that pleased if I was Scully to you and Mrs. Reedy here as well."

"And I'm Mags," Mags insisted, "always have been, always will be, and there wasn't never any Mr. Reedy. I'm just plain miss."

"Not just 'plain' anything," Scully murmured with a wink, "now or ever."

"Now that makes everything wonderfully cozy," Gracechurch's mother dimpled. "How delightful, and how delighted Joseph would've been had he been able to be here. He longed to meet you, Scully, for he had so many questions for you. Now, as I'm sure you're 'gut-foundered' after that long journey, and having to eat heaven-knows-what prepared heaven-knows-how in heaven knows what sort of impossible places, let's regale ourselves with this wonderful tea Lady Phelps provided. So thoughtful of her, but then that's always been her way."

Gracechurch could feel the blood draining from his face, the skin growing cold despite the warmth of the day.

"Suzanne Phelps provided all this?" he managed.

"And more. There's a ham, and wine, and a pair of ducks and a goose, and I don't know what all. You'd have to ask Mags. It was she and Cassie unpacked the baskets. Lady Phelps wanted to be sure our larder was well stocked against your return, for things haven't been precisely comfortable since your father died. It was she had the shed made into a true stable as she was certain you'd have mounts, and as for the cottage? There was no stopping her," his mother chuckled, "so I didn't even try. There are times when it's wisest to say 'Thank-you,' and leave well enough alone. I don't want you offering her the insult of insisting on paying for everything."

"I couldn't afford to," Gracechurch said automatically. "Good Lord, Mother—Suzanne paid for everything?"

"With the exception of my piano, your father's books, and the few things at the vicarage that were ours rather than belonging to the position? Yes, everything, and what was ours she had refurbished."

As Gracechurch collapsed in the chair where only moments earlier Suzanne Phelps had been sitting and buried his head in his hands, he insisted his laughter was merely bitter, not hysterical.

"You drive," Suzanne said as soon as she'd untied the pony and clambered into the cart, handing her sister the reins. "And don't say anything. Not a single word, Cassie."

"So *that* is the infamous Stephen Gracechurch all the fuss was about years ago. I wonder you gave him a second glance," Cassie muttered, expertly backing and turning the cart, then setting off toward the village. "He's not much to look at, and even less to speak with. A rude, insufferable boor, if you want to know."

"I don't." Then, more gently, Suzanne said, "War changes a man, I'd imagine."

"Not that much. You must've been all about in your head, creating a person who didn't exist from a fine uniform and the boredom of a wet spring. I suppose being eighteen offers an excuse, though I'm only fifteen and I doubt I'd make such a gross error. At least Sir John was civil when he noticed we were about—which wasn't often, I'll grant you that—if his gout wasn't troubling him."

"Yes, Sir John was exceeding civil."

Suzanne held her head higher than ever, grateful for the bonnet's deep brim. Had she a veil, she'd've pulled it down. She wasn't certain whether she couldn't think, or whether she didn't want to, or if she was thinking far too much and that made it appear as if she wasn't thinking at all. No matter where the truth lay, she didn't want the villagers to see her while she went about doing whatever it was she was or wasn't doing. When they learned of Stephen Gracechurch's return they'd remember how she appeared down to the finest detail. She wanted nothing in the least remarkable or memorable about her when they thought back on the moment. If there was, the old whispers and sly glances would begin anew. Unfortunately, the only way to be unremarkable in Chipham Common, especially if one were the widow of Sir John Phelps, was to be invisible.

"Miss Pemberton is waving to you," Cassie murmured.

"What? Oh—where?"

"By the draper's."

"Thank you." Suzanne turned, smiling automatically, waving automatically. "Yes, it's a lovely day," she called in response to the little spinster's cheerful panegyric regarding the weather. "No, I'm enjoying the sun, Miss Pemberton, and don't need to raise my sunshade. The brim of my bonnet protects my face, you see. No, I shan't need the excellent complexion restorative your brother has invented, but thank you for the suggestion. Keep driving, Cassie," she muttered. "Don't stop, whatever you do. I'm not up to social niceties at the moment."

Was this how she'd have to spend the rest of her life, being reminded to perform the simplest actions? Being informed it was time to eat, to sleep, to bow to this one or nod to that one? Hardly! She wouldn't permit it of herself.

No, there was no sense creating a Cheltenham tragedy out of what had been, were one honest about it, merely an unpleasant encounter. There'd been a moment in the garden when she'd feared she wouldn't escape without disgracing herself. Stephen would learn the truth soon enough and, unless he'd changed beyond all recognition, come to stiffly beg her pardon, driven by pride if not compunction. She'd almost rather he didn't bother.

It had been the shock of it, she decided, first seeing him so unexpectedly and then, unfortunately, hearing him. The former had been a joy so deep she'd thought she'd die of it. The other? Well, she'd thought she'd die of that, too. Apparently dying was a deal more difficult and complicated than she'd believed. At least for her it was, for she hadn't been able to die on her wedding day, either. She hadn't even been able to faint, and oblivion would certainly have proved a welcome escape that time.

"The vicar," Cassie hissed. "And Mrs. Browne and the boys. At the vicarage gate. Either Mr. Browne's just returned from paying calls, or else he's about to go out on 'em. Wave to the Brownes, Suzanne."

Suzanne smiled and waved. Then they were past. She dropped her hand, closed her eyes. Only the Pembertons' apothecary shop, a few more cottages, and the blacksmith's. Then they'd be out of the village, and she wouldn't have to worry about people remarking her looks or her expression or her manner. That release couldn't come soon enough.

She sighed, then smiled ruefully.

The moment in the parlor when, boy-like, as much the prankster as he'd been years ago, Stephen'd announced tea pretending to be a butler from one of the great houses sprinkled about the countryside? She'd wanted nothing so much as to dash across the room and hurl herself into his arms, sobbing out her joy at his survival and safe return. What a shock to them all, even dear Mrs. Gracechurch, had she behaved so. Now that dream had vanished into the realm of impossibilities.

She'd expected formality at first, coolness, even to be ignored. She hadn't expected his white-hot, bitter rage—not after this many years. It hadn't been only his words that flayed her. It'd been his eyes, once so warm and tender, now so cold and remote.

Stephen, she decided, wouldn't't've acted in such a manner. Not the Stephen she'd known. He'd've understood what had happened, and that all of it had been against her will. He might not've taken her in his arms as soon as they were private, but all would've been forgiven and forgotten. Within days he'd've begged her to marry him, only too grateful time and a weak heart had made her a wealthy independent widow rather than leaving her the daughter of an impoverished, social-climbing country squire out to barter his daughters in order to line his pockets, or the spouse of a decrepit local luminary who only wanted an unpaid housekeeper to run his establishment and an unpaid governess to see to his daughters' education, and not a wife at all.

Or, would he? How well had she known Stephen Gracechurch, after all? It had only been a matter of the few weeks of his leave, beginning with Mr. Gracechurch's beaming introduction following services of a rainy Sunday morning.

There'd been the seemingly chance meetings when she was out walking, the few dances at country entertainments that aped London's famous Season. She'd been on the block, known it, but hadn't given Sir John Phelps's attentions a passing thought. He was, she'd believed, merely being polite to an old acquaintance's shy daughter. Then had come Stephen's declaration followed by his confrontation with her father. She'd been called into his study at the end of it, the unwilling witness to the humiliation of the proud young officer she'd adored and would've gladly followed to the ends of the earth, counting no privation excessive so long as she wasn't deprived of his company.

They'd managed to meet just once more—that same night, after the countryside was asleep. She'd sworn to wait for him. She managed it for almost a year. Unfortunately, a year wasn't enough when one wouldn't achieve one's majority for two more, and be free to marry wherever one wished so long as one didn't mind being cast off by one's parents. Her single attempt to join him in the Peninsula had ended in hushed-up disaster. Three months later, weak from a diet of bread and water, pale from incarceration in her bedchamber, she'd stood at the altar and recited her vows as ordered.

"Suzanne, Mr. Pemberton's standing in the middle of the lane waving at us with both arms. He wants something. I'm going to have to stop or run him down."

"What? Mr. Pemberton? Why, Cassie?"

"Suzanne, I'm stopping. It would be wise if you'd return to Chipham Common for the next few minutes."

"I've been here all along," Suzanne murmured distractedly. "Indeed, I've never left the neighborhood but the once, for all the good it did me then or now."

"Suzanne!"

"Yes," she sighed, "I'm very much rooted here, however much I may devoutly wish I were elsewhere, and I see Mr. Pemberton as clearly as you do. Myopia's not my current problem, however much it may've been at one time."

Suzanne gave herself a shake. The past was the past, its errors and sorrows as irremediable as they were unimportant. Stephen Gracechurch had been beyond her reach then, though hardly beneath her touch as her father'd claimed. He remained just as far beyond her reach now, however great his physical proximity. Repinings and regrets would change nothing. Neither would being characterized as having taken leave of her senses or entering into a decline. Into each life some rain fell. That she'd endured more than her share of downpours was neither here nor there.

"Good afternoon, Mr. Pemberton," she called. "Such a lovely day, isn't it. Do you require assistance?"

The spindle-shanked apothecary bustled to the cart's side, smoothing the sparse hairs dislodged from his pink pate by the summer breeze, the tails of his rusty black coat flapping about his knees.

"Miss Phelps and Miss Aurelia Phelps stopped to say your mama-in-law required more of her stomach settlers, some headache powders, a jar of her rheumatics salve and three flasks of her fortifying cordial," he rattled, voice as gratingly high-pitched as ever, "but they refused to wait, saying they were expected elsewhere, and I can't leave the shop as my sister's gadding about the village as usual. Could I prevail upon your good offices, Lady Phelps?"

"Of course. We'd be delighted."

Pemberton, effusive in his thanks, and declaring that he'd add a flask of his most excellent complexion restorer to the order gratis as Lady Phelps insisted on going about without her sunshade, backed from the cart's side as if he were in the presence of royalty, then darted to his shop.

"So that's why you insisted we take the cart rather than the carriage," Cassie grumbled. "Bet Aurelia and Delphine were far more uncivil than Mr. Pemberton hinted."

"Probably. The girls have no more affection for Mother India than she has for them, which is understandable I suppose. As for this afternoon, they'd been invited to a *fête champêtre* at the Dennings', and didn't find it commensurate with their dignity as the daughters of a knight to arrive in a pony cart, and the smaller carriage is being repaired."

"While it was totally in keeping with your dignity as his widow to travel about the countryside any which way? Typical."

"At least we weren't afoot, and using a wheelbarrow to transport everything. I far prefer arriving at Mrs. Gracechurch's in a pony cart to the overblown state of either of Mother India's carriages," Suzanne returned mildly, "complete with coachman, groom, and liveried footman, and a horse pistol in the side pocket for protection."

"There's that," Cassie giggled, good humor restored. "Why, I doubt anyone'd've been able to pass through the lane unless they were riding shank's mare, the blasted thing's so cumbersome."

"Precisely, though I do wish you'd avoid using cant," Suzanne returned on a low chuckle. "Besides," she said more seriously, "it's not polite to pay a call in state when one's hostess can't match that state. I'd never for the world play the grand lady with dear Mrs. Gracechurch. The less consequential we appear, the more comfortable for everyone."

Chapter Three

"You'll never believe the wonderful gossip we heard while passing through the village," fourteen-year-old Aurelia Phelps simpered, throwing her bedraggled bonnet at a table by the door to Rose Cottage's drawing room and missing it by a mile, then running a thin hand through her dark, tousled curls as she glanced at her stepmother through wide blue eyes.

Suzanne looked up from the mending with which she'd occupied her fingers, if not her mind, since midafternoon.

The girls had been so long in returning from their excursion Suzanne had considered sending to learn of their whereabouts and the reason for their extended absence—a proposal her mother-in-law had rejected. It might be coming on to dusk, the sky stained a sullen red on the western horizon. And yes, it was well past the appointed hour. But, treat them as tardy schoolroom misses? The chaos that would engender would make their usual tantrums pale by comparison.

Aurelia and Delphine were too well known in the neighborhood for them to come to harm. Besides, between coachman, groom, footman and a pair of abigails, in how much mischief could they indulge?

And now they were back, just as Mother India had insisted they would be, and as self-important as ever.

"Indeed, you won't," Aurelia continued, breaking in on Suzanne's abstraction. "Why, a dozen people must've stopped us with the news."

"It was most gratifying," Delphine—the elder by two years, and equally raven-haired and blue-eyed, a legacy from their mother—crowed as she followed her sister into the room, "and proves their comprehension of our importance in the neighborhood as our father's daughters, for they clearly felt we must be instantly apprised of anything of note that occurs."

"Good evening, girls. A dozen?" Suzanne said, returning her attention to the charity box mending—a far safer place to rest her eyes than the insolent pair, gowns stained with punch, hems tattered, lace mitts and reticules lost or forgotten, faces flushed.

She repressed the urge to reprove her stepdaughters' gauche entrance and lack of civil greeting. Even the mildest comment yielded only increased rudeness these days, full of themselves as they were.

"Surely not so many," she protested mildly.

"Oh, far more." Delphine tossed her torn sunshade aside and helped herself to a handful of sugarplums from the dish by her grandmother's chair. "Why, it was three dozen at the very least, Stepmama," the plump sixteen-year-old caroled, popping one of the confections into her mouth. "And infinitely gratifying, as I've already said. You should be pleased the countryside is according us the deference that is our due. Each hardly had time to regale us with the news before the next came bumbling up with another detail to impart," she continued around the sticky sweet. "They were so full of it, they were dancing on their toes. It was really quite amusing, in addition to all else."

"Colonel Stephen Gracechurch? The vicar's son?" Aurelia picked up the tale when Delphine became unintelligible thanks to the surfeit of sweets crammed in her mouth, throwing Suzanne and then Cassie a speculative glance. "The one involved in some ancient scandal no one's ever been willing to tell us about? The one who's supposed to be deliciously dangerous? He's returned. Isn't it exciting?"

India Phelps's mouth closed in mid-snore. Her snowy head, 'til then lolling against the back of her chair, jerked as her gaze darted sleepily from her granddaughters to her daughter-in-law.

"And an entire month before he was expected, too," Aurelia crowed. "Weren't you supposed to take tea with fusty old Mrs. Gracechurch this afternoon? Certainly that was the excuse you gave for not accompanying us as any decent stepmother would've even if she wasn't invited and would've been entirely out of place—especially a stepmother whom Papa only married for the purpose of having someone to see to us. So perhaps you already know all about it? Perhaps you've even seen him."

The old lady shifted in her chair, pulled a shawl more

tightly about her shoulders and blinked furiously. "Well?" she snapped when neither Suzanne nor Cassie responded.

"Yes, we were aware Colonel Gracechurch arrived unexpectedly this afternoon, Mother India," Suzanne admitted with a sigh.

"Then why didn't either of you mention it at dinner? Is there always to be a conspiracy of silence in this household where I'm concerned? There's little enough of interest happens in this benighted place. Might've spent the rest of my life not knowing Stephen was back, confined as I am, and gone to my grave ignorant as a fish."

"You've seen him? What's he like?" the girls chorused, descending on Suzanne.

"He's a gentleman very much like any other: a head, two eyes, two ears, a nose, the usual."

"Well, is he handsome? At least you can tell us that," Delphine pouted.

"Certainly Cassie didn't find him so."

"No, I didn't," Cassie said from where she sat curled in a chair well away from the others, a book in her lap. "I found him most unattractive. He was dirty and dusty and smelled of soiled linen. As for his togs, they were of the cheapest sort and badly worn. I doubt if he was the first to own them, either. And he was incredibly rude."

"Cassie, he'd just completed a long journey on horseback," Suzanne protested. "He was clearly exhausted, and hadn't taken time to regularize himself out of desire to see his mother as quickly as possible. Do show a little understanding."

"That's no excuse for his lack of courtesy. I don't see why you'd want to leap to his defense, for he was every bit as rude to you."

"Took you for a servant, did he, Cassie?" India Phelps chuckled with uncanny accuracy. "And put your nose out of joint, no doubt. If you'd act and dress the young miss instead of clumping about like a hobbledehoy who belongs in the stables, you'd be recognized for a lady rather than a lad and such insults would vanish."

Cassie flushed and returned to her reading.

"Well, he shan't be rude to *us,*" Aurelia declared, tossing her midnight curls. "He wouldn't dare, for he must know who our papa was, and if he doesn't we'll tell him."

"Much good that'll do you. Besides, he knows perfectly well who your father was," the old lady snapped. "Knows better'n most, I'll warrant, as far as that's concerned. Leave those alone," she barked, slapping Delphine's hand away from the dish of sweetmeats. When the girl persisted, she seized her cane and rapped her smartly across the ankles. When that had no effect, she prodded her posterior. "They're mine. Shoo! Get away with you, Greedy Gus. You're already far plumper than is pleasing, Delphine, and you're forever throwing out spots. It's all that sugar you gobble, as I've told you time out of mind."

"It's not! It's the sun causes my spots. My complexion's unbearably fair, Grandmama," Delphine protested, thrusting out her lower lip, but nevertheless prudently moving out of the walking stick's range. "Mama was just the same. Nurse told me."

" 'Sugaring and greasing make a plump miss infinitely less pleasing,' " India Phelps snapped, "and those're the things you're best at, Miss Sauce. As for your mother, she never threw out a spot in her life."

"Well, it doesn't matter if he's rude," Aurelia said, returning to the main point. "We'll teach him to behave properly if we must, as Delphie intends to have him. We settled that on the way home. Then we'll be able to move out of this dreadful house where life's dull as ditchwater, and have some fun."

"The gentleman just may have something to say about that."

"All men have to marry, and he's reached the age for it," Aurelia returned as she attempted to glide elegantly across the room, instead giving the impression her boots pinched. She sank onto the *tête-à-tête* in front of the empty grate, plumped a handful of cushions behind her back and slung her legs over the opposing arm, swinging them from the knees and absently kicking the already much-abused upholstery. "He'll be infinitely grateful for Delphie's condescension in even considering him, for marriage to her would set him up in the neighborhood as nothing else could, just as marriage to Papa set our stepmother up. Delphie's infinitely popular with the gentlemen, and then there's her dot. She'll only have to smile at him, and he'll come running. I could manage it just as easily if I weren't only fourteen, but I am so we decided she must be the one."

"Infinitely popular with striplings, not gentlemen," India Phelps proclaimed on a bark of laughter. "You'll find there's a difference."

"Horace Whiting danced attendance on Delphie all afternoon." Aurelia leapt to her feet, scattering a rainbow shower of pillows, hands rising to her hips, arms akimbo. "And he paid her ever so many compliments. Pretty ones, too."

"Doesn't say much for Whiting's intelligence," her grandmother snapped. "That, or he was either bored or making mischief on a dare."

"You're a mean old witch," Aurelia muttered, "and as jealous as you can stare."

"Poor as churchmice, all the Gracechurches are," India Phelps continued, either ignoring or not hearing the girl's ill-natured complaint. "You two are a pair of expensive fillies."

"Then it's a good thing Papa left us well-dowered, isn't it," Delphine said airily, darting in to sneak another sugarplum.

"Not that well-dowered, Miss Barely-Out-of-the-Schoolroom-Who-Should-Still-Be-in-It. To think I have such a wet-goose for a granddaughter. Gracechurch is old enough to be your father, you silly chit."

"Our stepmother married Papa, and he was old enough to be her grandfather. Why shouldn't I marry a gentleman old enough to be my father? Especially as he's convenient and would be easy to convince of the advantage to him?"

"Because no one's forcing you to it, goose. Besides, your brother wouldn't permit it and neither would I, and he and I between us must approve your intended or your dowry shrinks to the size of a dust mote."

Suzanne fumbled with her mending, setting a stitch wrong she'd have to pick later, feeling her mother-in-law's eyes boring into her. Dear heaven—would she never be able to spend three hours running in this room, or any room in Rose Cottage for that matter, without at least two of the four pulling caps? And making peace, the task she'd set herself within a day of making the move from Placidia? Any attempt only caused the combatants to turn on her, claiming she lacked any understanding of the issue at hand.

Reluctantly she raised her eyes to meet her mother-in-law's

assessing glance, and flushed uncomfortably. The look at the back of those almost black, snapping orbs was unfathomable. With a sigh she retreated to her mending.

"You'll have to permit it if we fly to Gretna Green," Delphine insisted. "Nothing much either of you can do then but put a good face on it and release our funds."

"Have it all planned, do you?" The old lady made threatening motions with her stick as the girl's hand crept toward the sugarplum dish. "I wonder how much you'll enjoy life in a cottage without a groat to soften the way—or any love, either."

"Gretna Green was Aurie's idea." Delphine eyed her grandmother warily, clasped her dimpled hands behind her, then backed several steps. "I thought it'd be more fun if we went to Paris, but she says there's too much chance of our being stopped before we sail."

"Don't be more of an idiot than necessary, Delphine. Stephen Gracechurch may be many things, including every bit as ill-mannered as Cassie claims, but he's never resorted to havey-cavey behavior that I know of. As honorable as they are poor, all the Gracechurches. Besides, he's far more of an age to consider someone such as Suzanne," the old lady said absently.

"Now you're being silly, Grandmama," Aurelia laughed. "Our stepmother, remarry?" she continued as if Suzanne weren't in the room, and hearing every word. "Delphie has youth and looks on her side even is she is a bit plump, while *she's* nothing but a dried-up old stick. He'll be sure to want to set up his nursery. *She'd* fail utterly in that, being far past it.

"Besides, Oren wouldn't permit it. Then everything Papa left her would go with her, rather than coming back to Oren as it will when she dies unwed. We heard him tell her so following the reading of Papa's will, and not to have any foolish ideas about changing her situation for he'd put a stop to it before she could blink an eye. Oren says she should contract a convenient inflammation of the lungs now we're grown and she's no longer needed, just as the vicar did. Nothing else is convenable."

"Viper! No, Cassie, don't say a word in your sister's defense," the old lady ordered, raising an imperious hand as Cassie sprang to her feet, book cast aside, mouth open, fingers

curling into claws. "It's not worth it, and will only lead to
more brangling, which I refuse to tolerate. This was my home
before it was yours, and I find all your presences unbearably
wearying. Not in the least suitable for an enfeebled old woman
suffering from dozens of complaints who's given notice to
quit at least once a week, and only hangs on from pure stub-
bornness, and perhaps a touch of curiosity as to how life will
work out for the rest of you.

"As for you, hussy," she snapped, spearing Aurelia with
arctic eyes, "one day you'll learn your brother doesn't have
quite the power either he or you appear to believe he has.
Was there ever such nonsense? Suzanne's in her prime, and
remains unwed from choice, not duty or necessity. I know for
a fact she's had five offers, and good ones, for they applied
to me first. Why she rejected 'em is her business, but I can
tell you this: it had nothing to do with Oren's greed, or his
wife's either, and Sophia's quite his match in that department.

"Now, out with you. Neither your behavior nor your disheveled appearances are suitable to the presence of ladies."

The brief and violent altercation that ensued gave the lie
to India Phelps's claim of advanced decrepitude. As ever when
they occurred, which was with daily regularity, the old lady
emerged triumphant, her granddaughters by her son's second
wife storming from the room and threatening dire vengeance
for the insults to which she constantly subjected them.

"Now *that* was invigorating," the old lady chuckled as soon
as she'd chased Cassie from the room a few minutes later
with far more gentleness than she had her granddaughters.
"How does it happen such a pair of ninny-hammers were
born of individuals supposedly in possession of their senses?
Fit for Bedlam, both of them. Of course John always had
more hair than wit, even if he was my son, but Amelia didn't
lack for intelligence whatever her other short-comings, and
they were legion. Indeed, you're the only pleasant daughter-
in-law I've had."

She settled herself more comfortably in her chair and
draped a light shawl over her legs, studying Suzanne's downcast face. It was ever the same: the little harpies insulting
beyond belief, Suzanne foolishly accepting their cruelties

because life and her father had convinced her she deserved no better.

There were times when she almost lost patience with the child. No, if truth were told there were often times when she lost patience with her entirely, for all she rarely let her disgust show. In the past there'd been no remedy—not to Suzanne's situation, and not to her own. Foisting a youthful widow, the young woman's even more youthful sister, and Amelia's two brats on her wasn't the act of a respectful grandson, but that was what Oren'd insisted on as soon as John's will was read.

"Not about to try to make a marriage of it with two giddy schoolgirls and a graceless hoyden and a weeping widow cluttering up the place," he'd ranted when she protested the invasion of her peaceful retreat in the cottage orné—actually a commodious modern country house complete with ten bedchambers and the very latest in appointments and improvements—famed for its roses. "I want room to breathe, dammit, Grandmother. Ain't been married but six months, and Sophia's increasing. One female's enough for any man, especially in that condition. Often too much, come to that. Freshets and vapors all over the place, and that's on the good days.

"Besides, Aurie and Delphie'd go about countermanding all Sophia's orders, and telling everyone how she hasn't any respect for how things were done in Papa's time, and then she'd come complaining to me. Happened already, if you want to know, and it's been just three days since Papa died. I won't endure them, and that's all there is to it."

Rose Cottage served as dower house—there was no arguing that point. His father was dead. No arguing that one, either. Rose Cottage was where Sir John's unwanted young relict belonged, along with the infantry that went with her. If his grandmother wouldn't share houseroom with them, then she could find other accommodations. Lord knew, the place was big enough to shelter a dozen such *ménages* with room to spare, for all the spacious house with its multitude of bedchambers and plethora of parlors was dubbed a cottage—a misnomer if ever there were one.

And so here they'd been, cheek by jowl, for the past five years and more. Suzanne would've been a delight were she not cursed with dragonning her stepdaughters, and far too retiring for her own good.

Cassie was exhausting, but it was an exhilarating exhaustion. She'd gladly bear the girl's presence to the end of her days if there was a need. The point was, there wasn't. Cassie belonged with her parents, not making her sister seem old before her time by implying there was such a great difference in their ages that Suzanne might as easily be her mother as her sister. So she'd informed Squire Hodges at every opportunity, and so she'd continue to inform him until he listened, the penny-pinching old fool. The putative excuse of a wider and more elevated acquaintance to enhance Cassie's marital prospects had crumbled with John's death when the chit'd been but ten, and Oren chased them from Placidia. Now they lived as retired as nuns at Rose Cottage—not that Placidia'd offered much in the way of entertainments following John's third marriage, gouty old frump that he'd become by then.

If either of 'em'd had the requisite scrap of intelligence, she'd've thought Oren and Squire Hodges had formed a conspiracy. As it was, she could only conclude avarice and stupidity in one fostered stupidity and avarice in the other.

As for Aurelia and Delphine, the sooner a professional *duenna* was hired and they were set up in an establishment of their own, the better for everyone. Unfortunately, Oren held the required purse strings and wasn't about to loosen them, blast him.

"Not that I'd admit I enjoy these set-to's to anyone but you, Suzanne," the old lady continued after a thoughtful pause. "Better than a tonic. Gets the blood flowing, and helps me maintain my reputation of a bad-tempered old woman who's not to be trifled with. Keeps the fools at bay—including Oren, whom I can't abide for more than five minutes at a stretch."

"I apologize for their lack of manners," Suzanne said, pausing in her mending to throw her mother-in-law a contrite glance. "Cassie's, too. The fault's mine for not better regulating them. They all behaved unpardonably."

"The girls are no more ill-mannered than their mother, who was as unpleasant a creature to listen to as she was fair to look upon. It's in the blood. Only decent grandchild out of the entire crop's Emeline, and she escaped at the earliest opportunity, more's the pity—not that Roger Dight's not a decent enough fellow, for all Emmie has ten times his intelligence. Seems to work well enough in their case, for a blessing. Rarely does, for in such unequal matches both generally seek more congenial companionship outside the marital bond and create a scandal. But there, they share their love of horseflesh, Dight's seat is actually superior to Emmie's, and apparently that's enough for them. And, I suppose he may have more in his brainbox than I credit him with. Not likely, but it's possible.''

"You intimidate him," Suzanne murmured, returning to her mending. "One's never at one's best when intimidated."

"As I said, a gudgeon. As for Cassie, she's not ill-mannered, merely forthright."

"You'd defend Cassie to the death."

"Reminds me of myself when I was her age. An inveterate hoyden, Oren has that right, but a good-hearted one. She'll do once the edges're knocked off. Time takes care of that, unfortunately. One only hopes too many won't be knocked off, leaving her spineless. It happens. Of course you were never a hoyden."

India Phelps was delighted to see her daughter-in-law flush at her accusatory glance. One message delivered. Good. And now for a few more, along with some information gathering. There just might be a solution to the overpopulation of Rose Cottage, for all Oren would fly into the boughs at the notion. When he did, he could stay there permanently as far as she was concerned.

"Open the windows, would you, Suzanne?" she requested, fussing among the cordial flasks on the table beside her. "Those sillies insist on dousing themselves with the most unsuitable perfumes, and spread the miasma about as if it were fairy dust. The air wants clearing."

As soon as her daughter-in-law's back was turned India Phelps observed the young woman with more than usual care. Still graceful. Still slender. Still light of foot. Hair barely tarnished by time. And, she had all her teeth. Not even Delphine could claim that distinction, enamored of sweets as she was. Of course the hideous grayed lavender gowns worn in deference to John's memory would have to go, and high time— he hadn't earned the right to such punctilious observance of custom in any case—so would the habit of hiding in corners whenever there was company, and never appearing to have

an opinion concerning anything but the weather, and that
only offered in the most tentative fashion.

"Of course, Cassie wasn't very charitable where Stephen
Gracechurch was concerned," she continued, once more
rooting among her flasks as Suzanne returned to her seat.
"Or," she essayed, glancing from the corner of her eye as
she made a great business of pouring some of her favorite
raspberry cordial, "was she actually being charitable where
he was concerned, for all she didn't realize it?"

"I wouldn't know," Suzanne replied, picking up the child's
nightshirt she'd been mending and once more plying her
needle with determination.

"Good heavens—you were there, weren't you?"

"Yes, I was there."

"And knew Stephen Gracechurch in the past, I believe. Is
he greatly altered?"

"No more than one would expect from his experiences
during the war, I suspect."

"Will you cease prevaricating! I know all about your abortive
betrothal and your scotched attempt to join Stephen just
before your father forced you to accept John. Don't protest
it was a ramshackle thing to do. At least you showed some
gumption in that instance—something you haven't done
since to my knowledge. Told your father at the time he was
playing the fool cutting young Stephen dead in front of the
entire village. Sympathies were entirely with him, not your
father. A wounded officer, after all, and a hero of the Corunna
retreat? Idiotish thing to do, and caused the very attention
to the relationship your father was attempting to scotch.

"Oh yes, your father's quite the fool even without trying,
and your mother with not an ounce of control over him.
Quite a scene, that was. He'd be laughable if he didn't make
such a mull of others' lives. But there, Winifred Scanlon was
ever a cloth-head, and changing her name to Hodges when
she wed didn't alter her predilection for folly or her worship
of position and purse. Matches your father perfectly in those
departments."

The poor girl was ashen, actually trembling where she sat.

"I don't blame you for any of it," India Phelps said more
gently. "That you should tumble top over tail for a brave

young officer with his arm in a sling is as natural as breathing. Do you still fancy him?"

"After nine years? I barely know the gentleman now," Suzanne returned with a certainty that said far more than her words. "Our acquaintance was of the briefest to begin with. How would that be possible?"

"Cassie was correct, then. He's become little better than a boor. Pity. Another thing that Corsican monster must answer for when his turn comes. Stephen Gracechurch was both well-spoken and courteous when I knew him—even to an old lady who bored on about subjects that interested him not in the least, and whose only claim on his consideration lay in a childhood friendship with his maternal grandmother and an acquaintance with his mother. Indeed, he was perfectly willing to propel a Bath chair along garden paths for hours at a time even if he suspected its occupant was as capable of ambling about as he was. She was, too, but she enjoyed being pushed about by a gallant young officer. It reminded her of her salad days, you see."

A low rumble of thunder broke the silence that followed India Phelps's evocative words. The air had become oppressive, and not just because of the depressing nature of the conversation. The lemon-yellow damask draperies had stilled in the last minutes. A robin, disporting itself long after the hour it should've been abed, broke off in mid-song. Lightning filled the evening sky with harsh white light, dimming Suzanne's work candle and the lamps on the mantel by contrast. This time the crash of thunder was closer.

"I do believe it's coming on to rain at last," Suzanne said as a sudden gust set the draperies to dancing once more.

"Perhaps you'd best close the windows. At least it no longer smells like a brothel in here."

India Phelps waited and watched, timing her next thrust for the moment when Suzanne was battling billowing yards of heavy yellow fabric. "Well, what *did* you think of Stephen?" she demanded.

"We made our departure after the first flurry of welcomes—a matter of minutes at the most," Suzanne responded, her voice muffled.

"You can do better than that," India Phelps grumbled. "It's just you won't. Either way, you're going to prove uncommonly difficult, that I can tell. Well, if he won't do I'll find another candidate somewhere who will."

Suzanne emerged from her battle disheveled and rumpled, closed the windows, latched them, and drew the draperies.

"What did you say? I couldn't hear."

"Nothing for your ears, my dear. Merely an old woman's maunderings."

She absently brushed her hand against the unstopped flask of raspberry cordial as Suzanne passed on the way to her chair. The flask went flying, spewing ruby liquid over Suzanne's lavender gown and crashing to the floor where it shattered into a thousand splinters.

"Oh, dear—now look what I've done," India Phelps exclaimed, gazing in horror at her daughter-in-law. "I'm such a clumsy old thing. The stuff's ruined your lovely gown, and just look at the carpet. Can you ever forgive me?"

The next three days passed in highly unpleasant fashion at Rose Cottage, for the storm that broke on the night of Stephen Gracechurch's return proved far more extensive and long-lasting than any would've anticipated. Rain fell steadily, sometimes in torrents, sometimes more gently, miring the lanes and depressing spirits to an unusual degree even for that household.

The carpet, a miniature Aubusson that had been one of India Phelps's treasures, proved stained beyond remedy. Her tears as it was rolled up and carted away were too copious to be doubted.

And Suzanne's lavender dinner gown? That too proved beyond remedy, and was relegated to the rag bag—though what anyone would want of lace-trimmed silken rags not even India Phelps could explain. Unaccountably, two more of Suzanne's grayed lavender gowns—her other summer silk and a light muslin—vanished from her dressing room, no one knew where. Other muslins were found to be stained, or with worn spots so obvious and extensive she was forced to discard them.

It all came, India Phelps grumbled, of her daughter-in-law lacking sufficient interest in her appearance to see to the regular refurbishing and replacement any lady's wardrobe required. The harpy who saw to her, a relic who'd served John's first two wives and been inherited by Suzanne, had never cared for the third incumbent. The combination was lethal, she declared. Why, even she—recluse though she was—showed more pride in her person than a woman so many years her junior it was ridiculous.

She instructed her daughter-in-law to acquire a proper abigail who'd be loyal to her alone, and insisted she summon the local dressmaker to Rose Cottage at the same time. It was that, she declared, or else Suzanne would soon find herself parading about either naked or in rags. While the ensuing brouhaha was sure to enliven what promised to be a dull summer despite Stephen Gracechurch's return, providing entertainment for those of insufficient imagination to entertain themselves shouldn't be anyone's goal. It certainly wasn't, she declared tartly, hers.

Suzanne bore the nattering with her customary good-humored fortitude. When, lacking her usual lavender summer evening gowns, she appeared at dinner on Friday in a *démodée* black silk from the first year following her husband's death, India Phelps's dismay was almost comical. The young woman's explanation that she never discarded anything unless it was past all use didn't sit well with her irascible mother-in-law, but there was little she could do or say beyond few muttered grumblings.

Life at the little Gracechurch cottage was, by contrast, all that was peaceful and pleasant despite the inclement weather—if one didn't count the hours Stephen Gracechurch spent staring at the rain, forehead contracted in a furious scowl, or else pacing the rooms with a repressed fury that would've made one think he'd just suffered defeat at the hands of a hated enemy. Scully avoided the main part of the cottage, suspicious of what ailed the former colonel and only too glad to escape his disgruntlement.

Matilda Gracechurch, even more awake to possibilities than Scully, watched and held her peace except when she remarked on the excellence of the meals Mags Reedy prepared. Wisely, she never again mentioned the source of the delicacies, nor did she appear to notice when every bite seemed to lodge in her son's throat. That the liberal provisions of excellent brandy, wine, and Madeira remained untouched she ignored.

Stephen, she was convinced, would come around. Precisely how far that would take him she left to fate, and perhaps the benevolent influence of the spirit she was convinced lingered among the well-worn books on the parlor shelves. That Stephen had made enough of an idiot of himself for it to cause him extreme unease wasn't necessarily a bad thing. Hearing what had passed in her garden hadn't been needed to understand that. His reactions when he'd joined them in the parlor after Suzanne Phelps's departure had been hint enough. Stephen, like it or not—and that he didn't like it in the least was clear—was going to be forced to offer his former love a sincere apology. With any luck, propinquity and that fair-mindedness without which he would never've risen to the rank of colonel would lead to more.

The first Sunday of Gracechurch's return didn't dawn clear, but at least blue skies and sunshine were making appearances through brief breaks in the heavy clouds. Flowers tattered by the storm lifted weary heads, their bruised petals showing dark spots not even Matilda Gracechurch's skill could heal. Trunks were black, splattered with mud, leaves drooping. The lane before the cottage was all puddles, but it was passable if one were determined.

Stephen Gracechurch was determined.

He dressed with what care he could given the intentionally dilapidated state of his wardrobe. While shaggy and in desperate need of the attentions of a decent barber, his dark hair gleamed and he was meticulously clean-shaven. Shirt points remained yellow and frayed beneath a liberal application of chalk. The seams of his well-brushed coat shone. There was a green cast to the cheap cloth of his pantaloons unintended by the weaver, and not all the blacking in England could eliminate the scuff marks on his cracked boots. The aroma of musty trunks rather than sandalwood clung to him, not overpoweringly, but carrying its subtle message nevertheless: Here was a man who'd returned from the wars in worse case than he'd departed for them, pockets to let and with only his pride to see him through.

The troubled expression at the back of his mother's eyes when he joined her in the parlor just before leaving for services made Gracechurch doubt the reasonableness, if not the justice, of his masquerade. Then he thought of the squire and Suzanne Phelps, and his shoulders straightened.

"I hadn't realized you were in such desperate case, Stephen," Matilda Gracechurch said gently as he paused in the doorway, giving his perfectly-tied but obviously mended neckcloth a last twitch. "However do you manage to pay Scully?"

"I don't. His pockets're as shallow as mine, or mine as his, whichever you prefer. We've been sharing what little we have, and making the best of it. At least there's a roof over our heads now, and food when we're hungry," Gracechurch ground out, despising himself for what amounted to a lie, but knowing there'd be no way his mother would keep his secret if she knew the truth. "There's many have returned from the Continent in this fix." That, at least, was nothing but the truth.

"I have a little put by," she said, fingering his sleeve with a concerned frown. "It's not much, but it could see you decently garbed, at the least. There's no need for what amount to rags."

"Thank you, but I'll do as I am for the moment. No desire to bowl them over with my magnificence as yet," he returned gruffly, skirting the truth, but hinting at it nevertheless through the bitter sarcasm. "I just want to spend some time quietly with you. Then we'll see what eventuates. Don't concern yourself. My togs may not be in the latest style, but they're clean and they're paid for, same as my mount and Scully's. Not much style to them, either, but they get us where we need to go. These togs'll do the same."

"Your father would insist—"

"He might've tried, were he here. He's not, though, and we must muddle through as best we can without him." Gracechurch put a gentle arm around his mother's plump shoulders. "I don't mean to make light of the situation, but there's no sense pretending things haven't changed, because they have. I don't look forward to seeing another in Father's place this morning."

"Now there you're being unbearably foolish," Matilda Gracechurch protested, busily gathering shawl, umbrella, gloves and reticule. "Mr. Browne is an excellent young man, and will become as beloved as your father in rapid order. As it is, he's well-liked and respected. We're fortunate to have him and his wife is a miracle, for she manages to see to things without treading on toes. There's been not a scrap of malicious talk about her or the boys. You know how rare that is.''

''I do indeed.''

Whatever Mr. Browne's strengths or weaknesses as the new spiritual leader of his father's small flock, it wasn't to be that Sunday on which Gracechurch was able to judge them. He'd wanted to enter the little Norman church late and so be one of the first out the doors, lying in wait for Suzanne and counting on a crowded churchyard in which to make his apologies relatively unobserved in the general turmoil of country greetings and gossip that invariably rounded out the services.

He'd forgotten about life in places like Chipham Common. The quiet moments of private mourning and abashed apology weren't to be. The return of the vicar's son? After a nine years' absence? Hardly a personal matter.

When he entered through the heavy oak doors with his mother on his arm half the village trailed behind them. Residents had been watching to see if he'd attend services on this first Sunday of his return, or whether—as most of them had hoped to do—he'd permit himself the excuse of uncertain weather, muddy roads, and lack of any transportation for his mother but her own feet.

They should've known better, Gracechurch thought wryly as he ushered his mother into a pew at the far rear of the little church, determined he wouldn't be on exhibition any more than necessary this once. Vicar's widow and son were as likely to stay cozily at home of a Sunday, no matter what the weather, as they were to dance naked around the village pond.

He knelt, head supposedly bent in prayer, hands clasped over the back of the next pew, closing his eyes so he wouldn't have to see the familiar place with the wrong man standing before the altar. Closed eyes made no difference. The rustle of prayer books, the whispers, the very smell of the place made hiding from either past or present impossible. He saw every detail of the stonework, every brass, every curve of the wooden altar screen as clearly as if he were gazing about him like the scrubby boy he'd once been. Saint George still battled the dragon in the liquid light high above the altar, sparkling gold and red and blue and green, shield raised, sword thrusting. Even the faces were there, peering at him, though many he saw in his mind were long departed and time had wrought changes in those who remained as surely as it had in him.

Finally, with the utmost reluctance, he took his seat on the slick pew. His timing couldn't've been worse. The ladies of Rose Cottage had just made their grand entrance, and were beginning their procession down the short aisle to the Phelps pews toward the front. He kept his eyes on Saint George as heads swiveled and voices murmured. Even so, he could tell Suzanne Phelps glanced not once in his direction. The dowager, leaning heavily on Suzanne's arm, was less circumspect and far more curious. He felt her eyes raking him like one of Saint George's spear-thrusts. As if compelled, his gaze met hers.

India Phelps hadn't changed much. Her eyes were as dark and penetrating as ever, her back as straight, her frown as she swiftly assessed his appearance as forbidding. The sudden twitch at the corner of her lips, the slight nod came as a surprise. Then they were past, little Cassie Hodges with her nose in the air, the pair of giggling schoolgirls behind her pausing to gawk insolently at him and his mother. He tried to stare them down, found it beyond him, again sought refuge in Saint George's perpetual battle against evil.

The service began. Gracechurch sang with the rest, rose and sat and responded and knelt by habit, attention wandering between Saint George, the pew at the front, and the new plaque honoring his father's memory, its inscription indecipherable from where he sat. The new vicar had a pleasing voice and a pleasing manner, that much he noted absently. No histrionics, and no mumbling either. His father would've approved. The few phrases of the man's sermon that penetrated his abstraction were well-constructed and thought provoking without overtaxing the intelligence or attention of the majority of his parishioners, though what the topic might be Gracechurch couldn't've said from one minute to the next.

And then, blessedly, it was over and he'd survived it. He was raising his head—if not his eyes—following the benediction, gathering up prayer books and umbrella, pretending preoccupation with the little businesses of putting the place where he'd supposedly worshipped in proper order to avoid watching as the occupants of the first Phelps pew, by custom usually the last to enter and always the first to leave, made their stately progress to doors once more open to the fitful summer sunshine.

Again his timing was amiss. He'd just straightened and turned toward the aisle when Squire Hodges paused by their pew, his wife skittering ahead of him as if anxious not to witness the confrontation. Hodges gave him a hard, sneering look, his eyes like bullets as he took in the worn coat, the yellowed linen, the cracked boots. Then he was past. The coarse, bandy-legged earthenware jug hadn't changed a bit. Gracechurch's father's parishioners clustered about him with cries of welcome, and Gracechurch learned the true meaning of the word "purgatory."

Chapter Four

If he learned the meaning of purgatory inside that little church on the Sunday morning following his return, it was in the churchyard Stephen Gracechurch learned the definition of hell—a term he'd always reserved for the aftermath of battle. Of course, he admitted wryly, the churchyard and the lane before it constituted a battlefield of sorts, if one were both honest and fanciful.

Trapped by well-wishers and the curious, receiving congratulations on his safe return on the one hand and condolences regarding his father's death on the other, at first he was convinced he'd never escape. The opposing generals—William Hodges and Oren Phelps—couldn't've planned it better, though nothing could be more certain than they hadn't planned it at all for Hodges was playing pompous squire among the wealthier residents in the area and Phelps wasn't there at all. Certain things simply happened in certain ways in the country, no matter how maddeningly inconvenient.

He wanted his encounter with Suzanne over and done with, the words said, his apology accepted no matter how stumbling or awkward that apology and no matter how reluctant the acceptance of it, then to be able to forget the incident in his mother's garden and move on to more important matters.

Strangely, he'd almost've sworn he had an ally in India Phelps, who stubbornly resisted her granddaughters' efforts to encourage her toward one of the family carriages, and was apparently exchanging still room recipes with his mother. Finally he managed to break away from Andrew and Abigail Pemberton after enduring an interminable lecture on remedies for the stomach ailments he was certain to have contracted on the Continent, and the necessity to partake of them copiously and often lest he succumb to a wasting sickness or a foreign fever. Only a solemn promise to stop by Pemberton's apothecary shop and permit himself to be physicked and tonicked secured his escape. Pemberton's insistence on a diet of plain tea and gruel for the next month he ignored as if the suggestion hadn't been made.

Hat in hand, boots squelching unpleasantly in the mud, he strode across the churchyard to where Suzanne Phelps waited just beyond the Rose Cottage carriages, staring across the lane to the sodden fields.

"Lady Phelps?" he said, repulsed by his tentative tone, even more repulsed by her black poplin gown, plain black straw bonnet with its heavy concealing veil, black gloves and black Spanish jacket. "Good God, can't you dress any better than that?" he blurted before he could stop himself. "You used to have at least some sense of style."

She was very still, not even seeming to breathe. Then she turned, her gaze sweeping him from bare head to cracked boots. She lifted a single brow, but said nothing. At least she'd acknowledged his existence. That was perhaps as much as he had a right to expect.

"I'm making a mull of it again," he muttered.

She gave it a moment, then nodded and said, "Good morning, Colonel Gracechurch."

"I, ah, learned the provenance of that splendid tea immediately after you left," he tried, more uncomfortable than if he'd been facing a dressing-down by Wellington for some piece of idiocy.

"I assumed you would."

"Which was why you said nothing, of course."

She nodded, gazing at him through eyes that were neither

soft nor hard, welcoming nor forbidding. They merely observed, slightly curious perhaps, offering no judgment or encouragement, no censure, no reproof. Offering nothing. Neutral, in fact. Not a thing he'd ever experienced from her before. It was, to put it mildly, disconcerting.

"Not very forthright of you," he said when it became clear she had nothing to add.

"What was there to say, Colonel?" Her eyes remained locked on his. No bashfulness there, either. They might've been meeting for the first time, no history of love and betrayal between them. "Besides, you gave me little opportunity to speak, being so full of the scold you wanted to deliver. I knew no words of mine would stay the flood."

"Unfair, Suzanne," he murmured, disconcerted by the composed woman before him who'd replaced the gentle girl he remembered. "What was I to think?"

"Whatever you pleased."

"And I did, didn't I. And you said nothing to disabuse me. You're not making this particularly easy, you know."

"Making what easy?"

"Dammit, Suzanne," he growled, "you know perfectly well why I wanted to speak with you this morning. Will you accept my most heartfelt—"

"Here you, Gracechurch: what d'you think you're doing talking with Lady Phelps?" a voice he'd never forgotten boomed behind him. "Didn't you learn your lesson nine years ago?"

Rigid with ill-contained fury at the insult, jaws clenched, hands involuntarily balling into fists, Gracechurch turned to face the squire. This was what he'd wanted, wasn't it? What he'd planned? Why he'd returned as he had, presenting the appearance of little more than a pauper? Certainly, it was. And now it began. The first part of the game would be unpleasant. The rest? Retribution of the most delightful sort. He mustn't forget that.

"Well, get away with you. Go back where you belong, and stay there," Hodges barked, though his bark was perhaps slightly less impressive than Gracechurch remembered.

"Papa, don't," Suzanne said on a pleading note.

"As for you, missy, your mother wants you." Hodges flapped his beefy hands, as if chasing barnyard fowl. "On your way, now. Scat! I won't have you bothered by this paltry fellow. Pockets to let as always, eh what, Gracechurch?'' Hodges finished on an insinuating laugh.

"Go on, Suzanne," Gracechurch hissed on a slowly expelled breath. "Play dutiful daughter. That's your most famous role."

"Here now, who said you could be calling Lady Phelps by her given name?" Hodges bristled.

"I did, Papa." Her head was high, her face chalk-white against the black bonnet and veil, but for a miracle she was standing her ground. "Have a little charity, if you please. The colonel is but barely returned, and deserves a kinder welcome than this."

"And would do best to take himself off again," the portly squire blustered. "Preferably to the Antipodes."

"Colonel Gracechurch has done nothing to earn your contempt, and everything to earn your respect. You're making a spectacle of us all," Suzanne returned coolly. "Is that your desire, Papa? Because if it is, you're succeeding marvelously well."

"I'll have none of your sauce, madam," the squire growled. "As for you," he continued, swinging back on Gracechurch, "y'may take in the middling sort, but you won't cozen me, nor anyone else who matters. Y'won't be received anywhere, that I can promise you, no matter who your father was, nor'll you be invited to ride with the hunt come fall. I'm the Master; the decision's mine. Any who don't like it may go hang."

"I shall doubtless perish of the lack," Gracechurch murmured.

"You won't, but your mother may not find your presence to her liking if you're cut at every turn, and her along with you."

"Petty tyranny reigns rampant."

"Colonel, please."

It was the first sign of emotion he'd seen in her—a slight widening of the eyes, and mortification as severe and painful as he'd been enduring at her hands only moments before. Hodges remained the same self-important lout he'd ever been. Blind, in fact, to anything but himself. In the long run that should make things easier. As for Suzanne Phelps's mortification, that was hardly his concern.

"Had it reported to me you're hanging on your mother's sleeve," Hodges continued as if neither had spoken. "Village is full of it. There're those who think you should be chased from the place."

"An opinion you're doubtless encouraging?"

"Don't need encouragement," Hodges laughed. "They've more than fluff in their brainboxes, don't you see? Not like some I could name." His pointed glance at his daughter was all that was insulting.

"Oh, I see. I do indeed."

"Won't have you buzzing about Suzanne, who's a titled lady now thanks to the good marriage I arranged for her, and not a green girl with no more sense than to tumble for a plausible rogue's fancy words," Hodges declared, drawing himself up. "Above your touch then, farther now, what? Won't have you buzzing about my Cassie, either. Living with her sister, has entry into the best homes. Intended for better'n the likes of you."

"I'm not hanging out for a wife, if that's what troubles you," Gracechurch returned with a silky smile, eyes locked on the squire's, forgetting his company. "If I were, being a man of taste I'd not be hanging out for a hoydenish schoolgirl or a superannuated widow. If you like, I'll sign an affidavit to that effect, and so relieve your mind. Would you care to draw up the document?"

The words hung in the air like so many gobbets of mud, echoing in Gracechurch's ears. He reddened painfully, but there was no way he could or would call them back. Suzanne would simply have to understand. Why she should he didn't trouble to ask himself.

"So there you are, Stepmama dear," a young voice shrilled behind them, breaking the bristling silence. "Whatever are you about, lollygagging so? You're as bad as Grandmama. It must be age, I think, rendering you unconscious of your surroundings. It's coming on to rain again, and we want to return home before our bonnets are ruined."

"You may wait in the carriage, Aurelia," Suzanne said.

Dammit, she didn't seem in the least ruffled by his unpardonable insult. This determined neutrality of hers was becoming wearying. It was also troubling. He'd expected to be the one to pass her by without a thought or a glance. Having the tables turned wasn't what he wanted.

Gracechurch glanced at the source of the youthful voice from the corner of his eye. One of the schoolgirls who'd followed India Phelps and Suzanne into the church, a skinny, pert miss with bold blue eyes and a cloud of ringlets rapidly turning to frizz in the damp, stood tapping her boot, splattering mud on the hem of her overtrimmed yellow muslin gown. Just behind her hovered the plumper one garbed in fussy pink, simpering and posturing as if her life depended on it.

"Well, aren't you going to introduce us, Stepmama?" the scrawny one demanded, giving Gracechurch an assessing glance, much as if she were considering him for a position of some sort.

The plump one batted her lashes and attempted to twirl the lacy parasol of which she was apparently immensely proud.

"My stepdaughters," Suzanne said, voice lacking any inflection, "Miss Phelps and Miss Aurelia Phelps. Girls, this is Colonel Stephen Gracechurch."

"I'm Delphine," the one in pink simpered, once more batting her lashes as she sauntered up to him with hand extended. "I'm the elder. That's Aurelia, but *you* may call us Delphie and Aurie. That's not an honor we grant just anyone. We're Sir John Phelps's daughters by his second wife, who was a famous beauty. I'm considered the belle of the region and a tremendous catch, for I've an enormous dowry. Aurie's dowry is enormous too, but she's only fourteen and so not really out yet though we go everywhere together and even share a bedchamber, being inseparable."

"I see," Gracechurch managed, choking back a bark of laughter as he gave a quick bow. "A pleasure to meet you, girls."

"We're not girls. We're young ladies," Aurelia snapped. "Can't you tell the difference?"

"My pardon. I wouldn't insult you for the world. My eyesight's not of the best, unfortunately, being quite aged myself, and I've only just returned to England after a very long absence. What constitutes a young lady on the Continent is apparently quite different from English requirements," he said, sliding an amused glance at Suzanne as Hodges fumed at her side, cheeks puffing like a bellows.

"You're bamming us," Delphine caroled. "You are, aren't you?"

"Not entirely."

"Then you're flirting. That's even better," she giggled, darting over to place a possessive hand on his arm, and gazing into his face with calculation in the back of her eyes. "I do like a man who flirts. You do it so differently from the boys hereabouts, and so much better. I declare, Continental manners are everything I've been told."

"Delphine, a little comportment if you please," Suzanne murmured.

"You'll escort me to my carriage, won't you, Colonel?" Delphine gushed, tossing her head and ignoring her stepmother. "It's right over there, the big one that's much grander than any of the others, so you won't have to go out of your way. I wouldn't," she simpered, lashes once more seeing action, "want to inconvenience such a distinguished gentleman."

"I'll be seeing you to your carriage if you've become so weak y'can't make it on your own, hussy," Hodges barked, seizing the girl's shoulder and attempting to drag her away from Gracechurch. "This fellow ain't nobody whose acquaintance your brother would encourage. Should've been here today to see to your welfare himself, but he isn't, more's the pity."

"There you are, Stephen!" India Phelps strode up as if neither rheumatics nor rain affected her in the slightest, back ramrod straight, eyes sparkling with amusement as she prodded Delphine aside with the muddy tip of her cane. "I've been looking for you positively everywhere. Welcome home, my dear boy."

She seized Gracechurch's head in lace-mitted hands, bussed him soundly first on one cheek, then the other, in full sight of everyone lingering in the churchyard.

"There—I've been promising myself I'd do that the first time I saw you upon your return since the day you left. One should always keep one's promises to oneself." The meaningful glance she threw first Suzanne, then Gracechurch, had both of them flushing uncomfortably. "Now, dear boy," she continued, tucking her hand in the crook of his arm and turning him toward the larger of the two Rose Cottage carriages, "it's all been decided between your dear mother and me. You're both coming to dine with us. Girls," she tossed over her shoulder, "you can ride in the smaller carriage, for we won't have room for you in the family one what with Suzanne, Mrs. Gracechurch, and the colonel."

"See here, Mrs. Phelps," Hodges blustered behind her, "this ain't right."

The old lady paused, every inch the *grande dame*. She turned, forcing Gracechurch to turn with her by a steady pressure on his arm.

"Yes, Squire? What isn't right? I believe we had you and Mrs. Hodges to dine only two weeks ago. Surely you don't expect to be invited again so soon? Especially as we've received no return invitation?"

"Ain't that," Hodges protested. "Shouldn't be having this fellow at Rose Cottage."

"Whyever not? I consider him a dear friend."

"Y'got girls in the house. Ain't to be trusted around females that're well-fixed. No man is whose pockets're to let."

India Phelps looked Suzanne's father over from the top of his iron-gray Stanhope crop to the top boots protecting his feet from the mud.

"You, Sir, have always been an idiot," she declared, voice carrying clearly. "It would, however, be incumbent on you to be no more of an idiot than you find absolutely essential for maintaining your position as one of the leading lights of our limited society."

"Say what you like, old woman," he growled, thrusting out his chest, fingers hooked in the bulging waistband of his smalls. "I know what I know, and one thing I know is my duty. I'll see this scoundrel chased from the area, and not all the entertaining at Rose Cottage or bussing in the middle of the churchyard'll make a particle of difference. In the meantime," he said, turning on Suzanne, "you and Cassie'll be coming home with your mother and me."

"I think not, Papa," Suzanne returned. "Neither the colonel nor Mrs. Gracechurch have done anything to merit such rudeness."

* * *

Dinner that day was no more trying than Suzanne anticipated. Delphine, encouraged by Aurelia, made a spectacle of
herself attempting to flirt with Stephen Gracechurch, more
than hinting at attachments, summer betrothals, fall weddings
and spring babies, talking across the table, posturing and
preening, and interrupting her elders as if that were the
accepted form.

Cassie, who'd been cornered by her mother following services and so missed the contretemps in the churchyard,
ignored Stephen's existence no matter how desperately he
tried to make amends for his incorrect assumptions the day
of his arrival, her thick-headedness exceeded only by her
deference to his advanced years and gray hairs, both of which
she referred to at every opportunity—an odd sort of ignoring
that would've had Suzanne chuckling had it not distressed
her for Mrs. Gracechurch's sake. Indeed, the minx was treating him as if he were a doddering octogenarian with the same
pertinacity Delphine exhibited in treating him as an object
of youthful ardors and maidenly dreams.

If one had been in the mood to be amused, it was a splendid
farce. To her dismay, Suzanne was in no mood to be amused.
At least she kept her own counsel. Being seated as far from
Stephen Gracechurch as the table permitted made that relatively easy. It also made it supremely easy for him to pretend
obliviousness to her presence, a result that alternately pleased
and irritated.

India Phelps, clearly considering them all fools with the
possible exception of Matilda Gracechurch, was in no mood
to be amused either. Neither was she of a mind to hold
her tongue, no matter how often Suzanne cast her glances
imploring restraint. Finally, on threat of hiring a governess
no matter what Aurelia and Delphine claimed regarding her
having no say in the matter, the redoubtable old lady managed
to banish the girls to their room. Then, once the rest gained
the relative peace of Rose Cottage's drawing room, she commanded Cassie to exhibit her skill in the form of something
lullaby-esque on the pianoforte in a far corner, declared she
and Matilda Gracechurch were in great need of a postprandial

nap, and ordered Suzanne to show Gracechurch the gardens. There had been improvements since his last visit.

No protests regarding the dampness of the paths, the likelihood of a sudden shower, or an incipient headache did the least good. Whether her mother-in-law truly desired to rest, or merely wanted privacy in which to enjoy a comfortable visit with the vicar's widow, the result was the same. Suzanne reluctantly fetched a light summer shawl and the plainest of her black straw bonnets, accepted Gracechurch's arm, and they stepped through the open french doors onto the terrace.

Behind them, India Phelps complained at Cassie's selection of a vigorous sonata. Lusty Beethoven was replaced by tinkling Clementi, the performance so sugared and naively child-like that it brought an involuntary smile to Suzanne's lips.

"If you're truly feeling unwell, we've only to take the path leading toward the wilderness, turn at the sundial by the goldfish pond, and return to the west side door by the box hedge path," Gracechurch murmured as soon as they were beyond earshot.

"I'm aware of the design of the grounds," Suzanne returned graciously, "having wandered them quite often during the past five years."

"No one'll be the wiser," he insisted, guiding her down the broad steps to the garden itself. "You are rather pale, and I shouldn't want to see you come to grief merely to placate Mrs. Phelps."

"Trying to rid yourself of my company so soon, Colonel? By all means, let us proceed as you suggest, then," she said with a laugh that sounded brittle, even to her. "There is a quicker way, however: Through the rose garden by the lily pond to the front of the house and—surreptitiously, of course—through the main entrance and up the principal stairs. You'll find the library where it always was, lacking any books of genuine interest and reserved for the use of gentlemen callers—of whom we've none with the exceptions of Oren, my father, and the vicar—wishing to blow a cloud."

"I'm merely concerned with your comfort."

"Naturally. That's all that concerned you Wednesday last, either. I don't find promenading in gardens with you a pleasant exercise," she murmured with a touch of sarcasm she knew to be unforgivable, for he was being all that was both correct and conciliating. She dropped his arm once they reached the grassy parterre and storm-raked paths, and struck out toward the corner of the house on her own.

"You used to like it well enough," he snapped, hurrying after her, footsteps crunching on the wet gravel.

"Perhaps I'm older and wiser now. Superannuated, as you put it so aptly."

"Your father had driven me past endurance. I said the first thing that came to mind."

"And the first thing that comes to mind when you set eyes on me is 'superannuated?' How elevating."

He grasped her arm, slung her around to face him in full sight of the drawing room windows, were anyone troubling to watch. "I suppose you'll throw those words in my face whenever we meet from now on," he said through clenched teeth.

"Oh, they're accurate enough, as my stepdaughters remind me at every possible opportunity and in every possible manner."

"They're idiots, both of 'em."

"But highly acute in their assessment of both my person and my position here. My duty is done now they consider themselves young ladies ready for the adventures of ballroom and secluded walk, you see. With the exception of my mother-in-law, all are anxiously awaiting my demise, which I'm unconscionably delaying. Most inconvenient for them."

"Blast it, Suzanne—"

"Oh, but it is. Each has spent my inheritance a hundred times over in dreams if not fact, including Oren. Concerning yourself with my health is hardly a kindness to them, nor is it wise. As Delphine said, she and Aurelia are considered the belles of the neighborhood—if only among the very junior set. Act counter to their wishes and you'll lack invitations to the more pleasant of our country jollifications.

"Now, if you'll be so kind?"

Her pointed glance at his ungloved hand, fingers curled tightly around her arm, should've been hint enough. Instead, contrary as ever, he turned her toward one of the paths leading to the wilderness, grip too firm to be broken without an unseemly tug of war, half propelling, half dragging her with him.

"Colonel, please," she protested breathlessly.

"I have a need to speak with you privately, no matter how you feel about it," he said in an undertone. "As for the Phelpses, with the exception of the old lady and Emeline they can all go hang. Unfortunately Emmie's not here. She might be able to make you listen to reason even if I can't."

"Yes, it's quite clear: My feelings regarding being forced into your company aren't of the slightest importance."

"True enough, at the moment they're not."

"Goodness," she snapped for lack of anything else to say that would be cutting, "is there a battle raging around the goldfish pond that will be lost saving your presence, that we must go at such a pace?"

"No, but there will be if your stepdaughters catch us up. They're lying in wait in the rhododendrons. The flashes of pink and yellow were unmistakable. I take it the headache was an excuse?"

"Not any more."

"It would appear your father did me an immense service nine years ago," he ground out.

"No," she returned with a syrupy sweetness she knew would infuriate him, not caring in the least how he felt or what he thought of her as she almost ran to keep his pace, "I believe it was I to whom he did the favor. I shall have to thank him the next time I see him."

"Dammit, woman, button your mummer!" he roared.

"Dear me—I presume this is what they mean by parade-ground manners. I'd always wondered, you see, having been informed they're entirely different from what a lady is accustomed to, but no one has ever been willing to further enlighten me on the matter."

His ill-tempered grunt had her all but laughing. Strange how, when one no longer cared, one could find amusement in the oddest things.

They entered the little wilderness, Gracechurch selecting the path leading down to the rain-swollen stream that flowed past the village. Violets were everywhere, the scent of their crushed petals heady in the still air. The path was muddy, of course, its mossy verges slick. Her boots would be ruined, and her gown as well. At least it was one of her least favorites, dating from the period when she wanted to present a forbidding appearance to forestall the annoyance of potential suitors.

Not bothering with further protest, Suzanne stumbled along beside Gracechurch, determinedly watching her footing and only wishing it were secure enough to safely disengage herself from his grip. A root seemed to leap from nowhere, snagging the heel of her boot. Still they forged on, the loosened heel now wobbling uncomfortably.

"I, ah, earlier attempted to apologize for my misapprehensions of the other day," he said finally, voice strangled.

"Don't give it another thought, Colonel," Suzanne panted. "Certainly I haven't."

"Well, you should've."

"Why?" She stopped and turned to him in the wet, eyes innocently wide beneath the deep brim of her black straw bonnet.

"Because what I said and implied was unpardonable," he admitted with the slightest touch of hesitation in his voice.

"And yet you're asking my pardon?"

"Yes, dammit."

"You have it," she said with a shrug, "if that's what you want."

"So quickly? No protests? No reproaches? No recriminations?"

"Why should I reproach you? It was a natural enough assumption, given your opinion of me." With every ounce of determination at her command, she turned to gaze about them. "Aren't the violets lovely? A shame the rain battered them so, but they'll spring back as soon as we have some sun, I believe."

"And then I learned it was you who saw to my mother's comfort," he continued, "and not Oren at all."

"A minor matter. And the ferns are beaten down as well. Poor ferns."

"Bother the ferns! Will you please listen to me?"

"I've listened. You're making too much of what was truly very little. I saw to the cottage because Oren refused, and I felt it would reflect poorly on both your father's memory and my husband's if someone didn't make an effort. It was little enough I had done, heaven knows, and cheap enough as well. The shed had fallen down long ago, and the cottage was truly uninhabitable. It was see to it, or become a scandal in the village."

"And so having it all rebuilt wasn't for my mother's sake after all. You were merely playing your usual game of avoiding comment and censure no matter what the cost. At least you're right: in this instance no one suffered from your worship of conventionality and the opinions of others. Lady Dutiful at her best."

"Nurse died shortly after Sir John," she continued as if he hadn't spoken, "and the place'd been left untenanted as Oren insisted the expense of rendering it habitable would far exceed any income it might produce. Unfortunately, he persisted in that opinion even when it was the only housing available for your mother, and so I took matters in my own hands. Now, enough of this tedious topic."

"You find a gentleman attempting to apologize tedious?"

"I find gentlemen tedious in the extreme. There's no need for qualifiers. Now, shall we return to the house? You've said what you wished to say and achieved whatever it was you wanted to achieve, I presume?"

"Not quite. I intend to reimburse you for any expense to which you were put, Suzanne," he insisted, clearly uncomfortable.

"With what?" She glanced from his cracked boots to his worn coat, brows rising.

"I'm not entirely the pauper your father takes me for."

"The cottage is part of the Placidia holdings. Its upkeep isn't your responsibility, but Oren's. You're not fool enough to put your hard-earned pounds in his greedy hands, are you? The furnishings were my gift to your mother. Attempting to pay me for them would far exceed your rudenesses of the other afternoon and this morning."

"Ah! At last you admit I was rude?"

"Oh, that I've never argued—merely the point as to whether one should place any importance on the fact. It's my belief one shouldn't."

"My God, but you've become impossible," he muttered.

"I don't believe I've changed in the least," she said, looking at him directly, "any more than I believe you have. Accident, first in the form of my father and then in the form of tangled traces and a broken axle saved us both from a dreadful error."

"A broken axle?"

"Never mind—a slip of the tongue," she said, turning abruptly away.

"What slip of the tongue? What broken axle?"

"You know what an impulsive, foolish child I was in those days. I had an abortive adventure is all—one that ended badly, and which I'd rather not discuss. Now, you'll have to excuse me as I truly wish to return to the house. My boots are sodden, my hem mired, and my head aches unbearably. More to the point, I don't wish to continue this pointless conversation."

"What broken axle?" he shouted after her as she turned back the way they'd come, slipping and sliding in the muck in her haste. "What tangled traces?"

The nap India Phelps had claimed to want, and then found she actually needed after the morning's confusions and the strain of hostessing a gathering that included a pair of icily polite armed combatants, a pair of determined foragers and an undisciplined *guerrillera* who took pot shots at everything in sight, was interrupted by a sudden commotion at the French doors leading to the terrace. She opened her eyes sleepily in time to witness Aurelia and Delphine babbling protests and self-justifications as they tumbled into the room.

Matilda Gracechurch, she noted absently, was on her feet, shushing the impossible chits and calling for Cassie, who'd already sprung from the piano, to run a reconnaissance. Much good polite shushing would do with that pair.

"Silence," she roared in a tone of which a sergeant-major would've been proud, rapping the floor with her cane.

"It was *not* my fault," Delphine howled. "No matter what she says, it wasn't, Grandmama. Our stepmother is nothing but a clumsy ox, and that's all there is to it."

"Well, you did bump into her to keep from slipping," Aurelia carped.

"I did not. She was slipping, and I tried to save her from a nasty fall. Besides, you said I was to—"

"Will you be silent!" Aurelia and her grandmother chorused, then stared at each other in surprise.

"You keep still as well, Aurelia," India Phelps snapped.

"And what were you doing in the garden? I'd specifically sent you to your bedchamber."

"We wanted some healthful exercise before it rained again," Aurelia returned self-righteously. "Surely you can't object to that?"

"You'd be amazed what I can object to," India Phelps muttered, "starting with having my peace cut up."

"Where's my sister?" Cassie demanded, rushing to the terrace doors. "What've you two cats done to her now? Oh, merciful heaven, Suzanne—are you all right?"

"It's not half so bad as it looks," came a rueful, panting chuckle from the steps leading to the parterre.

Slowly, effortfully, Suzanne Phelps gained the terrace, leaning heavily on Stephen Gracechurch's arm. Her black poplin gown was muddied and torn past repair, her crushed bonnet dangling down her back from its narrow ribbons.

"I'm only limping because the heel of my boot's broken off," she explained at the cries of horror greeting her. "There's no need for a fuss, though I do believe my gown's seen better days."

"*You've* seen better days," India Phelps snapped, turned to Stephen Gracechurch. "Ankle's twisted?" she said, ignoring Suzanne.

"I believe so, though she claims the contrary. She wouldn't stand for being carried, but with your permission?"

"*She* is present," Suzanne declared, pulling away from Gracechurch, "and perfectly capable of speaking and walking for *herself.*"

India Phelps cast an assessing glance at her daughter-in-law, who was now attempting to cross the room, her erratic course taking her from table to chair to settee. The silly fool's head was high, but she gripped her lower lip between firm white teeth, and the smallest of puckers drew her brows together.

"Of course, Stephen. Cassie, show Colonel Gracechurch the way up, and then remain with your sister until Mr. Pemberton arrives," Mrs. Phelps instructed.

"I will not—" Suzanne began.

"You will, and now. I've lost all patience with you. Carry her up, Stephen. If she protests, I suggest a wisty castor. That's the term, isn't it?"

"It'll do," Gracechurch said with a chuckle, sweeping Suzanne up in his arms. "Where did you learn that bit of boxing cant?"

"This is Chipham Common, not ultima Thule," the old lady returned tartly, "and John was a roguish devil before he transformed himself into a tiresome, self-consequential bore. Men aren't born with the gout and constipated souls, no matter what you've heard. They have to work at acquiring 'em. Perhaps you'd care to go with them, Mrs. Gracechurch? The proprieties must be observed, I suppose."

"But *I'm* the one who's twisted her ankle," Delphine protested.

Gracechurch, his mother and Cassie paused in the doorway, turning to watch as Delphine demonstrated her incapacity by stumbling across the floor much in the manner her stepmother had employed.

"*I'm* the one needs to be carried upstairs. *I'm* the one needs the apothecary," she insisted, throwing Gracechurch a pathetic glance and calling up a tear that glistened like a rain drop on her rosy cheek.

India Phelps's lunge with her cane sent the girl nimbly scampering out of the way.

"*Ha,*" she crowed. "Caught you out in that one, missy."

"You're an evil old woman," Delphine whimpered. "My ankle's paining me excessively, but anyone'd get out of the way when you swing that thing."

"It is? Show me. Walk."

Delphine again hobbled across the floor as Aurelia cast her eyes to the ceiling.

"Caught you again," India Phelps crowed. "Last time it was the left. This time it's the right."

"Well, they *both* hurt."

"Then take them both upstairs to your bedchamber. Your sister can assist you if you've really a need of it—which I highly doubt."

"There's no need for the apothecary," Suzanne insisted from Gracechurch's arms as Cassie turned to lead the way with Mrs. Gracechurch playing rear guard. "A clean gown, some soap and water for my face and hands, a cool compress and a tray in my room tonight, and I'll be right as rain in the morning. Nothing for anyone to concern themselves about."

"Well, I shan't be," Delphine declared, plumping into a chair and giving every appearance of intending to take root there. "All right, that is. Colonel Gracechurch shall carry me to *my* bedchamber as soon as he's done with our stepmother. I'm far more in need of his assistance than she is. Aurelia can come with *us* to play propriety," she simpered, "and he can keep me company and distract me from my agony by telling tales of his glorious exploits on the Continent. Come back quickly, Colonel," she called after Gracechurch's retreating back. "Unlike our stepmother, who never feels anything, I'm delicate and in ever so much pain. She doesn't need you—I do."

"Join me as soon as you have Suzanne settled, Stephen," India Phelps called. "Don't worry, there shan't be a vixen about the place to trouble your peace or mine when you return."

Then there were only herself and her two granddaughters left.

"You have a choice, *ladies,*" she snapped. "You can take yourselves to your bedchamber instanter, or I'll have you carted there. If necessary, I'll have a pair of grooms summoned to do the job."

"You wouldn't dare," Aurelia sneered. "You try it, and we'll tell Oren."

"Who'll say it was high time," the old lady returned. "Make no mistake—I've not the patience of your stepmother, and I have every intention of seeing to it she no longer has so much patience with you, either."

"This is our home as much as it is yours. In fact, it's far more our home than yours. You're only a Phelps by marriage. We're Phelpses by blood," Aurelia declared, taking a seat by her sister. "Delphie suffered a grievous hurt in attempting to assist our stepmother, and now you treat us as if we're the criminals when Delphie should be considered a heroine. I call that monstrously unfair, but then it's to be expected, I suppose. You're forever taking her part."

"Now you're calling Suzanne a criminal?"

"Well, it certainly was criminal of her to walk in the wilderness with an unattached gentleman," Delphine pouted. "She had no business doing so, especially when I declared my intention of wedding the colonel yesterday."

India Phelps prolonged her insulting laughter as long as she could. When it began to ring false even in her ears, she ceased it abruptly and eyed the two girls.

"I'll have the truth of what happened out there," she snapped.

"It's just as Delphie said. She attempted to stop our step-mother from suffering a nasty tumble, but the woman's so impossibly clumsy there was nothing she could do to save her. It's a miracle Delphie didn't fall to the ground as well. I don't see what's so difficult to understand about that."

"Nothing at all," India Phelps admitted with deceptive mildness. "And that's the truth?"

Delphine nodded vigorously, setting her dusky curls to bobbing.

"Because I shall be asking precisely the same question of Colonel Gracechurch. Do you think his account will tally with yours?"

"No gentleman would ever dream of contradicting a lady," Aurelia declared. "Besides, he was way behind her, and couldn't've seen a thing—not clearly anyway. Indeed, I believe he must've taken liberties she no doubt at first encouraged and then found less to her liking as he became more enthusiastic, for she was running away from him as fast as ever she could, and her face was all blotchy and red."

"What nasty-minded chit it is," India Phelps grumbled. "That the game you play with those boys who're forever chasing after you both when you're not chasing after them? In case no one's ever told you, most often an accuser is guilty of the crimes she attempts to lay at the door of others. The reputation of being a tease can be a dangerous one. Watch you don't come to grief when some man who's not entirely a gentleman decides to teach you a well-merited lesson."

She struggled to her feet and gave the bell rope hanging beside the fireplace a sharp tug.

"Well, which is it to be," she asked, "a pair of grooms, or your own two feet?"

Noses in the air, hips swaying, the two girls decamped with all the speed of which they were capable.

"How do you know so much about teases, Grandmama?" Aurelia shot over her shoulder once they were out of cane range. "Could it be you've personal experience?"

And then they were gone in a flurry of petticoats, saucily twinkling ankles, and giggles.

It wasn't until just before retiring that India Phelps paid her daughter-in-law's bedchamber a brief visit. Suzanne was already asleep, the faint light of the little veilleuse on her bedside table the sole illumination. The young woman's bound foot was propped on a pillow outside the coverlet. Wind rattled the windows, a fitful draft setting the undrawn bed curtains to stirring like ghostly shrouds.

She stood there for some time studying the exhausted, tearstained face exposed to her. It wasn't a twisted ankle or a wrenched foot that ailed Suzanne, of that she was certain. It was a wrenched heart.

Things, she decided, were progressing nicely. Of course it would take a bit of effort to achieve her goal. Her granddaughters weren't the only idiots with whom she had to contend. It was time for consultations and reinforcements. They'd come about if she had to beat some sense into every last one of them, including her dratted grandson. Rose Cottage's peace must be restored while she still had the health and energy to enjoy it. After eighty-three summers, she wasn't certain how many she had left in her.

As for the squire, a horsewhipping was too good for him.

Features lit by a self-satisfied little smile, India Phelps quitted the room, walking stick tucked high under her arm.

Chapter Five

Oren Phelps, merely an untitled country gentleman of no particular distinction—which impediment to unquestioned preeminence in Chipham Common rankled unbearably at times like these—stared beyond the streaming windows of his study, hands clenched beneath his coattails as he watched the rain mire his gardens.

He was in as foul a temper as the weather, and didn't care who knew it. Honors that couldn't be inherited—such as his father's knighthood, bestowed for some long forgotten service to royalty—would be banned if there were the least justice, he grumbled silently, but of course there wasn't. As for females being granted control of their own purse strings, that was insanity. The catalogue of indignities such blunders engendered was one he reviewed at every opportunity. Recently those opportunities had been unpleasantly numerous.

Item: His blasted stepmother took precedence over his wife, and would until she died—a welcome outcome—or remarried, a consummation to be avoided at all costs.

Item: Said stepmother refused all such superior counsels as would have permitted him to touch the interest, if not the principle, of the fortune his father had left her.

Item: He was shackled by the necessity to maintain at least a semblance of amity with said stepmother.

Worst of all, he couldn't order a person or persons to leave the neighborhood, especially not one who—on the surface, at least—had every right to be there.

It wasn't like the days when a gentleman was undisputed master of all he surveyed, no matter what Sophia claimed. No dungeons waited below to accommodate the unaccommodating, no oubliettes to disoblige the disobliging, nor was there even one faithful retainer about the place possessed of dirk and lacking conscience to dispatch interlopers—not that he would consider such a maneuver even under the most dire circumstances. Well, not seriously, at least.

What, after all, could he claim in justification? That Stephen Gracechurch, blast his conniving hide, intended to cheat him of every farthing his father had bestowed on his third wife, robbing son, daughter-in-law and posterity in the process?

Because that was the penniless rotter's purpose in returning to Chipham Common. Old Hodges had the right of it there, however adrift he might be on other matters. Delphie and Aurie playing the strumpet in an effort to catch Gracechurch's eye, indeed. They knew what was owed their father and position better than that, giddy schoolgirls though they might be.

Yet what could he or Hodges do, either of them, however unpalatable the situation? The entire neighborhood would applaud if their Peninsular hero pulled it off.

No, Phelps fumed, he was as trapped by circumstance as any careless piece of horseflesh mired in a bog, and the squire right along with him. Pretty soon they'd both be blowing mud bubbles. The trick would be to send the mushroom packing with the village cheering his departure. The question was, how?

He shuddered, still staring out the windows.

How unlucky Suzanne paid unending calls on the vicar's widow. How doubly unlucky Gracechurch had chosen one of those afternoons to arrive. How triply unlucky his grandmother—blast India Phelps's desiccated hide to perdition—had decided nothing would do but to invite Stevie Gracechurch and his mother to Rose Cottage for dinner following services yesterday. How quadruply unlucky the weather had kept him closeted at Placidia with the vaporish Sophia for over a week without the least opportunity to intervene given Hodges had proved unequal to the task.

A solitary figure was slogging along the graveled drive astride a nag whose head hung low and sides heaved, at once the epitome of dejection and determination, diminishing in size and detail as it drew away. The bearer of ill tidings and unending tattle regarding Gracechurch's activities since his return. A daily visitor, no matter what the weather. And as displeased by events as ever he could be. Hodges, bumptious and sententious, little more than a truncated mustard pot, and with a weather eye to increasing his importance to his elevated neighbors come what might. Blast the man, couldn't he've forestalled the folly of that totally unnecessary invitation to Rose Cottage?

Phelps turned at a sharp knock. His study door squealed on unoiled hinges. How many times had he complained about it to Sophia? But no, she was too ill to see to that or anything else—increasing again, and constantly complaining of the discomforts and discommodations her condition entailed. As a result, on top of everything else he was cursed with a home ill-run and meals ill-prepared, a spouse who was alternately fretful and scolding, and immuration at Placidia at the very moment when he should be bestirring himself on all their behalfs.

Phelps drew himself up, watching his rib—as pale and bloated as she was unkempt—slip into his sanctum and close the door, gaze darting about the room.

"Is he gone?"

"Squire Hodges?" he said, employing infinite forbearance.

Wasn't it obvious no one was to be found in the room but himself? "Yes, my dear, as you can see if only you'll look about you."

"Well, what did he say this time? Anything to the point?"

"Only more of the same."

She murmured something he didn't quite catch as she lumbered to the chair just quitted by the squire and lowered herself into it.

"What was that, my dear?"

"Like the squire, nothing to the point." Sophia pointed to the hassock just beyond her reach. "Looming like a grampus won't accomplish anything, Oren. Do join me or we shall be shouting across the room like a pair of fishwives, and I have the headache. And bring me the hassock. You don't want me crippled for life, do you?"

"No, my dear," he sighed, eyeing the shapeless thing that was his wife.

The only miracle would've been were she not suffering from the headache. Had females any notion how confoundedly unpleasant having children was for a fellow, they'd manage the process in a more sensible manner. But no, they were unrepentantly selfish, glorying in their incapacity and chaining poor fellows to their sides.

"And I could do with a glass of Mr. Pemberton's fortifying elixir," Sophia droned on as if he hadn't spoken. "In that goblet I'm so fond of, Oren. You know the one. Suzanne presented it to me when I was increasing with Bitsy," naming the eldest of their daughters. "I couldn't abide the one he prescribed then, either. It has an etched foot and silver filigree on the stem. I do believe the elixir tastes better in it, for all it remains incredibly foul. It's on your drinks table, and the elixir too, if you'd be so kind? Ten drops, you'll remember—neither more nor less."

"Of course, my dear."

And so he was trapped playing lady's maid despite paying a handsome sum to the woman who supposedly catered to Sophia's needs. It never changed. The moment she was increasing, Sophia commandeered him as her personal slave. Why did he tolerate it? Any man in his situation would've responded with a question of his own: Four children and not a lad in the lot? What else could he do after six interminable years of marriage?

There was, he conceded as he measured out the amber drops and added the water which turned the mixture a sickly pale chartreuse, precious little he could do about it. Sophia had already lost two in the early months, both boys, besides the girls she'd carried to term. He was damned if he'd risk her losing the possible son and heir she currently carried, and for which he'd sacrificed tranquillity and freedom. Pride might be a bitter pill to swallow, but there were yet more unpleasant ones. Besides, she never importuned him in front of others. Sophia wasn't entirely unintelligent, for all she was little more than a coddled brood mare, and an unsatisfactory one at that.

"Here you are, my dear," he said, handing her the filigreed goblet. "And how do you do this morning?"

"With this weather? How do you think I find myself?"

"Out of sorts?"

"Frumpish and blue-deviled, and that's the best of it. You don't want to know the worst. Ah, that's better." She gulped the noxious concoction, her face contorting, then patted her belly. "At least I pray it shall be. Now," she said, setting the goblet on the dusty pie crust table at her side, then folding her hands and gazing at her husband through bright, bird-like eyes, "precisely what did the squire have to say this time?"

Phelps shrugged, sank into the chair across from his wife. "Gracechurch is playing impoverished hero at every turn, has the village fawning over him, even the new vicar. And my blasted grandmother invited him and Mrs. Gracechurch to dine at Rose Cottage yesterday."

"And Suzanne was there? She and Cassie didn't join their parents at Trillings?"

"What do you think?"

"Oh, dear. Is that everything?"

"Some nonsense about the girls fawning over Gracechurch as well."

"Now that may be useful," Sophia murmured. "Just Aurie and Delphie, or Cassandra as well?"

"Don't matter. Passel of lies," Phelps snorted. "You know the squire."

"I do, and he hasn't the cleverness to invent such a tale."

"Ain't as dull as you think—not by long shot. Clever as he wants when he needs to be."

"Besides, what purpose would false tales serve? He's our friend in this, whatever your past disagreements. No, if he said it, it's true—you may depend on it. Was the colonel always so popular in the neighborhood?"

"A thorn in the side of every right-thinking man—I've told you that countless times."

"Yes, you have. I'd hoped your song might change in pitch, if naught else. Everyone loves a rogue unless he carries roguishness too far. Has he always been one to catch the ladies' eyes? More to the point, did they catch his eye?"

Phelps hitched his shoulders, clearly uncomfortable at the direction of her questions. "Left early on to join the army," he mumbled. "Still little more than lads then, really. Ain't been about much since, except that one time just after Corunna when he was recovering from his wounds and encountered Suzanne."

"So the village isn't that well-acquainted with the man, for all they knew the boy well enough?"

Phelps nodded, stirring uneasily in his chair.

"That's the way to handle it, then," Sophia said placidly. "The lower orders will believe most anything if you drop a hint here and there. They'll spread whatever news you wish about for you. No need to involve yourself beyond the first whisper or two. You are Sir John's son. That still counts for something even if he has been dead these five years and more, and left off entertaining before he married Suzanne."

"Not sure I like what you're suggesting."

"I haven't suggested a thing as yet," Sophia protested on a trill of laughter. Then she sobered. "Pounds to pence your colonel hasn't the slightest interest in Suzanne if she treated him as I've been told. But if he remains in the district? Heaven knows what may happen—you and the squire have the right of that, if nothing else. It's most inconvenient, his returning at precisely this moment. If ever she's to remarry, now's the time she'll do it. Couldn't he have waited five more years before returning, or ten? Then it wouldn't've mattered."

"Don't like it."

"Soon or late, your sisters are going to need their dowries. Your daughters as well."

"They're mere babes," Phelps grumbled, rising to pace the room. "There's time yet."

He paused at the window, hands once more clasped beneath his coattails, bouncing on the balls of his feet and treating his wife to the sight of his back.

"The time will come, a point on which we've already agreed, as I remember it," she droned on behind him. "I'm not suggesting pistols at dawn or pillorying, Oren—merely that the villagers be convinced to encourage him on his way before any irreparable harm's done. Surely you don't balk at that notion?"

He shrugged. Horsewhips, fisticuffs—those he understood. Those he condoned. Blustering and threats had their place as well. This female propensity for little games, as Sophia called them, set his teeth to grinding and gave *him* the headache.

"We'll see," he mumbled, back still turned.

"Mark my words, husband," Sophia cautioned, pulling herself from the chair and rubbing the small of her back, "on the day Suzanne sets aside her mourning you'd best do more than just 'see.'"

India Phelps timed her visit to perfection.

Report had it Stephen currently passed the latter part of the afternoon (and often a good portion of his evenings as well) in the Tipsy Parson's taproom renewing old acquaintance, more often than not in the company of his former batman. While she didn't necessarily approve the practice— ale thickened the waistline, port led to gout, and Stephen was too well-looking a man to succumb to either at so young an age—at least it got him out of the way for the time she required.

If matters eventuated according to her desires, Suzanne's influence would bring a halt to that insidious practice. Generally speaking, men who frequented taprooms with regularity were bored at home, a not unsurprising situation where Stephen was concerned when one considered the eventful life he'd been leading and the retired manner in which his mother passed her time.

Report had it his consumption was moderate—India Phelps

was nothing if not careful where her daughter-in-law's welfare was concerned—shallow pockets leading to shallow tankards as both he and his batman were too proud to accept hospitality they couldn't return. The situation could've been worse, for no matter how much she desired to regain the peace Rose Cottage had once offered she wouldn't foist a genuine tippler on Suzanne, any more than she'd've foisted a gamester. They made the very worst sort of husbands. But a man who was bored with his manner of life? Ripe for the plucking, as the saying went, and grateful when it was accomplished.

As it was, on this drizzly afternoon Suzanne and her step-daughters were paying a duty call on the ever demanding Sophia. Cassie roamed the countryside on her gray despite the inclement weather, insisting Duro required exercise or he'd go mad.

Only the servants remained to witness India Phelps's descent from her bedchamber, clad in what passed for call-paying regalia among the high-sticklers of Chipham Common and armed with her walking stick.

Only they knew she'd commanded the smaller carriage be brought round as soon as Cassie vanished down the lane at a gallop that would earn her a private scold from the old lady later, not because of social error, but for the danger in which she placed herself on mired roads riding a horse that hadn't been out of the stables in almost a week.

Only they were aware that, besides two bottles of exception-ally fine port, a pineapple purloined from Placidia's succes-sion houses, and a fine sirloin of beef, she'd ordered Rose Cottage's cutting garden stripped of its most exotic blooms, all the while admitting that bearing flowers to Matilda Gracechurch was tantamount to bearing coals to Newcastle.

And only Croft, the aged coachman she hadn't the courage to dismiss, knew his instructions were to take her to the cottage shared by Gracechurch and his mother not by the lane that passed through the village, but by tracks that twined among the outlying farms so her visit wouldn't be noted.

As planned, India Phelps arrived at the Gracechurches' door unannounced and unwitnessed.

She delivered her bribes.

She invited herself in, shushing the widow's apologies at being caught in the midst of housewifely duties with a good-humored twinkle that would've stunned her two youngest granddaughters, convinced as they were she was intent on making their lives as miserable as possible—an impression she fostered at every opportunity, stirring the pot until it boiled over and they ran complaining to their half-brother begging houseroom at Placidia. Heaven knew they were more legitimately his responsibility than hers or Suzanne's. The sooner the man-hungry chits were gone, the better. Eventually Oren's resolve would crumble, little though he currently suspected it. The first order of business, however, was to see to Suzanne's future.

The bustle of arrival, of divesting of pelisse and bonnet, of umbrella and shawl and gloves and scarves was quickly seen to, along with effusions that were both sincerely gracious on Matilda Gracechurch's part in acceptance of floral gifts and the more substantial offerings, and protestations that the gifts were a paltry nothing on India Phelps's part that were equally sincere.

Mags Reedy whisked the provision baskets to the kitchen, cooing over the sirloin and the port and promising to return faster than cream turned sour in August with the tea tray. The two ladies retired to the parlor, settled themselves on either side of the table before the windows to take advantage of the meager afternoon light, arranged skirts and shawls to advantage, and surreptitiously inspected each other. Unnoticed at first by either, the assessing silence grew.

Then, as if simultaneously recognizing the social gaffe of which they were guilty, "So kind of you to trouble stopping by in such unpleasant weather, Mrs. Phelps," the vicar's widow said; and, "How remiss I've been, leaving all effort at proper attention to Suzanne and robbing myself of the treat of your company into the bargain," the defunct knight's mother apologized.

They looked at each for another moment, brows rising. Then both burst into good-natured chuckles.

"There was a time when you called me by my name," India Phelps said. "I wish you would again, Matilda. Makes me feel years younger, and I can always do with a bit of that, especially when a nasty period of rain sets my bones to aching."

"We can all always do with a bit of that," Matilda Gracechurch responded with a twinkle.

India Phelps glanced around the parlor, taking in the well-worn books, the new carpet, the bookcases to either side of the fireplace, the engraving over the mantel. The worktable that had served the vicar as desk, now standing in a crowded corner rather than in the capacious study at the vicarage, gave her a turn.

"I know I said at the time how deeply I regret dear Joseph's untimely passing," she said, hesitating as she tried to find adequate words, "but—"

"Young Mr. Browne is filling his shoes to perfection, and with a geniality and circumspection that're infinitely to his credit," Matilda Gracechurch interrupted. "It can't be easy following someone so universally liked and respected. Much easier for him had Joseph been a prosy bore. Better yet, Joseph should've been a heartless ogre giving all his devotion to God's laws and none to His compassion and love. Then all would be cheering the new vicar instead of watching his every step and listening to his every word as if he were suspected of murder. Really most unfair of Joseph not to've been a monster, though infinitely more pleasant for Stephen and me."

"How you keep your good humor through everything I'll never understand," India Phelps murmured. "A husband dying well before his time, and a beloved son gone to the wars—for which I partially blame myself of course, but it was what he wanted and Emeline was at her persuasive best that day. What was I to do?"

"Precisely what you did. One can't chain one's children to one's side and surround them with cotton wool all their lives, much as one might wish to. There's a time when they must try their wings. We'd've purchased Stephen his colors if we could have. Your generosity in sponsoring him was kindness itself."

"Which he repaid first by his gallantry, and then in hard cash just following Waterloo. He always swore he would one day. Stephen's a man of his word."

"And Stephen survived, so our prayers were answered. As for Joseph, we had many good years. It's not how many there are, but their quality that matters, I think."

The widow's expression softened as she gazed wistfully at the barren worktable and the empty chair before it, almost as if she were attempting to conjure up a vision. Then she gave herself a little shake and turned back to India Phelps, eyes sparkling.

"A pity for Mrs. Browne that I hadn't the grace to die when Joseph did, for her situation is even more uncomfortable than her husband's," she chuckled. "I've stayed as out of the way as I can, and refused Abigail Pemberton's pleas to instruct the poor thing on how we customarily did things, and so she's doing just splendidly and those in need of assistance or advice are beginning to turn to her out of respect and fondness rather than desperation. While they'll make changes eventually—only natural, and not the insult to Joseph's memory Miss Pemberton claims—they've had the intelligence to hold off a bit. Joseph would be delighted with them, don't you think, and their sons as well?"

India Phelps cocked her head, smiling now the first uncomfortable moments had been gotten through. "Their sons above all, I believe, irreverent young scamps that they are. Popping out from behind churchyard markers shouting boo, indeed!" Her twinkling eyes belied the note of reproof. "It pleases me no end to see little boys playing in the vicarage garden again," she prodded slyly. When that effort elicited no response she deepened the subtle barb, continuing, "How you must regret things turned out as they did nine years ago, for otherwise you'd've been sure of a bouquet of grandchildren to keep you lively, for all your borders might've become a bit tattered."

"I've always believed things eventuate as they ought." Matilda Gracechurch retrieved a child's pinafore from the basket of charity box mending beside her chair, eyes downcast, threaded a needle, and set to work on a split seam without so much as a murmur of apology. "God's plans are wiser than man's."

"I also believe your husband was fond of saying He helps those who help themselves. There's a pair of young fools in desperate need of our assistance, to say nothing of the delight we'd find in foiling old Hodges and sending my dratted grandson to the roundabout."

Matilda Gracechurch's eyes remained fixed on her mending as her needle wove through the cloth, never pausing, never faltering.

"Then there's the two of us to consider," India Phelps forged on. "I, for one, may dearly love my daughter-in-law, but I wish with equal fervor that she were someone else's daughter-in-law, living a life more in keeping with her youth and leaving my house to me. As for Aurelia and Delphine, they belong with their half-brother and his wife. Let someone else deal with their vapors and effusions."

And still the vicar's widow kept her eyes on her work and her opinions to herself.

Was she glad of Mags's appearance with the tea tray and the distractions it offered? There was no way to tell, though with a servant present India Phelps broke off her importunings in favor of more general conversation on such innocuous topics as the weather, the state of the roads, the latest news of Emeline and her husband, and Mr. Browne's sermon of the day before. Agreement was instant, the weather being declared abysmal, the condition of the roads following a hard winter and wet spring abominable, Emeline's impending annual visit a joy to be anticipated, and Mr. Browne as having spoken both feelingly and well concerning the plight of Wellington's penniless discharged troopers and their families, and the duty of every Christian family to stand in the guise of Samaritan to them. Tea was poured, consumed and declared the ultimate restorative, toasted stale bread fingers filmed with last year's quince preserves pronounced delicious.

Through it all India Phelps's eyes flared with irritation, her voice almost too mellifluous for credulity.

"It won't do, you know—pretending nothing's amiss," she snapped as soon as Mags retrieved the tray and vanished toward the kitchen attached to the rear of the cottage. "The individual with whose plans such an eventuality didn't accord is slightly lower placed than Heaven's throne, whatever he may think about the matter. Hodges was as much of a fool then as he is now, and broke more than one pair of hearts is my guess."

India Phelps watched the needle poke through the worn fabric, setting fine stitches that might lend the tiny garment a little additional life.

"What would you say, Matilda?" she insisted with growing impatience "Was it only his daughter and your son who were affected by his silly determination to see Suzanne cut a dash in the neighborhood?"

"Leave it be. What's past is past, and probably beyond remedy."

"You think so? You really think so? After yesterday's display?"

Matilda Gracechurch's needle flew through the thin cotton. "What happens or does not happen is Stephen's business," she said, "and perhaps Lady Phelps's. I wouldn't presume to interfere."

"That's where we differ. I intend to interfere."

"Such interference is more likely to produce unwelcome results than welcome ones. Do have a care. Both have changed in more than years."

"I never would've thought you a poltroon. Certainly you weren't as a girl."

"And I," Matilda Gracechurch returned sternly, "would've never believed you an interfering busy-body. Stephen has earned the right to wed where he will, and if he wills it. He may not, you know. I'm far from convinced he's returned to seek a wife. Certainly his circumstances would make such a step imprudent, for he can barely see to his own needs. Heaven alone knows when Mr. Bates last received his wages. A wife and children into the bargain? Out of the question at the moment," she sighed. "Such a wealthy young widow as Lady Phelps? All would call it creampot love, and sneer at him behind his back even if they didn't do it his face. No, no matter what Stephen's desires may be, he's trapped by circumstance."

"Stephen? Genuinely penniless? Don't tell me he's imposed on you so."

"I'm afraid it's the truth." Matilda Gracechurch set her mending aside, gazing earnestly in her old friend's face. "He was comfortably fixed at one time, he says, but there came an opportunity to triple what he'd saved. It was a risky business, but well worth venturing he thought. In the event instead of becoming quite wealthy or else remaining merely comfortable, now he's as near to destitute as makes no difference."

"And pigs will fly over Saint Paul's in the morning," India Phelps muttered too low for her hostess to hear. "Whatever can he be about? Well," she said more loudly, "if that's the truth of the matter I'm sorry for it. Stephen always impressed me as having more intelligence than to fall into such a self-destructive trap."

"We can all be fools on occasion. He wanted to lord it over Lady Phelps and the squire—he's admitted that much. Not very generous of him, and now he's paying the penalty for his lack of charity. So often that is the price of improper pride, you know, and the desire for revenge, for all his fine plans quite blew up in his face."

India Phelps kept her doubts to herself and turned the conversation to less unsettling topics after gaining Matilda Gracechurch's assurance that while she might not assist in any plots to bring Suzanne and the colonel together, neither would she join forces with the squire and Oren Phelps to foil them. With that she had to be satisfied for the moment.

"The squire was so kind as to call earlier," Sophia trilled when the tea had grown cold, the last cake crumb been consumed, the girls banished to window seats overlooking the rain-soaked garden, and the conversation languished, thick as the weather and twice as dull.

Suzanne remained apparently unmoved under her daughter-in-law's suggestive glance, merely murmuring, "How thoughtful."

Around them the inconvenient, démodé room sank into a silence broken only by Delphine and Aurelia's occasional titters as they poured over old copies of *La Belle Assemblée*, prattling of gowns and beaux and entertainments.

No flowers softened the graceless mantel or clumsy antique tables. Dark paneled walls, smoke-stained ceiling, deep burgundy draperies, worn brown and gold carpets—all were as oppressive and shabbily opulent as they had been when Suzanne came there as a bride. The only change lay in the dullness of the oak furnishings, which she'd seen were at least kept gleaming with polish in those days, and the now perpetually tarnished brass firedogs and fender on the hearth.

The lack of proper housekeeping, the absence of the slightest touch of cheer was, Suzanne knew, a determined ploy on Sophia's part to bring Oren to his knees. He had yet to sanction the massive—and costly—redecoration of Placidia his wife demanded. What had been good enough for his father was good enough for her. So had Sir John claimed the one time Suzanne broached the subject, desiring to refurbish the schoolroom for his daughters' sakes. On a sodden day such as this the atmosphere was more tomb-like than ever, carrying with it an aura of ancient drains, musty cellars and dank ashes, the pervasive dust teasing nostrils like cheap perfume.

Suzanne sighed, remembering only too well the hours of boredom she'd endured in this room, keeping out of Sir John's way and attempting to instill a trace of proper comportment in his daughters. Avoiding Sir John's notice had been by far the easier task.

It was here she'd been sitting when Sir John's physician announced her entry into the widowed state. It was here she'd been sitting when Oren ordered her and the girls from the house the day following his father's funeral.

"We were so anxious for news," Sophia continued, breaking in on what, given her surroundings, Suzanne could only characterize as a brown study, "being penned here by the weather and my condition."

"So inconvenient for you."

"Yes, ah well—duty, you know. One must do what's best for the coming generation, no matter how contrary to one's own desires. Or, perhaps you don't." Sophia's eyes dropped, then rose to peer speculatively at Suzanne. "The squire said that fellow accosted you. You know the one, the son of the previous vicar. That you actually spoke with him."

"We're old acquaintances. You believe I should have cut Colonel Gracechurch in front of the entire village?"

"Nothing so extreme as that, but his presumption in approaching you passes all that is pleasing. Merely a country mushroom with nothing then to recommend him in face or figure or manner or fortune then and nothing now, according to your father. Oren concurs. You should consider your position."

Suzanne stirred restlessly on the lumpy settee across from her stepdaughter-in-law, then forced herself to stillness at the sudden light of triumph in the woman's eyes. "And what position is that?"

"You are a Phelps. You're the widow of a knight. You must

maintain a certain distance or they'll be calling you giddy all about the countryside, and anxious to buy yourself a husband. You shouldn't like to be the subject of such gossip, no matter what the truth of the matter."

The sly glance, the insinuating tone combined with the superior smile gracing Sophia's features were almost more than Suzanne could bear. She longed to box the slightly younger woman's ears, to slap her silly—most unaccustomed emotions. Customarily Sophia merely bored her.

Instead she said, "I see. It would've been wisest, you believe, to cause a scandal in front of the entire village?"

"Hardly that, but I do feel you should be cautioned Stephen Gracechurch isn't quite the thing. A rough military sort, and without a *sou* to call his own?" Sophia glanced at the rings decorating her fingers. They gleamed with gold, sparkled with sapphires and emeralds and rubies despite the uncertain light, all old family pieces Suzanne had elected not to wear. "Granting him notice would debase your standing, both in the countryside and within the family," Sophia continued. "Oren doesn't desire his acquaintance, and neither do I. What does anyone know of him beyond what he claims for himself, after all? Your father said you spent an inordinate amount of time chattering with the fellow, though he did his best to send him packing and instill in you a sense of your position and duty. You should be guided by older, wiser heads in this. I tell you only to maintain harmony in the family, you understand, for I shouldn't like to see Oren forced to call you to task regarding the matter."

"How kind of you to caution me." Suzanne managed a smile that felt like a death rictus as it bared her teeth. "A pity Mother India isn't with us today, for it was she invited the colonel and Mrs. Gracechurch to dine with us at Rose Cottage. Are you going to caution her as well?"

"I'll leave that in your capable hands," Sophia returned with another sidelong glance. "Neither of us would care to see dear Oren compelled to exert his authority as head of the family where she is concerned. Most unpleasant, that would be. Family disagreements are inimical to my current state. Neither you nor Mother India would care to endanger the child I carry, I'm sure?"

"Naturally not, though how our dining with the vicar's widow and his son could do that I fail to understand."

"But then you always were something of a goose, weren't you? And hardly capable of seeing to your own or anyone else's best interests. That's why Oren insisted you settle with Mother India—who can unfortunately also play the fool at times—rather than permitting you to set up your own establishment and sending the girls away to school where they truly belonged. You wanted occupation and overseeing, and we ensured you had both. That was all decided between your father and Oren and me at the time, and a wise decision it has proved given current circumstances."

Suzanne choked down a sudden blinding rage, clenching her hands in her lap until the knuckles showed white. At least that stopped their trembling. There was nothing she could do to still her heart, no matter how she tried.

"I see," she said at last.

"I was certain you would. I've always been told I have an excellent way of explaining things."

"Did Oren commission you to inform me of all this?"

"Oh, dear me, no. He wouldn't presume. I shouldn't have done it either, were I not convinced you're merely heedless and perhaps a trifle vain rather than actively malicious, and require only a gentle hint or two to put you right. After all, you are confirmed in your solitary state. You've rejected several suitors, and well-fixed ones at that. No reason to engender misconceptions at this late date."

"No, no reason at all."

"And every reason not to. Much more comfortable for everyone, and far more in keeping with your status as Sir John's widow."

"I'm only surprised," Suzanne muttered too low for her words to reach Sophia, "you didn't all require me to throw myself into his grave and cover me over with dirt."

"What did you say?"

"Nothing of consequence."

Suzanne's gaze flew to where Aurelia and Delphine still pored over fashion plates, now squabbling about which costumes would be most likely to find favor in Colonel Gracechurch's eyes and lend Delphine the desired air of sophistication. Their only points of agreement lay in the absolute necessity for daringly plunging décolletages, sheerest muslins and dampened petticoats. Then Aurelia was pulling Delphine's jet curls and calling her a mindless idiot, Delphine whining that she had every bit as good a sense of style as Aurelia and doing her best to land a pair of sharp kicks to her sister's shins.

"Girls, cease that this instant," Suzanne snapped, rising. "Whatever will dear Sophia think?"

How clever. How infinitely efficient the solution to the problem of a wealthy young widow her father and Sir John's family had selected. If poor Stephen had been the man she thought him years ago, she'd almost be tempted to throw her cap over the windmill just to spite them.

As it was, Mother India probably had the right of it. A little more independence was called for. And perhaps a few slightly more modish gowns? There was no reason for her to continue in half-mourning, after all. That had been her own choice, and made with excellent reason. As Sophia said, the neighborhood had finally accepted her status and conceded she had no intention of changing it. No suitors came importuning her these days. At every country fête and ball she was left to sit with the other widows, listening to stale gossip and fetching innumerable cups of watery punch, rather in the manner of a superior lady's maid or a poor relation. She was sick unto death of it.

A few minor changes should be safe enough.

Chapter Six

Squire Hodges hadn't returned to Trillings following his visit to Placidia.

Instead he'd jogged about the countryside for the rest of the day, damp from the drizzle, disgusted by Oren Phelps's equivocations regarding potential steps to rid them of Chipham Common's unwanted Peninsular hero, and morose in the knowledge that wherever he turned Stephen Gracechurch was welcomed with smiles and slaps on the back for his father's sake if for no other reason while he, a noted landowner whose family had been prominent in the neighborhood since before the Flood and who should have received more respectful treatment despite his diminished circumstances, instead was generally accorded little more than a shrug or, at best, a reluctant tug of the forelock.

Too, Hodges was loath to return to his wife with news that nothing had been settled. That was precisely what she'd predicted. She didn't need to be apprised of her triumph so quickly. Having her be even partly right in such an instance would have been insupportable. Admitting she'd been entirely right was beyond him at the moment, and the harpy would be certain to force the truth from him. And revel in it. She always did.

He despised those moments as much as she delighted in them, and she'd been enjoying far too many of them lately, starting with yesterday morning. Quite ignoring his superior wisdom in such matters, she'd insisted Suzanne had never forgotten the impoverished former officer, cared nothing for titles or money or position and, if permitted, would exchange pleasantries and more with Gracechurch at every opportunity as soon as he returned.

Right, right, and right again, blast it. Suzanne was lost to all propriety. A fool. A goose, feckless as they came, with naught but fluff in her cockloft and the memory of a pea-hen. She'd clearly forgotten the period between Gracechurch's departure and her marriage to Sir John, and needed to be reminded what he, the squire, would tolerate and what he wouldn't. She might be a widow. She might be far wealthier than he. That gave her no right to independence of thought or action. He was, after all, her father. That still counted for something, at least in his mind and in this part of England.

Hodges had mulled the visit to Placidia as his mount plodded across sodden fields and along mired lanes. He'd twisted its unsatisfactory tenor this way and that like a rotten tooth one knew required a trip to the drawer and an agonizing session with pliers and straps. Nothing had gone as he'd planned—nothing.

For Phelps insisted Suzanne remain under his own eye rather than agreeing to a return to her childhood home and her father's control. It was high time, however, for Cassie to

rejoin her parents, if Hodges wanted the truth of the matter.
With her mother-in-law, Aurie and Delphie to cheer her days
and enliven her evenings, Suzanne had no need of her sister's
presence, which was an unwarranted drain on her pockets
and, by extension, his.

Well, Cassie would stay precisely where she was, no matter
what Phelps pretended. Growing girls were expensive and
flighty. He refused to stand the nonsense when Suzanne's
pockets were far deeper than his own. As for flightiness, a
female was far better equipped to deal with such vagaries than
he, and Suzanne was sensible enough except when it came
to herself.

Worse yet, Phelps had insisted Hodges leave the matter of
chasing Gracechurch from the neighborhood to him. Hodges
did not have, Phelps claimed, the necessary turn of mind to
pull the thing off. He'd botch everything, and they'd be in
worse case than ever. Besides, Hodges's dislike of the man
was too well known, and had been exhibited for all to see
only the morning before. If any had forgotten the incident
in the churchyard nine years before, they'd been forcefully
reminded.

No, Hodges would have to content himself with watching
from the sidelines and following whatever lead Phelps in his
wisdom deemed best.

Hodges didn't like following another's lead. That it should
be Phelps's, who was little more than an oversized gawk and
Suzanne's stepson into the bargain, rankled. No proper deference to gray hairs. No understanding of the fact Hodges had
been uncommon kind in bringing news of events following
services the morning before. Phelps'd taken it as his due,
blast it, sitting there with his bloated stomach and his almost
broad shoulders and his almost not thinning hair, garbed in
his almost tailored-in-London jacket with his almost aristo-
cratic nose poked in the air. It wasn't to be borne, and Hodges
was damned if he'd bear it.

He was also damned if he'd stand by and watch Suzanne
throw away the handle he'd been at such pains to acquire for
her, and never lift a finger to prevent it. Such foolishness
would make him the laughing stock of the neighborhood.

Late afternoon found the squire in Chipham Common,
more irritable than ever, nursing a pint of mulled ale and a

fine case of the sniffles at the Tipsy Parson and observing Stephen Gracechurch and his current cronies—Andrew Pemberton; Lambeth Scowden, one of the more affluent local landowners, and possessed of three unmarried daughters; and Duward Sanwiddy, the sacristan—from his self-appointed place of honor by the fire. An apothecary, a gentleman-farmer, a sacristan, and a profligate, penniless, sold-out soldier playing the jovial companions? Nappy had a deal to answer for, not the least of which was the nasty turn of democraticality the military'd taken during the long war years, and which'd been copied since by all and sundry.

The bounder was playing diffident returned hero as usual, and being treated with a fawning deference that set Hodges's teeth on edge. Also as usual, his former batman held court at the main communal table, detailing yet another of his master's supposed exploits in a whisper that carried like the baying of hounds on a fine fall day, and being attended to with breathless anticipation by every soul within hearing. This latest one held Gracechurch had sneaked a fortune provided by some Jew moneylender through enemy lines so Wellington's troops could be paid, foiling both French agents and a band of deserters intent on relieving him of every pound, and saving the moneylender's brother's life into the bargain.

Not a particle of truth to it, of course. Wellington and his paymasters having traffic with moneylenders? Hodges wasn't such a fool as to believe a word of it, but there were clearly those who swallowed every scrap and begged for more. No, it didn't appear to matter how many lies the scrawny batman told, and the bigger the better as far as both host and patrons were concerned.

The temptation to call the man's bluff was almost irresistible. Instead Hodges contented himself with lumbering over to the table, gripping the fellow's shoulder, jerking him around and hissing, "Next I suppose you'll be telling us your master had to do with Wellington himself."

"He did," the batman protested, "and many a time."

"And danced at the Duchess of Richmond's ball, I suppose?"

"That he did, and had many a fine partner. Not much left of the uniform after Waterloo, though."

"If he saw Wellington," Hodges muttered, retreating to

his place by the fire and ignoring the scowls that followed him, "more like it was because he'd been called up on charges for a sound drubbing."

"Ain't the only duke what he's acquainted with, neither," the batman shot after Hodges, "nor is the Duchess of Richmond the only one what he's saluted the hand of. As for nabobs and earls and such, they're a farthing a gross."

Blast the man's insolent grin!

"Duchess of Petticoats and Duke of Panderers, I'll warrant, and Chairman of the Right Honorable Muslin Company," Hodges muttered, hoping his voice carried well enough that the gist of his jibe would be caught without its being so clearly understood some fool would take exception to it and demand a retraction.

Village needed to be given a disgust of Gracechurch and his henchman, that was the plain and simple of it, and his daughter brought to a sense of the man's iniquities. But, how?

He was a vicar's son, known to have treated every soul with equal respect as a boy—or disrespect, come to that. And played only such pranks as were acceptable, and even smiled on as proving a lad possessed sufficient bottom to see him through life. One who'd been wounded, and returned after years of war not enriched as some had, but with less to call his own than when he first departed in service of King and Country.

That was one scrap Hodges might turn to his advantage if only he could determine how, but so far as he knew it was the only one. Gracechurch was hanging on his mother's sleeve, no question about it, and she a poor widow. Living in a cottage that'd been a tumble-down ruin until Suzanne squandered heaven knew how many hundreds of pounds seeing to its repair while not lifting a finger to assist her parents. People shouldn't like it—that Suzanne had seen to everything rather than Gracechurch sending his mother the necessary funds, and so by implication Gracechurch owed the roof over his head to her. People should turn their backs on Gracechurch because of it.

But that wouldn't be enough. It was only a detail he could toss in as yet another example of the man's depravity after something truly horrendous came to light. Problem was, Gracechurch wasn't depraved and never had been. That was the simple truth. So was the fact that he was disgustingly honest in his dealings with men and women alike, and disgustingly forthright in his opinions and attitudes. Nothing of the loose fish about him, nothing of the gamester, nothing of the sot, nothing of the ne'er-do-well. Finding something serious enough to cause the villagers to cut him would be quite a task.

But, Hodges determined as he stretched his legs towards the fire, watching the proceedings from beneath lowered lids, he'd find it. He had to. There was no choice.

Gracechurch spent the rest of that second week continuing to reacquaint himself with old haunts and former companions just as any returned soldier might have, whether penniless and seeking preferment or wealthy beyond avarice and on the prowl for some deferential toadying.

He ambled afoot, armed with an umbrella against the persistent rains that began the day following his return, never venturing far from the center of the village, chatting amiably with everyone he met and avoiding the directions of Placidia and Trillings, the squire's ramshackle holding, as if they harbored the plague.

Avoiding the Pembertons' apothecary shop and physicking against some unspecified but dire Continental sickness proved a trifle more difficult. In the end he'd had to resort to the old gamester's trick of tossing a vial of noxious liquid old Pemberton fetched from his shop up the sleeve of his coat in full view of everyone in the inn's taproom, praying no betraying green drops would trickle down his fingers. He'd gotten away with it, but only thanks to its being late in the evening, the room dim, and his companions rather well to pass. Cleaning the blasted coat had been another matter.

As for the summonses to tea he received from India Phelps, his excuses and apologies had been all that was clever and courteous, and equally all that was insincere. Even the hint that she desired to be private with him, that Suzanne and the girls would both times be at Placidia bearing Sophia Phelps company made not the slightest difference. Much as Gracechurch wanted to avoid his former love, he desired even more to avoid her all too perspicacious mother-in-law. He wasn't certain what he was about anymore. The prospect of having India Phelps discern his intentions before he did rankled as much as it annoyed.

If he suffered twinges of conscience because of the half-truths with which he treated his less astute and more trusting mother's questions, he insisted circumvention was justified. And if Scully's scowls and muttered remonstrances grated, so be it. Scully's barracks-room grumblings would cease with time. He, not Scully, knew what was best. He, not Scully, was responsible for their futures. He, not Scully, had suffered the torments of hell when the letter arrived from his mother informing him of Suzanne's nuptials. He owed his younger self a debt and he was damned if anyone, including his current self, would renege on that debt.

Tell his mother he could purchase an abbey if he wished, and intended the equivalent? That there was no need to choke down cheese rinds in lieu of more palatable fare, or be faced with either pigeon pie or rabbit in a thousand guises each evening? That they could easily afford Suzanne Phelps's delicate gifts for themselves? That it was all a game for the edification of some and the punishment of others?

Hardly.

The news would have spread across the countryside within hours without her having the slightest notion how or why. For all she'd never have revealed anyone else's secrets, and had been the most circumspect of vicar's wives regarding those who called at the vicarage in distress, his she'd spread to the winds since he took his first step with one sole exception: his abortive betrothal to the squire's daughter. It was the nature of mothers, he admitted ruefully, to chatter about their sons as if they were lay figures and not real people at all—witness the fact that at every turn he was greeted with embellished retellings of the contents of every letter he'd sent his parents over the long years.

Now, on this first fine Thursday afternoon after more than a week of drizzle and rain he garbed himself with exceptional care, certain he'd see Hodges at a distance—as he had almost every day since his return—and be inspected by that gentleman with his usual mistrust. How the pugnacious squire realized something was not quite as it should be Gracechurch had no notion, but it was clear the man did.

As of the moment, however, Gracechurch was desperately avoiding yet another skirmish with his tenacious former batman.

"Circumspection," he snapped at Scully's monotonous grumblings about his refusal to ride the countryside now sunshine and drying roads offered inducement.

He seized the yellowed neckcloth hanging over Scully's arm, tied it in no recognizable style, inspected the result, rumpled it a bit, then made an apparent attempt to smarten it up that only made matters worse. "I want 'em accustomed to seeing me about," he continued more equably, tweaking his shirt points awry, then crumpling the tips. "Told you that. And I want 'em convinced there's no more to me than meets the eye. Hodges especially. Told you that, too. Misdirection, that's the ticket. Leave be, my friend."

Gracechurch turned to don the shiny-seamed coat Scully held at the ready, thrusting his arms in the sleeves and scowling at the crack of tearing lining.

"This thing'd better last me long enough to get the job done," he muttered.

"Told you that cannon won't fire, Colonel," Scully returned with a look of satisfaction. "Said it in the beginning, and I'll say it now. Fact is, dratted plot's likely to blow up in your face. Powder burns and worse ain't exactly pleasant. When're you going to give over your playacting and behave like a sensible man?"

"When I've made a chosen few sensible of their errors, and perhaps trodden on a few maidenly sensibilities and caused a few despairing tears." If he'd shed none of his own in the past, it'd been only because he refused to let any woman bring him so low. Sauce for the gander was, in the old parlance and turning it about a bit, surely sauce for the goose as well. He had a tureen of the stuff ready to empty over a certain lady's head.

"Playing fast and loose with hearts ain't never been your style, sir," Scully persisted, "nor yet words into the bargain."

"Well, it's my style now—not that there're any hearts involved, merely pockets of varying depths and grasping fingers anxious to pick up the odd yellow boy to fill 'em up. That's the way it was then, and that's the way it is now. Quickest way to make 'em see the error of their ways is to prove I could buy and sell 'em ten times over if I'd a mind to—after first convincing them I haven't a groat to my name."

"Not how Mags—Miss Reedy, that is—sees it. Not that I've said a word regarding your true circumstances, but according to her—" Scully's voice trailed off at Gracechurch's impatient scowl. "Don't see as how none of what you're planning's going to make for a cozy billet," he grumbled, "nor yet as why you can't begin reconnoitering for—"

"I don't want to appear to have the slightest aim in my wanderings. A man afoot implies aimlessness. A man astride implies business at hand. A man with pounds and to spare has business and an aim. A man with his pockets to let has neither. We've discussed this before."

"But that house as you're wanting, the one where you'll lord it over 'em all, and that pretty Lady Phelps the most of all—what of searching that out?"

"Plenty of time later. There's never been much available hereabouts. It's merely a case of learning who's died or run into dun territory, and what's to be had at a fair price."

With the goal of appearing both aimless and shiftless the former colonel had dressed with as much care as he had for the Duchess of Richmond's ball on Waterloo eve, if with different results. A glance in the spotted pier glass proved he'd achieved his goal to perfection. Boots shone mirror-like, which only emphasized their cracks. His coat was brushed until hints of lining showed through its worn elbows. He remained in need of a barber, his longish dark locks—frosted with silver at the temples—lending him the air of a doomed Byronic hero.

"I'll do," he muttered. "Dignified poverty—that's the ticket."

"Ticket to Bedlam, if you're asking me."

"I'm not." Gracechurch shrugged, then bent his elbows and crossed his arms at chest level, straining back and shoulder seams. "We may have to replace this coat, Scully."

"What? You're not going to ask Mrs. Gracechurch to mend it? She's as fine a needlewoman as ever was born."

Gracechurch almost met his manservant's eyes in the mirror—almost, but not quite.

"Have done, Scully," he muttered.

"Poor lady was almost in tears t'other day, seeing as how

she'd given all your father's togs to the poor and now you have need of 'em and she hasn't so much as a waistcoat or a pair of smalls to offer you."

"Blast you, Scully, have done!"

If there were moments when the masquerade caused Gracechurch to cringe inwardly he ignored them, as now. His old friends would understand and approve in the end. So would his mother. The others didn't matter. Neither did Scully, who hadn't been there nine years ago when Hodges turned his back, or when the letter arrived announcing Suzanne's marriage to the most elevated, wealthiest—and oldest—man in the neighborhood. Scully didn't understand the stakes. Only another man who'd suffered those indignities could, and they were in short supply at the moment.

"I'll not be stopping by the inn today," Gracechurch murmured, giving his neckcloth a few extra creases. "Must be seen to watch my pennies. No need for you to trail after me this time. I'll pay calls in the village, and plan to stop by the vicarage afterward. Something for those rascals." He retrieved a longish parcel shaped like a walking stick from beneath the bed, tucked it under his arm, then retrieved his hat and gloves from the dressing table.

"By the bye, I've received an invitation to dine at Scowden Lodge Wednesday next. Mr. Scowden has three well-dowered daughters. Eldest pair are butter-toothed antidotes and shrews into the bargain just like their mother, but the youngest isn't too bad. Any billet in a storm, the old fellow thinks, and he's anxious to rid himself of at least one of the lot. The courting's begun without my lifting a finger or offering the slightest inducement. You can imagine what it'll be like once the truth comes out, Scully—one of the reasons I intend to avoid it as long as possible, and make my choice before it does. You'll have to do what you can about my evening clothes. Don't air 'em, though. I want a touch of musty trunks and ancient dust about them."

That Thursday was finer than any day they'd seen in over a week: not a cloud anywhere, and the rain-washed sky so piercingly blue it caused an ache in Suzanne's throat.

She watched longingly from Rose Cottage's door as Delphine and Aurelia rattled off in the sun-dappled family carriage, garbed in their favorite muslins and best bonnets and shawls, intent on paying as many calls as possible while gleaning more gossip than was right or proper or good for them. And Cassie'd departed on another of her interminable horseback jaunts as soon as nuncheon was over, escaping courtesy duties as surely as the girls were, and with barely more compunction for all her excuses regarding Duro's need of exercise after so many days of wet, and no matter how fervent her promises of an early return.

With Mother India dozing in the back parlor, only Suzanne remained to receive Sophia—who'd sent notice she intended to call as the weather had turned fine at last. The physician in Timsborough recommended short dog cart jaunts interspersed with sedate takings of tea and cordials and chat as offering the most healthful exercise in her interesting condition. Where better to go than Rose Cottage, so conveniently close and so very comfortable, and where she could send such things as her favorite hassock ahead without seeming to insult her hostesses?

It was all Suzanne could do to keep from sighing. It was even more difficult not to join the others in playing truant, slip through the door and disappear into the fresh summer afternoon as if she hadn't a care or responsibility in the world. Instead she softly closed the door so as not to waken her mother-in-law, gray skirts swirling around her ankles, turned toward the back of the house and nearly leapt from her skin.

"They're gone?" India Phelps hissed, leaning on her walking stick and standing so close it was as if she intended intimidation.

Suzanne gulped and nodded, wishing her heart would slow.

"Well, what're we waiting for?" The old lady seized Suzanne's wrist, pulling her toward the stairs, stick tapping smartly against the floor. "Bridges that aren't crossed have a tendency to crumble as surely as those that aren't mended."

"You mean fences, don't you?"

"I do not. If I'd meant fences, I'd've said fences. Besides, how d'you cross a fence? Climb over one, yes. Leap one? That, too. I've done it myself, little as you may believe it. Even crawl under one if one wishes and is feeling particularly naughty.

But *cross* a fence? As impossible as scaling clouds or sculpting water."

Suzanne managed a weak smile at the old lady's determined sallies, and then they were in her bedchamber, with her mother-in-law firmly closing the door behind them and turning the key in the lock.

"In case they return too soon," that doughty lady said, then chuckled at Suzanne's open-mouthed gasp and staring eyes.

To some it would've seemed an ordinary thing—that rainbow of muslins and silks, of laces and gauzes and poplins spread across her bed and the window seats overlooking the garden. And everywhere, it seemed, bonnets daringly decorated with feathers and flowers and ribbons perched on chair knobs and candlesticks and lamps, all with brims begging to take part in decorous flirtations consisting of coy sidelong glances and flushed maidenly cheeks. And silk stockings festooning her pillows. And kid gloves of every hue imaginable. And sunshades arranged in a frothy bouquet like acrobats' parasols—not practical ones intended to block the sun such as Suzanne customarily carried if she carried one at all, but confections of the most stylish sort—pagodas and temples and delicate ruffled things that had no name at all. There was even a traveling costume of rich blue, the jacket trimmed in deeper blue with a modest stand of lace at the high neck, and a bonnet to match.

"Dear heaven, whatever have you been about?" she said weakly.

"Having a wonderful time, Miss Blevins and I. I've had her and two of her girls hidden here for the past week, stitching away in my bedchamber and sleeping in my dressing room. The servants kept the secret most wonderfully well, I think. Surprised?"

"Entirely, but—"

"But what? 'But I can't wear such colors?' 'But I'm in mourning?' 'But these styles are too girlish for a woman of my mature years?' "

"All that and more." Suzanne closed her eyes against the vision of carefree elegance.

" 'I'd be chased from town on a rail?' 'Sophia and Oren would be horrified?' " India Phelps struck the floor repeatedly with her stick, the picture of indignation. "And your parents as well, I'm sure."

"Well, they would—and rightly so."

"What business is it of your stepson's how you dress? Or of a stepdaughter-in-law who's your junior, all else aside."

"As a daughter-in-law should be, don't you think, even if it's only by two years?" The attempt at turning the subject and lightening the moment were futile given the derisive expression on India Phelps's face. The sigh Suzanne emitted was as heavy as it was deep-felt. Hints had given way to action. It was as if everyone she knew were attempting to pull her limb from limb without the least concern as to how she felt about it. "I have a position to maintain in the vill—"

"Balderdash!"

Suzanne went to the bed, twisting fingers hidden in the folds of her dull gray skirts. Behind her India Phelps sighed gustily. Then came the creak of a chair, the sound of silk skirts being settled.

"Your mother dressed you as a nun when you were a girl, why I've never understood because you were a pretty thing then and have become a beautiful woman since, for all you do your best to hide it. Nor yet why you didn't rebel at such irrational treatment."

Suzanne held her peace, knowing any arguments would be lost before they were begun, and leave her with improper longings and impractical regrets that had nothing to do with the realities of life in Chipham Common.

"No reason to continue the tradition in any case," India Phelps snapped.

"Mama and Papa maintained fine feathers attracted the wrong sort of cockerels," Suzanne murmured, reaching out despite herself to stroke a spangled gauze confection clearly intended as an evening gown. Beside it lay a gossamer dressing gown in the Greek style whose split sleeves would float like wings whenever one moved, as exquisite as it was improper. "Fribbles and rakes and such. I suppose they do."

"And my son was the right sort? Not that John was a fribble even in his salad days, but there're worse things than being a fribble. A humorless bore's one of 'em, and that he had become by the time you accepted him, the pompous, gouty old fool. Even a rake isn't so bad if he's the right sort of rake.

They do make the very best husbands if ever they reform, and certainly the most caring and understanding of fathers, both to sons and daughters. I should know, given both father and husband. Certainly my mother never had any complaints. Neither did I. Of course things were a bit freer when I was a girl, but that still doesn't excuse this.''

India Phelps's disdainful gesture encompassed Suzanne's overly plain room and equally plain dress. ''All you lack is a wimple and a bed of nails. A lash wouldn't be amiss, either. I presume there're a hair shirt of two in your dressing room? What have you been punishing yourself for all these years— that's what I'd like to know.''

''Nothing.'' Suzanne flushed at the doubting glance thrown her way. ''I am most comfortable so,'' she insisted.

''Habit or laziness or fear or guilt—only those would account for such travesties. You're not lazy, you're too young to've developed bad habits, there's no one about can terrorize you unless you let them, and you've absolutely no reason for guilt on any head. Now,'' India Phelps said with a determined smile, rising from her place by the empty fireplace, ''let's see how these fit. We'll start with that spangled gauze you've been eyeing. It's my particular favorite. The color will bring out the lights in your hair.''

''I can't wear any of these, no matter what you say.'' Suzanne sighed, pulling her hand back regretfully. They were so beautiful, all of them, and in such wonderful colors. Not a gray or a lavender in the lot. She turned her back with a firmness she was far from feeling. ''Perhaps they can be made over for the girls, or even Cassie, so the money shan't've been wasted. I do apologize, for I know you've only tried to help, but I'd feel twenty times a fool if I appeared in public garbed so.''

''Then wear 'em around the house at first. Accustom yourself.''

''The girls would laugh at me. So would the servants.''

''What do you care?''

''I've always cared what others think. That's how I was trained.''

''And far too well, if you ask me.''

''And they'd say in the village I was setting my cap at Stephen,'' Suzanne murmured, ignoring her mother-in-law's tart comment and flushing painfully. "Certainly it would seem so were I to change my style so soon after his return."

India Phelps's placid smile held nothing but satisfaction at that reluctant admission.

"Well, none of these ensembles are suitable for the girls." She hobbled to the bed, smoothed the spangled gauze Suzanne had been worrying. "The ones they'd like are far too stylish, and they'd turn their noses up at the rest as too dowdy. Eventually you may find a use for them. For now, hang them in your dressing room. The wrapper you can at least get some use of in the privacy of your bedchamber."

"I do intend to dress in a livelier fashion, you know. Soon, but not just yet. And the changes must be of my own choosing, and infinitely subtle. Besides, what would I do with a traveling costume? I never go anywhere. You do understand, don't you?"

"No need to apologize, child. Yes, I understand more than you may think I do. You're right, of course. A titmouse appearing in bluebird's garb would cause a deal of gabble at first. As for the expense, don't think a thing of it. There's less here than it appears. Miss Blevins and I spread all about before she made her departure so it would seem you'd happened on a cave of treasures."

"And it does. Oh, it does." Suzanne gave her mother-in-law a loving hug that took fragile bones and rheumatic joints into account. "I'm ever so grateful, and infinitely touched that you care so much about my happiness and pleasure. I only wish," she said with a wistful sigh, "that I dared wear just one of them, if only once and only at home, but it wouldn't do, don't you see? It wouldn't do at all."

"I'll concede the point for the moment, but only for the moment. One thing I promise you: The next time we're invited out of an evening, you will not appear in one of those hideous gray things you've worn since John died."

"We'll see," Suzanne murmured, turning to the windows at the sound of wheels crunching over gravel. "Oh dear—that must be Sophia already. I wasn't expecting her until much later."

"T'aint Sophia at all," India Phelps said, peering over her shoulder. "That's a gig. Sophia wouldn't be caught dead in a gig, not if her life depended on it, not even to come here.

I do believe it's Mrs. Sanwiddy. Looks like she's added another layer of lard since Sunday. About to burst the seams of her gown, and that's the truth. Now whatever can she want?''

"Gossip," Suzanne sighed. "That's all she ever wants— either to impart it or to glean it. The poor woman doesn't intend cruelty I'm sure, but that's usually what it comes to in the end—reputations destroyed and heads laid low and hearts broken, and all for a bit of entertainment. What she sees or hears she repeats like a parrot, and generally where it'll do the most damage.''

"There's no need for you to suffer through it however, my dear. Make your escape once I have her in the drawing room with her back to the windows. It's such a lovely day at last.''

"But what of Sophia?''

"I'm certain I can manage to entertain two such inconsequential females without bringing shame on our heads.''

"Oh, but—''

"Will you stop being so duty-ridden? You know you're longing for a brisk walk in that lovely sunshine. Develop a bit of a vertebral column. A touch of selfishness wouldn't be the least amiss, either. If you're going to protest, then I'll give you a commission or two in the village and use them to explain your lamentable but unavoidable absence. Will that suit your sense of rightness?''

Suzanne burst into helpless laughter at the twinkle in the old lady's eyes, entirely missing the grim determination lurking in their depths.

"You truly don't mind?'' she managed.

"Mind? Quite the contrary. I intend filling them up on tea and macaroons and bustling them out the door before they realize they've departed, and then having my house to myself for a bit. They'll be gone within the hour, both of them— that I can promise you.''

In the event it wasn't quite the single hour India Phelps intended. Sophia, in a snit following a spat with Oren regarding the best method to ensure the Widow Suzanne remained a widow rather than becoming a wife—for the fool had had the temerity to tell her he had all in hand, had even set events in motion that assured the desired end but refused to tell her what they were—arrived hard on Mrs. Sanwiddy's heels, great with both insult and child and anxious for sympathy for all she refused to specify the reasons for her pique.

Whisking Suzanne out the back way was a simple matter requiring only that India Phelps ignore the young woman's protests and self-recriminations at abandoning her mother-in-law to two of the most tiresome females in the neighborhood. Settling the ladies was equally easy. Beyond that even she was at point-non-plus, for each droned on as if the other hadn't so much as opened her mouth or drawn a breath, ignoring tea and cakes and each other and assaulting their hostess with a verbal barrage that rivaled one of Wellington's famous tongue-lashings.

India Phelps sighed as the waves of words washed over her, meanings indecipherable, intent—beyond attracting attention and so gaining importance—lost. She considered heart palpitations, dismissed the notion as too commonplace to be worthy of her. She considered splattering one of the women's gowns with tea, but misliked the thought of being considered too infirm to manage the pot, for the news would've traveled the countryside *ventre-à-terre* and forced her to submit to the false sympathy of all her acquaintance. She almost considered hysterics, and definitely considered rudeness equal to their own. No solution pleased, none attracted. And, she'd done it to herself. With Suzanne there, they could've separated the pair and at least lowered the volume, if not the banality, of the conversation—not that it could be called a conversation. A pair of self-serving monologues was more like it, with Sophia's megrims every bit as tedious as Mrs. Sanwiddy's gabble-mongering twaddle.

And then both Sophia and Mrs. Phelps came erect, ears at attention, brows rising.

"Would you repeat that, please?" they chorused.

The look of satisfaction on the sacristan's wife's face confirmed the importance of her news, if not its actual import.

"Caught you napping, did I?" The dumpling of a woman chortled, busying herself with inspecting the refreshments she'd so far ignored. "Well, I ain't saying it's true, mind you. Ain't saying that at all, just that I heard it in strictest confidence, and from one as should know if any does given who *he* had it from—not that I'm saying who that was, mind you, for I was sworn to secrecy and I've always been one as considers a secret sacred. One must consider the dear lamented Mr. Gracechurch, after all.''

Mrs. Sanwiddy gave a broad wink, took a sip of tea grown cold while she was in full spate, then selected a macaroon from the plate beside her, nibbling it with rabbity speed and showering her gown with crumbs that were certain to leave grease spots.

"Well?" Sophia demanded.

But the sacristan's wife apparently wasn't prepared to repeat herself immediately now she had their attention, instead drawing out the delicious moment with a sense of timing that would've done a tavern wag proud. When she'd almost lost them, when one more sip or nibble would've been one too many, she smiled. Dimples twinkled in her rosy cheeks. The joy of momentous information to impart sparkled in her pale eyes.

"That's precisely what I've heard," she said, and selected another macaroon.

"And precisely what was that?" Sophia snapped, eyes glinting.

"That he ain't what his batman claims, that's what," Mrs. Sanwiddy whispered after making a great show of glancing about to make sure no servants were present. "In fact, he's quite the reverse. A coward, don't you see, and the next thing to a traitor. Wellington knows him right enough, but not in any manner that does him credit. All a parcel with that business years ago when he was wounded, don't you know? Sent packing then, I've heard, though I never did know the particulars, and should be sent packing now—not that there's any'll have the courage for it would kill his poor mother, and she with so much to bear of late and him hanging on her sleeve, nor making the slightest effort to be of use. Shocking, I call it."

"But who gave you the news?" Sophia gasped, hope shining in her eyes. "This is positively wonderful."

"Don't expose yourself so, woman," India Phelps murmured too low for Mrs. Sanwiddy to hear. "Oren wouldn't thank you for it."

The malevolent glare Sophia threw her grandmother-in-law would've cowed a less stalwart woman. As it was, it merely caused India Phelps's lip to curl.

"Yes, who gave you the news," the old lady repeated. "Don't believe a word of it, myself."

"Well, it's true," Mrs. Sanwiddy insisted. "There's one as is saying one thing in public and another in private when his tongue's been loosened by too much drink, that much I will say, and if anyone should know the truth of the matter, it's him—at least so I've been told."

"You're referring to Stephen's batman, of course."

"You said it, not I, but when one considers how they've been welcomed by all and sundry, and the colonel—which he never was, not by a long shot, that being merely a rank he conferred on himself once he was where no one would know the difference, I have that on the very best authority—even invited to dine at the best homes, well!"

"We haven't had him to dine," Sophia protested. "Not once. Nor do we intend to."

"Didn't mean you," Mrs. Sanwiddy returned. "Oren ain't entertaining these days, any more than his father did. Skints, the pair of 'em, but *he's* been here to Rose Cottage ain't he? And he's to dine Wednesday next with the Scowdens, and he's dined at the vicarage twice, and the Dennings and the Whitings once each, and I don't know where else but I do know there's more, and him not here but a fortnight. Shocking, that he should seek to impose on us so, and his father our vicar for dunamany years. Someone had best warn Mr. Scowden is what I'm thinking, for *he's* thinking nuptials plain as the nose on your face when he should be thinking horsewhips and hangings at dawn, that's what I say—if there's any truth to the tale, of course."

"Oh, there's truth to it," Sophia said. "There's always truth to such tales, for how else would they begin?"

"How else, indeed," India Phelps murmured.

"You'll not be repeating it, will you?" Mrs. Sanwiddy pleaded. "I shouldn't want it thought I was playing fast and loose with a good man's reputation if it happens there's no truth to it, but I did think you should be warned. You especially, Mrs. Phelps," she said, turning to India, "for you had him to dine the very first Sunday he was here, and so have been the most dreadfully imposed upon of all."

Then she turned to Sophia, eyes bright. "And then all the neighborhood knows it's Sir John's widow has been assisting Mrs. Gracechurch. She'd best distance herself or it'll reflect on you and your children, don't you think, and Mr. Phelps as well? And the squire and his wife, of course, and poor little Cassie Hodges. She's such a hoyden—why, I do believe I saw her riding astride across the fields near Mrs. Gracechurch's cottage last week—that this would ruin her chances entirely."

"Her chances of what?" India Phelps snapped.

"Why, of a respectable match, of course."

"She's naught but a girl."

"Girls grow to women right quickly here in the country," Mrs. Sanwiddy said. "Don't know about Town nor yet the Continent, and they're nothing but heathens in the Colonies and so that doesn't count, but here they're playing at lottery tickets one moment and the next they're in a hay mow with their skirts above—well, be that as it may, it's not too soon to be considering her future, you know, if you care for her in the least."

"And all this merely because you think you *may* have glimpsed her at a considerable distance riding astride?"

"Well, it might've been Mrs. Scowden's nephew, the younger one. I did hear as how he was visiting for a bit, and he does have the air of a girl, more's the pity."

"Dear heaven, what a deal of pother over nothing," India Phelps came close to groaning. "I'll thank you to keep both tales to yourself, if you don't mind."

"Oh, but if it isn't a hum then everyone must know, mustn't they, so they can take the proper precautions? I think," she said, turning back to Sophia, "that the best thing might be to cut the man. Then he'd leave, wouldn't he? Certainly he did the last time, and if it *is* true that would be a very good thing, wouldn't it? Mr. Phelps should lead the way, perhaps, showing the rest of us how to go about it."

"But what if it isn't true," India Phelps threw in, an edge to her voice. "What if it's all a fabrication? What if—" and here her glance speared Sophia until the woman flinched and placed a protective hand over her bulging belly, "What if it's false witness being born by those so avaricious and self-centered that doing an injustice to an honorable man matters not in the least if only it makes their pockets heavier?"

"How would chasing a pauper from Chipham Common make anyone richer," Sophia protested, eyes wide with innocence, "unless of course the pauper were hanging on someone's sleeve or in danger of becoming a public charge, and then of course it would be a case of not becoming poorer rather than becoming actually richer."

"That's what one would need to consider, isn't it? And the reaction when such a tale was disproved and the culpability of those who originated it exposed. They'd not be in very good odor with their neighbors, I would think. Why, they might even be cut in their turn—something to consider."

"So long as one's position were unassailable one shouldn't have to worry about that sort of unfairness," Sophia returned placidly. "Money speaks. A great deal of money speaks very loudly, so loudly one could almost say it shouts."

Mrs. Sanwiddy, whose gaze had been flying from one to the other in confusion, helped herself to the last macaroon.

Chapter Seven

The walk into the village had offered all the privacy and time for thought Suzanne desired.

No stepdaughters lagged behind, dragging their feet and complaining of the distance, the dust, the thousand and one activities they would have preferred to walking along a country lane like common farm girls and ruining both their gowns and their complexions. No younger sister demanded to know why she bore it all so patiently. No passers-by stopped to offer her transportation only to realize they were a party of four rather than two and gig or cart would not accommodate them—and so instigate another tirade from Aurelia and Delphine as to the desirability of their taking advantage of the transport offered no matter which direction it was traveling, leaving Cassie and her to enjoy their walk in peace. There were times when that prospect was so alluring she came close to capitulating, no matter what the dictates of decorum and healthful exercise demanded regarding intransigence.

Suzanne had taken her time once the guilt at leaving her mother-in-law to face Sophia and Mrs. Sanwiddy alone dulled. She'd sat on a stile for a bit, watching the butterflies dart from blossom to blossom, listening to the hum of the bees and reveling in the warmth of the sun and the freshness of the breeze bearing so many spicy scents, and the absence of human complications to spoil it all. She'd picked a posy of daisies and fashioned them into a chain she wound around her gray straw bonnet, lending it an unaccustomed air of fashion. She'd even hummed as there was no one about to scold that she wasn't acting the proper widow.

It was, she decided as she licked the salty film of sweat from her upper lip and swung the empty basket she carried, the fringe of her gray shawl dragging in the dust, like being liberated from a very luxurious but infinitely constricting prison.

Strange—she'd never thought of Rose Cottage that way before. Even Placidia had been more velvet tomb than granite jail, though she certainly hadn't been reluctant to quit it for the dower house. As for Sir John, though she'd mourned him according to custom, his death had meant little more than the passing of a distant and generally pleasant acquaintance—which was all he'd been before their marriage, and all he'd been after. Sad—that she'd been unable to feel more at his sudden absence, but there it was: he'd been absent when present, if one could put it that way. As remote as the gods on Olympus. In fact, more so.

A whimsical smile flicked the corners of her lips.

If she remembered correctly—and she did—the Greek gods had had a nasty habit of descending regularly to muck about in the affairs of mortals. Sir John's descents from library or study, on the other hand, had been rare rather than regular, and never fraught with disaster for the mortals in his path. Indeed, most times he'd passed her by with a nod so vague she was convinced he had no notion who she might be or what business she had in his house.

But there it was: Rose Cottage had become a prison. That she'd only just realized it made not the slightest difference. She'd probably built the walls herself, just as she'd hidden behind the nunnish garb she'd adopted following her husband's death to keep the importunate at bay.

It was, she knew, time for a change. The neighboring widowers seeking unpaid housekeepers for themselves and nursemaids for their progeny had finally accepted she'd no desire to exchange what little freedom she had for another golden band around her finger and iron chains at her wrists and ankles. So had those with shallow pockets and little regard for how they filled them. Once was enough. Besides, she still bore responsibility for Aurelia and Delphine, no matter how little she liked it or how unjust the burden.

That, at least, could be changed. There were sufficient funds to hire a governess-companion for them from their allowances—if ever she received those allowances. Indeed, she rather suspected she could lay such charges at her stepson's door. Certainly there was no reason she should continue to pay the girls' housing and clothing and food from her own pocket. That had hardly been Sir John's intention. She'd simply slipped into the habit when Oren had insisted on becoming their banker and been tardy with their allowances. Then, as she'd met one month's expenditures and part of the next, he'd stopped the girls' allowances altogether claiming he was setting the funds aside as part of their dowries as they clearly had no need for more than pin money living quietly retired and in mourning as they did.

Oren had next attempted to stop Suzanne's quarterly income, claiming she had no real need of it either while he did, placing the expense of both her and the girls on Mother India, and Cassie as well. That stratagem had lasted precisely three days. She chuckled each time she thought of it—Oren sputtering his good intentions and insult and need of extra funds with a house to run and wife to clothe and feed and a child about to be born and a position to keep up, Mother India threatening him with legal action and not in the least unwilling to spread the tale through the neighborhood if what was due his father's widow wasn't forthcoming—and promptly.

Perhaps the time had come to insist a genuine man of business handle their affairs? And not one of Oren's choosing, either. Nor one of her father's. Perhaps it was time for her quarterly income to be used to meet only her own obligations. Perhaps it was time, as Mother India put it, to develop a vertebral column.

The one impediment to such a scheme, all others aside, was she hadn't the slightest notion how to go about finding a man of business whom she could trust. Those in Little Stoking and Timsborough toadied Oren, self-interest being what it was. No sense striking a blow for independence only to come a cropper.

As Suzanne approached the outskirts of the village her steps slowed. It wasn't that she didn't want to go among these people she'd known all her life. Not precisely. But moments of privacy to consider her situation were as rare as they were precious, the inclination to do so even more rare.

She passed the Pembertons' apothecary shop, then the churchyard and church, and continued into the main part of the village. Mother India's commissions were quickly seen to: some rose ribbon and matching thread to refurbish last year's summer bonnet, a packet of peppermints and the latest Minerva Press offering to while away the small hours of the night. That the shopkeeper looked at her slightly askance, that those she greeted repressed titters behind quickly raised hands Suzanne hardly noted, having completely forgotten the ragged daisy chain gracing her bonnet. The day was too fine, her freedom too unaccustomed for her to concern herself about details of behavior that varied from the norm. And, if truth were told, she was too abstracted. As for the mysterious hints that new information had been received concerning Colonel Gracechurch, that he wasn't quite what he or his batman claimed, her air of polite disinterest stilled whispered comment and unwanted detail.

She purchased a tin of candied fruits for Mrs. Browne and three tops—merely brightly painted spindles with bulging bellies and fine points at either end—that could be set spinning with a twist of the fingers for the vicarage boys.

Then, boots and hems dusty, face glowing, she set off for the vicarage with her simple gifts, avoiding the end of the village where Mrs. Gracechurch's cottage—her customary destination until recently—stood. She heard the childish whoops, the cheers, the laughter while still well away from the vicarage with its commodious, if rather tattered, garden, and a deeper voice that must belong to the vicar.

The confusion of joyous, carefree sounds brought a wistful smile to her lips. Such abandon had never been permitted at Trillings. As for Placidia? Heaven forfend! Sir John's home had been aptly named, or else strove to deserve its designation. Either way, only the quietest diversions had been permitted: checkers, backgammon, the occasional game of lottery tickets or patience in the schoolroom when lessons were over and improving works had been studied and discussed. At least Rose Cottage possessed a croquet ground, even if it was laid out well away from the house and seldom saw use.

Suzanne depressed the latch of the gate giving on the lane and let herself in. The three boys—Matthew, Mark, and Luke—were squinting at the old chestnut through whose thick foliage bright flashes of red and gold could be glimpsed.

"To the left, sir," Mark, the middle son, shouted, brown hair ruffled by the breeze. "Just a little more, and you'll have it."

An ominous crack announced that a little to the left might prove a great deal too much for the tree-climbing vicar.

"Twas the most wondrous kite we've ever flown," Luke, the baby of the family, mourned.

"But ungovernable," Matthew intoned from his lordly thirteen-year-old height, "and is now suffering the fate of all ungovernable things."

"Spoilsport," Luke muttered. "Just because you're the eldest doesn't mean you must prattle on like one of old Fordyce's sermons, you know."

"I'm not prattling. I'm stating an incontrovertible fact as applicable to kites as to people. Had you not wanted to let out too much string too soon—"

"Oh, hush!" the two younger boys chorused.

"Don't be tiresome, Matt. It was an unexpected gust was at fault, and not Luke at all," Mark protested. "D'you need a hand, sir?" he called, still peering into the tree. "I can scamper up in a trice. Done it lots of times."

The only response from the tree was a grunt and another ominous cracking of branches burdened beyond their capacity, followed by a muttered expletive that had very little of the man of God in it, and a great deal of the frustrated male. A small branch plummeted to the ground, followed by leaves that fluttered on the wind like butterflies caught in a sudden eddy.

As Suzanne watched, torn between concern for the young

vicar and amusement at his predicament, another muttered oath preceded Mr. Browne's sudden and uncontrolled return to *terra firma* to the tune of rending cloth and in a shower of broken branches and shredded leaves. He landed with a thud that drove the air from his lungs, cutting the oath off in mid-syllable—which was perhaps as well given its saltiness and the youth of his auditors. The man was unmoving, eyes closed, chest heaving, mouth working like that of a beached fish.

Suzanne's heart leapt to her mouth as she dropped her basket and darted forward, unconsciously uttering a gasp of horror. It wasn't Mr. Browne at all. It was Stephen Gracechurch who lay like one dead, ruddy complexion dulled to chalk as if felled by a French saber and not a children's kite.

"Oh, sir—I am sorry." Mark was kneeling at Gracechurch's other side, his own plump cheeks pale. "Are you all right?"

"Course he ain't, cawker," Matthew snapped. "Go fetch Mother, Luke. That's what we should do, isn't it, Lady Phelps? Fetch Mother?"

At the mention of her name the colonel's eyes opened, still glazed, still confused, but with a hint of laughter in them as Luke held his ground, unwilling to depart the scene of so much excitement now the colonel had regained consciousness.

"Trust you to appear when and where least wanted, Suzanne," Gracechurch gasped as she scrabbled among the folds of his neckcloth to loosen the knot. "I should've known if I chose to play the fool you'd be there to witness my disgrace."

"Hush," she murmured. "You're injured."

"No, merely humiliated, clumsy oaf that I've proved," he wheezed in snatches. "Here now, what d'you think you're about?" He seized her trembling hands in his, pulling them from his neck. "No need to garrote me."

"Oh, but—"

"I'm fine, I tell you. Just a trifle winded, and definitely wounded in my *amour propre,* which is a far more delicate organ than the human body, when all's said and done."

He struggled to sit, wincing, then shifted his shoulders beneath his ruined coat. The elbows gaped wide. The right sleeve had parted company with the rest, and the back was rent straight down the middle.

"Oh, Lord," he mumbled, inspecting what he could see of the damage, "I've gone and done it now."

"You have indeed," she said, flushing furiously as she sat back on her heels. "Whatever did you think you were about— a man your age to go climbing trees?"

"Playing the fool, quite obviously."

"He was fetching down our kite," Mark explained.

"No kite is worth this," Suzanne scolded, trying desperately to keep her voice even, torn between the desire to laugh and the desire to turn tail and run from the vicarage garden as fast as she could. "Besides, from what I understand one should fly kites from a hilltop, not in such a place as this."

"But it was a very special kite, don't you see?" Luke pleaded. "And we wanted to try it right away. The colonel brought it all the way from Paris, for Mrs. Gracechurch'd written him about us and he remembered as how he'd loved kites as a boy and things that come from unusual places, but the tree ate it."

"Well, in that case," Suzanne murmured, refusing to meet Gracechurch's quizzical glance. This man tallied too closely with the Stephen she remembered. It was unsettling, and unsettling she didn't want at the moment, not with everything else she had to consider. "Perhaps you'd assist the colonel to stand, Matthew?"

"I can manage on my own, thank you," Gracechurch said, suiting action to words. "Not in my dotage yet, Lady Phelps, no matter what you may think."

As he stood, the sleeve slipped from his arm and fell among the leaves and twigs.

"Mama can fix that," Mark said, picking it up. "Don't you worry about it, sir. She can fix anything."

"Not this, I believe." Suzanne took the sleeve from Mark, examining it closely. "The fabric's rotted clear through. Amazing it didn't give way before now."

"Yes, isn't it," Gracechurch agreed, really looking at Suzanne for the first time, and then chuckling softly. "What've you been about, playing Queen of the May?"

"What?" Her hand followed his eyes to her bonnet, fingers tangling among the damp, crushed daisies. "Oh, my heavens —I'd forgotten," she said, flushing.

"Obviously. No, leave them," he said as she attempted to

unwind the chain, gently pulling her hands from the faded blossoms. "It's pleasant to see you appear just the slightest bit rumpled and ruffled for once, Lady Phelps, however ungallant it may be to say so."

"You'll never believe what we learned today," Delphine said self-importantly as she flounced into the family dining parlor that night, late and with her dusky curls unbrushed, her voice slicing through the murmur of conversation between her grandmother and stepmother. "It's quite incredible, and definitely changes everything, don't you agree, Aurie?"

Aurelia—already at table and picking at her food— shrugged and nodded. "Cutting him when we passed him earlier was a bit stiff, though," she complained around a bit of asparagus. "If it eventuates there's no truth to it, you've ruined your best chance and we'll be imprisoned here the rest of our lives."

"Oh, là—there'll be plenty of others. After all, I'm the belle of the neighborhood."

India Phelps and Suzanne exchanged troubled glances as Delphine went to the sideboard and examined the platters set over warmers.

"Oh no," she moaned, "boiled mutton and parsnips again. At least there's turkey and other things, but mutton and parsnips? We need a new cook, really we do, Grandmama. Preferably a French chef such as Scowdens just hired from London who knows about sauces and pastries and things, and would never dream of serving boiled mutton at a respectable table."

"Mutton? Who cares about mutton? Stop being so silly, Delphie. There's none beyond Colonel Gracechurch so near at hand or ready to tumble," the younger girl shot at her sister. "No other paupers of good family about that I know of, and what you require is a pauper who'll be so grateful at being rescued from the poorhouse he'll let us do anything we please, and we can have a little fun for once. Then we can hire a French chef, for Grandmama will refuse to, that I can tell you."

India Phelps glanced pointedly at the two footmen dancing

attendance, her brows drawn in a frown of caution. Suzanne followed the direction of her mother-in-law's eyes, her own clouding. If the men's ears had been any larger they'd've been flapping, so interested were they in what Delphine and Aurelia had to say. Those blank faces meant nothing at all. It was in the eyes one spotted the truth.

"Don't be silly, Grandmama. They know—servants always know these things before the rest of us—and if they don't they will soon." Delphine plunked herself into her chair, grinned at the first footman, a fellow grown grizzled in her grandmother's service. "I'll take gobs of everything except the mutton and parsnips, Charles. I will not condescend to mutton or parsnips. And some jellies right off, too. I've a longing for something sweet. And a big slice of that pigeon pie.

"I'm famished," she continued, turning to her grandmother, "for we've been positively everywhere this afternoon, or everywhere that matters, though the refreshments we were offered were trumped up things quite clearly left over from when others had called—merely scraps of this and that. It was most insulting." She turned to Suzanne, eyes narrowing to slits. "We stopped first at the Scowdens' to see how Mary and Jane and Ann went on after all this rain. They're not very interesting, but this time it was worth the effort for you'll never believe what they told us."

"Later, Delphine," Suzanne reproved softly.

"Don't be silly. They know, I tell you." Delphine turned to the two men by the sideboard. "You know, don't you? About Stephen Gracechurch's disgrace?"

Hesitant nods met her question.

"Told you so," she said with a grin, turning back to her stepmother and grandmother. "You've heard Colonel Gracechurch was invited to dine at the Scowdens' Wednesday next, I'm sure? That's why the Scowdens hired a French chef—to impress him. It's been the talk of the neighborhood for days, so I don't see how you could help but know. Mr. Scowden was hoping he'd take one of them off his hands, nasty freckled things that they are. All that carroty hair? Pheh! No style, no style at all. Doomed to be old maids, and that's the truth of it."

"Delphine, a little decorum and a little charity if you

please," Suzanne protested by rote, knowing her words would be ignored as always, but making the effort despite that as always.

"Well, he isn't hoping now," Aurelia chimed in, not to be outdone as this was when the exciting tale was to be told. "They'll have sickened for something during the night, or at least that's what Mr. Scowden'll tell Colonel Gracechurch tomorrow or the next day, and cancel the whole thing. You see, Colonel Gracechurch isn't a colonel at all—nothing but a subaltern, and he was broken of even that rank for cowardice under fire. What do you think of that!"

"We've all been most dreadfully deceived," Delphine added with no little relish as soon as her sister paused for breath, ignoring her grandmother's and stepmother's desperate signals for silence.

"Well, I don't believe any of it," Cassie said. "Just someone trying to make trouble, and you're helping them."

"Just think—a vicar's son lying like that," Delphine continued as if Cassie hadn't spoken, "and the vicar and his wife too, if all that's said is to be believed. It was a conspiracy between the three of them against all of Chipham Common, don't you see, for the colonel is nothing but a braggart and a blackguard, but it wouldn't do for everyone to know that—not with his father the vicar—and so they devised a plot to trick us all."

"Where did you ever hear such nonsense?" India Phelps snapped.

"Oh, everyone's saying it, so it must be true," Delphine insisted airily between bites of turkey, jellies, and mushroom fritters.

"Fustian!"

"I heard the same thing when I stopped by the Parkinses' farm to see the twins," Cassie admitted reluctantly from her place by Suzanne. "The tale's everywhere, Mother India. They're even saying as how Colonel Gracechurch was a traitor and stole from the officers' mess, and has left debts behind him everywhere. Thousands and thousands of pounds. Debts of honor, too. They even say he killed his man. Dueling's been outlawed for years, so it was nothing but murder. It was hushed up, but then he insulted one of those who'd sworn to his being nowhere near where the man died, and so he changed his tale somehow. It's all moonshine, of course.''

"We heard it was nothing but a common tavern brawl, but the one he killed was his superior," Aurelia sniffed. "You've got that part wrong, for our source is certain to be better than yours, Cassie. And he turned and ran at Talavera and again at Santa Vitoria. That's a hanging offense.''

"But he wasn't hung as a traitor and a murderer, or shot, or whatever they do, because his father was a vicar which I say is shameful because the one has nothing to do with the other," Delphine threw in. "Think of all the needless deaths he caused.''

"And his batman's a thief, they say, and a housebreaker," Aurelia rushed on as Suzanne watched her in horror. "I always said he had a ferrety face, and now I'm proved right. That's how they were living in Paris, only the constabulary—or whatever outlandish thing it is they have over there—was hot on their heels and so they escaped to England just ahead of the law. His returning has nothing to do with his father's death. How could it? If he'd been in the least affected, he'd've returned immediately he received word.''

"Delphine, Aurelia, please," Suzanne pleaded. "Enough of this malice.''

"Oh, let them go their length," India Phelps said with a sigh. "They will anyway, and this'll get it over with the sooner.''

"There's talk of chasing the colonel and his mother from the neighborhood," Cassie admitted at the imploring look thrown her by Suzanne, setting her knife and fork on her plate and pushing it away. "Sally Parkins was full of it, and Tom muttering as I've never seen him.''

"I should think they'd be glad to go quietly now the truth's out," Delphine said piously. "No need to trouble ourselves chasing them off.''

"And Mrs. Gracechurch always pretending to be such a lady. Why, butter wouldn't melt in her mouth. They're always the worst sort." Delphine held out her plate to Charles. "I'll have some more of everything save the mutton and parsnips, and double helpings of the jellies and the mushroom fritters. They're uncommon good tonight.''

"It's lies—all of it," India Phelps snapped. "I'll thank you not to be spreading such ridiculous tales abroad.''

"They're abroad already," Delphine said with a pout. "Not a soul we told but didn't already know all we knew and more. I said double helpings of fritters, Charles, and the jellies as well. And another slice of that turkey. It's moist, for once."

"Dear heaven," Suzanne murmured, casting her mother-in-law a troubled glance. "It can't be true. It simply can't."

"Of course it isn't. Someone's making mischief."

"That's what I tried to tell the Parkinses," Cassie said, "but they wouldn't listen. There're always jealous people about, and so much's been made of Colonel Gracechurch since he returned that it's no surprise, I suppose. I think it's positively dreadful, for all the colonel and I have our differences. That's one thing, and personal, and perhaps it was a trifle amusing. This is another entirely. I don't like it."

"Doesn't matter if it's true or not," Delphine said with a wisdom far beyond either her intelligence or her years. "What matters is people believe it, and nothing anyone says will change their minds."

Stern words, frowns, nothing did the least good. Only sending the girls to their bedchamber following dinner stopped their flow of gossip and speculation. They insisted they—and all the countryside—had the right of it. Stephen Gracechurch, a mere vicar's son, actually a colonel? Unlikely in the extreme. And known to the Duke of Wellington? Even more unlikely, unless the reason were something to the discredit of the vicar's son. Vicar's sons, after all, were known to be wild. Little wonder this one was as bad as the rest.

The girls retired to discuss possible alternate suitors for Delphine's hand while Cassie stormed off to practice the pianoforte in the drawing room, scowling and muttering and prepared to attack Beethoven with unaccustomed vigor. India Phelps and Suzanne retired to the back parlor to take tea and see what could be done about what appeared to be impending disaster for the colonel and his widowed mother. Each reluctantly admitted that they'd heard rumors that afternoon of precisely the sort with which the girls had regaled them at dinner, a little less detailed perhaps, but equally destructive of the colonel's character and good name.

There was, they admitted ruefully, little they could do. Tracing such gossip to its source was hopeless. The perpetrators were generally too clever, protecting themselves from

discovery in ways that would never have occurred to more
honest folk. Anger at the injustice of it all was all they had,
and anger would serve no one, least of all the colonel.

More troubled than ever, Suzanne retired to her bedchamber at an early hour to sit on the window seat staring across
the moonlit gardens. She didn't approve of Stephen
Gracechurch. He was unsteady and volatile and always had
been, and those were the least of his faults. But a coward?
No, not that. And if his batman claimed he was well-acquainted
with the Duke of Wellington, that was nothing short of the
truth.

Still in the habit of following military notices in the London
journals after the years of war, Suzanne knew the duke was
currently in Town, a relatively short visit whose purpose had
been unspecified. The notice had been tucked in among a
plethora of other news, including the latest bulletins regarding Princess Charlotte who, like Sophia, was great with child.
Had the Iron Duke been fence-mending with his wife? It was
possible. Rumor had it they'd had their differences.

And then Suzanne scowled. She was as unpardonable as
the girls, devouring the latest London *on dits* with the avidity
of a starving dog leaping on a bone. So much for moral
superiority, she admitted bitterly. Life at Rose Cottage was so
dull that she sought diversion in the slightest, most inconsequential things.

But there was hope of stopping the tales about the colonel
before some unforgivable disaster occurred, no matter what
Mother India claimed to the contrary. One hope, and one
only. And there was a chance that hope could be realized,
but only if one were extremely brave and extremely determined, and not in the least concerned about one's own reputation or what was thought and said about one.

She glanced across the bedchamber to her dressing table
where she always kept a few pens, ink and paper. Then she
rose with a sigh. If she thought about it too much, she'd never
do it. Therefore it was best she do it immediately.

Unknown to Suzanne, two other ladies—one tossing fitfully
on an unquiet bed when she wasn't staring angrily at the
ceiling, the other pacing the floor of her bedchamber with
long, coltish strides—had reached precisely the same conclusion. One person, and one person alone, could pull Stephen

Gracechurch's irons from the fire. The only question was, would that very highly placed and busy individual feel it incumbent upon himself to do so?

Three letters were penned that night on dressing tables cluttered with the essentials of these three ladies' lives, the first two circumspect, hinting at more than they said. The third was blunt to the point of rudeness, though its author certainly didn't regard it in that light. The blotted pages, all six of them littered with myriad interspersions and covered on both sides with minuscule writing, and containing among other things a description of the deceased Mr. Gracechurch's final journey of mercy as vicar of his small parish and his subsequent illness, death and interment, and the impoverished state in which he left his widow thanks to his constant charity to others, concluded:

And so, your grace, it's up to you. Is a widow to be chased from the village and an innocent man—the son of one who was universally loved and respected—be unjustly vilified and cast out on the highroad because he's merely a vicar's son and hasn't two ha'pennies to his name, and so is proving most inconvenient to my half-stepnephew—or whatever Oren Phelps may be, for I've never been entirely certain what our precise relationship is and only wish it didn't exist at all as he's the prosiest and most sanctimonious bore in all of Christendom, and so full of himself and his father's knighthood that it passes all bearing—because of a prior attachment to my sister, who is Mr. Phelps's stepmother for all she's five years younger than he is?

(I knew a lot more of what was happening when Colonel Gracechurch came home on leave than any realized, and there wasn't any need to listen at doors, either. Suzanne became as silly as can be, blushing and simpering when she wasn't staring at nothing with a funny little smile, and the colonel—who was only a lieutenant then—was the complete mooncalf, and if that's not being in love, I don't know what is. But then my father, who didn't think a mere lieutenant who was a country vicar's son was good enough for Suzanne, refused the colonel's suit and he left after Papa cut him in the churchyard in front of the entire village, and his father and mother too, which must've been infinitely humiliating, and while Suzanne never shed a tear that I saw, she never smiled anymore after that either for the longest time, and a year later Papa arranged for her to marry Sir John because of his title and all his money and Placidia, which is a very grand house indeed, for all it's very musty and dark and I hated living there.)

It's clear as day Mr. Phelps wants the money Sir John left my sister to return to him upon her death, you see, having a rather expensive wife and being rather expensive himself for all he tries to hide it, and with four daughters to settle into the bargain though they're still in the nursery, and heaven alone knows how many more to come for he's determined to have a son and Sophia seems capable of producing nothing but girls, and I think he's terrified whatever there was between my sister and the colonel will revive now she's a widow and he's no longer absent. And are two silly chits—for that's all Aurelia and Delphine are despite their airs and graces—to besmirch a good man's name for the sake of a bit of gossip with which to amaze their friends and make themselves seem more important than the inconsequential gnats they really are? Especially as it's all a lie?

I leave it to your sense of justice. You have one, I'm told, despite your dreadful temper when you're not best pleased. Well, that's understandable. I have a temper too when I'm vexed, and at the moment I'm very vexed indeed, and am having a dreadful time not losing it. My temper, I mean.

You see, I'm convinced Colonel Gracechurch served you well, for all we have our differences. (He thought me a *servant* when we first met. *And* ordered me about as if I were one! I was quite out of patience with him for that, and still am, so you can see I'm merely performing an act of Christian charity in writing you, and not attempting to put myself forward in an unseemly manner—which Mr. Phelps, whatever relation he bears me, would claim were he to learn of it.)

Now it's your turn to be of service to him, if you

would be so kind. I'd dearly love to see Mr. Phelps's nose put out of joint, for it's he is behind these dreadful stories about the colonel, I'm sure of it. (It's him or Papa, who is every bit as bad.) And he makes poor Suzanne's life a misery, for all she pretends he doesn't and is too polite to complain, and holds back the girls' allowances as he acts as their banker, which isn't quite right I think, and so they're a charge on her even if they have money of their own. And Sophia is the greatest cat in the world except for Aurelia and Delphine, who I'm afraid carry off the honors in that department. Mother India, who's Mr. Phelps's grandmother and was Sir John's mother, can't abide them either, any of them, and she's a very wise lady, and quite wonderful for all she can be extremely crotchety when there are too many damp days in a row and her bones are aching. The only two Phelpses who're worth anything are Mother India and Emeline, who's Oren Phelps's older sister and the jolliest sort and rides neck-or-nothing in the hunt. She's even ridden with the Quorn, if you'll credit it.

I'm not one to grovel, but please, please, *please,* your grace, won't you come and set things right? It wouldn't take long as we're not so very far from London that it would be a great inconvenience. You'd only have to spend a single night on the road, I believe, for you must have the very best horses in the land and could travel faster than most people if you wanted. There'd only be a need to spring 'em, don't you see? And horses like to gallop, or at least Duro (he's my gray gelding who I named in honor of you) does, and so you'd really be doing them a favor as well as the colonel, for I've heard you like horses as much as I do and so would enjoy doing them a favor, wouldn't you?

Your humble supplicant,
Cassandra Mary Hodges, Spinster
Rose Cottage, Chipham Common

The next morning Cassie rose before dawn, splashed her face with water, pulled a brush through her tangled hair, donned her riding habit, tucked her letter to the Iron Duke in her pocket, slipped from the house, and saddled Duro.

She skirted the village at a relatively decorous pace, then took off cross-country at a neck-or-nothing gallop for Little Stoking, the nearest town through which the Royal Mail passed. The sun was just tipping the horizon when she arrived, gilding the tree tops and touching the market cross in the square with fire.

She smiled, thinking how fortuitous it was Nature appeared to bless her errand. The slowly wakening town seemed to be shaking itself, welcoming the new day. And it was pretty for once, the uncertain light hiding what was tired and run down, and bringing out the brightness of the flowers in the little plots before the houses.

Then her eyes narrowed and she frowned. The sun was highlighting something else as well.

Right by the posting house across the way, clearly intending to intercept the Mail just as she was, stood old Charles, the more prepossessing of Mother India's two footmen, beside the little gig used to run errands in the village and take baskets round to the Placidia tenants at holiday time.

"Drat!" she murmured. "How blastedly inconvenient."

He spotted her at the same moment, and they eyed each other beneath lowered lids. Then Cassie shrugged and trotted up to the man, ignoring the sleepy travelers waiting beside their traps to take their places on the Mail when it pulled up.

"What're you doing here, Charles?" she demanded over the calls of the ostlers in the inn yard, certain of the answer and hoping her assumption of authority would turn the trick. Servants could behave more like one's parents on occasion, and this was one occasion when she didn't want any parents, real or pretended, about.

"Might ask the same of you, Miss Cassie," the grizzled footman returned, eyes not quite meeting hers. "Shouldn't be gadding about alone at this hour. Could be there's highwaymen and such as haven't returned to their lairs yet. Not safe."

"Highwaymen? Here? Don't be silly. There haven't been highwaymen in these parts in years."

"Still don't explain what you're doing here. Proper young ladies're asleep in their beds at this hour."

"But then I've never aspired to be a proper young lady, you know that. It seemed too glorious a morning to waste lollygagging, and so I—'' She broke off at his derisive glance, shrugged. There was nothing for it but the truth. That's the way it always was with Charles. ''I've a letter to be got off to London fast as possible,'' she admitted, ''but I didn't want anyone to know about it, so I came myself.''

''You do, do you? Since my errand's the same, best give it to me before you're recognized and your father hears of it. No end of troubles for you if that happens, and Lady Phelps as well. I'll see to it for you.''

He held out his hand. Cassie shook her head.

''No, this is an important letter.'' She slipped her foot from the stirrup and dropped to the ground, reins and crop held firmly in her hand. ''I must see to it myself, Charles. How many are you sending off? Two? I'll wager it's two, for Mother India was spitting nails last night for all she didn't say much, and Suzanne as well. We must've all had the same idea.''

Charles looked at her from the corner of his eye, face impassive. Then he sighed and gave a single jerk of his head. Her assumption was correct, then. She wasn't the only one summoning reinforcements.

''Could I see them, please? I'll wager you a farthing they're all being sent to the same person.''

''Couldn't do that,'' he mumbled. ''Not right. Swore me to secrecy, both of 'em.''

''You mean neither's aware the other's written to his grace?''

He nodded, expression troubled. ''What His Grace of Wellington'll be thinking when he gets all three is what I'm wondering,'' he said absently.

''I'd love to be a mouse in the corner of his breakfast parlor when he opens them,'' Cassie giggled, delighted to have her suspicions confirmed by the footman's slip. ''I can imagine the style of both Suzanne's and Mother India's. Mine's a bit different, I suspect, for if one wants someone's help one should be totally honest about what's happened and why one can't see to the matter oneself, don't you think?''

''I think as how it's enough Mrs. Phelps and Lady Phelps've written his grace, and mayhap you shouldn't send your letter at all as it won't be needed. Chits shouldn't be writing to dukes.''

''Oh, it'll be needed. They've probably been so circumspect

his grace won't understand a thing of what's happened or why he's wanted. Much better to keep theirs and just send mine if we're to hold any back.''

"I couldn't do that," the incensed footman protested.

"Didn't think you could so we'll send all three, shall we? And not," she said sternly, doing her best to act the grown-up lady, "say a word to anyone about meeting here like this. Of course it won't matter once the letters're off, but I'd rather my sister and Mother India not know of mine, even if there's nothing they could do to call it back."

"I'll keep m'mummer shut if you do the same seeing as how neither knows about the other, and so I been paid twice for a single trip."

"You were, were you?" She laughed then, certain of her ground. "I'll keep your secret, Charles, so long as you keep mine. And not a word to anyone in the village or at home, either. Not anyone."

"No, I'm not going to be saying anything. Nothing comes of it, best that way. Something good comes of it, my words won't matter. Something bad? Well, there's plenty of time for that."

"It won't be bad for any but those who deserve it, for I'm convinced my letter'll do the trick even if Suzanne's and Mother India's don't. Best the good come as a surprise, for otherwise there're those who'd do their best to prevent it. That wouldn't be fair.''

"No," the footman agreed, shifting from one foot to the other, "t'wouldn't be fair at all. Always had a liking for young Stevie Gracechurch, y'know," he said, turning suddenly garrulous at the sound of a post horn in the distance. "Always came to see Mrs. Phelps when he could. Those visits set her up for days, they did. Wrote her while he was away, too. And he was a scrappy young one, taking no guff from any and treating all fair. No way the tales they're telling're true, no way at all."

"I couldn't agree with you more, Charles. He's as fair as they come, even if he can be dreadfully rude on occasion and leap to unwarranted conclusions."

The horn brayed again. Shutters were thrown back from the windows of the houses around the square. A baker's boy bearing a tray of currant buns hot from the oven circulated

through the crowd, crying his wares. Ostlers stood at the ready
with a fresh team stamping and snorting its impatience to be
off on the King's business, or at least the Regent's, while
others waited to unhitch the horses whose stage was over and
lead them to the stable and a well-earned rest.

"Give me your letter," Charles said as the Royal Mail swept
up to the posting house. "I'll see to it, I promise you."

The ordered confusion of the Mail's arrival, the speed with
which everything happened always stunned Cassie, no matter
how many times she witnessed it. She shoved her letter in
Charles's direction, eyes wide at the miracle of it all, and
shrank against the posting house's wall as she watched.

Sleepy passengers bundled in nightcaps and shawls were
shouting for bread and ale to break their fast. Two disem-
barked, yawning and stretching. Three more mounted the
step and vanished into the cramped compartment. Charles
was talking to someone. Money changed hands, she could
see that much. He was handing over the three letters one at
a time so she could count them and know he hadn't played
her false.

The horses had been changed. The horn sounded. The
yard cleared. Cassie's heart rose to her throat as, with a crack
of the whip and slap of the reins and a peal of the horn, the
Royal Mail rolled across the square gathering speed, and
then down the road and out of the town, bearing three very
different letters to His Grace of Wellington. There was a last
cry from the horn, and the Mail vanished southward in a
cloud of dust.

Then Charles was at her side, hand on her shoulder. "Letters'll be delivered tonight, late though it'll be," he said. "I
paid summat extra so one of the boys'd carry 'em around
directly they arrive in London."

"Thank you, Charles. That's wonderful," she breathed.
"How much do I owe you?"

"Nothing, Miss Cassie. Told you I was paid double. My part
in seeing things is set right, the way I look at it." He handed
her a bun. "Must be hungry as I am," he said, biting into his
own, "riding all this way at the break of dawn."

"I am, but I hadn't realized it 'til now. Thank you, Charles.
Procuring me a bun was ever so kind."

She smiled up at him and he winked, and suddenly she

knew that everything would be all right. The letters would be
delivered, and the Iron Duke would understand hers even if
he could make no sense of the others. And he'd come. He'd
come as fast as ever he could. What man wouldn't?

"A man acquainted with dukes and earls, a pauper?" she
murmured on a sudden flash of insight. "Why, I'd wager he
could buy an abbey if he wished. He's been playing games,
that's what it is, only I mustn't let anyone know for that would
spoil it all."

"What's that, miss?" Charles said, wiping the crumbs from
his mouth and then dusting off his coat with a spotless handkerchief.

"Nothing, Charles. Just talking to myself, which is a dreadful
habit I know, and unconscionably rude into the bargain. Do
forgive me. We'd best be returning home, don't you think?
Only I'm going to go cross-country as there's a call I must
pay before returning to Rose Cottage."

"At this hour?"

"At this hour, and it won't be pleasant, either. If anyone
asks, tell them I went out for an early ride, will you? It's the
truth as far as it goes. I left a note, but they mayn't trouble
to look and I shouldn't want Suzanne or Mother India to
worry."

And then she was in Duro's saddle and trotting decorously
out of Little Stoking before Charles could do more than
murmur his puzzled agreement.

Chapter Eight

It was damnably difficult to rouse himself, and totally unnecessary. The hour was disgustingly early. The bed was too comfortable, the covers too snugly tucked over his head shutting
out birdsong and sunshine. And he was stiff and sore from
yesterday's tumble, annoying little aches proclaiming he was
no longer a boy, along with a shoulder and hip that screamed
their annoyance at his carelessness.

He'd become a civilian again, dammit, with a Town gentle-

man's habits even in the country. Noon was the proper hour
for greeting the world, and not a second sooner. Preferably
considerably later. Besides, he had nothing better do than
sleep. No duties to perform. No business to conduct. No one
to see.

"Go 'way," Stephen Gracechurch muttered, burrowing
more deeply. "Tired."

"Don't care if y'are," Scully's voice grated on his ears.
"Told you as trouble was coming. Well, it's arrived. You've
got a caller."

"Devil I do. Send 'em away, whoever they are."

"It's a young lady, and you'd best see her."

Suddenly the covers were gone.

"Here now, what d'you think you're doing?" Gracechurch
roared, then winced at the sound of his voice. He might not've
made indentures the night before pondering the problems
facing him in Chipham Common and dulling the aches of
his ignominious tumble, but he'd come close with a bottle of
Suzanne Phelps's superior brandy. He rolled over, tugging
his nightshirt below his waist as he opened his eyes. "Dammit,
Scully," he said through a huge yawn, "I'll have you drawn
and quartered for this."

"That's as may be, Colonel. Y'can do it later if you're still
of a mind to."

"It isn't much past dawn," the colonel grumbled, eyeing
the low light streaming through the windows as he sat and
thrust his feet in a pair of threadbare tapestry slippers. "Can't
this wait?"

"Don't think so. She woke me out of a sound sleep, and
if I can wake, so can you."

"Misery loves company, eh?"

"You might say so."

He was standing now, and Scully was settling an old, cheap
banyan around his shoulders. It smelled of countless wearers,
none of them particular in their personal habits. He hated
the thing, though it served its purpose well enough and was
free of vermin, which was more than could've been said of
his uniforms in the Peninsula. And then he was being forced
in a chair and Scully was lathering his stubble of beard.

"Blast it, man," he growled, and received a mouthful of
lather for his pains.

He gagged and coughed and spat, then subsided. When Scully was in one of his moods there was no gainsaying him, and Scully was clearly in one of his moods. Gracechurch permitted himself to be lathered and scraped, his hair given a preliminary brushing. Then, a little more himself, he plunged his face in fresh icy water, came up spluttering. The towel Scully held at the ready was welcome in the extreme.

"All right," Gracechurch snapped as he emerged, "let's have it."

But Scully was now silent, perfectly ready to assist him in dressing and to pull on his ancient Hessians and equally unready to do anything more, such as explain this unwarranted and rude summons from the Land of Nod beyond the single fact that a young lady awaited his presence. Gracechurch considered a major dressing down, decided against it. He could hear his mother now, conversing with someone whose tones were considerably higher. Young lady, ha! He had a good notion who it was had come calling at this unconscionable hour. She was the one about to have her ears assaulted, not Scully, not that he'd be able to say everything he wished with his mother in the room. Still, he'd manage well enough.

He pretended he didn't recognize the voice, permitted Scully to cram him into his sole remaining coat, a hacking jacket even more threadbare and démodé than the one he'd ruined falling out of the old chestnut tree, gave his hair a final swipe of the brush without paying attention to how it lay, attached a cheap pot metal fob at his waist and donned the battered silver ring he'd worn all through the wars, then descended the stairs limping ever so slightly.

Scully, rather than remaining behind to regularize the Spartan bedchamber as he should, was following behind. Well, he'd settle with Scully later. Plenty of time for that. Plenty of time for everything, in fact.

He paused in the tiny entry, listening to the female prattle floating from the dining parlor that had once been a kitchen at the back of the cottage. Nothing of consequence, just as he'd assumed. Merely assurances that nothing at Rose Cottage was amiss, and the coffee and jam-slathered toast Mags had just served were perfection.

With a stern twist to his mouth and the fire of retribution

in his eyes, Gracechurch stalked into the parlor, ignoring his mother and bending all his attention on their guest.

"What d'you want here at this hour, minx?" he barked, arms crossed.

"Stephen, please," his mother murmured. "This is England, not a battlefield."

"Well, Miss Hodges?"

The growl was a particularly fine one, for the girl blanched and shrank back in her chair. Good. Then, hands trembling so cup rattled against saucer, she set aside her coffee, rose and dipped a creditable, if abbreviated, curtsy. That she was in a riding habit didn't render the task any easier, he granted her that.

"Good morning, Colonel," she said.

Was that a note of defiance he caught in her voice? He'd teach her defiance! He'd teach her to wake a man deep in his slumbers and make a May Game of him. He'd teach her to have a sister who caused him no end of difficulties, and caught him in embarrassing situations.

"What're you doing here?" he repeated coldly from the doorway, shaking his head when his mother indicated he should join them at the table.

"I need to see you about a matter of utmost importance," the chit said.

The note had definitely been one of defiance. It was still there, and a touch of something else. Reproof at his surly behavior? Dear God, but she had a lot of her sister in her. Suzanne had been forever telling him to moderate his tone in the old days, and reminding him, as his mother just had, that he wasn't on a parade ground or battlefield and no one in Chipham Common was under his command, dependent on him for the very blood that coursed through their veins to keep on flowing where it belonged rather than spilling on the ground.

"An unmannerly brat such as you?" he snorted. "Have business with a gentleman? And next you'll be telling me pigs have sprouted wings and taken to the air."

"With an *unmannerly* gentleman, yes."

"Good Lord, deliver me. Not only unmannerly, but cleverly rude into the bargain."

That should have sent her scurrying, but it didn't. Not

daring to meet his mother's eyes, Stephen Gracechurch strode across the room until he loomed over Cassie Hodges, hands now on his hips.

"Well, out with it. What d'you want?"

"D'you have a sore head?" Her own was cocked to the side, sparrow-like, as a dawning sympathy replaced the disgust in her eyes. "Because you're certainly acting as if you do."

Scully's stifled guffaw from the doorway was almost more than Gracechurch could bear.

"None of your business," he said, choking back a chuckle of his own. "Besides, young girls aren't supposed to know of such things."

"Rather difficult not to as Papa always becomes foxed because of the excellence of the wines and spirits when he and Mama dine at Rose Cottage. The stuff he has at home is much cheaper and infinitely inferior. Then he falls asleep, and when he wakens he growls at everyone just as you are. Mother India says it's because he has a sore head. Sore heads hurt dreadfully, she says—worse than the worst megrim. They make one want to cast up one's accounts, she says. Papa's done that several times at Rose Cottage."

The image of the iniquitous squire those words conjured came close to unmanning Gracechurch. As it was, after giving himself a slight shake he condescended to hold out Cassie's chair for her, then to seat himself and pour a cup of coffee he downed black, and then another.

"All right," he said more mildly once the coffee began to take effect, "let's have it. Why are you here? Briefly and clearly, if you please. I'm in no mood for roundaboutations or Cheltenham tragedies."

"Sore head," Cassie murmured in a confirmatory tone. "Coffee's an excellent antidote. You have that right."

Gracechurch's scowl didn't have quite the effect he intended, for the girl had the audacity to burst into giggles. She had bottom as well as sauce, he'd grant her that. Then, at the expression on his face—which he knew to be properly forbidding, and had cowed many a Johnny Raw in the Peninsula—she sobered.

"There's trouble brewing," she said. "Serious trouble."

"What would a child like you know of trouble?"

"I know lies are being spread about the countryside." She

hesitated, throwing an apologetic glance at Mrs. Gracechurch. "Ah well, you'll find out soon enough if I don't tell you myself, and in a far more unpleasant manner."

Mags loomed in the doorway behind Scully, ostensibly to provide another pot of coffee and muffins fresh from the oven, but the way her gaze darted from the colonel to his mother, then to Cassie told another tale. She paused, tray resting on her ample belly, as the young girl turned back to the colonel.

"Someone's put it about that you turned tail at Talavera and Santa Vitoria. And they're saying you stole from the officers' mess, and that the only way Wellington knows you is you were up on charges before him countless times. And they're saying you killed a man in a duel, and it was hushed up. They're saying you're a coward, and worse, and deserve hanging."

"'They.' The omnipresent, insidious 'they'—like the poor, forever with us. Is that all?" Gracechurch kept his tone lazy, almost disinterested—a damnably difficult thing to achieve, but essential. Only the tightening of his jaw, the white about his lips betrayed him. "Paltry stuff. I've had worse said of me, here and elsewhere."

"You don't understand. There's talk of chasing you from the neighborhood, and Mrs. Gracechurch too."

The girl's eyes were wide and troubled now. As for his mother's gasp, her incoherent protests, they broke his heart.

"Told you as there was trouble brewing," Scully said behind him, then stalked to the table and took a chair without being asked. "Cannon's begun misfiring, Colonel, just as I said it would. Pretty soon it'll explode."

Mags Reedy deposited her tray on the table and sat next to Scully. Words trembled on her lips, but after one quick look at the colonel she clamped them firmly.

"I know it's not true, any of it," Cassie continued, shoulders hunching, "and I've a good notion who's at the back of it, but, well, at the very least things're going to be unpleasant for a while. Is there anyone Mrs. Gracechurch could visit while it's all being sorted out?"

"I'll not leave Stephen, nor will I be chased from my home," that good lady said with a spark in her eyes that permitted no contradiction, "but who would say such things? And to what purpose?"

"Those to whom I pose a threat, or who consider me an inconvenience," Gracechurch returned easily, patting his mother's hand and giving her a smile that didn't reach his eyes.

"But who could that be, Stephen? You're the mildest-mannered man alive."

Scully's sardonic bark of laughter was quickly stifled.

"Don't trouble yourself, Mother. It'll blow over as quickly as it came up," Gracechurch said with all the assurance he could muster. Then he turned back to Cassie. "I appreciate your concern, but this is none of your affair. You'd best return to Rose Cottage, and perhaps avoid this end of the village for a bit. I shouldn't like to see you come to grief over it, and I suspect your father wouldn't take kindly to your showing either my mother or me any special courtesy at this juncture."

"I'm more likely to call here daily," the girl said, straightening her shoulders. "D'you think I'm the sort to roll over just because there're fools about? As for Papa, well, perhaps I'd better not say anything, but what'll you do? Where'll you go?"

"I'll go precisely nowhere, and I'll do precisely nothing."

"Could get a bit uncomfortable for Mrs. Gracechurch, you take that attitude," Scully threw in, scowling. "Mayhap now's the time to pay some calls. Duke of Rawdon's been importuning you, that I know, and so have many of your old comrades. Colonel DeLacey, what's now married and an earl, for one. His wife's a charmer, they say, and you know they'd be that glad to meet Mrs. Gracechurch."

" 'They' again? Deliver me."

"Ain't a bad notion, that one," Mags said. "Could do with a bit of a holiday meself. Niece up Timsborough way's had her latest, and I'm that anxious to see it."

"I will not turn tail and run. Don't you understand that's precisely what 'they' want? I refuse to be so accommodating."

"Well, them errands you said as how you'd see to once we were here a bit, then," Scully suggested over the sound of hooves clopping in the lane. "You'd still be in the neighborhood."

"Possibly. And just possibly I'll ignore all of it."

"That'll be difficult with people cutting you left and right."
Cassie's elbows were on the table now, her chin propped on
her linked hands as she stared unblinkingly at the colonel.
"And they will, you know. I have it on the best authority Mr.
Scowden's rescinding his invitation to dine on Wednesday
next, and that'll be only the beginning. People don't like the
idea of your hanging on Mrs. Gracechurch's sleeve, all the
rest aside. I doubt even the Tipsy Parson'll be comfortable
for you."

Gracechurch met Scully's derisive glance with a half-
hearted shrug and a sigh.

"I'll be damned if I'll turn tail," he said, but even he could
tell his tone was less determined.

"Stephen, please," Mrs. Gracechurch murmured. "You
aren't on bivouac."

A light rap on the front door was followed by the sound
of it opening. They all turned toward the entry.

"Matilda?" India Phelps's voice called. "Matilda, I can tell
you're up and about. Where are you? May I come in?"

Gracechurch glanced at Cassie, brows rising in amusement
at the sight of her ashen cheeks.

"You can climb out the window," he hissed with a wink,
"if you're of a mind to play least in sight."

But Cassie's shoulders were back, her head high.

"We're in here, Mother India," she called, rising from the
table and going to the dining parlor door. "Mags has prepared
coffee, and she's baked the most wonderful muffins—not
what we've had any as yet, but they smell positively delicious."

"Could've used that one on the Continent," Scully murmured. "Face down Old Duro for breakfast, floor Nappy for
lunch, and still be able to go a round or two with Gentleman
Jackson for sport in the evening."

Gracechurch broke into a reluctant, wry grin as he nodded.
"I'm beginning to think the minx is up to anything," he
murmured in response.

"Cassandra, *what* are you doing here?" India Phelps
demanded from the entry, stick tapping on the polished
floorboards as she made her way to the back of the cottage.
"And at this hour?"

Gracechurch and Scully rose, and then the others. There

was a slight pause as the old lady entered the room trailed by Cassie. She glanced at the assembly and sighed.

"So, Cassie's already informed you of what they're saying in the village," she said. "Probably without the least tact, either. I'm sorry for it, but it's quite true, all of it—not what they're saying, but that they're saying it. This is a council of war, I presume? With your permission, I'd like to join you. I've had Charles take the gig around back so it won't be noticed from the lane. Not to worry—he's in my confidence, but if we're to enter into a conspiracy it's best as few as possible know there is one."

Suzanne's night had been sleepless. She'd risen with the dawn to watch Charles depart in the gig with her letter, tempted to dash over the dew-spangled grass and take it back again.

The very thought of her audacity in writing such an elevated personage as the Duke of Wellington made her cringe. What would he think of her? Worse yet, would he understand her message, or had she been so circumspect that he'd toss the thing out in disgust after reading only the first few lines?

Even God seemed more approachable, and approach Him she had during the endless hours of darkness, however uncertain she was of His existence. Approached Him repeatedly and not the least humbly regarding her letter's being given a respectful reading and rapid positive response. Since it wasn't for herself, she hoped He hadn't deemed her importunings too rude if He did exist. Especially as they were for the benefit of one for whom she didn't particularly care, who confused her and with whom she was currently quite out of charity. Her sense of fairness, she hoped, had impressed Him.

Of course He wasn't always known for fairness: witness Job's misfortunes, and His refusal of Cain's well-meant gift that led directly to Abel's murder, when all was said and done. In human terms, God could be as capricious as the vainest *ton* belle, blasphemous though it might be to admit it openly. That, or He was entirely different from the fatherly portraits advertised, and totally incomprehensible to His creation. A sparrow might not fall that He didn't notice, true, but there were multitudes of starving children to whom He paid not the least attention.

As for the famous duke, she placed little more dependence on him than she did on God. Great men, too, were known to be capricious. Rank had its privileges, whether celestial or earthly.

She shook herself, banishing the uncomfortable thoughts. Charles had been gone for what seemed like hours. The sun was well up now. It was time she faced the day and the task she knew she must somehow perform.

Because she had to seek out Stephen Gracechurch, however little the prospect of another encounter with the former officer appealed, and warn him of what was being said in the village. Waiting until Sunday, when she could expect to encounter him after services and beg a few private words, would be too late. Too, if her father was there he'd make her self-appointed task impossible, and be there her father would on the chance she might be so lost to propriety as to seek the colonel out. The note he'd sent round yesterday cautioning her to avoid Stephen's company had been pointed in the extreme, his addressing her repeatedly as "my lady" indicating his reasons clearly enough. He liked having a title in the family, and didn't want it to vanish with a second marriage. He needn't have worried. There was as much chance of that happening as of her riding a broomstick to the Witches' Sabbath.

She sighed and pulled herself from the bed. It was an uncommonly fine day. Well, if one were to mount the scaffold so to speak, why not on a fine day with the sun shining and all the birds singing? Certainly that would provide a more cheerful exit than lightning and thunder and clouds blanking the horizon while rain pelted down. Stephen would provide those in any case once she'd had her say—glowering, short-tempered, impossible man that he was.

She rang for her abigail to bring hot water and tea, then went into her dressing room to select an appropriate gown in which to conduct her self-immolation, chuckling at the contradictory images she was conjuring. Flames and floods, indeed.

Everything that wasn't black was gray or lavender, of course. She ignored the butterfly-hued gowns she'd hung out of sight in the farthest corner, holding up first one somber ensemble to the light, then another. They all seemed unnaturally faded, somehow—dull and uninteresting, their sparse trims slightly frayed, the fine tucked cambrics and sheer muslins masking bosom and neck limp. Well, so was she. A limp, faded widow with two stepdaughters battering at the gates of womanhood, aspiring to fashion? The notion was ridiculous, even repugnant. Better a gray mouse no one noticed than a bird of paradise greeted at every turn with scorn and derision.

Her lips twisted at the notion someone might mistake her for a lightskirt. Not even in her salad days would that error have been made.

She pulled the least offensive gown from its peg—a grayed lavender with darker gray bands of narrow ribbon at the hem, the vandyked trim above echoed on the restrained puffs at the shoulders and on the tight wrists of the long sprigged muslin sleeves—wrinkling her nose in distaste. Truly, one could be a little less the mouse without being considered Haymarket-ware, couldn't one? Well, it was only Stephen Gracechurch she would be meeting. He expected no more of her than she did of him. A vague air of disinterested kindness, that was what she must project. Anything more would not only be out of place. It would constitute a lie of sorts.

She took down the bandbox holding her most severe gray bonnet and absently retrieved a short dark gray jacket trimmed in the military style and a lighter gray shawl. She'd do in those.

Dressing, once her abigail arrived with a copper can of hot water and she'd washed, was only a matter of fastening tabs and settling skirts. Dressing her hair in its usual plain knot took even less time, for there was no need to heat tongs and create the softening curls over which Delphine and Aurelia and even Sophia spent so many hours only to have their efforts degenerate into a messy frizz.

She studied her reflection in the dressing table mirror as her abigail bustled about straightening a room that was already neat as a pin, and making up the bed. She did have the air of a nun, Mother India had that right, or of a ghost. Unwillingly her eyes strayed to her left hand with its massive golden band. She'd never removed it—not since the day Sir John had placed it there while she choked back the tears that would have been her undoing. Hysterics at the moment when Stephen's father declared her eternally shackled to a man she barely knew wouldn't have been the thing at all, and caused no end of unpleasant comment.

Well, she hadn't known Stephen then either, apparently. But, both for the sake of the man she'd thought he'd been and the brave soldier he'd been in actuality, no matter what his other failings, she had a task to perform and she'd perform it. The question was, how? She couldn't accost him in the village. She couldn't go to the cottage now either—not without its being remarked and tales born to her father. And she had no intention of wandering the countryside, ostensibly seeking healthful exercise, but actually in hope of finding him more or less by accident. There were less exhausting ways of ruining one's boots and scorching one's skin if one really were of a mind to achieve those unpleasant ends.

No, it would have to be a note sent round to the cottage requesting a private interview in some secluded spot. The very thought made her blush.

And to deliver that note? It would have to be Charles, just as it had had to be Charles to carry her letter to the Royal Mail. According to Mother India he'd known Stephen since he was in leading strings. Charles was to be trusted, for there was no way he'd believe the tales being bandied about.

She dismissed her abigail, sat at the dressing table where she'd spent so many hours of the night attempting to say what must be said without revealing more than was essential, retrieved a sheet of cold-pressed paper and stared at its creamy blankness.

No words came to mind to cover a situation such as this. What she was doing would be considered fast in the most liberal of circles. In a place such as Chipham Common? She shuddered, selected a pen and examined it. The thing wanted mending. She dithered over that for a bit, nicking her finger with the penknife and making a regular botch of the job. Then once that pen was ruined she had to find another. Then she had to test it to see if it fit her hand. It didn't, and so she had to trim that one, too.

Each time she raised her head she was forced to meet her dark-rimmed eyes and acknowledge the smudges beneath them caused by a sleepless night. And her face was pale beyond the usual. Indeed, she appeared distinctly ill. And old—far older than she in truth was. Surely eight and twenty couldn't present such a haggish appearance?

It took considerable time and what seemed a thousand and one false starts—surely there were that many sheets of crumpled paper littering the floor—but at last she had a note that was both circumspect and neutral, and referenced nothing of either past or present. It merely requested a meeting as soon as possible at a time and place of the colonel's choosing. It wasn't even signed, but he would recognize her hand, wouldn't he? Certainly she'd recognized his on each letter he wrote during the long years of war.

She removed the japanned screen from before the fireplace, crumpled her discarded efforts more tightly and set them afire. It was infinitely pleasing to watch all those unsatisfactory words vanish up the chimney in puffs of smoke.

Then, head high and with a martial light glinting in her eyes, she set out in search of Charles.

"What the devil," Stephen Gracechurch muttered, setting aside the book he'd been reading and rising from his chair by the window when India Phelps's footman—who couldn't've been gone more than an hour—let himself into the front parlor. "Well, what d'you want, Charlie? More marching orders from Mrs. Phelps?"

Charles shook his head. "Lady Phelps," he said, shoving a folded and sealed note at the colonel.

Gracechurch's brows rose. "You don't say," he murmured, hands clasped beneath his coattails as he rocked on his heels. At least his mother wasn't present, given she'd gone to Rose Cottage for the day with Cassie and the old lady. Scully was back in his cubby in the shed, Mags to her elbows with baking in the kitchen. No witnesses, for a miracle, and for some strange reason he didn't want any. "I suppose you want me to read the blasted thing, and have been instructed to take back a response?"

"That I have, Colonel."

"And it'll be worth your position, I suppose, should I refuse?"

Charles shrugged, and again shoved the note at him. Ever

taciturn, old Charles. Never a word more than was absolutely essential. It'd given him an air of wisdom when Gracechurch was a boy. It had the same effect now.

Gracechurch sighed irritably, took the thing, broke the wax seal, glanced at it, then read it more carefully.

A matter of considerable concern has been brought to my attention. Fearing you may not have knowledge of it, I request the favor of a private meeting as soon as possible at a place and time of your choosing so that I may make you acquainted with the particulars and you may take such actions or precautions as you deem advisable.

There was no salutation, no signature, no seal impressed in the wax, not even a pair of initials. Just those few lines, as cold and impersonal as a bucket of water spilled over a drunken trooper to rouse him. The damned thing was an insult. Didn't she trust him with her name? More to the point, it implied she'd heard the village tattle—how could she not when both little Cassie and India Phelps were well-acquainted with it—but unlike them she clearly believed every word being said against him. Like father, like daughter. He'd been well out of it when she married old Sir John. Squire Hodges, not that he realized it or would've cared, had done him a genuine favor back then.

Well, he'd grant her a meeting. He'd endure her horror and recriminations and insults. Then he'd acquaint her with a few home truths, such as his resentment of her unwarranted intrusion on his privacy and his life and his thoughts. He might even bring her to book regarding her assumptions.

Gracechurch crossed to his father's worktable, dipped a pen in the ink well, and scrawled the words.

Midnight beneath the old oak just beyond the Weeping Sisters. Be punctual, as I shan't wait.

across the bottom of her note. The precise place and time of their last meeting, just after her father rejected his suit and cut him dead in the churchyard. Almost the same time of year. Would she remember? Undoubtedly. Would the memory disturb her? He hoped it would. Certainly that was his intention. A midnight assignation between a jilting widow and a gazetted wastrel? The impropriety of it should disconcert her, right enough, and he wanted her disconcerted.

Best of all, it was as lacking in common courtesy as her cold words.

He sanded the thing, waited a moment, then shook the stuff into a brass bowl set beside the standish for that purpose, folded the note and resealed it using a plain drop of wax. No signature. No initials. No seal impressed in the wax. Two could play at that game. Two would. And no retaining of her note. No hint that he might harbor tender sentiments and lingering regrets where she was concerned.

"I suppose you expect a shilling or two for your troubles," he grumbled, handing the thing to the waiting footman.

"No, sir." Charles shoved the note in an inner pocket. "Already been rewarded."

"I'm sure you have," Gracechurch murmured. "The only question is the manner of your reward."

Suddenly his neckcloth was being seized in a gnarled fist, twisted so tightly he had difficulty breathing.

"Here now, lad," Charles growled, "I took a birch to you for your sauce when you were a stripling. You continue in this vein, and I'll take one to you again, man and officer or not. That clear?"

"Very," Gracechurch choked out, face reddened by more than lack of air.

"Good."

The glare in the footman's eyes was astonishing. So Suzanne had made a fool of the old fellow, just as she made fools of any who crossed her path. Poor Charles, duped by a winsome smile and demure manner and a soft voice. Well, it wasn't his task to disabuse the man if he was so easily taken in, but he did his best to give glare for glare, hands curling into fists.

"You're a fool, Colonel," the footman said more calmly. "No more brains in your cockloft than in your privates, and that's a fact."

He gave the neckcloth a final wrench, then released it, turned on his heel and left without another word.

The rest of the day passed in unrelieved tedium. Seconds lagged and minutes crept. As for the hours, they advanced not at all. No book could hold Gracechurch's attention. No project in the little cottage appealed. The thought of riding about the countryside, the one diversion agreed upon as safe by all concerned, was repugnant.

He remained withindoors as India Phelps had recommended, not because he felt it was the best manner in which to proceed, but because of his mother's earlier tearful entreaties. This silliness had her genuinely distressed. At least she, unlike Suzanne, didn't believe a word of it, but the question of who could be slandering him, and why, had her in a most uncharacteristic frenzy—hence India Phelps's insistence she spend the day at Rose Cottage. There at least there would be none casting sly glances her way, and uttering phrases whose double meanings would have had her choking back tears one moment and imprecations the next as she went about her usual rounds in the village.

Scully he avoided as if the man had the plague. The former batman's superior looks, his very silence regarding what had happened spoke more loudly than the most acid recriminations. Gracechurch, with all his plots and prevarications, was to blame for everything. Well, it was true enough—not that he enjoyed having the fact shoved down his throat at every turn. No one would have dared the murmurings had they the slightest notion of his affluence.

As for the unpleasant confrontation with old Charlie Simmons, that had been beyond distressing. He'd felt a paltry schoolboy again, caught stealing buns left to cool on a sill—the infraction for which he'd received that birching so many years ago. Charles had been the winner then, and Charles was the winner now. What had possessed him to make that comment about Suzanne? He had no idea. The words had been there waiting, and they'd tumbled from his lips without so much as a thought on his part. That, more than anything else, troubled him.

Gracechurch ate a solitary dinner from a tray in the parlor after Mags chased him from the kitchen claiming it wasn't fitting for him to take his meals with the help, but probably more because she wanted the time with Scully to herself so they could review his iniquities and devise methods of bringing him to a proper sense of them. What that meal consisted of, however, he couldn't've said two minutes after rising from his chair. Then he paced, watching the hands creep around the dial of the carriage clock on the mantel, pausing every so often to tap its apparently unmoving hands in irritation.

Finally, unable to stand it anymore, at eleven he went out to Scully's shed to saddle Iago and be on his way. Lights still burned in the kitchen. Scully and Mags were at the table silhouetted against the glow, heads together. Plotting against him, no doubt. And finding ways to assist him despite himself. At least Scully wouldn't betray his secrets, that was certain. A few words in his ear after everyone left that morning had seen to sealing his lips.

Allowing an hour to reach the old oak was ludicrous, Gracechurch admitted as he mounted and turned his horse's head toward the village. A measure of how desperately he wanted this undesired encounter over and done with? Probably. It would be an unpleasant few minutes, but afterwards he'd be able to banish Suzanne from his mind for good and write *finis* to that entire lamentable chapter of his existence.

Once beyond the vicarage and the Pembertons' apothecary shop he cut cross-country at a comfortable trot, giving Iago his head and enjoying the moonlit landscape to the full. July had always been the best month in Chipham Common, the trees still hinting at the fresh green of spring, the birds with their plumage as yet untattered, the skies of a heavenly blue by day and a velvety inkiness by night so long as rain didn't threaten. Crops thrived. Flowers bloomed. Butterflies and bees went about their business with devotion. It was idyllic, a scrap of heaven set in the verdant English countryside to remind men of their duty to God and King, totally unlike the harsh mountains and dusty plains of the Peninsula, the wind blowing hot and dry off the Mediterranean and cold and damp from the Atlantic.

He shivered at the memory and blanked his mind. There were certain things it was better not to remember, for the memories served nothing.

They cut into the ancient woods, rider and horse, where legend had it once kings hunted and unicorns roamed. Gracechurch followed the trails as easily as if it had been nine days rather than nine years since last he was there. The changes were few beyond trees perhaps grown a bit larger and trails more choked with weeds. Night sounds greeted his

We'd Like to Invite You to Subscribe to Zebra's Regency Romance Book Club and Give You a Gift of 4 Free Books as Your Introduction! *(Worth $19.96!)*

If you're a Regency lover, imagine the joy of getting 4 FREE Zebra Regency Romances and then the chance to have these lovely stories delivered to your home each month at the lowest prices available! Well, that's our offer to you and here's how you benefit by becoming a Zebra Home Subscription Service subscriber:

- 4 FREE Introductory Regency Romances are delivered to your doorstep
- 4 BRAND NEW Regencies are then delivered each month (usually before they're available in bookstores)
- Subscribers save almost $4.00 every month
- Home delivery is always FREE
- You also receive a FREE monthly newsletter, *Zebra/Pinnacle Romance News* which features author profiles, contests, subscriber benefits, book previews and more
- No risks or obligations...in other words you can cancel whenever you wish with no questions asked

Join the thousands of readers who enjoy the savings and convenience offered to Regency Romance subscribers. After your initial introductory shipment, you receive 4 brand-new Zebra Regency Romances each month to examine for 10 days. Then, if you decide to keep the books, you'll pay the preferred subscriber's price of just $4.00 per title. That's only $16.00 for all 4 books and there's never an extra charge for shipping and handling.

It's a no-lose proposition, so return the FREE BOOK CERTIFICATE today!

AFFIX
STAMP
HERE

ZEBRA HOME SUBSCRIPTION SERVICE, INC.

120 BRIGHTON ROAD

P.O. BOX 5214

CLIFTON, NEW JERSEY 07015-5214

ears now as then, a haunting chorus of frogs and crickets and the occasional owl calling to its mate. It wasn't a lonely place, for all the old tales of witches and warlocks and fairies, the warnings of enchantments at full moon and curses when there was none.

He came upon the Weeping Sisters, by tradition five Druid maidens turned to stone for betrayal of their High Priest many eons ago when the world was young. Here there was indeed change. One had toppled. Another tilted, leaning against her nearest companion as if seeking comfort, their shadows stretching long and tortured across the clearing. Just beyond, the oak beneath which he and Suzanne had sworn undying love was split in two, the jagged rent showing black in the moonlight. Only the topmost branches bore leaves. It was impossible to tell if they were of this year's sprouting, or sere relics of a long gone summer. He sniffed the air as Iago shifted uneasily beneath him. The odor of old charring lingered in the air. Lightning? All too probable. The clearing was at the top of a little hill, the oak the tallest thing about. Amazing it had survived this long.

A shadow moved among the shadows, separating itself from the others.

"Stephen?" The one word, softly spoken, hesitant, the voice unmistakable.

So she too had been restless, unable to wait patiently for the appointed hour. That, or she felt what she had to tell him was of such great importance that she came early for fear she might be delayed or lose her way, and he would come and depart before she arrived.

He said nothing, dropping from the saddle and looping Iago's reins over a convenient bush. Then he turned, remaining where he was.

"Well," he said, "what d'you want?"

She came toward him in the moonlight, this ghost of the girl he'd known and loved, garbed in a dark hooded cloak surely too warm for the balmy night, her steps uncertain, almost reluctant. She stopped when there were still several feet between them, a neutral territory across which they could fire their salvos, and simply stood there regarding him, cloak blanched by the cool light of the moon.

"Well?" he repeated when the silence grew to unpleasant proportions.

"There's trouble in the village," she said. "They're talking."

"They always talk in the village, my lady." He was pleased with the tone he'd selected. Bored, indifferent, condescending—he'd managed all three in less than thrice that many words. Perfect.

"The talk is about you, Stephen."

"And so it's Stephen now, is it, and not Colonel Gracechurch? I've fallen so low in your estimation, given whatever it is they're saying, that now you feel free to call me by name as you would a servant?"

"My apologies, Colonel. I wasn't thinking."

"No, you weren't," he returned coldly. "You've brought me out at this hour and this far merely to tell me things are as usual in the neighborhood?"

"Time and place were of your choosing, not mine." Her head rose then, the moonlight striking her face despite the cloak's deep hood.

"So they were. I see you remembered the way easily enough."

She turned her back at his sarcasm, shoulders slumping.

"Well, what is it you wish to tell me?" he snapped as she started for the path that led to Trillings, Placidia, and Rose Cottage. "Certainly there's more."

"I don't know why I bothered," she murmured, but she did stop. "Yes, there's more—if you really want to hear it."

"I do, if you would be so kind. Curiosity, you understand, merely idle curiosity as to what it might be this time."

"All right," she said, voice barely audible.

Then, back still turned, she repeated the tale told by Cassie at dawn and confirmed by India Phelps not much later. This time he let the silence grow between them when she was done, a palpable thing carrying subtle messages of its own.

"And you believe it, of course," he said finally. "You believe it all, and have come to warn me from the neighborhood."

"You think that? You truly think that?" She turned then, eyes wide. "I never knew you, did I? I never knew you at all."

"No, you didn't, just as I never knew you. Given the evidence, it's as well. Must you be so officious on my behalf?

The great lady, come down from her lofty tower to dispense alms among the beggars at her door. Well, I'm not a beggar, Lady Phelps, at your door or any other's. I never was. I never shall be, appearances to the contrary not withstanding."

She had vanished among the trees before the bitter words were fairly out of his mouth.

"Come back here," he shouted. "I'm not done with you yet, dammit, Suzanne!"

Only an owl's call and what might have been a rustling of leaves answered him.

"I already knew," he roared after her, hoping she heard. "There was no need for all this drama of moonstruck midnight meetings!"

Chapter Nine

The ride back to his mother's cottage once he left the clearing—which had been considerably after Suzanne's departure given his need for solitary self-castigation once the fit of self-congratulation at his narrow escape from existing under the cat's paw had passed—was quickly accomplished. Iago longed for his stable. More importantly, Gracechurch had no desire to be out and about as the moon sank toward the horizon. By contrast, he had a very great desire for a tumbler or two of the brandy Suzanne had had delivered to his mother's cottage not three days before.

Besides, the hilltop had provided no more answers than any other place would.

What had come over him to behave in such a boorish manner? He didn't know. The hour perhaps, the darkness and the near anonymity it offered, and the years of carrying certain letters tucked in a hidden pocket of the wallet in which he'd kept important papers. At the time he'd insisted he hadn't burnt them so he'd have a reminder of eternal truths concerning females, fidelity, and fickleness—the Three Fs, he'd called them once in a drunken stupor. Perhaps they had served that purpose in the beginning. Now? Lord knew, for he couldn't think of a one other than taking up space.

He was only certain that each time he saw Suzanne he became more deeply infuriated with her, with her father, with the conventional wisdom that stipulated impoverished lieutenant did not wed with dowerless miss, nor did penniless vicar's son seek the hand of knight's wealthy widow—though that was hardly at issue now, or ever would be. Perhaps—and this he didn't want to consider too deeply—he was even infuriated with himself for not at least attempting more definite action all those years ago. Little as he liked to admit it, given his absence Suzanne had been caught in a maze from which there had been no exit other than the one guarded by her father and Sir John, the rights of fathers being what they were and the rights of daughters being non-existent. She'd resisted for a year. No one could ask more of a frail female.

Besides, what could he have done, he in the Peninsula and she in Chipham Common? Nothing. Precisely nothing. Unless a letter from his superior at the time, who'd conveniently born the name of Wellesley and hadn't been unknown even then, might've turned the trick? But no, it wouldn't do. The past was the past. He'd gone over it all so many times there were those who would've considered him obsessed were they aware of his agonizing. He'd been all that was honorable in the affair. And she? She'd been all that was dishonorable, cowardly and weak.

Unfortunately that mattered not in the least at the moment, for one thing was clear, all else aside: he'd put himself in the position of having to apologize to the blasted woman again the next time he encountered her. That seemed a perpetual activity these days.

He cut around the village rather than through it, not wanting his passage to be remarked with the hour grown so late, for he must have lingered on that hilltop trapped between bemusement at his own behavior and fury at hers, past and present, for over an hour. Then, as he approached the cottage through the fields, he paused in the lee of a convenient hedgerow.

What the devil?

Goblins tumbled about in the lane, darting now here, now there—shadows that bore solid form and substance, high-lighted by torch flames. He watched through narrowed eyes, at first puzzled. There were lights in the cottage. He could hear shouts. His mother? Mags? Scully? There was no way to tell, even this close, but those shadows bearing torches were stubbornly silent, and all the more terrifying for it. Shouts would at least have proved their humanity.

Then the chaos resolved itself into something slightly more organized, totally human and infinitely more unpleasant.

Gracechurch descended on the hooded mob with a bellow, an enormous black figure reaching for a non-existent saber as he spurred his mount. They scattered as he pulled Iago to a shuddering halt in the lane, some to the fields, some to the woods around and behind the cottage, one lashing at Iago's legs with a whip as he tore past.

How many had there been? Ten? Twenty? The entire coun-tryside must've descended on his mother while he was gone.

"Scully!" Gracechurch roared as the big bay reared and attempted to break after the vandal, well accustomed to chas-ing down the enemy. He pulled Iago down, knowing pursuit was as futile as it was ill-advised. The men who'd been here were as well known to him as he was to them unless Phelps had tired of waiting for him to be attacked and imported bully-boys from beyond Little Stoking. The possibility drew his mouth back in a snarl. "Scully, where are you?"

There was a rustling just beyond the gate. A figure separated itself from the trees, bent double, hand groping along the fence.

"Scully?" Gracechurch swung from the saddle, started for the gate. "Good God, man—what's to do?"

"Told you it wouldn't wash. Now'll you believe me?"

The words were barely a croak, the words catching in the throat. Gracechurch was through the open gate and beside his batman on the instant, reaching out to support the stumbling man.

"Where've you been, Colonel?"

"Had an errand to run."

"At this hour? Should've been here. An' you had, between

us we might've been able to chase 'em off. As it was, not much I could do. Too many of 'em."

Scully flinched beneath Gracechurch's tightening hand. The colonel took a deep breath and relaxed his grip, forcing himself to acknowledge that if there was one person who wasn't at fault in this, it was Scully.

"Did you see any faces?" he asked, voice shaking.

"Nary a one. They were that careful. Didn't want to be recognized, I'm thinking, in case you decided to bring charges. Nor did they speak, not a word. As there was but one of me they succeeded in what they came for."

Scully's weak gesture encompassed the uprooted flowers, the trampled garden, the gate dangling from a single hinge. Was that mud clinging to the cottage walls?

Iago followed them into the destruction, nibbling on crushed blossoms.

"I didn't dare use a pistol," Scully explained, "and they beat me with m'own cudgel."

"Oh, Lord," Gracechurch muttered. "Damn all of Chipham Common to hell."

"Might consider sending yourself there with the rest, it being as it's your games've brought this on."

"Stubble it. Let's get you to the cottage and see to your hurts. There's nothing to be done here until morning." Then Gracechurch glanced about him more carefully. "What's all the white? It looks like there's been a blizzard."

"Feathers, colonel. White feathers. Bushels of 'em."

The symbol of cowardice. The mob'd been pointed enough in its opinions—and destructive enough. The barbs didn't matter. The destruction did. And then Gracechurch wrinkled his nose. It wasn't just mud smeared over the cottage walls. And he'd brought all this on his mother. It didn't matter whether it was his neighbors who'd caused the destruction with little more than encouragement as their reward, or bully-boys imported by Phelps—who could easily afford it—or the squire, who couldn't. All would assume villagers incensed at the thought of an unpunished traitor in their midst had taken matters into their own hands.

He brushed away a clump of feathers clinging to his coat. Heaven alone knew where they'd gotten so many of the blasted things.

"I suppose I should make myself scarce for the next few days," he murmured absently.

"You do, Colonel, and you'll never be able to come back—not even when they learn the truth. Certain you want that? Seems to me now's the time to dig ourselves a few trenches and get down on our hunkers once we've evacuated the civilians."

And then they were at the cottage door, Mags holding a lamp high to light their way, his mother hovering anxiously behind her.

"Not a pretty sight out there," he said at Mags's concerned look, "but nothing that can't be remedied."

"Made a right fine mess of things," Scully agreed, shuffling across the threshold and turning to Mrs. Gracechurch. "Sorry for that, ma'am. Did my best to chase 'em off, but there was too many of them."

Scully looked even worse than Gracechurch had anticipated: eye blackening, clothes in tatters, tooth missing, lump on his forehead, and it was a good question as to which leg was causing him to limp, or if it was both.

"Damn them all to hell," Gracechurch muttered too low for his mother to hear.

"Amen to that," Scully murmured with a grimace. "We got some plotting of our own to do, Colonel. A deal of plotting."

"Later."

And then they were in the parlor, Mags setting the lamp on the table between the windows, his mother at the dresser pouring a tot of brandy in one of the glasses left there for his convenience. Gracechurch glanced about him, considering. No one would dare put a shot through the panes, no matter how clear Scully's silhouette against the drawn curtains. Murder hadn't been the object tonight—merely humiliation. Of course if someone'd accidentally been dispatched, he doubted either Suzanne's stepson or her father would've mourned for more than an instant. Scully's slight nod confirmed his assessment, but still the man hung back, clearly refusing to step on the carpet.

Gracechurch turned to Mags and his mother. "We'll want warm water and bandages. Soap. Some basilicum powder, if you've any at hand."

The stench of dung was overpowering. He scowled. Then

his brows soared as he glanced at the obvious source. Scully was covered with the stuff.

"God damn them," he growled, giving no thought to his mother's presence, "may they rot in hell forever."

But while she might not echo his words, from the expression on her face she was echoing his thoughts. He stared first at Mags and then his mother, hands spread in near helplessness. He was accustomed to a clever enemy, a devious one, even a needlessly cruel and heartless one possessed of a fanaticism so ingrained only a fool didn't take it into account. But this? And as he could prove nothing, he had no remedy or recourse.

"A bath," Mags said, shoving the brandy in Scully's bruised hands, "and those clothes to be burnt or buried. There's no savin' 'em, and that's the truth. And a hot soak might do a little to ease those aches of yours. They did you up right fine and brown, they did. You'll be a sight come morning—not that you were that much to look before, but at least your face was all of a color. As for moving about, you'll've gained twenty years in a single night if we don't see to you, mark my words."

"Stop your fussing, woman," Scully growled, but there was the slightest of smiles at the back of his swollen eyes. "I been worse'n this in the Peninsula with nary a bath nor any tending' to me beyond what I could manage myself, and that's the truth."

"But this," Mags declared furiously, arms akimbo, hands on hips, "isn't the Peninsula. I'll not be saying we're more civilized, not given this night's doings, but we try to be. I'll get the stove fired up and the kettles to boiling. Colonel, it'd save me a mort of time if you'd draw the water we'll be needing."

"See here now," Scully snapped, hobbling toward the door, "I'll not be having the colonel playing serving wench."

Gracechurch's restraining hand was as gentle as it was firm. "Don't be a fool," he murmured. "Right now it's we who follow orders, not we who give 'em. That'll come later."

Regularizing Scully took considerable time, and a trip to the stream before a more conventional bath was attempted.

The man had a spare pair of britches and an extra shirt and waistcoat, such as they were. Unfortunately, Gracechurch'd insisted—quite rightly, he'd believed as they scurried about London acquiring costumes of the correct decrepitude to portray the image he desired—the body servant of one so poor as he presented himself to be would hardly have two coats or more than a single pair of boots. That posed more of a problem, for he hadn't anticipated their royal reception.

He played inn's potboy scrambling after an extra shilling or two. Nothing would touch the boots, mostly because the filth had seeped through the cracks. Force Scully to wear dung-impregnated boots he would not. As for coats, he was down to one himself given his kite-retrieving adventures, his tawdry evening wear aside. As he'd murmured to Scully when Mags's back was turned for propriety's sake and his mother was busy concocting a posset, that posed an almost insurmountable problem.

He left Scully to Mags's ministrations once cleanliness and wounds had been seen to, and nightshirt and worn banyan made the man relatively decent. After cajoling his mother to return to bed and seeing to the stabling of Iago—whose breath would surely smell sweet in the morning—he stood guard across the lane from the cottage for the remainder of the night. Dawn found him pacing the dew-soaked weeds. His feet were cramping. His chin bore a liberal allotment of dark stubble. His face was dry, his eyes burning with exhaustion. His back and shoulders, still sore from his tumble from the tree at the vicarage, complained bitterly. All this would've been acceptable except for one detail: his watchfulness was too tardy to be of use to anyone.

The early light turned the feathers drifting in the lane and through his mother's destroyed garden to rosy curling petals. It was, if one didn't look too carefully, something out of a tale told to regale children, but no enchanted princess lay sleeping in the cottage. No dragon guarded the near-by hilltop on which he'd met Suzanne. There were no gallant knights about to come to anyone's rescue. As for last night's ogres, they were paltry fellows hiding behind hoods and darkness, and taking cup courage from anonymity and free ale.

He shivered, listening as the birds broke into such a racket he was reminded of winter camp, where lack of activity and too great proximity of too many men—and too few women to soften their irritabilities—led to fights and worse. It was almost as if one had opened the door to the infernal regions.

Then, stretching to ease stiffened joints and cramping muscles, he headed across the lane and around the cottage to the kitchen. There, as expected, he found Mags and Scully, as bleary-eyed and out of sorts as he felt, and equally sleepless.

Scully gave him a wry grimace, cocking a brow. "Time to evacuate the civilians?" he asked, but it was more statement than question.

"I told you I ain't leaving." Mags plunked another cup on the table and filled it with tea so strong it was almost black. "Here you go, Colonel. That'll loosen the kinks."

"Mutiny in the ranks? That's not like you, Mags." Gracechurch accepted the cup, choked the bitter stuff down. It was hot—that was the main thing. "I don't want my mother here. She's been through enough."

"Should've thought of that sooner, Colonel," Scully grumbled.

"Water under the bridge. What matters is now."

Mags regained her seat, watching the former officer through shrewd eyes. "We been discussing things, Scully and me," she said. "Herself goes—there I agree—if Mrs. Phelps'll have her to stay. Pounds to pence she will, but somebody's got to ask. And herself won't like it."

"I'm intending to head for Rose Cottage in a few moments."

"As you are?" Scully's brows rose. "Y'look like the devil, Colonel, and that's the truth. Won't let you through the door, is my guess."

"All the more convincing." Gracechurch sighed, setting his cup on the table. "I want my mother gone. You too, Mags. Lord knows when those ruffians'll return, but they will, and they won't be so easily scared off next time. For one thing, they'll be disgusted at letting one mounted man do a job it should've taken an armed squad had they decent leadership, for they had darkness on their side, and surprise. Angry men with their honor to avenge're determined men."

"Point is, they don't have that leadership—just someone who's paying 'em," Scully said with satisfaction. "Cowards're still cowards when there's no one to stiffen their spines, no matter how angry."

"Maybe you should consider applying for the post, Scully?"

The former batman snorted, then cocked a brow. "Might not be such a bad idea at that. A few conflicting orders here, a bit of countermanding there, and a constable arriving betimes to arrest the lot wouldn't go amiss."

"Wouldn't work, aside from the consternation it'd cause in the village. Least said or done, soonest mended."

"No, it wouldn't work—but it's a pleasant thought."

"Not to be considered, Scully. They'd tumble to you before you'd fairly begun, and what they'd do to you then I don't like to think. Bad enough as it is."

"I'll mend, Colonel."

"But how soon?"

"Soon enough. I've suffered worse and put in a full day's march after, as you'll remember."

"How many years ago was that, old friend? And you still pay the price when the weather turns damp."

Scully shrugged and winced. "There's that," he admitted grudgingly, "though it ain't in the least gentleman-like of you to remind me."

"I'm merely attempting to show a little sense for all our sakes."

"Too little, and far too late."

"We'll see. I think I'll start exercising Iago as you've been recommending, Scully. About time, I believe. He was frisky last night."

"Time, and more."

Mags had been following the acid conversation with quick turns of her head, her eyes questioning. Now she rose, went to the hearth and opened the baking door.

"The riding you should be doing is to Rose Cottage," she snapped, her back turned as she retrieved pans of freshly baked bread. "Herself'll be up and about in minutes, you mark my words, and fighting you every step of the way."

* * *

And so Gracechurch, after fortifying himself with several more cups of tea and a slab of bread, took off for Rose Cottage as instructed, avoiding the lanes where wagons traveled even so early. It was a good thing he'd taken the byways, for he'd no desire to encounter any who might've taken issue with his continuance in the neighborhood. The freshness of the morning, the clarity of the air had no soothing effect—not after the events of the night before. Suzanne or the bully-boys, it was difficult to chose which experience had been worse. Suzanne, perhaps, for there he'd been entirely at fault. Well, he'd probably been entirely at fault in the other as well, given his lack of forthrightness had encouraged such games.

His personal appearance and arrival at such an unreasonable hour caused no small degree of consternation in the housemaid who answered the door. Then old Charles pattered in on felt slippers, hushed her babbling and saw him to the breakfast parlor where India Phelps was making inroads on the contents of dishes set over warmers on the sideboard, and perusing the most recently delivered London journals.

She glanced at Gracechurch, eyes narrowing as she took in a tattered white feather caught beneath his coat collar, his dusty boots, his generally unkempt air.

"Been making indentures," she inquired tartly, "and sleeping with the chickens? Or have you been playing the fool?" Then, without waiting for a response, she gestured at the chair across from hers. "You'd best sit, no matter what your problem. You've an air of starvation about you, Stephen. No—hush until you've eaten. Not to worry, the girls won't put in their appearance for hours, and as I heard Suzanne pacing the floor half the night it's unlikely you'll see her, either."

Before he could more than open his mouth, a plate holding a thick slice of rare sirloin, grilled kidneys, and what must have been a half dozen eggs scrambled with cream and scraps of fried gammon was set in front of him by Charles, almost as if some had anticipated his arrival even if others hadn't. This was followed in rapid order by a basket of muffins, a tankard of ale and a pot of coffee almost as black as Mags's tea.

It was difficult not to sigh from pure pleasure at the luxurious meal. Given his continued refusal to let his mother in on his secrets, breakfast at the cottage generally consisted of porridge or bread. His single attempt at protest that his business with India Phelps was pressing met with a frown. Long accustomed to her ways, he gave it up. Truth to tell, once he attacked the food she proved to be right: little though he realized it, he was indeed starved. Gracechurch was just draining the last of the tankard when Croft, India Phelps's antiquated coachman, appeared as if on cue.

"Well?" she demanded.

"Just as you ordered, mum. Got most all the dead stuff out, Joe McTavish and his boys have, and replanted so clever none'd be able to tell there'd been aught amiss just hours ago unless they knew precise what flowers Mrs. Gracechurch had and where."

"What on earth—" Gracechurch spluttered, gaze flying from one to the other.

"Even roses is in place, though they ain't quite the same roses as Mrs. Gracechurch had before, nor yet the same colors or sizes, and Mr. McTavish is that worried they mayn't do well being transplanted in this season."

"I had your mother's cottage watched last night," India Phelps explained, raising her hand to silence the voluble coachman. "Stood to reason something unpleasant was about to happen, and happen it did. Too many for Tom, Croft's grandson, to take on by himself unfortunately, but he reported back once you'd taken charge. I sent Mr. McTavish and his crew over at first light with orders to hang back until you were on your way here, as I was certain you'd do your best to make difficulties were you about. You're too proud by half, Stephen, and always have been."

She turned back to Croft, eyes twinkling. "Mrs. Gracechurch is being settled into her room by my abigail, I presume?"

"She is that, mum, but there was no moving that cook o'hers, no matter what I said. Swore she'd stick by Mr. Bates and the colonel, Mags did—begging your pardon, Colonel, but we been acquainted all our lives, and argufying most of 'em—but othergates all's as you wanted it, mum."

"Dear Lord," Gracechurch murmured.

"A simple thank-you will do, Stephen. I know better than to try insisting you spend your nights here—only marginally convenable despite my presence in any case, given Suzanne and the girls—and I do realize it's not wise for you to skulk about, but shoving yourself under the noses of those who'd rather see you gone? Not advisable, either. At least not at the moment. Later? Even I'll enjoy the sight, though it's my own grandson you've been diddling along with the squire, which they quite deserve, and most of the village into the bargain, which isn't quite as justifiable."

"Diddling? I? I don't understand."

"You don't? Truly?" Her glance swept his thread-bare coat with its shiny seams, his cracked boots, his frayed linen. "Well, we'll leave it for the moment, then. I can imagine the tale with which you'll regale me eventually. In the meantime, you're not to be concerned about your mother. I'll keep her busy here until it all blows over."

At the sound of voices in the hall Gracechurch's hostess paused in her teasing, head cocked. Then she seemed to shrink, collapsing into herself. The hand that had firmly poured tea developed a palsied tremor. The mouth became slack, the eyes lost their sparkle and narrowed as if against pain. Charles spread a napkin over her half-consumed meal and whisked the plate away.

"I can see this may become distinctly inconvenient," she murmured. "I may even be forced to take frequent naps lest I become permanently incapacitated. Have a tray in my room as soon as I've set Mrs. Gracechurch to some task or other, Charles. And give me my walking stick. I believe it's in the corner. Wouldn't do to be caught without it."

The door opened just as she was hooking the stick over the arm of her chair.

"Matilda," she quavered in a voice so thin it seemed little more than a rustle of dry parchment as Gracechurch rose from his place, "I'm so relieved you've come. What I'd do without you—"

"You'd go on perfectly well," Matilda Gracechurch returned with a smile as sweet as it was pointed. "No play-acting if you please, India. I've been acquainted with your tricks these forty years and more. You here, Stephen? Ah well, I suppose I should've expected that. I'm not made of sand you know, that the first drop of rain sets me to crumbling. Sit down, for pity's sake."

"I, er, ah," Gracechurch attempted with the conviction he was strangling on his neckcloth, and subsided like a stripling caught purloining his father's cheroots.

She glanced at the sideboard, retrieved India Phelps's plate, uncovered it and set it before her. "Finish this," she commanded, "or you'll be in a foul temper all day. It's most unfair, you know—that you may eat anything you wish and still present a pleasing appearance, while if I but glance at such a plateful I become a bowl of dough left too long to rise."

"You're not all adither from the events of last night?" India Phelps inquired, voice once more firm.

Charles swept out the chair beside her and bowed slightly to the widow.

"Hardly. Unpleasant of course, but I've survived worse. Thank you, Charles." She sank into the chair, nodded at his offer of tea. "You've no idea the sorts of people who would come importuning Joseph in the middle of the night," she continued brightly, "nor the condition they'd be in. Thank heavens Stephen was a heavy sleeper or he'd've spent half his childhood terrorized.

"No, these were just rowdies bent on intimidation. They may've succeeded with Stephen and Scully, but certainly Mags and I know better than to be cowed by such poltroons. There are moments when I'm most uncooperative. Did I never tell you of the time an escaped brigand arrived on our doorstep, wielding a knife that was more like a saber and demanding all sorts of things, such as the Communion plate? No? Well, someday I must, that's clear. In the end I subdued him with a warming pan."

"Mother—" Gracechurch broke in.

"Enough! I'm here, be satisfied with that. For your sake I'll stay until there's no chance of a recurrence. Beyond that? Grant me a modicum of sense, Stephen. No lily-livered miss would ever've survived as your father's wife, not the way he took in every vagrant he encountered, and nine tenths of them not worthy of the kindness."

"You're unaccustomedly blunt," India Phelps threw in with a twinkle.

"I'm unaccustomedly infuriated by the wanton destruction of my garden, if you want the truth," Matilda Gracechurch returned, voice trembling with indignation. "I know Joseph would scold me for being illogical were he here, but such brutality always infuriates me. There, now you know my besetting sin. The destruction of anything of beauty is an offense in the eyes of God—or at least in the eyes of the God whom I worship. There's enough that's ugly in the world as it is without adding to the total. And I do thank you most sincerely for sending over Mr. McTavish and his boys to make what repairs they could. Even so, I'm still tempted to find a cudgel and go after the varlets."

Hard on those words the parlor door opened once more. Gracechurch sprang to his feet.

Suzanne stood hesitantly in the opening, face wan, eyes darkly smudged, hair severely pinned back, garbed in yet another of her lackluster gowns. But, there was a change, albeit a small one: The shawl hanging in graceful folds from her elbows was of a wool so fine it was almost transparent, the fringe deep and intricately knotted. And its hue? Better to say hues. It had the luster, the depth, the glow of the great rose window at Chartres, a French cathedral not far from Paris that he'd visited during the early days of the Occupation, having been told of its glories by his father.

"Good morning, my lady," he murmured. Then, lower still so no one could catch his words but Suzanne, "My apologies for last night. I don't know what came over me."

"Good heavens, Stephen, must you be so formal?" India Phelps snapped. "Well, don't just stand there, Suzanne. Come in or go out."

That day passed uneventfully for Stephen Gracechurch if one didn't count being cut each time he showed his face. He chose to publicly ignore the public insults, however he felt about them privately, pretending to an abstraction that made it a good question as to who was cutting whom. It would be easier in the long run that way. Of course there was the note from Scowden awaiting him on his return from Rose Cottage.

Mr. Scowden was deeply distressed to inform Mr. Gracechurch all three of his daughters were indisposed with an unnamed but highly contagious complaint whose symptoms, blah-blah-blah. It was with sincerest regret that he rescinded the invitation to dinner on Wednesday next, but he knew the company of such dull married folk as he and his wife, unrelieved by the beauty and sprightly manners of their fetching daughters, would be tedious to a young gentleman bent on establishing himself, blather-blather-blather, in addition to which Mr. Gracechurch would certainly not want to risk bringing the infection home to his mother, gabble-gabble-gabble.

The thing went on for a full two scrawled pages, almost as if Scowden weren't certain he should believe the tales being circulated and wanted to ensure if they proved false he could reissue his invitation without any questioning of his motives on either occasion. Gracechurch crumpled the thing and tossed it on the cold parlor grate.

As for the brief conversation he'd held with Suzanne following that most uncomfortable breakfast at Rose Cottage, it had been unsatisfactory in the extreme. He'd cornered her. She'd listened, eyes on her toes, saying nothing until he'd run out of words. That had taken longer than he'd expected, for unlike Scowden he didn't tend to rattle on forever. No military man did. At the end of it she'd merely murmured, "Think nothing of it, Colonel. The error was all on my side," eyes still downcast, and wandered from the room almost as if she were a lack-wit and comprehended not a word he'd said.

After that he'd beaten a hasty retreat before either India Phelps or his mother could more than make a comment or two, pleading a need to return to the cottage and ascertain all was as it should be.

There he'd found two of McTavish's boys scrubbing the walls under Mags's good-humored direction. Pails of whitewash waited at the ready. The gate had been mended, the detritus carted away. There wasn't so much as a feather to be seen, and though the garden wasn't as it had been—soil showed between some of the plants, and the blooms were fewer and perhaps smaller—its resurrection was a minor miracle of major kindness all the same.

But then came the incident late Saturday night while he was returning to Chipham Common. It might've been anyone and anything despite Cassie's insistence that it was someone distinctly particular. Still, once it was over he maintained it could've been anyone, only too conscious that putting Cassie's undoubtedly accurate interpretation on events would force him to actions he in no way desired to take.

For, after checking on Scully upon his return from Rose Cottage the morning following the destruction of his mother's garden, Gracechurch saddled Iago and took off cross-country. Scully was right about one thing: it was time to seek out the fine residence he'd promised himself when Nathan Rothschild's letter arrived announcing his sudden elevation to the ranks of the disgustingly wealthy following Waterloo.

And late Saturday he'd found it: Stormridge, an ancient manor on a steep rise overlooking the Chipple and its verdant flood plain just north of Little Stoking. The last family who'd occupied the place had lost everything at the time of Nathan's clever coup—a pity perhaps, but as they'd come by it in an underhanded manner according to local gossip, and their losses had sprung from greed rather than misfortune, there was perhaps a touch of justice there. The place had stood empty ever since, not even a caretaker to see to it.

He'd wandered the overgrown grounds as afternoon shadows lengthened, delighting in the view of the river, the remains of a leaf-clogged Elizabethan herb garden that might actually be original, and a bronze sundial almost black with age.

The house had been carefully modernized—the estate agent had had that right, though he'd cringed at the thought when listening to the man jabber in the local taproom. Windows soared. Doors had been knocked through walls linking the downstairs rooms to provide the popular *à suivi* succession of interior vistas. All was light and bright and in excellent taste, though the rooms lacked so much as a chandelier or a chair under holland covers, for all had been sold to satisfy creditors. Best of all, from what he could see peeking through windows, Stormridge only required a thorough cleaning and the essential in furnishings and window coverings and it would be habitable. Roof, walls, foundation—all appeared sound. As for the kitchen, Mags would be in raptures.

After inspecting the stables and a commodious barn, he returned to lounge on the terrace steps leading to the drive and the gardens at the front of the house, watching as the sun set over the river and triumphing in the knowledge that this superior property would be his home. The extensive grounds and gardens begging her touch would delight his mother, that was what counted. Whoever he eventually married would find it all that was pleasing, just as wives fortunate enough to acquire landed husbands always did.

He'd unearth the proper sort of mouse once the enemy was routed and the dust settled: youngish, but not so young she carried the milky air of the schoolroom with her; attractive, but not a tiresome bucolic belle, forever demanding attention and pretty words; not excessively vapid, but not too intelligent, either. Intelligent females had an unfortunate tendency to hold opinions that were not necessarily those of their husbands, and an even more unfortunate tendency to express those opinions at every opportunity. He wanted a peaceful home. He wanted a gracious hostess who would show proper deference to both himself and his mother. And, he wanted a healthy brood mare to provide heirs for his wealth. Beyond that, she could be anyone and anything she pleased so long as she stayed out of his way and was not totally repulsive when glimpsed at a distance or over the breakfast cups.

The sun sank behind the trees, casting long shadows across the scraggly lawns and firing Stormridge's upper windows. Bats darted through the darkening sky like demented black butterflies. He swatted at a mosquito humming annoyingly by his ear, stood and stretched. It was time to go. To leave the peace. To leave the gentle silence and the cooling air. To begin the battle again, and this time finish it. He took a late supper at the inn where he'd encountered the estate agent, listening to chatter about local issues with interest. Soon these concerns would be his. It was a strange notion, for his only concern for years had been the destruction of the Corsican opportunist who'd torn Europe apart in his search for *la gloire*.

He was just past Placidia's gates and Rose Cottage when he heard hoofbeats approaching from behind. He froze, hand seeking a pistol that wasn't there. Well, and why should he be traveling about armed, blast it? This was England, not the

Peninsula or Belgium. He'd left in daylight and had intended to return in daylight. The unexpectedness of discovering Stormridge had delayed him, and the volubility of the estate agent when provided with a bottle of port, a free dinner, and the opportunity to gossip with a stranger.

Scowling, jaws clenched, Gracechurch pulled Iago to a halt, then turned him in the lane. The pursuing mount thundered around a curve, its rider's cloak billowing, and skidded to a halt.

"Thought I'd seen you head out this way this morning," a light voice declared breathlessly. "I've been waiting for positively hours, and I had to claim the headache and then sneak out after they were all occupied to do it, and if I'm caught it'll be bread and water for months, and no doubt incarceration in my bedchamber and a thousand boring Bible verses to memorize into the bargain. Where've you been?"

"About my own business, which happens to be none of yours," Gracechurch snapped. So, now Suzanne's sister was spying on him? The chit had the blowzy air of a strumpet, even in the thin moonlight. Hair unkempt. Clothes every which way. A smudge on her cheek. And riding astride? This one would never pass muster, not now, not in a thousand years. "I see your sister hasn't managed to instill a sense of propriety in you as yet."

"Well!" Cassie gasped. "Of all the rude, overbearing, ungrateful wretches. Heaven knows what Suzanne ever saw in you. She must've been mad."

"And now that you've gone your length of rudeness—"

"Oh, I've barely begun. You know," she said consideringly, "perhaps I should just let you ride on and not say another word."

"I couldn't agree more." Gracechurch turned Iago's head toward Chipham Common and gave a low chuck of his tongue.

"Only Suzanne would be overset were you to be injured, and she has enough to bear as it is, what with me and Delphine and Aurelia to see to, and no real home of her own, and nasty old Oren controlling the purse strings. He's a skint of the worst sort, you know. There's only Mother India to make things bearable, and she won't live forever."

Now the chit was riding beside him, as easy in the saddle as he was. He ignored her, repressing the impulse to give her mount a smart rap on the rump and send her on her way. But, grant her the dignity of appearing interested in what she might have to tell him? Not he. The brat was entirely too full of herself.

"Oren's been busy," she said, appearing not to care whether he wanted to hear what she had to say or not. "I overheard two of the grooms at Placidia discussing last night's events with Oren's steward, and what they intended for tonight. And no, I wasn't listening at doors, not precisely. I'd taken Duro to be reshod for he'd cast a shoe while we were out this morning, and they weren't paying the least attention to who might overhear them. I can't be blamed for that, can I? Of course I haven't told anyone so I can't be sure, and grownups have the nastiest habit of finding things for which to blame one. They're just a mile ahead, by the bye, Boggs and Fidger are, waiting in a copse over the crown of the hill."

"Are they, indeed."

"And they're armed with more than cudgels, though there's only the two of them this time. The steward said as Oren wouldn't mind if, well, if you were encouraged on your way in the most forceful manner possible, or even sent on it permanently."

"Dunce!"

"Oren's no dunce, for all he's as cowardly and selfish as he can stare, and of course nothing can be proved against him as yet. But foisting Delphine and Aurelia on Suzanne the way he did when Sir John died? And there's worse, not that we've the time to discuss it just now. I thought you might want this."

He glanced at the girl out of the corner of his eye just in time to catch the glint of moonlight on the long and highly polished barrel of a horse pistol.

"Good God," he muttered, reigning to a halt. Then he said more sharply as he extended his hand while turning sideways to present the narrowest target possible, "Be careful with that, you little fool. I've no desire to meet my Maker tonight."

"It's not loaded. Here. It's the best I could do." She punctiliously presented him the pistol butt first, as if it were a pair of scissors or a knife. "It's customarily kept in the side pocket of the larger carriage in case of brigands. As if there were brigands in these parts. Croft tests it every Saturday, and then cleans it. Sometimes he lets me help, but he's never let me load it for all I've watched him time out of mind, so I felt it best to leave that to you."

She unbuckled a leather pouch from the saddle and handed it to him. Then, with a grin he could only term minxish, teeth glinting in the moonlight, she retrieved another item.

"I borrowed this from Oren's stable," she said. "I thought it might be best to start with something less lethal and infinitely more demeaning than a pistol. Pistols are for equals, I should think."

The longish shape resolved itself into a horsewhip such as coachmen employed.

"D'you know how to use it?"

"I do indeed," Gracechurch said, quickly checking the pistol was indeed unloaded and then cramming it in his belt. He took the whip, snapped it out. The crack was highly satisfying.

"Good. I took another for me, as I knew you wouldn't like it were I armed more effectively. Most men don't, and military men are the worst, I believe."

"What need have you for arms of any sort?"

"I know we've had our differences, but I can't let you continue alone, can I? Two against one isn't fair odds, especially as that pair are as big as bulls and twice as thick-headed, and have every intention of—"

"No," he roared, shocked. "Absolutely not. I'm grateful for your concern, Cassie, but I'm perfectly capable of seeing to things myself from here on."

"I'd almost suggest taking a circuitous route and avoiding the confrontation entirely," she babbled, ignoring him, "but at least this time you're warned. Another time you might not be. The point is to terrify them so utterly they'll never try to accost you again no matter how much Oren offers them by way of reward."

"No." He grasped her forearm, pulling her around in the saddle to face him. "If need be, I'll escort you to Rose Cottage myself, and rouse the house to ensure you remain there.

Which is it to be: a circumspect retreat with no one the wiser as to your activities tonight, or a brouhaha that'll make Donnybrook Fair seem calm by comparison? I can just imagine," he added with sly triumph at the girl's scowl, "the tales with which your two stepnieces will regale the neighborhood should you chose the latter option."

"Spoilsport," she muttered, but after an exchange of glares her shoulders sagged. "You win, I suppose."

"Naturally. I always do. Now, off with you. And my sincere thanks."

"I imagine you'll carry out your threat if I don't go?"

"I will indeed."

"Well, I call it most unfair," she sighed, "for you're robbing me of the best part of the adventure."

Then she sadly turned her mount and set off toward the track leading to Rose Cottage, shoulders slumped in resignation.

Chapter Ten

Gracechurch continued down the lane at the same steady, unhurried pace he'd favored before encountering Cassie, guiding Iago with his knees, loaded pistol in left hand, whip at the ready in right.

In the event, she proved wrong. It wasn't a mile that separated him from Phelps's henchmen, but rather less than a quarter of that distance. As for opportunity to employ whip or pistol, there was none. Amazing they hadn't heard him conferring with Cassie. A single shot rang out long before he expected it, startling in the peaceful night. Gracechurch gasped at the searing crease along his upper left arm as he slumped in the saddle, hanging low on the far side of Iago's neck.

It wasn't so much he was desperately wounded, for he wasn't. Nor was the pain that severe—not yet. That would come later. He was due for a few days of acute discomfort at the very least. For now his arm was primarily numb.

It wasn't even fear. What good was fear after the fact?

No, it was disbelief combined with growing fury. This was England. More specifically this was Chipham Common where he'd been born, spent his childhood and a good portion of his youth. He'd been well liked, his father and mother adored. And now Oren Phelps, weasely as ever, was doing his best to see him dispatched. And why? Because the fool believed he was trespassing. Because he envisioned Suzanne's inheritance from Sir John slipping beyond his grasp. Bloody hell! He had no more interest in Suzanne Phelps than in a toadstool. Less. Nor had he any need of Sir John's coppers, being well enough provided through his own efforts and Nathan's good offices. But convince Phelps of that? As easy to convince a vulture it should more properly sip nectar than gorge on carrion.

He dropped the whip, shifted the pistol to his right hand and slid from the saddle, doing his best to make it appear he was in worse case than was the fact. His knees hit the dusty lane tandem, folding convincingly as he tumbled on his right side protecting his wounded arm, and keeping Iago between himself and the woods.

"Jaysus! Y'weren't supposed ter more'n wing 'im."

"Is 'e dead, d'you think?"

"I dunno. Fell like a sack o' rocks, that's sartin. He is, we'll put it about as how we saw gypsies. Mayhap we should—"

A bloodcurdling howl shattered the night. Hooves pounded up the lane at a furious gallop.

"Oh Lord—*Cassie!*" Gracechurch moaned, sitting and training his pistol on the woods.

Iago, battle-hardened and steady, whickered in response, flanks quivering, but standing his ground without taking so much as a step. A tremendous crashing in the underbrush overrode the sound of hooves. Phelps's grooms, if grooms they were, had taken to their heels, Cassie in hot pursuit.

Gracechurch stumbled to his feet, grasping the saddle as he peered about him. The light seemed poorer than it had moments before, and his arm was beginning to ache. Worse yet, it felt extremely wet.

"Damn!" He hauled himself into the saddle, shocked at how weak he felt, how uncontrollably his limbs had begun to tremble. "Find Scully, old fellow," he ordered, looping the reins about his wrist, "take me to Scully," then slumped over

Iago's neck, arms dangling on either side. Something was trickling down his left hand, puddling in his glove. The wetness tickled annoyingly. "Damn."

How long it took he never knew, but the journey seemed interminable. That someone bound his arm to slow the bleeding and then held him in the saddle for a good portion of it, murmuring encouraging words through stifled sobs, he was aware.

Had he asked his savior to wed him? It seemed he had at some point, though when or why or how he didn't know. Nor was he at first certain, when that journey was over, precisely where he'd arrived. At first he imagined Badajoz, then his tent near Santa Vitoria, and then a fly-infested bivouac on the outskirts of Toulouse, even the shell of an outbuilding at La Haye Sainte. Eventually the world swam into focus: his mother's parlor; Cassie, bloodstained and wan, her eyes red and her cheeks tear-stained, trembling by the fireplace; Mags, thin-lipped as she cut away his coat and shirt; Scully, grimly steadying his arm and cursing softly and inventively.

"What a bother I am," Gracechurch murmured, trying a smile he could tell failed with all of them.

Then, clenching his teeth and gripping the chair arm until his knuckles turned white, he rode out the cleaning and stitching of the wound—which was indeed deeper than he'd at first thought—with resignation born of experience. At last a tumbler of Suzanne's brandy was thrust in his right hand.

"You'll do, Colonel," Scully said. "It's deep, but Mags here's that handy with a needle and thread. There'll be a scar, but not much of a one. Your coat's another matter, your hat's heaven knows where or in what condition, and your gloves're past praying for—not that they were much before."

"Spoken like a true valet. Always one to cut to the essentials, aren't you, old friend?" The wink didn't work any better than the smile had.

"It's a matter to consider while you're considering the rest of it," Scully continued stolidly. "We've a need of new togs, both of us, given your popularity in these parts."

"Should be able to find something in Little Stoking or Timsborough."

Scully shrugged and winced. "You feel up to jauntering

about in search of toggery? I don't. Why not send to London? Mrs. Rothschild'll see to—''

"Mrs. Roth's son wouldn't in the least enjoy searching through his father's used stock to find us something," Gracechurch cut in quickly, "even if we could be sure he'd get the sizes right. Lionel's as lazy as they come if you part him from his books, Scully—you know that. It's a perpetual condition of ten-year-olds. Besides, we could barely afford old Roth's prices last time. Now? Out of the question."

Scully's stunned expression almost set Gracechurch to laughing. Well, it wasn't so far off as all that. Mayer Rothschild, Nathan's father, had indeed dealt in used goods at one time in partnership with his brothers back in Vienna.

"Much more sensible to give Mags the wherewithal and have her shop for us locally," he insisted, glad he'd retained a certain glibness despite a light head. "Cheaper, too. We're not looking to cut a dash. And don't shrug, Scully. Scowling can't be too pleasant for you at the moment either, given the condition of your eye. Problem is, I'll need a coat tomorrow morning, for I've every intention of attending services, and there're no shops open anywhere at this hour."

"Oh, but you can't," Cassie gasped. "You bled so much. You must be dreadfully weak."

"Not as weak as all that. A bit of food and rest and I'll do." He grinned as she vigorously shook her head. "You forget, my dear, that I've spent the last few years rather differently than most men in these parts. It takes more than a scratch to lay me low."

"That's more than a scratch."

"Perhaps, but very little more. It's not as if they'd gotten me in the gut. A sling, however, may not be amiss. I'll decide on that later. It might be best to let them think they shot the wrong man, and wonder who it was and if he'll bring charges." Gracechurch shifted in his chair and gave Mags a cajoling smile. "How about some fodder? Something sustaining, Mags. Not one of my mother's possets, if you please."

That disposed of Mags. Scully he commissioned to bring Cassie's mount around from the shed, and then there were just the two of them. He coughed. He cleared his throat. He shifted uneasily in his chair.

"I seem to remember asking you to marry me at some point during all this," he said.

"You did." Cassie ducked her head, blushing furiously. "Not to worry: I refused you, understanding you'd taken leave of your senses."

"And if I hadn't? If I'd meant it?"

"I'd still have refused you," she mumbled.

"Am I truly such an ogre, then?"

Her eyes rose, calmly assessing, as she cocked her head. "No, I don't believe you are after all," she admitted, blush fading. "I think you're quite nice for an older gentleman who's so set in his ways he's become something of a stick, though I still think Suzanne must've been all about in her head to accept you all those years ago. Military men are forever issuing commands to those whom they've not the least right to order about if you're anything to judge by. That's not too much of a problem in a friend, for one can always laugh at him and say no, but in a husband whom law and custom say one must obey? Insupportable!"

"Then you're not going to hold me to my offer?"

"No, I promise you," she said with a guilty giggle. "We'd not only be December and April, but oil and vinegar as well. Disastrous, as I'm not very good at following orders."

"So I've noticed."

"And a good thing for you I'm not, for I doubt you'd've reached the cottage alive had I not bound your arm. It was bleeding all over everything. Would you like me to see if I can find you a coat at Rose Cottage? And perhaps some shirts and other things as well? There're all sorts of trunks in the attics. I explore there on rainy days when I don't want to be found."

"No, you've done quite enough for one night. I'm glad to see your current ensemble is more or less ruined. You'll have to discard it."

"Don't worry—there are plenty more where I found these," she said, grinning. "I told you the attics're well supplied."

And then Scully was at the door with her horse, and she disappeared with a twinkle of satin smalls popular in the previous century, and a swirl of velvet cloak.

*   *   *

"You've done what?" Sophia Phelps stared at her husband across the Sunday breakfast cups, eyes wide with shock. "I can't believe this, Oren."

Phelps shifted in his chair, rearranging the skirts of his dressing gown and hiding behind a week-old London journal. He gave the pages the emphatic rustle that signified he didn't want to discuss the matter because of preoccupation with momentous events only a masculine brain, with its superior convolutions, could fathom.

Unfortunately he was in for it now, and knew it. He should've said nothing. He should've let Sophia discover how clever he'd been in the usual way, through neighborhood tattle. He should've held his peace, but she'd been so supercilious only yesterday, scolding him about the destruction of Mrs. Gracechurch's garden, that he'd wanted to put her in her place.

Suddenly the lingering flavor of burned gammon and half-cooked eggs was as ashes on his tongue. As for the coffee, it had always been pond slime.

"Oren."

The single word, spoken with that flat calm that always presaged a storm. She'd already sent the servants from the dingy breakfast parlor at the first mention of Gracechurch's name. There was nothing to hold her back. Strangely, the storm didn't break. As if charmed, the stag at bay reluctantly lowered his journal and set his jaw.

"I said I've seen to the matter of Stephen Gracechurch, so you needn't concern yourself about him anymore," he repeated, natural pride creeping into his tone. "Rather permanently, if what Fidger and Boggs claim is true. Of course I've dismissed them—had to, you understand, as it wouldn't do to have them about where someone could come asking questions—but they've left with heavy purses and good recommendations, and the suggestion that they find new employment as far from Chipham Common as possible."

"Dear Lord," she murmured. "Why am I cursed with such a blockhead for a husband? It's a wonder our children aren't loonies, and I fit for Bedlam."

He caught the words, ears turning hot at the insult, but

managed to retreat behind his journal as if she hadn't spoken, and he hadn't caught her words even if she had.

"Didn't you realize I had everything well in hand?" she demanded more loudly. "Mrs. Sanwiddy regaled me with the tale I'd told my abigail not a day later. I told you that yesterday. It was everywhere! He'd've been gone within the week, and in such disgrace even his mother wouldn't've been able to show her face in public. As for Suzanne, she's so honor-ridden she'd've died of horror at the sight of him."

Phelps blanched at his rib's sharp tone, but continued his pretended indifference.

"So did Lady Macbeth," he muttered, "and see where it got poor old Macbeth."

"Only you're the one playing her role in this instance, and I tremble to think where *that* will get us. She at least was clever, even if her cleverness wasn't sufficient to see them through."

"Enough!" he roared, hoping it would work as he slammed the journal down and emphasized his words with a pounding fist, rattling china and silver. "I've done what I felt best, I did it for the sake of you and our children, and there's an end to it!"

"I wonder what fool named this place Placidia?" She was leaning as close as she could to him now, only the table and her belly separating them. "No, it's not over, Oren. It's barely begun. What reaction d'you suppose the neighborhood will have upon hearing their former hero's been wounded or killed?"

"They'll cheer."

"Will they? I don't think so. They'll remember his father, and they'll begin to wonder if the tales we've set about weren't false after all. There've already been contrary murmurs about the attack on Mrs. Gracechurch's cottage and all those white feathers. I told you in the beginning such stratagems wouldn't do. Why, oh why, couldn't you have left well enough alone? Unpleasant gossip would've turned the trick, and sooner than you think, without taking further action."

Phelps hunched his shoulders, expression mulish.

"I did what I felt was best," he grumbled. "Suzanne is entirely too independent for my peace of mind, especially with Grandmother aiding and abetting her. Father would've done far better to hire someone to see to the household. I told him so at the time, but would he listen? Oh no, not he. And then he ignored her completely so long as the girls were kept out of his way and the house ran smoothly. Whatever did he marry her for? He could've paid her a wage and left my inheritance out of it."

"I know. That's the saddest part," she sighed. "Well, what's done is done. No use repining. Now we must overcome it."

"Leave all to me," he blustered, making a fuss over filling his cup with cold coffee, and then adding several spoonfuls of sugar so he could choke the stuff down. "I know what I'm about."

"And Emeline and Roger arriving within the week for their annual visit. Was ever a poor female so set upon? But, we'll contrive. We must. Your sister is too clever by half. I don't want her nosing about, and as she's much of an age with the colonel I imagine they knew each other as children."

"Everyone knew Stevie Gracechurch," Phelps returned sourly. "He was a universal favorite, blast him—even with my own grandmother."

"And that rankled, didn't it? And still does, I'll warrant."

It had and it did—not that he would've admitted the fact to anyone, least of all Sophia. At least she was finally rising from the table, ponderous as a sow, steadying herself against its solid bulk, dressing gown gaping over her belly. He didn't bother to stand as courtesy demanded, instead leaning back and drumming his fingers against the dull oak surface in the traditional spousal signal of irritation and displeasure. She took a deep breath, pushing away from the table. In a moment she'd be gone, and he'd be able to summon someone and relieve his spleen by complaining about something. Finding a topic wouldn't be difficult.

"We shall have to be excessively circumspect, Oren," she was saying as she lumbered to the door, then turned. "You'd best dress for the day as that circumspection begins with attending services, no matter how little we may wish it. And playing shocked innocents at any news we're given before or after, and saying as little as possible. A gasp or two should do if worse comes to worst. A word of caution given last night's foolishness: If Gracechurch survived your neighborly attentions, we may even be forced to invite him and his mother to dine."

"*What?*"

"Think, Oren. You weren't the best of friends as boys, correct?"

He snorted.

"People mustn't be permitted to remember that."

"Oh, they'll remember it," he returned bitterly. "They always took his part, insufferable coxcomb that he was, while I went begging. No one showed me the least respect when he was about—no one."

She nodded, and then she was gone.

He considered ringing for someone. Demanding a fresh pot of coffee. Demanding more eggs, more gammon. Gave it up. He might not admit it publicly, but Sophia was far cleverer than he was, and he knew it. If she claimed he'd made a grievous error, then she had the right of it. He'd made a grievous error, no matter how noble his intentions or laudable his goal. And if she said they must attend services, then attend services they must, no matter how tedious the process.

He rose from the table in his turn, the taste of defeat bitter at the back of his throat. Damn Stephen Gracechurch! But it had ever been this way: Emeline ignoring him, and trailing after the slightly older boy. Emeline, forever quoting Gracechurch, claiming he was the wisest person she knew. And the kindest and most generous. Three years' difference didn't make for wisdom, no matter what she'd claimed. As for generosity, how could someone as poor as Gracechurch have been generous? He had nothing to be generous with, blast him.

At least his father'd ignored Gracechurch, but then his father'd ignored everyone.

Phelps sighed, went to the windows, stared over the grounds. The rain might've ceased, but the prospect was as bleak as ever. It would remain bleak until Stephen Gracechurch was gone, and Suzanne permanently a widow at Rose Cottage rather than a wife somewhere else. Stepmothers were damnably inconvenient creatures. His first one had had the grace to die young, but this one was hanging on unconscionably and causing him no end of bother.

* * *

They were lined up in the Gracechurch parlor like judges on the bench: India Phelps, his mother, Suzanne and Cassie. Shawls draped expertly from elbows—except in Cassie's case. Bonnets were tied perkily, skirts arranged to perfection—again except for Cassie, who retained her usual half-fledged look.

And their expressions were as stern, as accusatory as those of any four judges he could imagine. All they lacked were wigs and robes.

For a miracle, Suzanne was garbed in the cerulean blue that so became her rather than her customary gray, and both gown and short jacket had more than a touch of *á-la-modality* to them. A distinct improvement.

"I see you've gone bearing tales," Gracechurch reproved, pretending to ignore the welcome change in his former love and bending a glance on Cassie as stern as those the three older ladies were bending on him.

"I view it more in the light of reporting casualties to a superior officer following a close-fought battle," she retorted.

Scully's snort from just beyond the open parlor door set even Gracechurch's lips to twitching. He risked a glance at Suzanne, who'd had a delightful sense of the ridiculous in the old days. And there it was lurking at the back of her soft hazel eyes—the impish twinkle that had first drawn him to her, and later kept him firmly at her side until chased from it. A pity her character never matched those eyes.

"I must apologize for receiving you in my shirt sleeves," he managed in a voice that quavered only the slightest bit, "but I hadn't much choice."

"Part of why we've come," India Phelps snapped. "Scully's going through some things we brought. Should be a coat and shirt in there that'll fit you passably, and there're some decent neckcloths as well. Gloves and hats too, and some waistcoats given what Cassie reported to us. No boots, unfortunately."

Gracechurch turned to Cassie, avoiding his mother's anguished eyes as she attempted not to stare at his arm. "So—you weren't able to sneak in undetected after all, minx?"

"Certainly I was, but then I saw the light under Mother

India's door and thought it best to apprise her of the whole immediately rather than waiting until morning."

His brows rose as he received the confirmation he sought in India Phelps's nod. There was a deal more to Cassie than he would've dreamed. A pity she'd been born a girl, for she'd make some poor fool a handful when she came to marry. Gray hairs would be the man's allotted portion from the moment the vows were spoken. At least he'd never be bored, and he'd have as stalwart a helpmeet as fate could provide. Problem was, she'd've made the most intrepid of subalterns, and superior junior officers were forever in short supply, cannon fodder that they were. The thought gave him pause. Perhaps it wasn't such a bad thing Cassie was a girl after all. The thought of her lying broken on some blood-soaked battlefield was beyond bearing.

He met his mother's eyes then, having a fair notion of what she was feeling.

"I'm all right," he insisted, "truly. Good as new in a few days. Better, perhaps, given the predilection of medical men to bleed one at every opportunity. Probably did me a world of good, being winged. And that's all it was, Mother. I've suffered far worse and risen to fight the next day."

"But you said you were never—"

"There were things it wouldn't have served you or Father to know at the time. That was one of them."

She nodded, lips quivering. What surprised him was the sudden pallor flooding Suzanne's face, the anguished look in her eyes. What happened to him, good or ill, shouldn't've mattered to her now any more than it had then.

He drained the last of the brandy beaten with eggs he'd been sipping to fortify him against the jostling ride to the church in the Phelps carriage and the interminable time spent on a hard bench under the contemptuous eyes of the entire countryside. Dear Lord—had it been only a week since he first survived that? Except the looks had been approving then, beyond the squire's. Not now, however. Not now. He'd be fortunate not to be run from Chipham Common on a rail once the congregation was dismissed following the benediction, covered with those feathers that had so lately graced his mother's destroyed garden.

"We'd best be on our way since you insist on my arriving

with you. I've no intention of making a grand entrance following the beginning of services.'' He rose and strode to the
entry, keeping his pace as even as possible to avoid jarring
his arm. It was aching unbearably and he was lightheaded,
whether from loss of blood or so much brandy at such an
unaccustomed hour he wasn't certain. ''Find anything that'll
regularize my appearance among all Mrs. Phelps's largesse,
Scully?''

The coat was too big, which was all to the good given the
bandage on his arm. The gloves were too tight, the waistcoat
designed for a dedicated trencherman, and the hat had a
tendency to slip over his ears. Still, he didn't entirely resemble
a vagrant clothed from the rag bag. The cut of coat and
waistcoat was too good. He set the hat at a jaunty angle,
hoping it would stay in place, and then they were off.

The next hour passed in an indistinct haze. He entered
the church with India Phelps on his right arm, his mother
on his left, both supporting him rather than being supported,
Cassie and Suzanne trailing behind. And late despite his best
efforts. Services had begun. For a mercy there were no hisses.
Those would come later.

Faces swam before his eyes, advancing and retreating as
their small party went toward the front of the church: Scowden
turning his back, appearing to contemplate actually rising
and departing. And his daughters, all three the epitomes of
perfect health if nothing else, staring at him as if he were a
freak of nature, noses in the air, expressions disdainful. One
after another, backs turned. The sacristan's wife, whom he'd
known since he was a lad and who'd pressed peppermints on
him as recently as three days before, convinced he retained
a boy's sweet tooth and longed for his old favorites. The
Pembertons, after throwing him a look of such pained
reproach he almost felt the guilt of crimes he'd never commit-
ted. Only Squire Hodges didn't turn away, the look of triumph
on his florid face too clear to be missed.

Then they were at the Phelps family pew. It was already
occupied by Oren and a massively *enceinte* woman who had
to be his wife, and Suzanne's self-consequential stepdaughters.
Phelps had his nose buried in a prayer book, pretending no
one stood at the end of the pew. The girls peeked, simpered,
then stuck up their noses in imitation of the Scowden trio.

India Phelps coughed and jerked her head. Oren ignored her.

"This is where I sit, Grandson, as well you know," she declared loudly enough for the entire congregation to hear, poking Phelps—who was sitting on the outside—in the ribs with her walking stick.

"Oh, I say, Grandmother," he blustered, turning in a parody of surprise.

His eyes widened at the sight of Gracechurch, to all appearances unscathed if one didn't look too closely, and whom he obviously hadn't realized was there despite the stir among the congregation. Then his gaze traveled to Suzanne.

"Blast," he muttered. "Look at her, Sophia—colors! Did you ever hear of such a thing—my father's widow in *colors*. No sense of propriety or position, none."

"Told you it would happen," the woman hissed. "Told you what'd come next, too. You'd best have a care."

"Move your stumps, Oren. Into your usual pew, if you please, and take your sisters and Sophia with you," India Phelps snapped. "I need more space this morning, as I've brought guests."

Mr. Browne paused in the reading of the first lesson, clearly waiting for the situation to sort itself out as scattered titters broke out among the congregation. Somehow Mrs. Browne managed to keep their sons from turning their heads to see what the fuss was about.

"Mother India—*please*," Suzanne pleaded in mortified accents from behind them. "There's no reason we can't take the second pew."

"Hush, girl."

"Ain't fair to expect Sophia to move," Phelps protested. "Had a devil of a time cramming herself in here to begin with."

"Ain't fair to expect me to sit anywhere but where I'm accustomed to sitting," India Phelps retorted, retaining a firm grip on Gracechurch, who was beginning to waver. "You should've sat where you customarily do. This'll be yours soon enough. Don't try to hasten the day."

Then, head high, foot tapping, she waited.

"Thought you weren't coming."

And waited.

"You can see and hear just as well from the pew behind."

And waited.

"Besides, *I'm* the head of the family. This should by rights be *my* pew."

And waited.

"This is unseemly," he spluttered, ignoring Sophia's whispered injunctions and minatory tugs on his sleeve.

"You're outgunned," Gracechurch murmured too low for any but Phelps and his grandmother to hear. "Best abandon the position or there'll be the devil to pay later."

"I shall faint," Sophia complained loudly, hand rising to her forehead.

"No you shan't, blast it. Can't stand vaporish females— you know that." Face empurpled, jaws clenched, shaking with fury at the spectacle his grandmother was making of them all, Oren Phelps rose. "Come my dear," he growled, jerking his wife to her feet without regard to her delicate condition, "my grandmother hasn't the kindness or sense of decency to permit you to occupy her pew in peace. Instead she insists you move, and so move you shall, so she can play hostess to that—that—that penniless poltroon."

The hisses and soft cries of "Shame!" came then. Amazingly, Gracechurch realized, they didn't appear to be directed entirely at him.

There was a bit of confusion while Phelps moved his party, managing to jostle both his grandmother's rheumatic hip and Gracechurch's wounded arm in the process. India Phelps seized Suzanne's wrist and led the way into the contested pew, leaning heavily on her cane and limping, and muttering imprecations under her breath. Cassie followed, throwing Gracechurch a rueful little smile, then his mother. He slipped in behind her, feeling eyes boring into his back like a thousand stinging darts. Pages rustled as they found their places in prayer books. Silence fell. After glancing about the little church to make certain no other contretemps were brewing, Mr. Browne began the lesson again from the beginning.

Gracechurch closed his eyes, grateful to be seated at last. He hadn't been sure he was going to make it for a moment there—not when Phelps managed to punch him solidly on his wound. The involuntary groan that had drawn from him made him cringe just to think of it. He was becoming soft, that's what it was. Too much civilian coddling. Too much easy living.

What he found hardest to believe, however, was the swift and well-aimed kick his mother had sent to Phelps's shins when she realized what he'd done. The man would be limping for a week.

He must've drifted off during the interminable prayers for everyone and everything that were a part of the Church of England service if the vicar were so inclined, somehow regaining his seat without regaining consciousness. Noises woke him—a team pulling up outside the church, shouts, the church doors being thrown wide on protesting iron hinges. Prayer books rustled. Pews creaked. It began as the merest whisper. The whisper swelled to normal-toned voices laced with a combination of delight and disbelief, drowning out Browne's sermon. Browne stumbled to a halt. Good Lord— what now? Hadn't there been enough confusion this morning?

Gracechurch pulled himself erect and stared blearily about him, repressing a shudder. It was damnably cold. And then he heard the footsteps. By God—he'd recognize those anywhere. What the devil?

The gasps from the pew behind him, Phelps's curses, his wife's, "I refuse to believe it can be he. I absolutely, positively refuse to believe it. There's some mistake. It's an actor. It must be. That's it—they've hired an actor," gave Gracechurch all the answer he needed. Not the devil, but a most unlikely and excessively large-nosed angel had apparently come riding to his rescue. Whether by accident or by intention was the only question. He glanced down the line of female faces in the pew beside him, but they were blandly innocent. Too innocent? No way to tell. He'd delve into that later.

"Sorry, Padre, don't mean to interrupt," came the familiar parade-ground bark, barely moderated to suit the interior of a building. "Apologize for traveling on the Sabbath, but there it is—Affairs of State. I'm not my own master these days."

"P-perfectly understandable, your grace. No n-need for apologies."

"Wanted to see an old friend and comrade in arms is all,

and planned to be here in time," the well-remembered voice continued. "Could use God's blessing and a little of His help, what with one thing and another. Man of the battlefield, not a man of the Court, as anyone'll tell you. Dam—er, blas—er, pernicious axle broke. Delayed us considerably."

"Of c-course, your grace."

"Well, Gracechurch, and how do you do?"

Gracechurch rose shakily to his feet.

"Sir!" he said, turning and saluting smartly as he gripped the back of the pew in front with his left hand, then giving the matter a second thought and bowing as he wasn't in uniform, and never would be again. "Your grace. Welcome to Chipham Common."

"That the name of the place? Thought it was just Chipham, but last person we asked directions of said to come here, though he didn't say much else. Closed-mouthed, these country sorts. Not like the French. One of the reasons we beat them—Englishmen don't gossip, not *real* Englishmen.

"Well, shift over, Gracechurch—shift over. Don't want to stand here like a great lummox, holding up proceedings."

As always when the man entered any building, even a church, all others present shrank to insignificance—possibly even God. Those in India Phelps's pew had already moved. Gracechurch shifted down a place, making space as ordered. Wellington gave him a wink and sat, pulling him down beside him—unfortunately, by means of a firm tug on his right arm.

Gracechurch repressed a groan.

"What the devil sort of bumblebroth've you tumbled into this time?" the Iron Duke hissed. "You're wounded? Feels like a bandage under that sleeve. How did that come about? I'll be wanting an explanation, and it's best be an excellent one."

"You'll have it, sir," Gracechurch murmured, flushing painfully.

"I had the devil's own time getting away from London just now," Wellington grumbled on at full voice, for all the world as if they were warming their hands before a campfire rather than sitting in a church as the congregation leaned forward, anxious to catch every word. "Finally had to tell 'em it was get away for a day or two or go mad, and that was that. All's confusion, thanks to that blasted Frenchie conference in Aix.

Your old friend Nathan's causing problems. Family wants to float the next loan, but I suppose he's told you that. Someone doesn't listen up smartly, and he'll cause a genuine unpleasantness—mark my words.

"When Nathan Rothschild causes an unpleasantness, a lot of people become paupers. Most times they deserve to, but sometimes they don't. Of course there're those who profit by it when Nathan plays games. You did, certainly. We all did. Still, his games would've come to naught and the army gone unpaid if you hadn't pulled his irons from the fire, and young Kalmann's into the bargain, that time in the Pyrenees. Might've lost everything then, and that'd be a frog priest standing up there prattling in Latin. Someday I want to hear the tale of precisely how you got that shipment through."

The sound of a delicate female shriek from the pew behind them gave Gracechurch an entirely ungentlemanly, but most understandable, surge of satisfaction.

"How's that old reprobate always tags around with you?" Wellington prattled on uncharacteristically. "You know the one I mean—his name has something to do with Shakespeare. *Hamlet*, I think. He was mixed up in it, too."

"Scully, sir. Scully Bates," Gracechurch said clearly, following Wellington's lead and silently praying his father would forgive them both for behaving so in his church. "Yes, he was. He's here, though not at services this morning. Fallen upon by a bunch of hooded rowdies a couple nights ago, and he's a bit the worse for wear. I insisted he remain at my mother's cottage."

"You don't say? Sounds like a dangerous neighborhood. You'd best have a care to your own hide. Always see to the troops, though. Sounds like you haven't forgotten."

"No, sir, I haven't forgotten: Horses and troops first, and everyone else after."

Intimacy between them clearly established, Wellington turned to the front of the church with the courtesy that made him so popular among civilians wherever he went.

"My sincere apologies for the interruption, but I haven't seen this lad in some time and I've missed him," he informed Mr. Browne, and the rest of the congregation with him. "Keen mind, outstanding officer. I could use his services now, but I know there's no way I'll convince him away from his home unless there's another war and it's not just me who needs him, but England. Please continue, Padre. My soul could do with a bit of saving. I suspect there're a few others here in the same condition."

He folded his arms across his chest and waited.

Mr. Browne did his best, but it was clear he was unnerved by the presence of so august a sinner awaiting his guidance. The rest of his sermon developed a distinctly military flavor, complete with such phrases as bivouacking on God's battle-field, marching in His van, standing picket duty before His lines, and guarding His flank. As for the harried vicar's original theme—charity to one's neighbor—it sank into the morass unremembered and unlamented.

Gracechurch glanced at Wellington. An unholy twinkle lurked at the back of the great man's eyes, and there was a definite twitch at the corner of his mouth.

Finally the young vicar stumbled to a halt, gazing down on greatness with a bemused expression.

"It's an honor to have you among us, sir," he said with inspired simplicity. "Thank you for coming to Chipham Common. There's not a one of us here, I believe I may say without fear of contradiction, who doesn't hold you in deepest respect, and isn't grateful beyond counting for your coming to England's rescue in her hour of need."

Luke, the youngest of his sons, who'd been craning his neck to catch a glimpse of the hero of too many battles to count through the intervening forest of adult bodies, sprang to his feet.

"Three cheers for Old Hooky," he shouted, turning to his father's parishioners and waving his arms. "Hip-hip, hooray! Hip-hip, hooray! Hip-hip, hooray!"

By the third hurrah the entire company had joined in at full voice. Wellington gave a half-hearted wave, smiling sheepishly at the vicar and then casting an apologetic glance upward, perhaps at the vault, perhaps a bit Higher than that.

"Sorry about causing so much fuss," Wellington murmured, "but given the circumstances I felt it wisest to arrive in the most public and loudest manner possible, and I couldn't think of anything more public in an English village than interrupting Sunday services, or a place where I'd be less likely to be interrupted before I'd had my say. Wouldn't've mattered if you hadn't been here. I'd've turned the trick on my own if I had to, but there's not a one of 'em now'll doubt we're well-acquainted, and that you were indeed a colonel and something of a hero."

"But penniless, if you please, sir—absolutely penniless. I'll explain later."

"Up to your old games again?"

"Not precisely, though in a manner of speaking."

"Your excuses—and I suspect that's what I'll receive rather than explanations this time," Wellington murmured, regarding Gracechurch through narrowed eyes, "had best be excellent and irrefutable. You've been diddling those who care about you most. I don't like it."

Mr. Browne hurried through the rest of the service. It was clear he realized even the Second Coming might have proved anticlimactic at that point.

Chapter Eleven

Gracechurch, eyes reverently closed, head bowed, barely heard the words of the extended benediction flowing over the congregation. Diddling those who cared about him most? It was true enough, but how the devil would Wellington know that?

Ignoring propriety, he opened his eyes, raised his head and gazed down the length of India Phelps's pew.

His mother, Suzanne, Mrs. Phelps, even Cassie, hoydenism set aside for the moment, stood as the rest of the congregation did, supplicant statues all. Then, as if sensing his eyes on her, Cassie turned to face him, head high, expression defiant.

So that was it. He should've realized.

Somehow he kept his expression neutral, but a bubble of laughter grew that he had the devil's own time choking back. He could imagine the letter. He could imagine the duke's puzzled scowl during the first reading, then the twitch at the corner of his mouth as he read it a second time and comprehension dawned.

And, given Cassie, given the tedium of London, he could well understand Wellington's bolt for Chipham Common. Any port in a storm and London, with its plots and counter-plots and factions, was a stormy place these days. Chipham Common, by contrast, was placidity personified despite his own recent untoward experiences. Those could all be laid at one door, or perhaps two. The rest were merely sheep or hired agents. Sheep couldn't be blamed for following the bellwether. They were born to it. As for hired bullies, once their role became superfluous they'd disappear. Even Oren Phelps wouldn't be foolish enough to throw good money after bad, pusillanimous skint that he was. The long and short of it was Chipham Common needed a more reliable bellwether, but cast himself in that role? Not likely. He had done with being responsible for the lives and fates of others.

Then, to his amazement, Suzanne's head lifted. She was blushing, her expression every bit as defiant as Cassie's, though a hint of guilt lingered in her eyes along with what could only be extreme embarrassment. The frown he received from India Phelps seconds later held confession in it. It also contained a warning. *I will not be importuned concerning this. You're a nodcock, Stephen, a gazetted cloth-head.*

Well, perhaps he was. That didn't mean he intended a change in his plans. He'd proceed as he'd sworn he would ever since receiving Nathan's notification of his newly-acquired wealth while still in Brussels. The game would play itself to the end. He'd triumph. And after? "After" would take care of itself, just as it always did. You survived a battle or you didn't. Worrying about what came next was foolishness personified.

He gave himself a shake at the loud chorus of amens. One gauntlet successfully run, thanks to his trio of interfering champions and his unlikely guardian angel. One more to go. Pray his lightheadedness didn't increase to unbearable proportions. He'd find something to lean against in the churchyard and let events take him where they would. All eyes would be on the duke. He should be safe enough from prying importuners.

"Well, Gracechurch, aren't you going to present me to your lovely companions? Won't do to play dog in the manager. You've only two arms, after all."

If he'd needed confirmation of guilt, it was provided—

though not by the guilty parties themselves. Only with his mother did Wellington play the courtly stranger. The others he greeted as acquaintances of long standing, complimenting India Phelps on her vigorous good health, Suzanne on a face and figure that ensured her position as the belle of the countryside and a felicity of expression that proved she wasn't a vapid nonentity.

"Intelligent females are the only sort with which to surround oneself, you know," he tossed over his shoulder at Gracechurch. "The rest are such bores one longs to throttle them after a few hours' acquaintance. Across the breakfast cups? Justification for murder or suicide, choose whichever appeals to you more."

Then, ignoring Aurelia and Delphine Phelps, who had remained behind in defiance of their half-brother's urgings and were doing everything they could to attract the great man's attention, he turned to Cassie, eyes twinkling.

"Well hello, young lady," he said. "And so we meet at last. We could've used your services during the late unpleasantness, given your ability to cut to the heart of a matter and your determination to see the troops safely settled. You've a gentleman's sense of honor and justice and an unusual way of putting those principles into practice, for they're generally forgotten in the press of battle—unique attributes in one so young."

Cassie, eyes enormous in her slender face, dipped a perfect curtsy.

"Your grace," she whispered, a catch in her throat, "this is a great honor."

"The honor's all mine, my dear. You're what we fought for, you know—Gracechurch and I and the rest of us—you and your grandmother and your lovely sister, and Mr. and Mrs. Gracechurch, and places such as Chipham Common."

"What about us?" Delphine demanded from the pew behind them, unable to bear the attention being wasted on such a nonentity as Cassie a moment longer. "Didn't you fight for us more than for them? We're the daughters of Sir John Phelps, who was knighted for service to the Crown and is dead now. I'll be glad to show you his tomb if you like. It's most elegantly marked. There's even a stone angel. Quite proper, as he was the most important person hereabouts, and the most elevated.''

Wellington turned, gazing at youthful impertinence down his long and magnificently beaked nose. His brows rose. His lips thinned. His nostrils flared. His shoulders squared. Gracechurch, knowing the signs from long experience, held his breath and waited.

"And I'm the premiere belle of the countryside—not Suzanne," Delphine continued with a toss of her dusky curls, "who's naught but our stepmother and far too old to be the belle of anything, or Cassie, who's nothing but a hoyden and even rides astride if she thinks no one'll catch her at it. As for Grandmama and Mrs. Gracechurch, they're nothing but old bores, and have no standing among those who matter. If you'll give me you arm, my lord duke, we can dispense with their inferior company."

India Phelps caught Suzanne's arm, holding her in place and hushing her attempts to stop her stepdaughter from exposing herself in such a manner. The duke looked plump, dark-haired Delphine up and down, then sharp-featured Aurelia, as he appeared to consider their greater claims on his attention and their manifest charms as the daughters of so elevated a personage as a defunct knight whose tomb sported a stone angel.

"Delphie's right," the younger girl threw in. "Suzanne and Cassie are nobodies. We're the ones whose good opinion you should be courting."

"Besides, we're the prettiest girls in the neighborhood. It'll raise your status to be seen escorting us," Delphine explained. "Won't do ours any harm, either. A mutual benefit, don't you see?"

They simpered and bridled, batting their lashes. Delphine threw out her considerable bosom.

"Yes," the duke said at last, "I do believe we were forced to fight for you as well, though perhaps we might've reconsidered had we known you were part of the bargain."

As Wellington's set-downs went it was an exceedingly mild one, tempered perhaps to their tender years and the location, and certainly issued with the sensibilities of Suzanne and India

Phelps taken into account. And, anticipating the fawning deference their posturing customarily elicited, it took Aurelia and Delphine several moments to divine the duke's meaning.

"Well!" Aurelia spluttered, eyes slits, as Delphine's complexion reddened unbecomingly. "I'd heard you sprang from nowhere, a veritable mushroom. Ireland, I believe? Ireland's never been held in much esteem—nothing but bogs and ruins, and no one of any consequence whatsoever. Now I know the tales're true."

"You'll be welcome nowhere, for we'll spread news of your rudeness where it counts," Delphine added, tears of fury sparkling on her lashes. "No one's ever dared speak so to us—no one. I don't care if you are a duke."

"Perhaps someone should've spoken to you so years ago," Wellington returned with deceptive mildness. "Then I wouldn't've been forced to it, and you'd've been spared hearing a few home truths at a time and place where you'd rather've played great ladies than viperous brats. Of course perhaps someone made the attempt, and you were so impressed with yourselves you refused to listen. A pity, that."

"Well, that's rich!" Aurelia spluttered. "I've read you even consort with lightskirts, and you a married man. And probably scattered by-blows from Lisbon to Brussels. And left 'em to starve, I don't doubt."

"Your grace," Suzanne said, flushing furiously, "I must apologize for—"

"Don't you dare apologize for us, Stepmama," Aurelia snapped, "or we'll ensure you live to regret it. He's the one was rude. It's time someone put him in his place. Come, Delphie, the air's developed an unpleasant caste in here. Something from the tombs beneath the chancel, perhaps?"

Wellington chuckled as she grabbed her sister's hand.

"Not badly done for a neophyte," he murmured. "Give her a few years, and she'll be as vicious as any *ton* diamond when it comes to protecting her consequence."

They swept from the second Phelps pew, perfect exemplars of childish outrage. The result, Gracechurch decided, was rather pathetic—not that he had the least sympathy for either of them. Insufferable, and that was putting it mildly. How Suzanne bore them on a daily basis he had no notion.

"Well, now you know the best and the worst of us, my lord duke," India Phelps said, watching as they disappeared into the sunlight. "And you may be sure they intend precisely what Delphine threatened. That they're the ones'll be sneered at rather than you won't occur to them. My son was never known for a long head, and his first two wives were his equals in that department."

Wellington's understanding smile, his quick glance at Suzanne, couldn't be faulted. Why, then, did they grate so? And why, when Wellington graciously offered his arm did Gracechurch want to roar out that the duke had women enough of his own? Lack of sustenance combined with all the blood he'd lost and too much time spent sitting in a pew, he decided, offering arms first to his mother and then Cassie, and following Wellington and his two companions to the churchyard.

The duke held court in the shade of an ancient oak for something over an hour, keeping Gracechurch at his side, ensuring he leaned against the broad trunk and steadying him with a hand beneath his good arm.

It was, Suzanne decided as she watched at a little distance from the crowd, the most generous and kindest act she'd ever witnessed. His grace was all they claimed, and far more—an expert strategist on social battlefields as well as military no matter what he said, and a man anyone would be honored to call friend. So often great men were filled with self-importance, regarding only those who fawned on them with favor, high in the instep and higher in the flesh, loyal only to themselves. Not the duke.

What fawning there was came from a singularly unlikely source given her father's antipathy for Stephen, for the duke was certainly repairing every fence that had crumbled, and building a few extras in case of a recurrence: the squire was managing to ignore the man he considered his enemy while courting the one whose acquaintance he felt would elevate his status in the neighborhood above that of even Oren Phelps. It was clumsily done of course, as her father did everything clumsily. Oblivious to arctic glances her father forged on, wielding compliments like truncheons and adulation like a club. It was so usual a thing Suzanne felt only the slightest twinge of mortification.

Through it all the duke kept Matilda Gracechurch at his other side, telling tales of Stephen's exploits that had that gentle lady blanching even though he attempted to tailor them to a mother's sensibilities while ensuring the risks Stephen had run, the crucial role he'd played in events, his stalwart courage and determination to win through at any cost were clear. That the duke sent the occasional assessing glance in her own direction, almost as if the tales were told for her benefit as well, Suzanne ignored. Heaven alone knew what Stephen had said of her when in his cups, and it was her understanding all military men traveled that road regularly between battles.

As for her stepson, Oren had decamped as they were exiting the church, sweeping Sophia before him and halting his carriage only long enough to let the girls clamber aboard following an unseemly dash across the churchyard that displayed silk-encased ankles and lace-edged petticoats, and faces as stormy as a March day. That was after the Scowden trio had turned their backs. Moments before they'd been ranting ten miles to the minute while casting venomous glances at the church entry where the duke stood chatting with Mr. Browne. The little pantomime of insults traded and bosom bows falling out fell far short of the pathetic. It was clear the Scowden girls had an eye to their own advantage and cared naught for the offenses against their friends, for they had been among the first to come up to the duke and were now framing their faces with their parasols and wreathing them with idiotish smiles. The eldest, heaven help her, was even casting sheep's eyes at Stephen.

Scowden reissued his invitation to dinner on Wednesday next, his daughters being miraculously recovered, as all could see. Others among the dining families began to chime in, especially those with daughters in danger of being placed on the shelf did they not wed soon. Evening parties were proposed, fetes and routs and turtle dinners, and picnics at this beauty spot and that. Even a boating excursion on the Chipple was suggested as Stephen listened with glazing eyes, mumbling he wasn't sure of his plans.

And then, almost as if at an invisible signal, it was over.

The duke accepted Mother India's invitation to break his journey with them and put off his departure until the morrow, "Affairs of State" apparently not being so pressing now he'd carried the day in Chipham Common. It was quickly settled the Gracechurches would form part of the family party as Matilda Gracechurch was already staying at Rose Cottage. The vicar's sons, wide-eyed and flushed, were cheering once more as the duke led the way to the lane, still firmly gripping Stephen's arm and—in the opinion of at least one anxious observer—clearly supporting and guiding him for all he masked it well.

"You'll be riding with me, Gracechurch," Suzanne heard him murmur, "and the first thing I'll want to know once we're private is why you're gotten up like a beggar. I've never seen you so improperly garbed, not even when your uniforms were in tatters. There was at least some excuse for that."

"Not much choice," Stephen mumbled, "things being as they are."

And then they were beyond earshot, and she was following Mother India and Mrs. Gracechurch into the carriage, Cassie bouncing up after them. They set off for Rose Cottage to the continued cheers of the parishioners, the Phelps carriage in the van of the triumphal procession, Wellington following. Someone had unearthed a miniature flag from the time of the Waterloo celebrations, and was waving it wildly while attempting a bar or two of *"See the Conquering Hero Comes."* Cassie leaned out the window and returned the waves. Suzanne hadn't the heart to reprove her. Then they turned the bend in the lane, passing by the Pembertons' apothecary shop, and the noise faded. Cassie plumped herself against the soft squabs, grinning broadly.

"Well!" India Phelps said, settling herself, "I call that a most satisfactory resolution to the recent problems if I do say so myself." She gazed pointedly at first Suzanne and then Cassie. "I wonder which of us turned the trick. I'll warrant it was Cassie."

Matilda Gracechurch looked at them in turn, the slightest of frowns drawing her brows. "Whatever do you mean?" she said.

"Let's say none of us wished to see Stephen unfairly maligned, let alone chased from Chipham Common, and there was only one person to whom to apply for the necessary assistance. I believe it's termed 'calling out the big guns.' Thank heavens our big gun is currently in England, for had he not been I don't know what we should have done, any of us."

"Great merciful heaven—you summoned His Grace of Wellington? To Stephen's rescue?"

"None other. I'm delighted to see Suzanne made the effort as well—as her blushes prove—and that Cassie had the perspicacity to draw the same conclusions her elders did. You'll go far, Cassie."

"I intend to," Suzanne's younger sister said with such complaisance India Phelps burst into laughter and even Suzanne's eyes held a rueful twinkle.

The pounding of hooves behind them had Cassie leaning from the carriage window once more. "Oh no," she moaned, "*Papa*. I wonder who loaned him the horse, for he came by carriage and must've sent Mama home in it for fear of being delayed. Or perhaps she's behind us. Poor Mama."

The bellowed *halloo* gave confirmation to her words. Then the squire was by the carriage window, slowing his mount to their pace and sending clouds of dust billowing over the ladies as he leaned in the saddle.

"Won't do for you to receive such an exalted guest without a gentleman present to play host, Mrs. Phelps," he bellowed. "Y'aren't thinking of the proprieties, that's clear. I'll ride on ahead and see the servants're warned and there's sufficient wine decanted, and be there to greet the duke for you when he arrives. Here now, Cassie, pull in your head. Ain't seemly to be leaning from the carriage like that."

Then, with a great flourish of his battered crop and a digging of spurs, the squire galloped ahead, *hallooing* all the way.

"I do apologize," Suzanne murmured, casting her mother-in-law a helpless glance. "Papa insisted on joining us, but I told him it wouldn't do as I hadn't ordered a dinner extensive enough to accommodate him and Mama in addition to the duke and his secretary. With Aurelia and Delphine absent we might have muddled through. I never dreamed he'd ignore my refusal. Now? It's hopeless."

"Oh no, it isn't." India Phelps rapped on the carriage roof

with her cane. "Spring 'em, Croft! Don't want to be caught napping. As for that bumptious ox—begging your pardon, Suzanne, but we're none of us responsible for our parents— playing host in my home, we'll see about that."

It was the longest dinner Stephen Gracechurch had ever endured, following hard on the longest afternoon he'd ever passed. Even Waterloo had been less of an agony, or so it seemed to his pain-hazed sensibilities.

It wasn't just the company, though Squire Hodges was as overbearing as ever, consuming everything in sight and demanding more wine, refighting every battle of the Peninsular War, giving most the wrong names, often the wrong participants, and invariably the wrong dates and locations. The duke endured it with uncharacteristic patience, even to the point of merely raising a brow when told where he'd gone wrong, and how the squire could've won the war against the Corsican upstart in half the time at less than half the expense if offered the opportunity.

After a futile attempt to stem the tide India Phelps leaned back, cast an exasperated glance at her uninvited guest, a rueful one at the duke, and permitted the squire to go his length. A signal kept his glass filled despite his wife's best efforts to moderate his self-indulgence. The man's voice slurred. His face became flushed, then pale. His gestures grew expansive, then clumsy. Wine sloshed from his glass. Sauces decorated his waistcoat. At last he slid beneath the table in mid-diatribe, dragging his plate and cutlery with him. A sodden belch was followed by a hearty, rasping snore. The squire was bundled off to his carriage, his wife murmuring excuses and apologies as she trailed behind, then once she was beyond that lady's hearing quietly cursing India Phelps for providing so much excellent wine to one who was known to have a weakness for it.

The sighs of relief released by India Phelps and Suzanne were as silent as they were heart-felt. The detritus was cleared, an excellent trifle and bowls of fruit purloined from Placidia's hothouses set on the table, and the conversation turned to the grandeurs of Paris and the changes since the Revolution. The meal, so inauspiciously begun, finished in fine fashion.

No, once Hodges was gotten rid of it wasn't the effort of presenting a decent simulation of civility before what remained of the company that so troubled Stephen Gracechurch, or made every minute spent at that table a thing to be endured rather than enjoyed. It was his sense of utter confusion compounded by a splitting headache and a throbbing arm.

What business had Suzanne writing the duke on his behalf? India Phelps he could understand. Even little Cassie's interference, miffed though she'd been by his false assumptions regarding her position in the world the first time they met, wasn't totally unreasonable. For all she was a girl, Cassie held to a schoolboy's code of honor, a characteristic he found endearing rather than off-putting—witness her actions of the night before.

But, Suzanne?

And yet he had the proof tucked in his waistcoat pocket. For all its stilted circumspection, her intent had been as clear as it was incomprehensible: she'd pleaded his case to the duke as if her own life depended on her success as much as his. And yet there'd been a detachment to the thing, almost as if she were on some Olympian peak observing the petty squabbles of mortals, and finding the brouhaha as amusing as it was unfortunate.

He watched her from beneath lowered lids as the conversation flowed around him, a gentle murmur now the braggart squire and his alternately shrill and self-effacing wife were gone.

The blue gown became her despite her increased years. Truth to tell, she still had the look of a girl about her. Or perhaps it was an air of abstraction. In his fuddled state he couldn't be positive of the exact nature of the false note, but there was something about her that didn't match her widowed state, a certain lack of the assurance that should have come with being the wife of the most important man in the neighborhood, no matter what the reason for their marriage or however much or little she desired it.

As if sensing his attention, her gaze turned to meet his. There was nothing to be read in those impenetrable hazel eyes, blue-flecked today because of her gown.

"Are you quite well, Colonel?" she said softly across the table. "You appear fatigued."

"I'll do."

She regarded him seriously for a moment with that detachment he found so unnerving given it was entirely unlike the girl he'd known. Then she turned back to the others, joining in a discussion of the monuments Bonaparte had erected to himself.

"As bad as any of the Bourbons," India Phelps was saying. "Of course their names both begin with a B."

"That has nothing to do with it, Mother India," Cassie protested, then turned to the duke, "does it, sir?"

"No, I rather suspect that's pure happenstance."

"Ah well, he's suffering for his pride now, the poor man," Matilda Gracechurch insisted. "Exile must be a terrible thing for one such as he—almost like Lucifer cast out of heaven. And think of his poor wife."

"Think of all the deaths he caused, Mother," Gracechurch snapped before he could stop himself, "and reserve your pity for those who deserve it," then flushed and mumbled an apology for his sharp words.

After a moment the others turned back to their conversation leaving him to himself, the duke's narrowed glance lingering on him only fractionally longer than the startled gazes of the rest.

Gracechurch gestured for Charles to refill his wineglass and sipped thoughtfully as he returned his attention to Suzanne, not realizing he was staring. Slowly she began to flush, the color staining the base of her neck and traveling upward like a rosy sunset flooding a cloud. For some reason it gave him immense satisfaction to see she wasn't quite so detached as she'd have him believe. The goddess might reside on Olympus, but the attention of a lowly mortal could trouble her. The ghost of Suzanne Hodges lurked somewhere beneath Lady Phelps's carefully cultivated veneer.

And then India Phelps rose signaling the end of the meal, and the ladies retired to the drawing room. Charles, the second footman and a pair of serving girls made quick work of removing the covers, and placed decanters of brandy and port and a box of cigarillos on the table along with an enameled silver canister and a pair of tiny silver spoons.

Wellington's secretary excused himself, claiming pressing correspondence.

"Snuff? I see Mrs. Phelps keeps to the old customs," Wellington commented as the servants departed, their felt-soled pumps barely a whisper against the polished floorboards.

"I believe she enjoys the occasional pinch herself if there are no others about to shock," Gracechurch returned with a slight smile. "Sometimes even when there are."

"Does she? Not surprising given her generation. Well, let's have it now the walls have lost their ears. What sort of rig are you running here, garbed like a beggar and getting yourself shot?"

"I left a pauper. I want them all to believe I've returned in the same condition."

"But what the devil for? You're rich as Midas, thanks to Nathan Rothschild's sense of obligation and subsequent good offices."

"Let's say I have my reasons."

"Which include causing your mother's garden to be destroyed, and yourself shot and left for dead in the middle of the night?"

"I see little Cassie's been busy."

"And Mrs. Phelps. And Lady Phelps. They've all managed a private word or two with me despite the squire's best efforts. No, I didn't tell them the truth, but what in the name of all that's holy do you think to accomplish with this play-acting?"

"I'm accomplishing it, I believe." Gracechurch sighed as he unstopped the brandy decanter and pushed it within the duke's reach.

Behind them the sun set at last, casting fiery fingers across the room along with deep shadows that melted away as darkness grew. In the garden a nightingale called, its liquid trill achingly beautiful. Candles that had been primarily for show took on the real business of lighting the room as the draperies at the windows stirred in the evening breeze's first whisper.

"I've a few old scores to settle," Gracechurch continued at last. "Then I'll cry quits, purchase a decent home and play lord of the manor just as every returned soldier dreams of doing."

"But not you."

"No, not I. At least, not yet."

"Found the property you want?"

"I believe so. A place called Stormridge a few miles from here. It's a grand old house. My mother will love the gardens."

"And still you play games? Never took you for a vindictive person, Gracechurch. These seem to be fine people, every one of them, with the exception of the squire." The duke poured a finger of brandy in the bottom of his glass, warmed it between his hands, then took a small slip as another silence grew between them. A smile crept over his austere features. "Excellent," he murmured, "excellent."

Then, setting his glass aside, he turned back to the former colonel. "Well?" he demanded. "The squire's obviously no friend of yours, and neither's Lady Phelps's stepson from what Cassie tells me. She's also told me they're a pair of feckless idiots, and not worth your trouble so long as they behave themselves."

"Point is, Oren hasn't been behaving himself. I'm assuming it's he, for all that's happened bears the imprint of his weasely, jealous, cowardly little mind."

"Jealous of a pauper?"

"Concerned regarding the havoc a certain pauper might work on his pockets' prospects. Exceedingly concerned."

The duke kept his silence, leaning back in his chair and regarding Gracechurch through hard, narrowed eyes. It was a gaze the duke had refined to such a degree that now as always, and even with one who was far more to him than a former subordinate and was generally impossible to intimidate, it did its job.

"Lady Phelps and I were once affianced," Gracechurch admitted reluctantly, eyes falling as he toyed with one of the snuff spoons, "if only briefly and unofficially, following Corunna. That was before you came to the Peninsula, just after General Moore was killed. I'd been wounded on the retreat, and was sent home to recover once I could travel. Her father put *finis* to the affair, she swore she'd wait for me, I returned to Portugal, and the old sot bartered her to Sir John Phelps not a year later. The title was the attraction, you understand, and the deepest pockets in the vicinity."

"Still doesn't explain your playing pauper."

"That's the reason my suit was rejected: shallow pockets and no title. Hodges had ambitions—for his daughters and for himself. He wanted elevated connections and a chance to play kingling. My father was the vicar. Nothing in the least elevated about a vicar's son.

"Oren's in mortal terror we'll renew the connection, and Lady Phelps's inheritance from his father will fall to me if we meet at the altar. Not the slightest chance of that happening— she's a bit long in the tooth; I'd as soon wed Cassie, for at least there's not a traitorous bone in her body, only her teeth are perhaps a little too short—but I'm not entirely displeased he thinks there is. If Lady Phelps thinks so too, and hopes for it, all to the good."

"You're an ass," Wellington said, then drained the last of his brandy, but his gaze had softened slightly. He set his glass down, not bothering to refill it, and rose. "So there was more to it after all. Hannah suspected there was.

"Stopped to see her before I came—totally unofficially, of course, but there was a message I wanted to send privately to Nathan and it seemed the best way to do it now your services are no longer available. You know their latest's a boy? Mayer, named after his grandfather. Born a month or so ago. Handsome lad—or at least so I told his doting mother. Actually nothing but a scrunched-up monkey face and various unpleasant odors just like all babies, and a squall to wake the dead, but to listen to her Michelangelo chose the wrong model when he carved his *David*."

"I know. Both she and Nathan have written at length."

The great man rose, looking down his nose at his former officer. "I've one of your trunks with me. She doesn't approve of your playing pauper any more than I do. Less, perhaps."

"Hannah can be an intimidating woman."

"And a wise one."

Sleep was impossible.

India Phelps had insisted Gracechurch remain at Rose Cottage, unwilling to believe he was capable of enduring the short carriage ride through the village to his own bed. Now, a bit feverish and with his arm throbbing unbearably, he wished he'd ignored her vapors, pretended or otherwise, and courtesy go hang. Warm milk and biscuits were pap unsuited to a wounded man, and those were all that was available in his room.

A glass of brandy might help, he decided as he crawled from the enormous bed with its too-soft mattress, silk sheets and flowery embroidered curtains, and stumbled to the windows.

He threw them wide, gratefully breathing in the cooler air. The moon was setting, the stars lighting the sky like sparks from a burning city, but with a disinterested, cold fire that had nothing to do with human passion. Unlike his arm, which burned as if branded, there was no heat out there.

He sighed, thinking of the duke's stern words of reproof, of Hannah Rothschild's protests when he'd explained a little of his plans while depositing his trunks with her for safekeeping.

"It won't do, Stephen," she'd cautioned softly so the children wouldn't hear, going on to quote verse after verse of the Old Testament proving vengeance belonged to God, and woe to the man who took it on himself to see it accomplished. He'd listened politely, but ignored her even when she'd pleaded with him not to put himself in harm's way. "It will rebound on you," she'd said just as he was leaving, his gifts of silver mug and porringer for the as-yet unborn child placed unopened and unmentioned on a shelf to await the great day, the trinkets he'd brought the other five from Paris keeping them engrossed following a boisterous reunion. "You'll see: Your plans will crumble, and you'll find yourself in worse case than ever. The just man doesn't seek his own justice. Indeed, if one considers what happened to Job—"

"Enough!" he'd growled, but he'd softened his growl with a smile, and then he'd left, promising little Hannah—who considered herself very grown up at age three, and refused to attend to eleven-year-old Charlotte's hushes—that he wouldn't remain too long in the country and Lionel that they would fly his new kite—the twin of the one he'd given the vicarage boys—at the first opportunity.

That was all he wanted, if truth were told—a family like Nathan's, and a wife like his and comfort like his, and justice go hang. Except it couldn't, not if he were to remain true to his younger self. He had a debt to pay that man for all the

sleepless nights, the agony, the misery. He was one to pay his
debts, no matter what the cost.

Of course Nathan had his own devils driving him—witness
his most recent letters, filled with determination and fury and
not a little confusion. They were both blunt men, Gracechurch had written by return post. Bluntness didn't sit well
with the frogs, who made a ritual of everything from entering a
room to sneezing. They preferred their own polished bankers,
oozing *le savoir-faire* and *l'élégance*. Fine clothes and superior
carriages and overblown residences and bottomless purses
wouldn't turn the trick without generations of family background. A background that led directly to Vienna's Juden-
gasse and the sign of the red shield didn't count.

Perhaps a little subtlety was needed to capture financing
the loan, along with agents of impeccable social standing.
Agents who were as at home in ballroom or *salon* as counting
house. It didn't help that Lord Castlereagh was the British
representative, rather than one of their old friends from the
war days. If all else failed, there was always the Waterloo game
of depressing the market.

Gracechurch sighed again, hardly realizing he did so, as
he turned away from the open windows. Perhaps he should
go downstairs. A decanter of brandy waited on the dining
room sideboard along with a tray of fresh glasses given there
were gentlemen stopping in Rose Cottage that night. He'd
given Charles the orders privately just before retiring, and
had made sure the duke knew of them.

The forest green brocaded dressing gown with velvet collar
and cuffs fetched earlier from the attics slid easily over his
bandaged arm, the gold frogs not impossible to manage, the
gold tasseled belt only a minor inconvenience. A candle was
easy to light from the porcelain veilleuse on the mantel, where
he'd insisted on putting it rather than by his bed.

Silently, on feet thrust in soft morocco slippers from the
same source, Gracechurch traveled the upstairs hall and down
the gently curving staircase to the main entry, gripping the
banister and taking each step with exaggerated care. The
brandy was precisely where he'd requested. He downed a glass
in three gulps, then another more slowly, sitting at the head
of the table with his forehead propped on his fist, refusing
to consider either Nathan's problems or his own. A third

seemed a good idea as the first two sat so well and his arm
seemed to trouble him a little less, and so he poured that
too, spilling a little in the process. Well, and no wonder, with
only the thinnest thread of light streaming between the drawn
draperies.

That third glass took a little longer than the first two, or
perhaps he poured a fourth without realizing it. Not thinking
about something that preoccupied one was damnably hard
work. He was about to return to his bed, foot already on the
bottom tread, hand gripping the banister, when he turned
back toward the main door, brows rising. Not only was it not
locked and bolted, it was ajar, a slight draft moving the skirts
of the dressing gown against his bare ankles. He could've
sworn it hadn't been that way before.

"What the devil?"

He crossed the entry and pushed the door all the way open,
catching hold of the jamb to steady himself.

"Damn," he muttered. "Wound must be worse'n I thought.
Have t'see a sawbones if I'm not better in a few days."

The gardens called, almost as if they possessed a siren's
voice. Circe, come to England to lure him to his fate? An
intriguing notion, that. And they were dark, so dark and
peaceful, almost like a tomb. The tomb of his lost love. Could
be, or was he turning maudlin in his fever? For fever there
was, he could tell that for certain now, and a heart that thud-
ded with more effort than was usual. It must be his wound,
that and the loss of blood, that caused sweat to bead on his
brow. Too much had been drained from him on the return
to his mother's cottage despite Cassie's best efforts.

He descended the steps and followed the path away from
house and drive, eyes narrowing. Had that been a flash of
white by the lily pond at the center of the plantings that gave
the place its name? He'd best investigate. Marauders were a
constant danger. And naturally there was always the possibility
Circe had indeed left her native shores, and was now intent
on luring soldiers rather than sailors to their death. The wine-
dark sea had perhaps lost its appeal, or grown tedious with
too much familiarity. Forests beckoned, even if they were only
a wilderness at the edge of an English garden.

Almost invisible in the darkness because of his robe, and
silent in the soft slippers despite the gravel on the paths, he

stole down the slight incline, box hedges rising ever higher to obstruct his vision. He knew the way well enough though, having often played in those gardens as a child when his mother came calling and brought him with her.

He turned into the rose garden, heavy with the scent of blossoms at their peak. And then he was at the lily pond. The flowers were closed tight, black candle flames against the still water reflecting the stars. And, on the marble bench placed where one could enjoy the most pleasing prospect Circe, come to lure him to something, though heaven alone knew what that something might be.

"I see y'couldn't sleep either," he said by way of announcing his presence, placing a steadying hand on an urn containing geraniums and verbena that he'd always considered out of place in that spot even as a lad. Suzanne made a far better decoration.

The light wrapper did indeed give her the look of a sprite out of the Greek myths as she turned and rose, backing slightly from him, eyes startled: a dryad, perhaps, or a nymph caught dreaming where she shouldn't be, split sleeves flowing from rounded shoulders, bodice caught high about her breasts with silken cords, skirts clinging to slender hips and long, graceful limbs. All she lacked was a garland of some sort binding her hair. Amazing how much he could see. Or perhaps he was imagining what he couldn't see. There was always that possibility, but he would've sworn he could see it nevertheless.

"Stephen?" she said, doubt in her tone.

"None other. Disturbed t'see me here?"

"Surprised, rather. I'd've thought you asleep given all you've endured the past few days."

"Probably should be, but I wasn't. Arm's aching damnably."

"I'm sorry."

"Not your fault." He took a step toward her. She backed two. "What's the matter—'fraid of me?"

"Not at all."

"Because there was a time when y'wouldn't've been."

"People change."

"Yes, they do—an' become changeable."

He took another step. This time she stood her ground, a

touch of defiance in the set of her shoulders and the tilt of her head. That pleased him for some unaccountable reason.

"Why couldn't y'sleep?" he said more gently, not realizing until that moment his voice had held an unpleasant rasp.

"Fury at what Oren attempted, I believe. He is the most contemptible person, though most don't realize it, believing him merely self-consequential."

"An' so y'came flying to my rescue." He took another step. "Why'd you do that, Suzanne? Certainly I've given you no cause t'treat me so kindly."

"I'd've done the same for anyone," she protested. "I despise duplicity, and Oren is the most duplicitous man I know for all he doesn't appear to have the intelligence for it." This time she did back away from him, fetching up against some rose bushes. "Oh, drat," she murmured.

"Trapped? Let me see if I can release you."

"I'll manage," she said, and then he was at her side—perhaps the only way he could reach it with her as shy as a startled doe and twice as wary.

"Y've nothing t'fear from me," he whispered, believing he meant every word.

And then, whether it was their state of undress or the starlight, or the throbbing chorus of frogs singing to their mates, or the scent of roses—whatever the cause, he knew she couldn't trust him at all, any more than he could trust himself. Leaving the filmy skirts trapped in the thorns, he grasped her shoulder and pulled her around to face him.

"Why'd you do it?" he demanded huskily. "Why'd you come flying to my rescue?"

"So did Cassie and Mother India."

"I know their motives. I want t'know yours, the real one." Without waiting for her answer he pulled her into his arms and kissed her, tentatively at first, and then with a thoroughness that surprised even him as the familiar scent and feel of her drugged what little was left of his senses. "Why the devil did y'do it? Why'd you marry that old lecher? Why'd y'summon Wellington, devil take it?"

She was stiff in his arms now, and trembling like a hare caught in a gun sight.

"Come now, love," he murmured, blowing in her ear and chuckling at her sudden shiver, "you're a widow. Y'can do better than this. Grant a poor wounded soldier your favors. The old man must've plowed you day an' night once he got you in his bed. There's nothing t'fear. It's the oldest and pleasantest dance in the world. I promise you a more interesting ride than ever he could've given you.''

He groped for her breast and then he was sitting on the path, ears ringing. She wrenched away from the rose bush, leaving strips of filmy fabric behind.

"You're foxed, Stephen," she snapped. "I can smell it on your breath and hear it in your voice. When you've recovered, you'll do me the favor of forgetting this unpleasant incident ever occurred."

Were those tears sparkling on her lashes? They were, by damn.

"Suzanne," he shouted as she turned and dashed toward the house, "Suzanne, dammit, what's the matter with you? Y'did it often enough with him. Why not now with me? At least I won't leave you unsatisfied."

She had the experience to know what he wanted. Didn't she? Of course she did. Any widow did, and would provide ease and solace without hesitation. Widows were notoriously lonely. She'd been lonely for five years now, should be ravenous for a man's hands to soothe her.

And then he realized that while at first her lips had answered his just as they had when she was a girl, albeit reluctantly, they'd remained firmly closed—just as they had when she was a girl.

"My God," he whispered, staring after her. "My God!

"I'm sorry, Suzanne," he called, "I'm sorry. I'd no notion. How could I?" but only the frogs replied.

Chapter Twelve

There was nothing she wanted more following another sleepless night than to stay in her bedchamber and hide. Her head ached unbearably. Her ears rang with phantom music. Her eyes burned and her limbs trembled, and she was mortified beyond endurance. But there were guests at Rose Cottage, and one important guest who would be making his departure following breakfast, and it wouldn't do.

Suzanne dragged herself from her tangled sheets and ran shaking fingers through her hair as the sun kissed the horizon, refusing to think of the scene by the lily pond and her part in it. There would be time for that later, for admission of her culpability in escaping the house garbed so, for lingering after Stephen Gracechurch appeared unexpectedly rather than returning to her room on the instant. At least no one had witnessed the dreadful little encounter. No one had heard the disgusting words he'd spoken, words she barely understood—so unlike the Stephen she'd thought she'd known. Even being foxed didn't excuse them. Neither did a wound which, after all, was merely superficial—or at least so he claimed. If ever she'd needed proof of her youthful folly, she'd received confirmation last night.

Sighing, she stumbled over to the wash stand and filled the basin. She needed something to waken her. Cold water might do the trick if she were fortunate, and she was in no mood to summon her abigail, a tiresome old woman who'd served both Sir John's other wives and spent every minute she was in her current mistress's presence extolling the virtues of those ladies to the detriment of the present incumbent, chiding her for failing to do her duty and produce at least one child, and bemoaning the untimely loss of the departed Sir John.

Minutes later Suzanne was in her dressing room, toweling her face and arms. She reached for one of her grayed lavender gowns, paused. She already felt like a wraith. Garbing herself as one seemed ridiculous, especially as she'd had the temerity to fly in the face of her self-imposed custom and wear blue yesterday. Besides, her abigail wasn't present to grumble at her lack of proper reverence for the late lamented knight's memory. Defiance had been possible yesterday. Today it was mandatory if she was to see the morning through with reasonable composure.

She turned to the far corner where she'd stored Mother India's elegant gifts. The jonquil was pretty, but it would lend her a jaundiced look given her pallor. The green? Impossible, and yesterday's blue was too fine. Besides, it would emphasize the smudges beneath her eyes as much as the grays, and

Stephen had complimented her on it just before they went in to dinner, however unlikely compliments from that quarter might seem. No, the blue gown was definitely not what was required. There was no way was she willing to appear to court his favor.

Among the gowns suitable for a Monday morning on which one would bid farewell to a distinguished guest and face down a graceless roué and former love there was but one possibility given her temper and her faded looks: the rosy muslin sprigged in burgundy and trimmed with burgundy ribbons and touches of ivory lace. And as she was breaking with tradition and there were none present to gainsay her, why not one of the delicate lace-trimmed petticoats and an ivory shawl rather than the usual gray? And sandals rather than the practical boots she always wore? Neither her father nor Oren would be there to scowl at the solecisms.

Besides, what was improper about dressing to please herself? Sir John was five years in his grave. She'd extended the period of mourning past anything that was reasonable, especially given their May and December union and the fact that they'd never been more than courteous strangers. That it had suited her purposes to do so was neither here nor there.

As for the girls, if Aurelia or Delphine dared to so much as raise an eyebrow or venture a single titter, she's send them packing to their bedchamber for a week. Better yet, she'd pack them off to plague Oren at Placidia. That was where they truly belonged, after all. She rarely went about in society. Sophia was a gad-about when it pleased her, even as close to her time as she was, and far more suited to dragonning them.

Suzanne selected a lace-trimmed petticoat, took down the rose gown, grabbed a pair of sandals and returned to her bedchamber, jaws grimly set. Garbing herself was a matter of only a few moments. She sat at her dressing table and seized her brush. Dear heaven, despite her wan features how girlish the rosy color made her seem, even lending a touch of pink to her cheeks. As for the smudges beneath her eyes, now they gave her merely an interesting appearance rather than the look of a hag. But the manner in which she customarily dressed her hair? It would be totally inappropriate with

Mother India's gown. She'd have to contrive something a bit softer.

Contrive she did, and in the end wasn't entirely displeased even if it had taken her thrice the usual time. Released from its unforgiving knot, it had regained its natural deep waves during the night. Given the opportunity they dipped gently to frame her face, and the softer knot she'd fashioned was higher and infinitely more comfortable. She rummaged among her caps to find one that would suit. There were none. It was one of the drab gray things or wear no cap—unheard of for a wife or a widow. With a regretful sigh she picked up the least objectionable, then with a sudden muttered curse flung it across the room. Perhaps Mother India would have something suitable.

She didn't. Not only that, with a meaningful glance she said Suzanne had never been truly eligible to wear caps given John's condition, and yes, she'd been well aware of that condition. Wedding vows were one thing. Marriage was another entirely.

Thankfully, Mother India made no comment about the gown she'd donned other than to say that it suited her to perfection.

They descended the stairs together, Mother India gripping the banister and leaning heavily on her stick, Suzanne going before to block any sudden misstep, her hair gleaming like a helmet of polished walnut. From the drive came the sound of carriage wheels crunching on the gravel. Two portmanteaux and a single trunk waited by the front door. Gentlemen's voices floated from the breakfast parlor, followed by a bark of laughter that could only be the duke's.

"Goodness, it must be later than I thought," Mother India murmured as they reached the entry.

"No, they're early. His grace must be anxious to be on his way."

Matilda Gracechurch appeared at the head of the stairs, Cassie trailing in her wake, and then all became confusion as the gentlemen quitted the breakfast parlor, the duke protesting the ladies shouldn't've bothered to rise at such an unreasonable hour merely to wish him well on his return journey, his secretary seeing to the loading of the carriage, and Stephen Gracechurch—appearing much the worse for his recent experiences—doing his best to make himself invisible and failing utterly.

The squire's arrival, Oren hard on his heels, didn't help matters. Suzanne was roundly berated for dressing in colors by both local luminaries. The duke was fawned over, with the squire pompously presenting him to Phelps without regard to rank or Mother India's greater claims on the honor.

It was, in sum, every bit as unpleasant a scene as Suzanne had anticipated, if for slightly unexpected reasons. That her father should take it on himself to be there, and to declare loudly that without him the leave-taking would've lacked the necessary sense of ceremony as ladies never knew how to do these things properly, and that he should've brought Oren Phelps with him to witness his triumph, was mortification indeed. Even the rose gown didn't help, not even when the duke—lips downturned in disgust—scowled at the pair when they returned to the topic and informed the world at large Suzanne's gown became her very well, and was everything that was proper for so young a widow five years past the death of her superannuated and infirm husband.

"London manners don't do here," Oren snapped, "and she's not even wearing a cap!"

"I'm in colors," Mother India retorted, "and I don't hear you complaining of it."

"You're not of marriageable age, blast it, Grandmother!"

The silence that fell at those words had Suzanne wishing she could sink through the floor. Cassie's stifled giggles made it all the worse.

"I'd not be so certain of that, Mr. Phelps," the duke drawled. "I've several cronies would jump at the chance to make the lady an offer. Your grandmother's a real looker, and a charmer into the bargain. Besides, she sets an excellent table and her brandy's of the best—details dear to the soul of any gentleman worthy of the designation."

"If they're as penniless as Gracechurch over there, see you keep 'em in London," Oren growled. "We don't need any more basket-scramblers in the neighborhood. One's ten times too many."

Mother India lashed out with her cane, catching Oren smartly across the buttocks. He yelped, hands flying to his posterior.

"John should've seen to it that was done to you more often," she informed him before he could more than open his mouth to protest. "It would've done you a world of good and saved me a world of embarrassment."

"Grandmother," he roared, *"I'll see you in Bedlam before I ever permit you to do that again!"*

"Charming man," the duke said, brows rising. "I wonder he was never asked to join the diplomatic corps. An enormous loss to England, that."

He chuckled at Suzanne's babbled attempt at apology for Oren's and her father's behavior. "Think nothing of it, m'dear," he said. "You think this is unseemly, you should've witnessed Caro Lamb's cavortings with that Byron fellow. Kept London in a dither for several Seasons. These're a pair of talentless amateurs by comparison. Their histrionics lack the necessary grand style, you see."

Then, eyes still twinkling, he turned back to Mother India. "Well-placed thwack, madam. I compliment you, and encourage you to employ more of the same whenever it pleases you and the occasion suits."

"Been longing to do it for years," she returned, an answering twinkle at the back of her eyes.

"I can well imagine you have, and wonder at your self-command in not indulging yourself sooner. Well, Gracechurch, ready to break camp?"

Suzanne's gaze turned unwillingly to where Stephen stood conferring with his mother.

"What? Er, oh yes, whenever you wish, your grace."

"You're leaving us, Stephen?" Mother India said, scowling as she asked the questions Suzanne longed to pose herself. "Whatever for? Everything's fine now."

"Not entirely. I need to have this arm seen to. It's giving me more trouble than it should. And then there's the matter of regularizing my business affairs."

"Business affairs?" the squire snorted. "That'll take an eon or two and some long heads, I don't doubt."

"Possibly. As I've just told my mother, I'll return as soon as I can."

"I notice y'don't mention seeking employment."

"I don't believe that's any concern of yours," Gracechurch snapped, the officer he'd once been very much in evidence.

"Yes, well, be that as it may, you shouldn't be hanging on your mother's sleeve the way you are," Hodges muttered.

Ignoring the squire, Gracechurch strode over to where Suzanne stood beside her mother-in-law.

"The gown becomes you, Lady Phelps," he said, expression at once apologetic and pleading. "I hope you won't permit that pair to dissuade you from wearing it."

"I don't believe that's any more your concern than your business affairs or lack of employment are my father's," she returned with a semblance of calm that would have fooled any who couldn't see her eyes.

"Dammit, Suzanne," he murmured, "will you *please*—"

"Oh," she interrupted at full voice, "is that my given name now? Dammitsuzanne? Fascinating. Certainly that appears to be the only way you know how to say it."

Gracechurch stared at her, eyes turning to chips of ice. Then he was bowing as her throat constricted and her heart pounded painfully.

"My apologies, my lady," he said, "for everything, if you comprehend me, and my thanks for everything not comprehended in my apology. Mother, Mrs. Phelps, Cassie."

He spun on his heel and was out the door and down the steps before she could think of a retort cutting enough to suit the circumstances.

"Looks like I need to teach your son some manners," Wellington said to Matilda Gracechurch as he bowed over her hand. "I'll see what I can do on the road to London. No, don't apologize for him. He's been sorely beset these last days, and is currently in such a state of perpetual confusion that much must be forgiven him." Then he turned, regarding Suzanne narrowly. "Mustn't it, Lady Phelps?"

"I suppose so," Suzanne murmured, too distraught for more elegant speech.

Then somehow the duke was gone as well, bundling Oren and her father in front of him, and the doors were closing. Carriage wheels turned, rattling the gravel. A pair of hunters galloped across the lawns in the direction of Placidia. Suzanne spun toward the stairs at a small sound. There, at the foot, stood Aurelia and Delphine.

"We saw you last night, Stepmama dear," Delphine said

sweetly, "promenading in the garden, and we were that concerned for you that we followed."

"All the way to the lily pond," Aurelia tossed in. "And we stayed, becoming increasingly concerned for your welfare. We stayed a considerable time."

"You did? How interesting. You must tell me about it sometime," Suzanne snapped.

"More to the point, perhaps we should tell our brother and your father."

"I don't know what business it is of theirs, any more than I can discern what business it was of yours."

"You've no right to be consorting with Colonel Gracechurch," Delphine screeched. "He's mine! I'm the one should've received those kisses."

"'Colonel Gracechurch', is it now? Not 'that blackguard?'"

"He's been reestablished," Aurelia said airily, "so I've decided he's once more a suitable candidate for Delphie's hand. Mary Scowden needs to be taught a lesson."

At Mother India's step forward and raised walking stick the two girls fled up the stairs, but not before Aurelia shouted, "Delphie'll have him yet, just you wait and see, you old hag. Wearing colors, indeed!"

"Kisses by the lily pond? Well-well-well, no wonder the duke said poor Stephen is confused," Mother India murmured to Suzanne. "What have you been about my dear?"

"Nothing that's of the least importance, not that it's any of your concern any more than it is the squire's or your grandson's."

Head high, grateful for the courage rose gowns trimmed in burgundy and lack of caps imparted, Suzanne swept down the hall to the breakfast parlor.

With Stephen Gracechurch gone to London and all the countryside coming to call at Rose Cottage to assure his mother they'd never believed any of the nasty tales being circulated about him, India Phelps finally agreed it was safe for Mrs. Gracechurch to return to her cottage at the far end of the village. Life resumed its normal tenor, which is to say it became tedious in the extreme, relieved only by bickering between Aurelia and Delphine over the best way to go about capturing Stephen Gracechurch's heart and hand, and the slightly more acrimonious disputes between Cassie and the two girls regarding the likelihood of that event ever occurring if Delphine were the lamb bleating at the nuptial altar.

The few changes—the girls calling on Sophia uncajoled and uninvited, and paying court to their brother in an effort to persuade him to hold a dancing party when Gracechurch returned to Chipham Common as their grandmother had categorically refused to consider sponsoring such an entertainment—were as easily anticipated as they were banal. Oren refused their pleas, and Sophia chased them away.

After tentative overtures the rift with the Scowden girls was repaired. Besides, Aurelia and Delphine had other acquaintances on whom they regularly called, and several more on whom they could call if they felt particularly condescending. One of them might have parents who proved more accommodating. A dancing party didn't necessarily need to be held in one's own home to turn the trick. What was needed was moonlight, violins, and possibly a waltz or two if the Mrs. Grundies of the neighborhood could be persuaded the daring new dance from Vienna was entirely proper, performed by those of the highest *ton*, and not in the least lascivious. A little wine in the fruit cup wouldn't be amiss, either.

Suzanne found herself wandering the gardens perhaps slightly more than customary. If she occasionally lingered by the lily pond—never one of her favorite spots in the past— none noticed, or would've cared if they had.

Emeline Dight and her husband arrived for their annual visit to find Sophia still very much *enceinte*, and complaining bitterly of her uncomfortable condition. They settled their string of hacks in Placidia's commodious stables, themselves in their old-fashioned guest chambers, and proceeded to pay visits about the countryside, absenting themselves from Placidia as much as possible, stopping by Rose Cottage almost daily, and often inviting Cassie to join them on their jaunts. If Emeline regarded Suzanne's listless demeanor with concern and surprise, she kept her opinions to herself beyond a hurried conference with her grandmother that left her frowning thoughtfully.

The days slid into a week, and then two. Oren Phelps, never overly fond of his sister—how could one be fond of such a horse-faced female, let alone one who displayed her unwomanly intelligence at every turn, and whose laugh reminded one of a braying mule—decided to accompany the squire and Mrs. Hodges on a brief pleasure trip to London, not in the least concerned that he might be absent when his hoped-for son and heir would be born. After all, as he said, given the odds it was probably nothing but another girl coming to join the others in the nursery. As for Sophia's complaints regarding her condition and his abandonment, it was the lot of women to bear their husband's children. Why should she repine at something so natural, and make his life a misery into the bargain? Besides, if she complained less he might be less anxious to absent himself.

The Hodgeses and Oren Phelps departed. They returned. London had been hot and steamy, the miasma from the Thames particularly unpleasant. They saw three fires, one of which destroyed a house in its entirety despite the best efforts of the fire companies, and two more formal theatrical presentations. Mrs. Hodges contracted a stomach complaint that confined her to her bed for three interminable days. A cut-purse made off with the squire's pocket watch and fob, which he had to replace at considerable expense. Beyond that, nothing of interest had occurred, no place of interest been visited, no person of interest encountered. No, they mumbled, reddening slightly around the ears—or perhaps it was a trick of the light—they hadn't encountered Stephen Gracechurch. They traveled, after all, in more respectable circles than did penniless sold-out officers.

Shortly after their return Matilda Gracechurch began to wear a slight air of preoccupation, a minuscule frown creasing her brows. If encountered in the village, she seemed anxious to be on her way. When visitors came calling, she was always on the point of going out and could stop only a minute. Circles darkened beneath her eyes, a sad droop pulling down her mouth. Friends blamed her recent widowhood and her son's absence, and increased their attentions.

And still the days flowed, unvarying in their wearisome rhythm. Crops matured, promising an excellent harvest come fall. Suzanne stubbornly continued to wear colors, ignoring the reproofs of her father and stepson. She even commissioned more gowns from Miss Blevins, much to India Phelps's delight and her father's fury.

And then came the first break in the tedium. While returning afoot from the village after filling several commissions for her mother-in-law, Suzanne was overtaken by Mrs. Sanwiddy, the sacristan's wife, traveling as rapidly in the direction of Rose Cottage as the nag pulling her gig would permit.

"Such news," she burbled, pulling the old horse to a halt. "I was just coming to inform Mrs. Phelps, for I know how little she gets about. And you too, of course. *Such* news. You'll hardly credit it, either of you. Would you care to ride with me? I must wait until we're with your dear mama-in-law before telling you the whole, but you'll hardly credit it: Stormridge is being purchased at last."

"Indeed?" Suzanne sighed and climbed into the gig, depositing her parcels at her feet as she murmured her thanks for the favor of being taken up.

"Indeed it is. And by a most wealthy gentleman, I understand. Hey-ya, Brownie, you can move along now."

Mrs. Sanwiddy clucked and slapped the reins against the mare's back. Brownie shambled forward, plodding down the lane and raising clouds of dust that drifted over the gig's passengers.

"A stranger," she babbled on, not in the least discommoded. "There's an agent from London come to act on his behalf—a very self-important sort and not at all what one would prefer to see in the neighborhood, unfortunately. Salt to sand it's some cit wanting to give himself airs with a country property, for there's no expense to be spared in refitting the place if indeed he does purchase it, whoever he is. And likely a wife and children into the bargain, and expecting to be invited to dine everywhere and even ride with hunt and giving themselves airs too, which won't do at all if *he's* not what one would like either. City folk are so encroaching, thinking themselves more elegant than we solid country folk."

"Oh, my," Suzanne said as something seemed to be expected of her. "Stormridge? Isn't that the old manor overlooking—"

"On the banks of the Chipple. Lovely prospects. Elegant rooms, and completely refurbished. Workmen there for months, you'll remember, and then the family not receiving—

or worthy of being received either, you understand. Such a loss, that was! It's stood empty these three years. The last family owned the place were dreadful people, lost everything at the time of Waterloo. Don't you remember? It caused quite a scandal, for they'd speculated shamelessly and been most successful at it, and *then* their losses came when they believed the dear Duke of Wellington had lost the day and Bony was about to invade England, which of course could never've been the case, for the dear duke would've never permitted such a thing to happen.''

"Of course not," Suzanne murmured.

"He told me so himself, you know, when he was here. 'Mrs. Sanwiddy,' he said, 'I could never've permitted Bony-Party to come to England. Think of the havoc he might've worked in Chipham Common. Your comfort would've been entirely destroyed.' Which is true, of course—it would have been, and more besides.''

What more there could be to tell Suzanne had no notion, especially regarding a property some miles distant that might or might not be purchased by a man who might or might not be wealthy, and who might or might not possess a wife and children. Still Mrs. Sanwiddy droned on, insisting all the while she was reserving the best for when they were with Mrs. Phelps.

At last they turned in the gates of Rose Cottage and plodded up the drive as Suzanne stifled her yawns and sneezes. Horse and gig were entrusted to one of the McTavish boys to take to the stables rather than being walked. Mrs. Sanwiddy clearly intended a long coze and anticipated a magnificent tea in recompense for the news she was peddling.

The news, the "best part" as the sacristan's wife termed it, was saved until after refreshments had been consumed to the last drop of tea and crumb of cake, and Charles sent to fetch a pitcher of the superior lemonade for which Rose Cottage was famous and of which Mrs. Sanwiddy had been speaking longingly.

Then, eyes darting about the drawing room to make certain no unwanted ears lingered to hear the great news, Mrs. Sanwiddy leaned forward.

"You'll never guess what I've learned," she whispered hoarsely as Cassie slipped unnoticed into the room, the skirts of her old brown habit looped over her arm, crop in her hand.

"No," Mother India snapped, patience with the endless speculations concerning Stormridge clearly at an end, "I don't suppose I ever will. Why don't you tell us?"

"It's so exciting! And makes the dear duke's visit all the more wonderful, I believe, for he said not a word about it and he must've known, don't you think?"

"You haven't told us what it is yet, so we don't know what to think," Suzanne interposed quickly at the sour expression on Mother India's face.

"Oh, do get on with it, will you?" that lady snapped, undeterred. "If it'd been you giving the commandments, poor Moses would still be on the mountain."

"Well!" Mrs. Sanwiddy protested, cheeks puffing out.

"I do believe my dear mama-in-law is suffering from, from—" Suzanne apologized helplessly, unable to think of a malady mild enough to permit Mother India to be in company but severe enough to mandate her being forgiven a certain irritability of the nerves.

"From anticipation, of course! I should've guessed it myself," Mrs. Sanwiddy declared, once more all smiles, "but only I was hoping to give you both pleasure by drawing it out, don't you see? In Mrs. Radcliffe's novels things're always drawn out to make them more exciting, and I thought I'd try the same trick myself."

Suzanne ignored the choked giggle behind her.

"And whispering too," Mrs. Sanwiddy continued, dropping her voice. "When they're not shrieking with horror or fainting from terror, they're whispering, don't you know. And blushing when they're not turning pale, of course. That's always when the villain is importuning them, or else the hero throwing himself at their feet while declaring they're saints and angels and he shall die if they don't wed him."

"What, all of them? At the same time?" Suzanne murmured, unable to help herself. "I thought we'd become more civilized than that."

"I don't understand," Mrs. Sanwiddy said in genuine bewilderment. "All of what?"

Mother India rolled her eyes to the ceiling as she reached

for her walking stick. Suzanne quickly whisked it from sight, slipping it behind her skirts.

"I do believe you'd best tell us your news," she said smoothly, voice overriding another stifled giggle. "I know how anxious Mother India is to hear it, but she appears frightfully fatigued. I shouldn't like her cheated of hearing it, or you of imparting it."

Apparently satisfied that she'd made things sufficiently exciting for her auditors, Mrs. Sanwiddy leaned forward. "It's Mr. Gracechurch," she said. "The colonel, you understand, not the vicar." She paused. Mother India gave a little growl. "He was seen inspecting Stormridge not three weeks ago," she said quickly. "At least, a gentleman who was garbed most tawdrily and who resembled Mr. Gracechurch in every particular was seen inspecting it. And inquiring about it, too. What do you think of that!"

Blank expressions greeted her great news.

"Don't you see? Mr. Gracechurch—Colonel Gracechurch, I should say—has been toying with us all along. It's clear as crystal he came to Chipham Common merely to search out a property for this wealthy Londoner—for if he'd come for his mother's sake he should've arrived much sooner, you know—and has been playing the pauper to keep the prices low. He's not unemployed at all—he's the purchaser's agent's advance agent. What do you think of that!"

"I'm not certain what to think," Mother India murmured, a distant look coming into her eyes.

"Well, I am. There's no question but what Mr. Gracechurch's been diddling us—not quite nice of him, for all there isn't any law against it of course, at least not that I know of, just as I told the squire when I encountered him in the village before coming here, but then the vicar's son was always something of a jokester as a lad. He was just leaving the Tipsy Parson, don't you know—the squire, not Mr. Gracechurch, who's supposed to be in London, though I don't know how he can be as the squire and Mr. Phelps said they never encountered him while they were there, and one would've thought they'd see him in the natural course of things, being in the same place—and about to mount up and so I reined in Brownie and told him all about it. The squire said he'd look into the matter. So good of him. So careful of the welfare of everyone in Chipham Common.''

Mrs. Sanwiddy took a deep, revivifying breath and sat back in her chair, folding her hands primly in her lap.

"I've never been one to gossip," she said, "but I really thought you both should know.''

The narrowed glance she directed at Suzanne had her blushing as rosily as any of Ann Radcliffe's heroines. Smiling slightly, her presence still undetected by either of the older ladies, Cassie slipped from the room, then noisily reentered with Charles and requested a glass of lemonade while warmly greeting Mrs. Sanwiddy and, with a wicked glance at her sister, asked that worthy what news she had to impart of happenings in the village. On those words Mother India began searching for her walking stick in earnest.

"Better, now?''

Stephen Gracechurch turned his head at the softly spoken words, the gentle hand sweeping sweat-clogged, overlong locks from his brow.

"Hannah?" he murmured, half way between sleep and waking, eyes still closed.

"You've been most unwell, my dear.''

"And an infinite bother to you—and you with a new babe to care for.''

"Mayer is fine. He has an excellent nurse and his brothers and sisters to see to him. Hush. Don't trouble yourself.''

"Most women would still be lying on their beds with shawls covering their feet, sniffing their salts and complaining of their infirmities—not nursing a great lummox with more hair than wit. How long have I been here?''

"Over three weeks.''

His eyes opened then. Everything was hazy, as if seen through a thick fog. "Good Lord—they must believe I've died back in Chipham Common, which would satisfy several of them very well indeed.''

"You came close enough to it, foolish man. Traveling to London in such a condition! Who ever heard of such a thing? And then insisting on conducting business the moment you arrived, exhausted and feverish though you were. Even the duke concurred.''

"You don't say.''

"I do, though he did claim there was no stopping you and so I didn't scold, not even gently. As you know, that took considerable restraint.''

He tried moving his left arm. For a miracle there was no pain, only soreness and the sensation that it was made of lead rather than flesh and blood and bone. Trying to move his head from the pillow, however, set the room to spinning like a child's top.

"Whoosh!'' He waited for the room to cease its cavorting. Then, with extreme care, he shifted his eyes to peer where Hannah Rothschild stood. She remained a gray blur, more ghost-like than real. "Who saw to me? I seem to remember a sawbones and a deal of disagreement and grumbling. And loud voices. I remember that, too. There was an altercation of some sort?''

"Two examined you. In the end a young Scotsman of whom I'd heard took charge. Anything was preferable to having your arm removed, and that was what the surgeon recommended by the duke intended.''

"An army surgeon, no doubt. That's always their first thought: to hack away. Hannah,'' he groaned, eyes seeking a ceiling that might or might not be there, "thank you from the bottom of my heart. I owe you a debt I'll never be able to repay.''

"Hush! What's an arm compared to a life? And Nathan's own brother's at that?''

She was by the bed again, wiping his face with a cool cloth, then holding something to his lips. He sipped. Lemonade. Nothing had ever tasted so good. A chip of ice slipped between his lips. He held it in his mouth, letting it melt as he scraped his furred tongue against it. Nothing had ever felt so good, either.

"Where did you get ice in this season?'' he croaked when the last drops had slid down his throat, then took another swallow.

"Gunter's has an inexhaustible supply, or so I've been told. A minor matter, to send to them daily. The children have enjoyed it as well. So have I.''

"You won't permit me to thank you, will you?"

"I've written your mother as I didn't want her to worry at your long absence and lack of communication," she continued as if he hadn't spoken, setting the glass down and moving away, losing what little reality she'd had by the bed. "Mothers worry, you know, even when they claim they don't. Time enough for that if it became necessary to fetch her. I pretended you were dictating to me because of an annoying cut on your hand, and saved copies so you'd know what I claimed on your behalf and make no errors later. Fear in retrospect is almost as dreadful for a mother as fear at the time."

The words washed over him, gentle as spring rain, soft as a summer breeze. "Clever, clever Hannah," he murmured. "Hannah, the kind and caring."

With infinite effort he blinked. Gradually, after many blinks, the elegant bedchamber he often used when in London swam into focus. The draperies were drawn against the late afternoon sun, only a small crack letting in both fresh air and a band of gold that sliced across the room like a bar sinister. At least his head was clearing, even if he was damnably weak.

"I'm most dreadfully sorry about this, Hannah," he said. "Please accept my apologies."

"We have traditions. And then there's Kalmann," she tossed over her shoulder. "What would've happened to him without your interference I tremble to think, for all I'm not supposed to know a thing about it."

"He'd've escaped, or else talked his way out of it. Kalmann's a clever fellow."

"You think so? Surrounded by French spies in a mountain pass far from all civilization, and carrying so much money? That an agent who'd been trusted so long could turn traitor for a few pieces of silver—Ah well, that's in the past now."

"Yes, it is. Leave it there. As you say, you're not supposed to know anything about it." He coughed and cleared his throat. Blast, but he was hoarse. "Nathan would call me out if he knew I'd answered your questions," he continued in short snatches, "though how you could suspect I blackmailed him into assisting me I shall never understand. It's as I told you at the time, Nathan offered, after the incident in the Pyrenees. Offered? He insisted. Blackmail Nathan? I'd like to see anyone try!"

"We're vulnerable. You know that." She returned to the bedside and smiled down at him, expression resigned. "In this world, we'll always be vulnerable. Wealth protects us, but only to a degree, and then only until someone decides to take it from us and passes new laws. True friends not of our own people are rare. Loyalty is ever rarer."

"You're not to think of that. It'll never happen in England, at least. You're secure here. Besides, women are to be protected, business matters and the worries they cause left to husbands and brothers. Business causes furrows on the brow—most unattractive in a woman," he said with attempted lightness.

The look she gave him in return as she tugged the bell rope by the head of his bed had him flushing. He smiled ruefully, struggled to sit, but it wouldn't do. Weakness held him pinned. He sank against the pillows, scrubbing at the heavy growth of beard on his chin.

"Three weeks?"

"And more. You collapsed shortly after conferring with the agent who was to see about Stormridge. An agreement's been reached, the papers are signed and witnessed. The first moneys've been paid."

"Discreetly, I hope, with no mention of my name?"

"An agent of Nathan's, lack discretion? You insult me. I selected him for you myself. He's sent the papers back by courrier, and is waiting for your orders regarding opening the house and clearing the gardens. Furnishings you'll see to here in London. No—not today. You can concern yourself with that when you're stronger. No, not even pattern books, my dear, nor will I summon any cabinet makers to meet with you here."

She was bustling about the room now, placing screens before the windows so the light wouldn't trouble his eyes and then opening the draperies a little more to let in the fresh air, such as it was.

"Is it hot, or am I still feverish?" he asked, giving up on the problem of furnishings for his new home for that day.

"It's hot. Your fever broke during the night. If it hadn't, Nathan had written I was to summon both him and your mother."

"I was that ill?"

"You were that ill. He specified the length of time before your mother was to be sent for. I've already dispatched a messenger to let Nathan know you're no longer in danger, and another letter to your mother. Your arm is healing well. You've encountered old comrades and are having a glorious time attending the theater and staging impromptu races in Hyde Park, drinking a little too much and enjoying yourself hugely—at others' expense, as you still pretend to poverty."

Her narrow glance had him flushing uncomfortably once more.

"Have pity, Hannah," he said.

"Perhaps eventually. Who is Circe? And why did you meet her by a fountain and then assault her?"

"Oh, Lord," he muttered, "I babbled, didn't I."

"Incessantly. Who is Circe?"

"A Greek goddess of some sort."

"Truly? You were composing an ode to her in your delirium. At least that's what you claimed. I wrote down the first bit. The rest degenerated into the unintelligible." She was retrieving a sheet of paper from the leather-covered writing table by the window, then unfolding it.

" 'Circe, untouched goddess whose voice calls
   Across the starry night
   Transforming men to pig and boar and lout,' "

"Enough!" he growled. "Give me that. Better yet, burn it."

"But there's more, Stephen," she protested, eyes wide. "It becomes most—ah, pointedly descriptive, one might say—in the next lines. And you found a rhyme: 'snout'. That's the first one in the entire thing. You're no Keats, nor even a Byron, and have very little sense of verse structure, but somehow I suspect you speak of a real woman, not a Greek myth. Circe, by the bye, was a sea nymph, not a goddess." And then, at the expression on his face, she laughed. "You may destroy it if you wish, but only later." She placed the thing on the bed beside him, eyes serious once more. "I think you should read it. It's most instructive, if I understand it correctly."

And then the hall door opened. Little Hannah tripped in carrying a plate of thin biscuits in her chubby little hands, eyes wide at being permitted the honor; behind her came Charlotte with a tray holding a bowl of soup, a napkin and a spoon. The distinctly uncomfortable moment was over.

The next morning, much strengthened after a night of true sleep, Gracechurch insisted on at least donning a dressing gown, being shaved, and sitting by the window. That night he demanded roast chicken rather than chicken soup. After a mild quarrel, Hannah capitulated. The following day he made it to the garden behind the house, if still garbed only in a dressing gown, and while he didn't attempt to fly the kite with the boys, he did watch and enjoy the spectacle. And, on the day following, with the Scots surgeon's agreement, he dressed and descended the stairs unassisted.

It took a bit of convincing, but Hannah finally summoned her town carriage so he could tour the warehouses and inspect what was available in the way of furnishings and fabrics. But, she cautioned him just before he climbed in, it might be wise not to purchase more than the essentials. Circe's taste, she informed him with a twinkle in the depths of her eyes, might differ materially from his. A pity, to spend money only to have to spend it again.

Chapter Thirteen

The expression on her father's face should've given Suzanne fair warning. The squire never smiled so openly unless he'd gained the upper hand over someone. This morning he was positively beaming.

But her mind was distracted. Even his calling her "Lady Phelps" and "my lady" loudly so all would remember her elevated position in their little community, and therefore his elevated position as her father, didn't grate as much as usual. Beyond the customary abbreviated courtesies, she paid him not the least mind as she crossed the churchyard, Mother India leaning heavily on her arm and thwacking the heads of inoffensive daisies and dandelions with her walking stick as if intent on destroying them to the last one. Cassie and

the girls trailed behind as always, Cassie thoughtful, Aurelia
and Delphine giggling and throwing come-hither glances at
butcher's son and baker's boy as there were no more elevated
sprigs in evidence with whom to flirt. For once Suzanne didn't
attempt to correct them. She had troubles enough already.

The church's interior was dim and cool, the sun already
so high it barely kissed the stained glass windows, the candles
burning on the altar mere smudges against the dark stone
walls. Suzanne waited until the girls had filed into their pew,
then assisted Mother India to sit and organize herself. Then,
after acknowledging Emeline Dight's toothy grin and hoarse,
"Halloo, young fillies; halloo, Grandmama," and chuckled,
"Halloo, 'Mama,'" from the pew behind, Roger Dight's
friendly nod and the elephantine Sophia's cooler one, she
took her place at the end and knelt, jonquil skirts billowing
like sunstruck mist, folded her hands on the back of the pew
ahead and murmured a brief prayer without attention to what
she requested, remaining on her knees long after the petition
had been sent on its way.

She'd been right. Over and over it had been proved to her.
Over and over, from the day he first returned, she'd accepted
the fact that Stephen Gracechurch was far less than she'd
thought.

Why then this desolation each time more proof was offered?
The incident by the lily pond should have banished any lingering doubts as to his true character and her lucky escape.
Clearly it hadn't, much as she'd believed it had when she
boxed his ears, backed away from him and then returned to
the house with all possible speed, as enraged at having permitted his effrontery as she was by that effrontery.

Was ever a woman so inconsistent? For at that moment
she'd wanted nothing so much as she'd wanted his speedy
departure from the neighborhood, and never to be forced
to encounter him again. And then, contrary as always, once
he was gone she'd longed for his return.

And now? Now she wished him at Jericho and beyond.
Permanently.

All the long years when he was in the Peninsula she'd
prayed. All the long years of her marriage. All the long years
of her widowhood, wearing half mourning not for her husband but for him in the hope that if she wore it then, never

would she have to wear it for him later, if only in her heart. A man who didn't exist. A man who'd proved what he was by the lily pond, and countless times before. A man whose London letters proved what he'd demonstrated so clearly that night.

Stephen Gracechurch was the very lecher he'd accused poor Sir John of being.

Lightskirts. Gaming. Debauches of every sort. Perhaps worst of all, permitting others to frank his entertainments, just as he'd permitted his mother to house and feed him without the slightest compunction or effort to lighten her burdens.

A tear trembled on her lashes, fell to her folded hands.

The reason for Mrs. Gracechurch's recent air of abstraction, the slight furrow between her brows, had been explained. Letters that hinted at more than they said, after a frustrating and unsatisfactory trickle, had arrived in a flood, some written when Gracechurch must have been foxed almost beyond coherence, handwriting barely legible, expression at once awkward and gross, one when he was more himself for all his hand remained execrable, the worst of them intended for a Dorinda Pettigrew whose profession could be deduced from contents including payment for services rendered, and had been accidentally misdirected.

That it would be extremely unlikely for a gentleman to mention such matters as opera dancers, magdalens and gaming hells to his mother—even euphemistically while in his cups—never occurred to Suzanne. Neither did the unlikelihood of a man of Gracechurch's acuity misdirecting a letter intended for his current convenient to his mother. Hearing scraps of the abominable letters whose existence Mrs. Gracechurch had just divulged as she begged Mother India's advice concerning what to do about the one intended for Miss Pettigrew and the funds it contained had left her beyond thought or reason. True, it had only been a matter of moments, huddled by their carriage as Aurelia and Delphine waited impatiently in the churchyard, but those moments had been the nadir of her life. Even pledging her troth to Sir John had not been its equal.

Better Stephen Gracechurch had never returned than he should return transformed into such a dissipated monster. Never—never had she been so deceived in anyone. A chasm yawned where apparently love had continued to dwell until that very instant despite her best efforts to banish it. The pain of its absence was close to unendurable.

Surreptitiously Suzanne wiped away a second tear while pretending to sneeze, and took her seat.

"Y'quite all right, Suzanne?" Emeline asked from behind without attempting to whisper, hand as hard and firm as a man's gripping her shoulder. "Y'look off your feed."

"Quite all right, thank you."

"Wouldn't want t'see you foundering," her stepdaughter insisted, "nor yet developing a colic. People get 'em too, y'know, in a manner of speaking."

"Hush, Emeline," Oren hissed. "After services, if you please. This isn't seemly."

"God'd approve, even if you don't, y'puffed up woodcock," Emeline returned at full voice. "Not a sparrow, as they say. Come to think on it, y'look unsettled more'n anything, Suzanne. Oren been plaguing you? I'll take my crop to him if he has."

But she subsided nevertheless to Suzanne's immense relief as India Phelps chuckled. Across the aisle her father beamed triumphantly at her look of distress. She shuddered, shrinking into herself, then stared determinedly at the altar.

As so often in their little world, word had traveled. Her father had learned of Stephen's letters, and gloried in her disillusion. Scully, perhaps, tongue loosened in the taproom now that he could make his way about again, or even Mags, so loyal to Mrs. Gracechurch anything that overset that kind lady had her muttering without thought as to whether she might be overheard or by whom. What was overheard was often exaggerated in the retelling. Unfortunately, in this instance exaggeration would be impossible.

Mr. Browne entered. Words flowed over her, soothing in their familiarity. She knelt, stood or sat as convention demanded, pretending to be unaware of her father's pointed glances. Attention to the service, however, was impossible. And then kneeling and repeating the words of the Lord's Prayer as if they had no meaning, her voice faltered.

"'As we forgive those who trespass against us,'" she repeated beneath her breath, and fell silent.

When it came, the text of Mr. Browne's sermon could not

have been more apt had he chosen it with Stephen
Gracechurch's degradation in mind. "Let he who is without
sin cast the first stone."

The notion was too fanciful to be given serious consideration, and yet it was as if someone were intent on sending
her a message. More confused than ever, hardly hearing Mr.
Browne, the two phrases ran through her mind until they
became a litany of their own, syllables made meaningless by
too much repetition. Deeply abstracted, waging a war in which
she took one side and then the other, she was at first unconscious of the sudden commotion at the back of the church,
of Mr. Browne's voice stumbling to a halt, of a child complaining and a woman demanding to be heard in a voice so penetrating it reverberated in the vault. And then of a sudden the
words were all too intelligible.

The stranger shrilling, "I arst, where is Stevie
Gracechurch's ma, damn yer! I've a bone or two to pick with
'er, let me tell you. Vicar's son, phah! They're all the same,
vicar's sons, expectin' all ter be given to 'em fer free, and
God ter take care o' the results."

Her father's voice, a roar in the sudden silence, "Here
now, madam, y'can't come interrupting honest folk at their
prayers! Out with you. Shoo!"

Suzanne opened her eyes.

A woman of perhaps thirty years garbed in a manner that
might have been well enough for Covent Garden or Haymar-
ket, but was as out of place in a country church as a peacock's
plumage in a hen house, stood even with their pew. She
gripped a dirty boy by the hand, twitching him this way and
that to ensure he remained visible. In her other she bran-
dished a furled sunshade. Brassy curls peeked from beneath
a fuchsia bonnet so laden with scarlet feathers and ribbons
it was a wonder the thing didn't topple over her ear. Carmined
lips drew back in a snarl. Kohled eyes gleamed balefully.

"Think you're better'n me, do you?" the woman sneered.
"Well, let me tell you, me fine boy-o, Dorrie Pettigrew ain't
going ter be choused of what's rightfully hers!" She stalked
to the head of the aisle, turned, dragging the ragamuffin with
her. "Well, which one of yer's Mrs. Gracechurch? You?" she
demanded, pointing her sunshade at Mother India. "I warnts
me money. Stevie said as how he sent it to yer by accident,

an' if I warnted it I was ter come an' fetch meself as he
ain't about t'be bothered. Havin' too much fun with his new
innerst, y'unnerstand, t'see to me or his brat."

Gasps echoed in the little church. She jerked the filthy
boy's arm.

As if on cue, "I warnts me gram," he howled. "I warnts
me pa!"

"Here, now, enough of this, I tell you!" The squire strode
up the aisle as the rest of the congregation sat frozen in shock.
"Get yourself out of here. The very idea! Why, you being here
is an abomination in the eyes of God."

"Such effrontery," Oren murmured behind Suzanne
clearly enough to be heard by all.

With the theme of his sermon standing before him in the
flesh rather than the abstract, Mr. Browne cast a despairing
glance at his wife and another at the vaulted ceiling. There
was a deal of difference between theory and practice, especially when practice arrived in so blatant a guise. Unfortunately, assistance arrived from neither quarter. Instead Dorrie
Pettigrew raised her sunshade en forte and gave the squire
such a solid poke in the chest that he landed on his rump in
the middle of the aisle. Again she twitched the boy's arm.

"Me pa says as me gram's got a house where I can sleep
wivout hearin' me ma goin' at it wiv ten differnt fellers at
oncet sincet me pa won't give us no money an' she's gotta
earn our keep any way she can," the child blurted in Mother
India's direction over Hodges's curses, "an' a worman what's
named Mags as'll feed me good. You me gram, old worman?"

Mother India stood, the slightest of smiles twitching the
corner of her mouth, and prodded Suzanne with her walking
stick to make her move out of the way.

"He's overplayed his hand, as usual," she murmured.
"There's no reason to be ashen-faced, little goose. Quite the
opposite. Your Stephen is as blameless in this as new-fallen
snow."

Then she was stepping over the squire and strolling up to
the strumpet. She looked the woman up and down with a
glint of unholy amusement in her eyes, then gently took the
child by the chin while Suzanne watched, as bewildered as
the rest of the congregation. He flinched. Giving the child

a reassuring wink, India Phelps tilted his head toward the windows.

" 'ere now, watcher think yer doin', puttin' yer mitts on me boy?" Dorrie demanded, retaining a firm grip on him, though there was perhaps a touch less assurance in her tone. "I'll have yer up on charges, I will, y'harms a hair on 'is head."

Still silent, eyes narrowed, Mother India pulled the boy's sleeve back, then examined his free hand, patted it, nodded and turned to the pulpit.

"Mr. Browne, the benediction, if you please," she requested, retaining the child's hand in hers. "Then we can repair to the churchyard and cast a stronger light on this matter. God will approve I know, as He doesn't care for those who bear false witness, and it was His Son said, 'Suffer the little children.' " Then she turned toward the pew where Matilda Gracechurch sat, lips parted, tears running down her cheeks. "He's not Stephen's," she said, "nor yet this hussy's either, I'll warrant, but you may want to take him in eventually given your fondness for sparrows with broken wings. If you decide against it, I'm tempted to house him myself and make him my heir."

"Over my dead body!" Oren Phelps roared. "I'll see you in Bedlam first!"

"And now who's behaving unseemly?" Emeline demanded with obvious relish, then burst into laughter at her brother's spluttered protests.

"What's your name, child?" Mother India continued as if there'd been no interruption.

"Willie," the boy answered, eyes wide. "Yer really gonna keep me? Allus?"

"Perhaps, if you're very good."

"I dunno how ter be good, missus, just how ter clean chimbleys."

"Just as I thought, given the soot ground in your hands and the scabs and scars on your poor arms." She glanced up at the pulpit. "And please ask for a special blessing on Willie's head, Mr. Browne, so that he may learn to be good enough to keep. He's not at fault in any of this, being more sinned against than sinning."

The look she cast the squire sent him scrambling for his

pew while muttering about interfering old women who didn't know their place in the world. Then her gaze shifted to Oren Phelps sitting in the pew behind hers, her expression inscrutable. Emeline Dight's understanding grin split her face.

"Y'don't want him, Grandmama," she said, "Roger'n me'll be glad enough to take him on. No sense bothering poor Stevie with him, and that's who'd end up in charge of him, boys being boys. He's got troubles enough of his own. Looks like Willie'd make a good tiger, and mine's growin' like a beanstalk. Y'like horses, Willie?"

"Yes, missus!"

"Then pray for him to stop growing, Mr. Browne, along with the rest of it," Emeline barked. "Tiger gets too big, you turn him into a stableboy. I've got plenty of those already."

Once in the churchyard India Phelps favored the battered carriage waiting in the lane, its mismatched pair and scurvy driver, with a single derisive glance. Then, still holding the boy by the hand, she seized Gracechurch's supposed cast-off by the chin as she had Willie, though in a far less gentle manner.

"I thought so," she declared as the congregation gathered around them. "Suzanne, what color are Stephen Gracechurch's eyes?"

Blushing furiously, "Pale gray," Suzanne replied, ignoring Aurelia and Delphine's hissed protests at the ignominy of their grandmama having to do with such people as a London lightskirt and her climbing boy brat, and Cassie's repeated tugs on her sleeve. "In certain lights blue or silver depending on his humor."

"That right? Pale gray with a blue cast? You're certain?"

Suzanne nodded, wishing she could vanish into thin air. "Yes, they're pale gray." What in the name of heaven was her mother-in-law about? Asking her the color of Stephen's eyes all but shouted to those assembled she had a personal interest in the subject, and she didn't. Not a single scrap of interest, drat it. Not anymore. "I'm certain."

"Except when he's infuriated, yes, I suppose they are," Mother India admitted after appearing to consider the matter.

"Were he here now, I imagine they'd be the hue of a thunder cloud."

Then she turned and scanned the crowd, apparently considering potential assistants. Her gaze paused at the vicar, standing slightly apart with his wife and sons. With a smile that held very little of the contrite sinner in it, and a great deal of the determined *grande dame*, she waved her walking stick in the air.

"Mr. Browne," she called. "Mr. Browne, in the name of justice I have a need of you, if you please," then waited until he reached her side. Her smile became all that was reassuring. "Mr. Browne, what color are this woman—Dorinda Pettigrew's eyes? Unfortunately, I can't tell. Weak vision, you understand."

The vicar, with a bracing glance at his wife, turned to the lightskirt.

"Miss Pettigrew's eyes," he declared poetically after careful examination, hands clasped behind his back, "are like the sky at dawn—a delicate and liquid blue."

"And, gentlemen," India Phelps snapped, turning to where Phelps and the squire had been conferring moments before, "what color are—Oren! Oren, come here this instant, if you please. There'll be plenty of time for you to decamp later. You too, Mr. Hodges. I've a need to consult you."

Quickly she disengaged the little scrap of London stews bait from his supposed mother and pulled him against her skirts, gesturing for Suzanne to take the child's other hand so they presented a united front against the world of Chipham Common.

"Mother India, don't draw me into this—please!" Suzanne whispered.

"What, missish, Suzanne? I'd never've believed it of you," the old lady hissed in return. Then, "Oren, I'll have you here on the instant, if you please," she called.

"Sophia's feeling most unwell," Phelps bellowed from the lane, unceremoniously bundling his wife into their carriage. "Got to get her home, summon the midwife."

"A likely tale!" Emeline Dight was at her brother's side on the instant, pulling him from the carriage and turning him toward their grandmother. "Though it'd be most convenient for you if it were true. Come along peaceably, Oren, or I'll box your ears as I did when we were children. You too, squire. Wouldn't mind having the boxing of yours, either." As the villagers grinned, she marched the two men over to India Phelps, Willie and Suzanne. "Here they are, Grandmama," she declared, keeping a firm grip on their arms. "What d'you want of 'em?"

"Willie," India Phelps said, turning so the three of them faced Phelps and the squire, "open your eyes wide, child. I want these gentlemen to tell everyone their color."

Cassie's hand was suddenly gripping Suzanne's arm, giving it a firm squeeze. Suzanne glanced at her from the corner of her eye. The look on Cassie's face, at once determined and triumphant as they faced their father together, gave her pause.

Mother India waited as squire and knight's son pretended to glance in the boy's direction, then away as quickly. "Well? What color?" she repeated.

"Hazel," Phelps mumbled.

"Grayish green," Hodges countered.

"Interesting. And what color are mine?"

"Brown," they chorused, not troubling to look. Everyone in the region knew the color of India Phelps's eyes: a brown so dark as to be almost black, and carrying a hint of the devil in them when she wished.

"Emeline, you have a look. You too, Roger. Keep a good hold on those scapegraces. That grown men should behave so! The color of my eyes?"

"Brown."

"The color of Willie's?"

"Brown."

"Lighter or darker than mine?"

"The same," they chorused without hesitation. "Almost black."

Suzanne frowned with the first glimmerings of understanding. The look she cast on her father seethed with contempt. Then her features softened as she glanced at the tiny scrap of humanity clutching her hand as if terrified someone would tear him from these great people who apparently wanted nothing more of him than that he stand there quietly and permit himself to be stared at.

"Might have a bit of gypsy to him," Emeline boomed,

squinting in the bright sunlight. "Gypsies're good with horses. I'll take him, Grandmama, just as I said."

"We'll see. Y'breed a milk-white stallion with a snow-white mare, Emmie, d'you get a coal-black foal?"

Emeline Dight laughed and shook her head, clearly anticipating the direction in which her grandmother traveled. "White," she grinned, "every time. Snow or milk, it makes no difference. How about the boy?"

"I said we'll see. I find I'm taking a considerable liking to him, given his eyes and mine're the same. No gypsy to me that I know of. Spanish blood, more likely, from the time of the Armada. Could be there's a family connection there, for all it would be a distant one and not necessarily proper to mention publicly. I've always fancied a page."

Mother India scanned the crowd, searching for the face she wanted. "Mr. McTavish," she called to her gardener over the intervening heads, "you breed a white rose with a white rose, d'you get a red?"

"No, mum," he called back, clearly enjoying himself, "you get a white. Every time," he added.

Mother India turned back to her grandson and the squire, expression derisive. "The principle is the same with people, you idiots," she snapped. "Pale gray eyes and blue eyes do not yield eyes of so dark a brown they're almost black."

"Don't know what you're talking about," the squire blustered.

"Has nothing to do with it," Oren insisted. "People aren't roses or horses."

"It doesn't? This lad can't be this woman and Stephen's son—not given his eyes. They'd have to be gray or blue. It's the little things've always tripped you up, Oren, ever since you were in leading strings. The details you ignore, assuming everyone will be foolish enough to ignore them as well. The inconsistencies, such as jam smeared in your hair while you insisted it was your sister stole the tarts from the kitchen.

"There's another problem as well. When this child was fathered, Stephen was in Spain."

"Y'don't know that," the squire protested, but it was clear he was protesting for form's sake. "Brat could be any age."

"How old are you, Willie?"

"Dunno, missus." The boy scrubbed his toe in the dirt,

clearly sorry to disappoint. "I was at the foundlink 'ome, an' then Scabby Sam what's a sweep come buy me fer a crown, an' then her," he explained, pointing to Dorrie Pettigrew with both their hands, "bought me offen 'im fer three shillings cause I'll be gettin' too big fer the chimbleys soon. I'm good fer a few months more mebbe, an' that's all."

"She *bought* you?"

"Yar."

Mother India winked at Suzanne. "She's not your mother?"

"Her? Her kind knows better. Gets rid of 'em if they starts one, quick as a wink."

"You little—" Dorrie Pettigrew hauled back to give the suddenly cowering boy a vicious slap.

The thwack of walking stick on overblown bonnet was loud in the sudden silence. "Only a fool punishes a child for telling the truth," Mother India informed the trollop. "That teaches him to lie. How much did they offer you?"

"I don't unnerstand," Dorrie Pettigrew snarled, settling the thing back where it belonged. "Strikin' a poor innorcent woman, indeed."

"I'll do more'n strike your bonnet if you don't tell the truth, my girl. Out with it!"

Dorrie turned on the crowd, eyes flashing. "Ain't none o' you gentlemen going ter come to me rescue? Y'don't, an' you ain't no gentlemen!" When only Emeline's braying laugh answered her plea, she turned on Mother India. "I'm going t'have you up on charges, y'old witch. Ain't nobody here can stop me, neither. That's the law."

"We'll see about that later. Claiming to be someone you're not carries certain penalties, as well as certain risks. How much?"

"Boy's mine. He's just tryin' ter cause me trouble the way he allus does."

"I never!" the child shouted. "Y'ain't even fed me, an' you promised!"

"An' he's Stevie Gracechurch's get right enough, too. Color of his eyes has nothin' t'do with it. We was together three year afore he left me. At's when Willie was bornt."

"You were? Oh, dear me, I am sorry. I've made the most dreadful error."

As Suzanne watched, India Phelps seemed to deflate, her

shoulders slumping, her face crumpling. She released Willie's hand, reached out, clinging to Roger Dight for support. Cassie slipped to Willie's other side and quickly seized his free hand in hers, giving both him and her sister a reassuring glance.

"When were you together?" Mother India quavered, appearing on the point of collapse. "Because Stephen Gracechurch was a colonel in His Majesty's army, you know, and has spent the last nine years in the Peninsula and then in Belgium and France. To my knowledge he was never in London during that time."

"I follered the drum," Dorrie snapped with a venomous glance at her tormentor. "That's where we was together."

"You're quick—I'll grant you that. What is the name of Gracechurch's batman?"

"Don't know. Never seen him. Stevie kept me private-like." She glanced at the men in the crowd, seized on Mr. Pemberton as a likely sympathizer. "Y'can unnerstand that well enough, sir," she simpered, batting her lashes at the spindle-shanked apothecary. "I'll warrant you'd've done the same, now wouldn't yer, if y'had a toothsome filly like me t'see to yer?"

"His horse?" India Phelps demanded, apparently regaining her strength in a flash and ignoring Mr. Pemberton's incoherent protestations and his sister's faint shriek.

"We had better things t'talk about than 'is horse," the woman smirked. "In fact, we didn't do much talkin' at all when he come calling. Entertained ourselves otherwise, don't yer know. How d'you think I come by Willie here?"

"Oh, really? No, I don't imagine you did much chatting— as you've never seen Stephen in your life. Name me three towns in Spain. Come—you must know the answer to that one if you spent so long there?" India Phelps smiled at the woman's sulky expression. "All right, I'll give you an easy one: Describe Stephen Gracechurch, if you please, as you're so well acquainted with him."

"Gray eyes," the woman declared triumphantly.

"You learned that here. How is he built? What is the color of his hair?"

The woman glanced about, then pointed to fleshy Oren Phelps. "Like him," she said. "Big. A solid one, he were. Rode me like a stallion. An' his hair was yeller, like mine."

Her crestfallen expression at the laughter that greeted her assertions had India Phelps smiling.

"I believe," she murmured to Roger, "that I would have made a most excellent barrister had I been born a man."

"I believe you would've at that, Grandmother Phelps," Roger returned.

"It won't do, you know," she continued, turning back to the London petticoat. "Stephen's hair is brown, not 'yeller', as you put it. Dark brown."

"Sun musta lightened it, then. Sun's hot in Spain."

"And has been since he was born. And he's not above medium tall. My grandson outweighs him by several stone, and tops him by several inches. How much did they promise you?"

"Stevie's ma's got me money," Dorrie Pettigrew insisted, trying to brazen it out. "Arsk her."

"Fifty pounds? So much? Yes, I know the contents of that letter. I'm amazed! I'll double the sum if you'll tell me—and all these good people—who hired you to play this charade."

"A hunnert pounds?"

"No: their fifty, and my hundred. You'll be nicely fixed for a bit."

"Let me see it."

"Don't be foolish, girl. No one carries such sums with them. But, if you wish I'll have our vicar bring out a Bible on which I'll swear before the entire village the sum shall be yours tomorrow. If you don't agree, you'll likely not see a penny for your troubles as I shall insist the funds contained in the letter sent to Mrs. Gracechurch be distributed among the deserving poor."

"Then it'll come to me anyways," Dorrie snapped. "I ain't got three coppers t'rub together most times."

"I specified the *deserving* poor."

Dorinda Pettigrew recognized intransigence when she met it. She shrugged, turned and again pointed to Oren Phelps.

"Him," she said. "The flash cove."

"Oh, I say—" Oren blustered, attempting to pull away from his sister.

"Not his companion as well?"

"Never seed the one with the belly before in me life. Big

one come in the stews and found me and promised me fifty pounds t'come here."

"And the child?"

Once more Suzanne gave Willie's hand a reassuring squeeze. There was no way the lad was returning to London with this female, no matter what it took to prevent it.

"Was up t'me t'find a brat. Didn't matter if it was a girl or a boy. Hired the carriage, an' told me when t'come. Wanted me ter interrupt services of a Sunday so everyone'd know."

Sophia's shriek of rage, her tears, her moans that her children were ruined, and she along with them, flooded from the carriage.

"See here, Grandmother—you can't believe this, this—" Oren spluttered. "I've never seen the female before in my life."

"He's got a wen on 'is bum the size of a shilling," Dorrie said, grinning as she fell into the spirit of the moment, "an' he's a grunter oncet he gets going."

The words hung in the silence as their implication sank in. From the lane, Sophia could be heard ordering the carriage to return to Placidia instanter.

"Shame, Oren," India Phelps murmured. "Oh, shame— and your wife carrying yet another babe of your getting."

"Caught with your breeches at midmast again, eh, Oren?" his sister chortled.

"Woman's a liar," Oren roared. Then, at the general laughter, he blustered, "Well, a man has needs! When his wife can't or won't accommodate him, he must look elsewhere, mustn't he? I'm sure all the gentlemen here understand my predicament. But the rest of it's a lie," he shouted over the whistles and catcalls. "The baggage followed me wanting more money. I sent her packing, and she chose this road to get it, and that's the long and the short of it. All this foolishness about my hiring her to pretend she'd a babe by Gracechurch—well, that's all it is, foolishness. She spotted you for a soft touch, Grandmother, and you've played right into her hands."

"There's jam in your hair again, Oren," India Phelps returned sweetly.

Some wag had climbed the church tower. From above them, the bells pealed. The tune—a scrap of a bawdy ditty popular during the late wars—had Mother India's lips twitching once she recognized it. She rounded on Suzanne, eyes glinting.

"You must always look before you leap, my dear," she said. "Or perhaps in your case that should be, 'Consider before you weep.'"

Oren Phelps decamped the next morning, ostensibly on an extended business trip long in the planning. Squire Hodges waited for him in a copse half way between Chipham Common and Little Stoking as arranged, hat pulled low, collar turned up despite the heat to avoid recognition. It wouldn't do for them to be seen together, not after the scene in the church-yard the day before.

He clambered aboard the already dusty carriage after tying his borrowed nag behind, scowled at his coconspirator and let fly a diatribe that surprised even him with its extensive and vitriolic peroration. Phelps, already out of sorts thanks to the previous day's debacle and his wife's refusal to so much as speak to him, drummed his pudgy fingers on the arm rest, scowling like a fat baby contemplating a tantrum.

"And don't you go saying Mrs. Hodges and I didn't warn you," Hodges snarled, finally grinding to an end. "Told you your gram was too clever by half to swallow the tale, not even with child and doxy in front of her, and I'll say it again. Up to every rig and row, always has been. Bane of every man in Chipham Common, and quite a few beyond it. Still could've pulled it off, though, if y'hadn't insisted on getting some good of that Dorrie for your money."

"Have done," Phelps growled.

"And got it," Hodges pressed with a leer. "A wen on your bum, eh?"

"Have done, I say! You've no call to go nattering like an old woman."

Hodges settled himself against the squabs, watching idly as the familiar countryside lurched by.

He'd managed to convince his wife he'd known nothing of Phelps's plans, though she'd still been casting him sly, reproachful glances as recently as that morning, and saying as how everyone knew what bosom bows he and Phelps had become these last weeks, with Phelps even joining them on their jaunt to London. The looks she'd given him then, her carping about the time she'd spent confined to her bed while he'd been gadding about Town and consorting with heaven-knew-whom, had been so pointed they'd been an accusation he was hard put to ignore.

"Problem is," he said after a bit, "what do we do? No one'll believe a word against Gracechurch now."

"Give it up," Phelps shrugged, "since you're not willing to burn the cottage down around their ears."

"Wouldn't work. Your gram'd take 'em in, just as she did when the place was ruint the last time, and likely my blasted daughter would rebuild it for them."

"I wash my hands of it. Stephen Gracechurch is a curse none of us'll survive. As for my blasted stepmother, she'll do as she pleases. Always has, when all's said and done. You're about to acquire a penniless son-in-law, and I'm about to lose a fortune."

"That you won't. I forbade the bans once. I'll do it again."

"On what grounds?" Phelps snorted. "She's of age, and as independent in her purse as she is in her mind thanks to my father's largesse, unnatural parent that he was."

"I'll not be letting her change from a 'my lady' to a 'mis-sus'," the squire insisted. "That's the plain and simple of it. Bargained hard with your father to get her that handle to her name, and then it was all I could do to force her to meet him at the altar. Not about to sacrifice all that work, nor the handle neither."

"Work? As I remember it, your work consisted of eating and drinking at my father's table. Always called when dinner was about to be served."

"Only time I could be sure of him. And listening to him bore on about when he was a man of parts after, you'll remem-ber. Think that was easy, staying awake while he droned on about London and being presented at Court, and all the swells he met? And pretending to be interested?"

"No one forced you to it."

"I like having a daughter as people call 'my lady.'"

"All in the past, and quickly forgotten. Mark my words: Stevie Gracechurch'll have her if he wants her, and my guess is he wants her—if only to spite us both."

Hodges scowled, staring out the window once more. Phelps

had the right of it, even if the man's wits were more often begging than present. And then an idea glimmered, slowly took form. It could work. By damn, it had to work.

"Mayhap I'll help the fellow to a different bride with well-lined pockets if all else fails," the squire said, trying it out to see how it sounded. "Scowden's chits, now, one of them'd do fine. Lambeth Scowden was that anxious to bring him to the point until we put him off. Get Gracechurch foxed, have him compromise one of 'em, he'll have to marry her or quit the country. Either way, he'd be done for far as Suzanne's concerned."

"Won't work," Phelps grumbled, expression sour. "Wish it would, of course, but mark my words: it won't. Nothing'll work against that damned soldier! Lives a charmed life. A hundred years ago we could've claimed witchcraft. Now," he laughed bitterly, "it's us they'd chase from the village if we tried it, or lock us in the attics with guards to keep us there, and tell all the world we'd gone soft in the head."

Hodges subsided, scowling. Phelps had the right of it again, however unlikely that was.

"Got my eye on whoever's purchasing Stormridge for Cassie," he said finally, turning the topic to a more pleasant one. "Time she was off my hands."

"She hasn't been a charge on you since you sold your daughter to my father as a housekeeper," Phelps retorted with a nasty laugh.

"Be that as it may, it's my responsibility to see Cassie married off, and at as much profit to myself as possible. Way any man with more than fluff in his brainbox does it. Why I'm going to Little Stoking—to find that agent Mrs. Sanwiddy told everyone of, feed him a good meal and considerable brandy after. Ain't any fellow so shallow in the pockets he has to work for his keep won't fall into the trap. Always anxious for a free dinner, that sort is, and any other entertainment they can find at no expense to themselves. Need be, I'll hire him a doxy to loosen his tongue, and have her tell me what he says after."

"What if the purchaser's married?"

"Always knew you were a fool," Hodges said on a roar of laughter, pulling a silver traveling flask from his coattail pocket and indulging in a generous swallow of blue ruin to fortify himself against his coming endeavors. "The troubles those two females put me to," he muttered. "The effort, blast it—not that they ever appreciate it, ungrateful wretches that they are." He wiped his mouth with the back of his hand and made a great business of returning the flask to his pocket without offering Phelps a portion.

"What's being a fool got to do with it?" Phelps ground out. "No law I know of says a man can't be married and purchase a respectable property."

"And too many as says he's got to marry or burn," Hodges returned with a sly glance that had his companion reddening about the ears. "Trouble is, married or not, you burn anyway.

"Point of fact, if he was leg-shackled you may be sure his wife'd've been there going over the place like it was her first-born and the midwife just told her as it wouldn't live above a week, and finding fault with everything."

"Y'don't say."

"That's what wives do—find fault. Only reason God put 'em on this earth. Why, the woman'd've created such a fuss the whole countryside would've known of it. No, I've found a rich husband for Cassie, and I'll see she takes him as there're not many of those about. Only thing is, I've got to find out who he is first and convince him she's the one for him. More trouble. More expense. But there it is, I'm a devoted father."

Hodges leaned against the worn squabs, crossing his arms and beaming with such satisfaction Phelps's hands balled into fists.

At the crossroads a mile before Little Stoking the carriage paused as previously arranged. Hodges, with a derisive glance at the defunct knight's temporarily disgraced son, awkwardly descended, unhitched his horse and heaved himself into the dusty saddle. Then, mouth twisting, he watched as Phelps's coachman started off once more, this time at a much faster pace, turning the team into the lane that would eventually lead to the Brighton road. Soon they were over a rise, and disappeared down its opposite slope.

It was many hours later, the sun long set and himself perhaps almost as foxed as his prey had become, that William Hodges found himself again at that crossroads. He looked down it in the direction Oren Phelps had taken, raised his hand in a lewd salute, then burst into raucous laughter.

Finding the mysterious agent had been close to impossible—not because he wasn't in Little Stoking, but because he didn't want to be found. Shillings had crossed palms, and crowns, and finally an entire pound before anyone at the inn had been willing to point out Jacob Metz, a red-headed fellow with more knobs to his knees and bumps to his elbows than a half-grown stripling, reading a London journal at a table in the farthest corner of the taproom. Making his acquaintance had been a near-run thing requiring more shillings, and meals delivered to the wrong tables. Metz, the squire had been informed, kept strictly to himself. It was true enough so long as there wasn't one around willing to trick him, and stand the expense of it into the bargain.

As for loosening the man's tongue? That had taken the drops with which he'd provided himself at the apothecary's. Not from old Pemberton, of course. Wouldn't do to have the slightest hint of anything untoward about the matter—especially now.

No, he'd gone to the apothecary in Timsborough days before, claiming various complaints that led the man to concoct precisely what he wanted without realizing the purpose to which it'd be put.

Hodges turned his horse's head toward Chipham Common, burst into laughter once more. He'd had a choice, and he'd made it that night. He could laugh, or he could roar with fury. Rage such as he was feeling could lead to an apoplexy. Far better, far wiser to laugh. No matter what India Phelps thought, he was a wise man. And a clever one. Hadn't he just proved that?

Not that the agent had been specific as to name, not even after the drops had been added to his drink while he was visiting the necessary. But, he'd said enough. Oh yes, indeed—he'd said enough.

Cassie would have a wealthy husband.

And Suzanne?

She'd had her chance. That he'd been the one to spoil it for her, that if he'd left well enough alone she'd've had a far wealthier husband than old Sir John Phelps mattered not in the least. No title went with the current candidate, not even a knighthood. Everything was very well as it was. The oldest had the title. The youngest would have the man the oldest had wanted, along with all his pounds. If a few of those pounds found a home into his own pockets, all to the good. Cassie would understand her duty once he explained it to her.

But what a wonder!

The trick would be to let none know what he'd discovered, not even his wife. A secret was safe if one person knew it. If there were two, then soon there would be twenty.

As for Stephen Gracechurch diddling them all, if Cassie led him a dog's life it would serve the rotter right. In fact, once the knot was tied he might encourage her in it. The vicar's son had definitely earned punishment of some sort. Likely he was the only one who'd be willing to see punishment done.

No, once they knew the truth they'd come fawning it in droves. It had been bad enough before. Now it would be a thousand times worse. At least he'd get some good out of it. That was what counted.

Chapter Fourteen

Part of one day and all of another with Willie the Climbing Boy in residence had left Suzanne exhausted. Not fretful, as she often was when Aurelia and Delphine were up to their tricks. Not in despair, as she often was over Cassie. Merely exhausted. Perhaps even, she thought with a humorous glint in her eyes, pleasantly so. Certainly she'd slept the past two nights as she hadn't slept in nine years. It was a joy to view the new day knowing so much that was unanticipatable would occur.

From beyond the breakfast parlor windows came joyous shouts. Willie, after permitting his face to be washed, his hair combed and his hands inspected, and manfully consuming a bowl of porridge with a spoon under Cassie's supervision— and managing it without spilling a drop—was being rewarded with his first riding lesson. The girls' old pony, brought in from the pasture, had been pressed into service. Much of yesterday had been spent in the stable tack room, teaching

Willie to polish leather and clean brass, and then in the small box stall with brushes and curry comb.

Feeling younger than she had in years despite her exhaustion, Suzanne rose from the table and went to the open windows to watch.

The boy had cleaned up well, no question there. Scrubbed, vermin banished, sores tended, garbed in one of the simple shirts, breeches, a miniature waistcoat and a cap selected by Mrs. Gracechurch and Mother India in Timsborough the day before, he looked like any farmer's child, albeit a pathetically thin one.

Cassie was in her element, leading Puck along the graveled paths on a rope and paying strict attention to such niceties as heels pressed down, knees gripping saddle and elbows pressed firmly against sides. Strange though it might seem, the boy appeared to have a natural seat, moving easily with the pony's loose-limbed gait. Most wonderful of all, Cassie's tendency to hey-go-mad impulsiveness when not directly under adult eyes had suddenly been tempered by a sobriety few would have recognized as belonging to the same child.

Turning from the open window at the sound of heavy footsteps and the door opening, Suzanne found herself facing her father.

"Still wearing colors?" he snapped at the sight of the rose gown she'd worn the day of the Duke of Wellington's departure. "That toggery's far too stylish for a proper widow, and so I keep telling you, but you won't listen. Making a scandal of yourself, that's what you are. Well, t'won't be a complete loss, for you can have that made over for Cassie. The rest of 'em as well. Chit's in need of a few fine feathers. You're not."

"Good morning, Papa," she responded, ignoring his words and remaining by the windows.

He strode to the breakfast table and seated himself at its head, tossing hat, gloves and crop in the direction of the empty sideboard. They fell to the floor, the crop rolling behind the draperies.

"Well, aren't you going to order me some breakfast," he growled, eyeing the pot of tea, the plate of cold muffins and compote of fresh fruits with disgust. "Nothing here fit for a hungry man. We have matters to discuss, and I'm not much good at discussions when I'm gut-foundered."

"You should've thought of that before you came."

"Unconscionable early t'roust myself," he rambled on, "but I know my duty. Besides, it's best we have things straight right off."

"Whatever happened to 'my lady?' " she murmured. "And 'please' and 'thank you'? Ah yes, those're reserved for the churchyard."

"Enough of your lip. Stir your stumps."

"You should've eaten at home, Papa. This is all there is," she returned, "unless you'd care for the rest of Willie's porridge? I believe there may still be some in the kitchen, though it may've already been fed to the pigs."

"Bread and cheese, then, and some ale and some meat pie. You must have a meat pie about the place. What'd you eat last night? I'll have what's left. Certainly you've got the wherewithal to feed you father a decent meal in this house?"

Head high, mouth dry, she stood her ground. Her father had never called at Rose Cottage uninvited since Mother India threw him out when he came demanding the gift of a few pounds just after Sir John's death. At least he hadn't until Stephen Gracechurch's return. Whatever it was brought him here now, it must be momentous indeed.

"Mama's not unwell, is she?" she asked out of duty combined with a touch of guilt at not thinking of that potential reason for her father's unusual call before.

"Don't know. Ain't seen her this morning. Keeps to her bed 'til noon most days. My breakfast?"

Suzanne regarded him with an attempt at charity and found very little of it resided in her soul at the moment. She wanted him gone. She wanted him as far from any room in which she found herself as possible. The day, so sunny moments before, had developed a definitely unpleasant cast. Even the children's voices were fading now, lesson apparently over.

"This is a household of ladies, Papa. Our larder doesn't extend to the sort of things a gentleman would want."

"Y'fed Wellington well enough."

"He was an invited guest. We made preparations."

"Fine thing," he grumbled, pulling the plate of cold muffins over without being asked and helping himself to one, slathering it with butter and then ladling on a hefty layer of conserves, "when a father can't call on his daughter and expect better treatment than this. Eggs and gammon'll do," he said around the muffin. "I know you've those to hand."

Realizing she'd have the air of a child called into its father's presence following an infraction of familial rules if she remained standing, Suzanne took her place at the table. Somehow she managed to keep her expression neutral, how she had no idea.

"What is it you wish to consult me about?" she said.

"That Cassie I heard out there?"

She nodded, heart sinking.

"Good. I'll tell her when I'm ready. Don't want to consult you about anything." The squire reached for another muffin. "Merely came to tell you of my decision, and see you do your duty. I've decided I've been wrong about the vicar's son."

"You have?"

"Not a bad sort, when all's said and done. Served his country, after all."

Suzanne's brows soared, but she held her peace.

"Cassie needs a husband," the squire forged on, reaching for another muffin. "At the age when she'll get into trouble same way you did if she doesn't have one. So, I've decided to marry her off to him. Steady man. He'll keep her in line, and that's what's wanted."

"But—"

"Know you fancied him for yourself," her father blustered, busying himself with the conserves, eyes not meeting hers, "but it wouldn't do then and it won't do now. You're the eldest, you've got a secure position, and there's a handle to your name. No need of Gracechurch for you. I won't have Cassie playing giddy miss the way you did when she reaches the age for it. She'll marry now, and she'll marry the vicar's son, and there's an end to it."

He'd gone mad, that had to be it. Suzanne stared at her father, ignoring the sudden weakness in her limbs. Totally mad. Only he didn't seem mad. He seemed more in control of himself than usual.

"But what'll they live on?"

"That's their affair. Mayhap you can frank 'em, lack of anything better. Good use for all of those pounds Sir John left you as you're not willing to hand 'em over to me what has a use for 'em when you don't, and sired and housed you, and fed and clothed you too from the day you were born to the day you married. Considerable expense, that was. And got you a fine husband.''

"Papa," she pleaded desperately, "Cassie's but fifteen."

"Sixteen in a bit. That's old enough to accommodate a husband."

"But he's twenty years her senior. Isn't one such marriage in the family enough?"

"She'll liven him up and he'll steady her down. What I want you for is to smarten her up, dress her like a woman rather than a girl. Cut her hair, something stylish. And have that new toggery of yours made over for her."

"Papa, you're all about in your head. Cassie's barely more than a child!"

"No she ain't. Just looks and acts the child because you permit it. Never should've given you the raising of her, but there it is: I was concerned you'd be lonely at Placidia. It's a gloomy place when all's said and done, for all it's exceeding grand. Wanted you to have a familiar face about. You owe me something for that, for all you ain't ever thanked me properly for thinking of it."

He looked at her expectantly.

"Thank you," she managed.

"And now you'll pay your debt and have those fancy new rig-outs of yours cut down for her as there ain't time to order anything special, nor any need to go to the expense either, and you'll go back to wearing gray or black as a proper widow should, and you'll foster the match, you hear? You'll tell Cassie as how I've decided she's to marry the vicar's son, and you'll see to it she does."

"Papa—"

"And when the seamstress makes 'em over, have the necks cut low, y'understand? Push her up a bit, and let him see it. He's young enough to like pillows. And damp her petticoats. Got to show him what he's getting or he won't buy."

"But I don't understand. Why this change of heart regarding Mr. Gracechurch?"

"I have my reasons."

She regarded him silently as his complexion passed through innumerable shades of red and purple.

"Why should one of Scowden's chits have him?" he growled

at last. "Or your ninnyhammer stepdaughters? Not that many unwed men in the neighborhood—not ones as I'd permit to have the sister of a knight's widow, don't you see? Gracechurch is respectable, and his mother's well-liked. Won't lead Cassie a dog's life—you'll see to that as you'll live with 'em and manage the household for Cassie. *That's* what she's a bit young for, not the other. Now, where's my breakfast?"

"You've had it," she said coldly, rising and going to the door. "Good day, Papa."

Just out of sight of the open window Cassie scowled, expression mutinous, lower lip out-thrust. India Phelps's face wore the identical expression as she distanced herself from the breakfast parlor door, but there was a more considering look to her eyes.

The door opened. Squire Hodges stalked out, muttering. He threw his daughter's mother-in-law a venomous glance.

"Y'got an ill-regulated household, old woman, and an ill-regulated daughter-in-law," he snarled. "See to 'em!"

And then he was out the front door, bellowing for his horse.

Stephen Gracechurch descended from his luxurious traveling carriage and contemplated his new property, scowling and rubbing his aching arm. It had healed well enough, though the strength wouldn't return for some time. One day he'd have a reckoning with Oren Phelps. Not a childhood reckoning such as their others had been, all bluster and fisticuffs. A gentleman's reckoning. Or perhaps not quite that, for it would be done silently. In fact, as he intended to borrow a page from Nathan Rothschild's book, it wouldn't be in the least gentlemanly. At the end of it Phelps would be ruined in purse as well as reputation.

"See to unloading the trunks and stowing them in the entry. Take the portmanteau to the dressing room off the master's apartments and leave it there. Then wait," he said to coachman and guard. "I shan't be long. Once you've delivered me to Little Stoking you can return, stable the team and settle in your new quarters."

This should've been a joyous occasion. Metz had seen to the cleaning up. Lawns stretched smooth and green, scythed as carefully as if the Regent were about to pay a visit. Dead leaves might never've existed. Windows gleamed. Flowers in neat beds lifted brilliant heads to the sun. The encroaching woods had been pushed back. It had required an army of gardeners and considerable expenditure, but the exterior, at least, was all it could be until his mother took a hand with the garden design, and she could be trusted to enhance rather than spoil its antique charm. Stormridge was even more gracious, more handsome than he remembered.

But there was no joy, no triumph.

All his precautions had been for naught. He'd just left Jacob Metz in Little Stoking, waiting at the posting house for the Royal Mail to carry him back to London. The poor man had been close to stuttering with distress, but clear enough in his descriptions. There was no question: Squire Hodges, lout though he was, had sufficient intelligence to deduce the identity of Stormridge's purchaser from the hints he'd been given. Not Metz's fault. Not anyone's fault. Drugs loosened the tongue as nothing else could. Hodges had outfoxed him. The only question was, how many others were aware of his wealth.

With a sigh he strode to the front door, let himself in. The rooms were as cool, as spacious, as welcoming as ever, even with the windows unopened. His memory hadn't deceived him. He wandered the place for a bit, footsteps echoing, trying to recapture the sensations he'd experienced when first he happened on the place. He'd peopled it with wife and children then, if only in his imagination and faceless though they might have been. Now? Still faceless. Perhaps, he admitted with a wry twist to his mouth, perpetually so.

He checked his pocket watch and shrugged. He'd written his mother that he'd arrive in Chipham Common by dinner time. It was barely noon. Scully wouldn't be in Little Stoking with Iago for several hours. There was no hurry.

He stood contemplating the main drawing room, its fine Italian marble fireplace, its imported wallpaper with a popular Chinese motif, wondering how his mother would accommodate herself to so much space and splendor. The vicarage had been a pocket handkerchief by comparison, the cottage far less than that.

Hannah had warned him. Scully had warned him. Even Nathan had warned him. As for the Iron Duke's opinion when he heard the whole, there hadn't been words enough to express his disgust and ridicule. Well, they'd been right, every last one of them—not that he'd ever give them the satisfaction of admitting it openly.

He slipped his hand in his pocket without conscious thought, fingering the folded pages in Hannah's hand, his *Ode to Circe*, as she called it.

Yes, he'd read it. And reread it. And read it yet again until he'd almost memorized the blasted thing with its faintly familiar echoes and moments of harsh revelation. Execrably expressed though it was, schoolboy twaddle of the worst sort, somehow its incoherencies gained a coherency of their own in the manner of a drug-induced nightmare before they degenerated into total incomprehensibility. His mind had delved where he would have banned it had his body not lain fever-chained and helpless for three weeks, delved and rooted and pruned in poisoned vineyards. As Hannah had said, what it regurgitated during those excursions was clear enough in part and salacious to the point of barracks-room erotica in others, if marginally better expressed and lent a touch of respectability by classical allusions and words of more than two syllables.

And, its message had been clear enough, she was correct about that as well: He'd been indulging in the art of self-delusion to the point of idiocy. The problem was, what was he going to do about it? Indeed, what *could* he do about it? Anything at all? Or, had he trapped himself with too much cleverness, locking himself away where honor and compassion and understanding couldn't exist?

The charade had taken on the air of irretrievable error. He could end it now if he wished. His curricle and pair had been delivered several days ago. The stables were inhabited, and well seen to. There was no genuine need to change from the elegant togs he now wore, to don yellowed linen and frayed waistcoat. He could arrive in all his glory, turn his back on Hodges and then laugh at his dismay. It was a notion, and not necessarily a poor one. Still, he probably wouldn't do it. He wasn't quite ready.

The sound of voices drew him back to the entry.

"Good Lord—what're you doing here?" he spluttered at the sight of Cassie, dusty and flushed, garbed like a stableboy and with her hair bundled under a cap. She flicked a battered crop against her boot, scowling.

"I had to see you. I explained all to Scully, and he brought me here. He has Iago outside, but where did you get those clothes?"

"London, minx—an advance on my pay," he added, thinking quickly. "I need to change before returning to Chipham Common. Wait for me outside."

"Not likely. Scully said I'm to stay out of sight. He's already sent the coachman and guard on their way. Whatever are you doing here?"

"I've signed on as bailiff."

"You? You don't know a thing about farming."

"There's no need to be so contemptuous. I'll learn. Come, why're you here?"

The girl stared around the empty entry, and beyond it into the empty rooms. "Isn't there anywhere we can sit?"

Gracechurch shrugged, pointed at the staircase. "That's about it at the moment, I'm afraid," he said. "Family hasn't taken up residence yet, as you can see. Furnishings should arrive tomorrow, what they have of them, and staff as well. Intending to purchase more later once they see what's wanted."

"Then you *were* the agent's man" Cassie said with a crest-fallen sigh. "I'd so hoped Mrs. Sanwiddy had that wrong, and was sure it was you was purchasing Stormridge. She'll be full of herself when her speculations're confirmed, and Mrs. Sanwiddy full of herself is even more tedious than Mrs. Sanwiddy in a dither of uncertainty. She doesn't just bore on forever then. She bores on *eternally.*"

The girl strode across the entry and plunked herself on the next-to-bottom step, leaned her elbows on the one above and stretched out her legs, crossing them at the ankle.

"I do believe you should call a halt to gadding about in the guise of a boy," Gracechurch said, turning away.

"I know. It's most unfortunate, but one does grow despite one's best intentions—and in all the wrong places. Don't let it put you out, for I'm not. Well, come sit," she ordered, patting the step beside her. "A lot's happened while you were gone."

"It has? In Chipham Common?"

"Now who's being contemptuous? Yes, indeed it has. Two days ago a London lightskirt arrived during services with a child in tow, claiming she was your, well, you know, and the child was yours."

"*What?*"

"Don't worry, Mother India and Suzanne saw to it *that* was exposed for the lie it was. We've kept Willie. He was a climbing boy. I'm teaching him to ride, and Mother India thinks he'll make a perfect page, though I'm not so certain about that. He'd much rather be a tiger or a stableboy, and Willie can be stubborn when he wishes. The doxy'd bought him from a sweep for three shillings as he'll be too big to be of use soon. Then Mother India paid a hundred pounds for him."

"She did? So much?"

"I suppose that's what it was, though one can't really buy and sell people in England, can one? Oh, and Oren has decamped. He has a wen on his bum, you see. I suppose you could say *he* paid fifty pounds for the boy, too."

"Did he indeed?"

"Or maybe it was for the doxy. I don't mean to sound stupid, but I'm not quite sure about that."

"Oren Phelps has departed, you say?" Gracechurch choked out. "With a wen on his, ah—"

"His bum. That's what Dorrie Pettigrew called it. For an extended journey. Sophia didn't like everyone in the churchyard hearing about the wen on his bum, and that he's a grunter. It was he hired the doxy to besmirch your good name. You don't know a Dorinda Pettigrew, do you?"

"No," Gracechurch said, caught between a desire to laugh and the sudden impulse to break everything in sight—of which there wasn't much available but windows. "Dear Lord, you're right—a lot has happened."

"Well, sit down," Cassie ordered. "You see, that's not the worst part, and before hearing the worst part I do believe you'd best be seated. When I heard it, I certainly wished I'd been. In fact I almost did sit right where I was, and if I had I'd've been caught and you'd have no warning, so it's a good thing I more or less kept my composure despite everything."

Gracechurch joined Cassie, watching her face through narrowed eyes and carefully avoiding glancing at the rest of her—

a milder version of the look he'd employed with fractious recruits.

"Listening at doors?" he said after a moment.

"Not precisely, and certainly not intentionally. I'm not like Aurelia and Delphine. It simply happened—and a good thing for you it did. A good thing for me too, I suppose." She paused a moment. Then, "Papa intends me to marry you," she blurted, "and I don't want to. I know you haven't the slightest desire to marry me either, though we do very well as friends now you've stopped being so starched-up, but when it comes to marriage Papa never cares about that. He makes up his mind, and one does as he wants or one's starved, and I don't want to be starved. It's most unpleasant."

"Starved?"

"That's what he did to Suzanne when she refused to consider Sir John's suit."

"Fustian!"

"That was after she tried to run away and was caught. I wasn't supposed to know, and was told she was merely ill, but that wasn't the truth even if Dr. Smythe did have to be summoned from Timsborough when she became truly ill from not being permitted anything but water for what seemed like weeks. Papa grumbled ever so much at the expense, but Mama insisted. Why, Suzanne was so weak she couldn't even sit up."

"Cassandra Hodges—" he ground out.

"There's no need to make your hands into fists or to look at me like that. Twasn't I did it. The one time I tried to sneak her something—it was only an apple, but it was *something*— I was caught and birched and locked in my room, and I didn't dare try again. Besides, that was all a long time ago. We've more pressing problems. Papa lies when it suits him, you see. I think he intends me to compromise you, for he was speaking of lowered necklines and dampened petticoats."

Gracechurch stared at his hands. It took an immense effort to unclench them, but finally he managed it. Then, after a deep and shuddering breath, he turned to the girl, trying to keep his tone light and his expression humorous.

"You're right, it was a long time ago. Don't you mean he intends I should compromise you?"

"No, I mean precisely what I've said. Haven't you learned yet that I don't say things I don't mean? All Suzanne's new

gowns are to be cut down for me, and I'm to become modish
and alluring. She's to teach me how, I believe, and I'm the
one who's to do the compromising. Then we're to be married,
and Suzanne's to frank us and run the household. The point
is, what are we to do?"

"Nothing," Gracechurch said. "Absolutely nothing—
except that we'll make sure we're never alone in each other's
company after this. That shouldn't be difficult."

"It seems a bit paltry. I'd hoped for something grander
when I rode all the way here to warn you."

"For which action I'm infinitely grateful, believe me."

"You see, even if he doesn't manage it this time Papa will
force me to wed now he's taken the notion, and if it's not to
be you then it's certain to be someone like Sir John. I don't
want that. Can't you contrive something that will spike Papa's
guns?"

"I'll give it some consideration."

"Well, think of something—please. Think of it quickly.
You're an excellent friend, but you'd make the most positively
dreadful husband. Besides, I don't want to wear dampened
petticoats. That would be horrid."

Suzanne got through what remained of the morning as
best she could, setting little Willie to practicing his alphabet,
conferring about the menu for the evening meal with Cook,
and listening to Delphine and Aurelia plan Delphine's next
assault on Stephen Gracechurch's heart while pretending to
busy herself with the Rose Cottage accounts. When at last the
girls sought their bedchamber to review Delphine's wardrobe
once more, Suzanne leaned back wearily in her chair and
rubbed her forehead.

There were mornings that had equaled this one in misery—
the one on which she'd capitulated to her father's demands
regarding marriage to Sir John for one, the morning of the
Duke of Wellington's departure for another. And then there'd
been the day of Stephen Gracechurch's return to Chipham
Common. That it had been afternoon rather than morning
mattered not in the least. The misery had been acute.

Well, this time she hadn't capitulated, for all the good it
had done her. Unfortunately it was little more than a staying

action. As always, her father would wear her down eventually, at least in the matter of the gowns. It was the activity at which he was most skilled. For now she'd sent Miss Blevins—who had arrived prepared to perform the necessary surgery as ordered by the squire—on her way with a shilling to compensate her for her trouble. Anything for a little time during which to settle her unsettled mind.

Morning blended into afternoon. Willie was sent to the stables for more lessons in currying, and to keep him out of the mischief into which he invariably tumbled when Cassie disappeared for more than a few moments. Cassie returned from one of her rambles, uncharacteristically close-mouthed, habit rumpled, hair windblown, expression perhaps a bit mutinous, and tossed their father's old crop in Suzanne's lap, telling her she'd found it in the breakfast parlor. Suzanne sent her to regularize her appearance, and had just returned to the accounts when Charles knocked at the parlor door.

"Callers, my lady," he said, then specified, "The squire, the colonel, and Mrs. Gracechurch," at her questioning glance. "I've put 'em in the drawing room. Squire's ordered brandy and madeira for the colonel and himself, and lemonade for Mrs. Gracechurch. That affable, he is. And he wants Miss Cassie fetched."

"Nothing about Mrs. Phelps or myself?"

"Nary a word, my lady, except to say you weren't needed."

"Oh dear."

"Just so, my lady. Thought you should know. Colonel said as how it was you and Mrs. Phelps he came to see, but the squire said that was entirely unnecessary as you were both undoubtedly occupied, and not receiving this afternoon."

Suzanne sighed, closed the accounts book and rose from the escritoire. "If you'd be so good as to alert Mrs. Phelps, Charles? I suppose Cassie must be fetched as well, but tell her to take her time."

A glance in the mantel mirror showed she presented a respectable appearance, if not a particularly blooming one. She pinched her cheeks and bit her lips, but these customary encouragements did little good. Worse yet, it was the same gown she'd worn the morning of the duke's departure. Well, there was nothing to be done about that now, either. Cassie must not be left to flounder solo.

With another sigh, she was out the door and down the short hall. She stopped before the drawing room door and gave herself a shake. Behind her Charles was ascending the stairs. There was no help for it. This first true confrontation since the incident by the lily pond must be gotten through. Unfortunately, the sounds coming through the door weren't encouraging. Her father was playing host as if in his own home, effusive in his gallantries to Mrs. Gracechurch, clumsy in his jovialities to Stephen, extolling Cassie's freshness and originality to the skies.

Had ever a man been so transparent? And so transparently self-serving? Was this how he'd prattled on regarding her while courting Sir John as his son-in-law? The notion was mortifying. Only his motives puzzled, for at least in Sir John's case he'd been courting wealth and position. In Stephen's he courted precisely the opposite.

She depressed the door handle.

"Ah," her father boomed, "that must be my dearest little Cassie now."

His expression when she rather than Cassie entered the drawing room would have caused laughter in a theater. In one's own home? Mortification beyond any mortification she'd ever endured.

"What're you doing here?" he snapped as Stephen rose. "Told that footman there was no need to fetch you. Cassie's the one what's wanted."

"Good afternoon, Mrs. Gracechurch, Colonel," Suzanne said, ignoring her father's words and doing her best to portray the very essence of calm and cool correctness. "How lovely to see you, and how kind of you to call. I hadn't realized you were returned, Colonel. I hope your presence among us once more signifies complete recovery from your late injuries." Then, turning as she took her customary seat by the tea table, she gave a brief nod. "Papa."

"Get gone," the squire snapped. "You're not wanted here, Madam Marplot. And what're you doing in that gown? Commissioned Miss Blevins to see to cutting it down for Cassie. Supposed to come straight out this morning, have it ready by this afternoon. Ain't she been here?"

"I sent her on her way, Papa. Neither this gown, nor any others of mine, are suitable for Cassie at her age."

"Selfish, that's what you are! Always were, always will be. She's selfish, that's what," the squire declared, turning to Matilda Gracechurch, "an unnatural daughter, and as head-strong as a mule. Led poor Sir John a dog's life, and that's the truth of it. Always a commotion of some sort. Frivolous an' expensive, too—not like my little Cassie, who's the very pattern card of all a young girl should be. She's got broad hips, too," he added, leering at Stephen. "Not like her sister, who's skinny as a broomstick."

"Oh dear, I hardly believe—" Mrs. Gracechurch began, giving Suzanne an apologetic glance.

"Your sister needs some new togs," the squire fulminated, paying no attention to the fact that he was interrupting a lady, "and she needs 'em instanter. Colors're suited to a girl. You're a widow, and a brazen one at that."

Suzanne gave her father a cloying—if falsely bewildered—smile and turned back to Stephen, gesturing for him to regain his place by his mother. "How did you find London, sir? You lingered there some time."

"Much as it always is in this season: somewhat lacking in company, and excessively hot. I came to thank—"

The drawing room door burst open. Delphine posed in its frame, hastily cut-down neckline revealing far more of her charms than would've been considered seemly even in a London ballroom, the merest scrap of lace tucked in to play propriety, a silk rose peeping from among her curls. Aurelia hovered behind, twitching her sister's skirts to make them fall more gracefully.

"Colonel Gracechurch! You are returned at last!" Delphine enthused, darting across the drawing room, hands extended, once she'd given the company the opportunity to admire her décolletage.

"See here," the squire growled, surging to his feet, "where'd you spring from, hussy?"

"I've been positively pining away while you've been gone," Delphine rushed on, tilting her head coquettishly to the side and ignoring the squire's question. "Why, I almost fell into a decline, Colonel, truly I did! I should have been informed the moment the colonel arrived," she declared, glaring at her stepmother, "as well *you* know, for I positively idolize him. Why, I do believe I'm his greatest admirer in all the region!"

As quickly as Stephen was on his feet Delphine seized his hands, attempting to pull him apart from the rest. When he remained immovable she appropriated his arm, clinging to it as she turned to Mrs. Gracechurch. "You'll cede me your place, dear Mrs. Gracechurch, I'm sure," she trilled, "for you know how distraught I've been over the colonel's absence, how desperately I've longed for his return. Why, I've been positively mopish!" She batted her lashes impartially at son and mother, simpering and preening.

"See here, y'little—"

But what sort of "little" the squire had been about to call Delphine those in Rose Cottage's drawing room were never to know.

"My, this is quite a gathering," Mother India said from the doorway, eyes dancing as she surveyed the company, voice slicing across the squire's for all its volume wasn't that great. "Entirely unexpected, too. Delphine, what have you done to your gown, cut away half the bodice? Totally unseemly. Fetch your sister a shawl, Aurelia, if you please. A thick one. Immediately! No—no protests. You may wait in the hall until you're properly garbed, Delphine. Glad to see you've returned at last, Stephen. Well, don't just stand there. Come give me your arm, you silly man, and help me to a chair. A kiss on the cheek wouldn't be amiss, either."

"Where the devil is Cassie?" the squire roared in the sudden silence. "Y'got her locked up somewhere? Five females, and not a one of 'em the one I want!"

When at last Cassie made her curtsies just as the company was finishing their tea, she presented precisely the opposite appearance of the one her father desired: shapeless gown hanging like a sack, slippers scuffed, hair tied at the nape of her neck with a ribbon, she had the helter-skelter air of a coltish schoolgirl interrupted at her studies. She even carried a natural history book in one hand to complete the illusion while grasping Willie's hand with the other. Gracechurch gave her the slightest nod as her eyes sought his desperately for approval, though it was all he could do to refrain from bursting into laughter. All that was missing was a film of milk and crumbs surrounding her rosy mouth, the minx.

The squire made the best of it after a single growl of frustration, pointing out what a wonderful mother Cassie would be—as witness her care of the London climbing boy. Then, in a voice ringing with a joviality belied by the fire in his eyes, he ordered Willie to come perch on his knee and examine his pocket watch so Cassie could join the colonel and his mother. Willie, clearly remembering the squire from the churchyard and no doubt sensing the signal Cassie sent him through a tightened grip on his hand, clung to her all the more determinedly.

Hodges next attempted to bribe Willie with the last jam tart while ordering Gracechurch to view the gardens with Cassie as his guide. There must be improvements since the last time the colonel was at Rose Cottage, he insisted. It had, after all, been several weeks. That brought Delphine and Aurelia mincing from the widow seat to which they'd temporarily retreated, declaring Cassie knew nothing of gardens and flowers, and if anyone should give the colonel a tour it was Delphie, who was the only one present of the proper age and accomplishments to ensure he enjoyed the pastime.

The squire's spluttering protest brought deep blushes to Cassie's cheeks and an unwelcome pallor to Suzanne's.

Gracechurch observed the little war with no small amusement, grateful for Cassie's forewarning. He'd have protected himself from unwanted entanglements and compromising situations somehow, being a man as well as a gentleman, and not entirely unobservant, but knowing they threatened at every turn certainly helped matters. The rueful glance he sent India Phelps, while it didn't precisely beg for assistance, definitely hinted it would be welcome.

"An excellent idea," she declared as if on cue. "Healthful exercise on such a pleasant afternoon? What could be more proper. Delphine certainly gobbled too many fairy cakes for the fit of her gown, and will benefit from it."

Caught between insult and triumph, Delphine opened and closed her mouth like a beached fish, slipped the shawl from her shoulders, patted her curls, thrust her bosom forward, and extended her hand to Gracechurch.

"Colonel, why don't you and Suzanne oversee the children at their play?" India Phelps continued, ignoring her granddaughter. "I presume there's a ball about the place, or perhaps a hoop they can teach Willie to use."

"I am not a child!" Delphine protested. "The rest may be, but *I* am *not!* Better our stepmother, who's too old for such activity, remain here where she won't squander her strength. Besides, I'm the lady of the most consequence here. I'm certain the colonel would much prefer *my* company. *We* can oversee the children. After all, I'm young and pretty, and she's nothing but an old hag!"

"That's the truth with no bark on it," the squire chortled, "but my Cassie'll be far the better guide. You take my Cassie on your arm, Colonel, and if you should happen to lose sight of the others for a bit, I won't mind in the least."

His lewd wink had poor little Cassie blushing.

"Nice day for a bit of dallying," the squire concluded in an insinuating tone.

Jaws clenched, hands balled into fists, more deeply enraged than he had been since just after Bussaco, Gracechurch rose in the sudden silence. *This* was what Suzanne, cast in the role of the luckless Cassie, had had to endure following his departure? Along with all the rest? Amazing she managed to resist for so much as a year. The man was nothing but a panderer, for pity's sake—and of his own daughters.

"But then, Miss Phelps, I should doubtless hinder you in your play," Gracechurch said tightly. "Far better that we antiquated relics stick together, rather than attempting to join in your games. I, for one, haven't the stomach for 'em, being nothing but a rough military man who more often than not speaks his mind all too clearly."

Ignoring India Phelps's shout of delighted laughter and his mother's horrified gasp, he turned to Suzanne.

"Lady Phelps, may I prevail upon you to show me the gardens," he said smoothly, offering her his arm. "The day is so clement you needn't trouble with sunshade or bonnet, I believe."

Her eyes glittered as if she were about to burst into tears, damn them all, and her hand as she rose and laid it on his arm quivered like a hummingbird's wing.

"That sounds most delightful, Colonel Gracechurch," she said.

Blast it, even her voice trembled.

"Here now, I won't have you go waltzing off with Suzanne," the squire growled, struggling from his chair. "You insist she gad about, I'll take her on my arm. Totally improper otherwise. She's Sir John's widow, after all. You take Cassie, Colonel."

"What about *me?*" Delphine demanded from where she'd been whispering with her sister. "You give Cassie or my stepmother precedence over me, and I'll see my brother hears of it. Oren shan't like it a bit, you know, and he's the most consequential person in these parts now Papa's dead. It won't enhance your standing to put him out."

"Your brother's consequence can go hang, Miss Phelps, as well as your own," Gracechurch said with a bow so punctilious at first the girl simpered. "I don't care in the least what his opinion may be, never having been on particularly easy terms with the man. I believe he's not in the neighborhood at the moment in any case, having in some fashion irritated his good lady.

"With my apologies for abandoning you in such company, my mother excepted, Mrs. Phelps. My lady, Cassie, Willie, shall we?"

And then they were on the terrace and descending the steps to the garden, Willie scampering ahead in the direction of the stable path, Cassie dashing after him.

"My dear, you mustn't permit those harpies to overset you," Gracechurch managed through clenched teeth, his grip on the hand that lay on his arm perhaps a little too firm in his desire to offer support and comfort. "If I'd had a horsewhip about me, I'd've been sorely tempted to use it these last minutes."

Suzanne's responding stifled giggle had him frozen in place.

"What the devil?" he muttered incredulously. "Are you laughing?"

"It was such a magnificent set-down," she said, smiling at him much in the manner she'd had as a girl, their eyes nearly on a level, "almost as wonderful as the duke's. Sophia, 'irritated'? That's rich! The best of it was, at first Delphine didn't understand, the little ninny. None with Phelps blood flowing in their veins is overly intelligent with the exception of Emeline, but then you know that, having been acquainted with them all forever. Thank you, Stephen. I've longed to do that for years, but never quite dared, and now you've done it for me.''

"Think nothing of it." He gave her an answering grin. "My pleasure entirely.''

Then, as if nothing of moment had just occurred, she was turning him toward the gardens, and they set off once more. In the distance Cassie shouted for Willie to wait, then disappeared behind a clump of yews so tall and old they resembled a small forest.

They strolled down the path in the bright afternoon sun, footsteps crunching on the gravel. He cast repeated glances at her out of the corner of his eye, but her face remained turned from his. There was too much of the past between them, strolling along like this, and far too much of the present, for ease or comfort. The one had to be laid to rest, the other seen to, though he was as damned as ever if he knew how he'd manage it. As always, Suzanne was proving highly uncooperative.

"We're still in sight of the house, aren't we," she said just as her silence was beginning to unnerve him.

"Yes. Why?"

"I merely wondered. Is you arm quite recovered?"

"Yes."

"Goodness, but you're curt."

"I came here with the intention of thanking you and Mrs. Phelps for leaping to my rescue Sunday last. Leaping again, I might add. Rather heavy weather there for a bit, but now I can manage the courtesy, I believe. I seem to be forced to be either perpetually thanking you or apologizing to you these days.''

There—he'd said it, for all he'd babbled a bit, and he'd called up a smile to go along with it. Of course more was needed—much more—but it was a beginning. Would ever this woman, with her cool composure, stop transforming him into an imbecile? Or was that something he managed without benefit of her assistance?

"Unless," she countered with a tight smile, "you're leaping to mine.''

Unconsciously he turned their steps toward the rose garden and the lily pond just beyond it.

"I don't believe it's wise to go in that direction," she murmured.

"What? Oh."

Blast her! More to the point, would she forever hold that night against him? He'd been feverish, ill, and foxed into the bargain. And there'd been a lot he hadn't realized then, such as the precise nature of her marriage to old Sir John and the manner in which that marriage had been brought about. She should have told him. His mother should have told him, or his father. Blast it, *someone* should have told him!

Of course his mother had tried, but she'd dealt in so many circumlocutions and he'd been so bitter that he'd dismissed her words as meaningless. That had been his second error. The first was not abducting Suzanne from her father's house all those years ago rather than meekly attending Sunday services and then permitting the squire to go his length in front of the entire village. He'd been tempted, Lord knows. He'd even hired a traveling chaise and bribed one of the squire's stableboys to assist him, but then he'd remembered his duty to his father's position and chosen patience as the wiser course, the more fool he.

Suppressing a sigh, he turned their steps toward the little wilderness beyond the yews. The shade there was cool and inviting. So was the privacy the screen of trees and shrubbery would offer, given his present mood and inclination.

"I just attempted to thank you, Suzanne," he reminded her as they came to the first trees.

"I had very little to do with it. Mother India took charge. From that moment Miss Pettigrew hadn't the slightest hope of succeeding with her lies or Oren with his machinations. Are we out of sight of the house?"

"Yes, I believe so." He turned to look behind them. "Only the roof and chimneys now, and they'll be lost in a moment. Why?"

She slipped her hand from his arm.

"What?" he growled, turning on her as they reached a fork in the path, one branch leading to the stream that first passed through Placidia's park on its way to the Chipple, the other, with many twists and turnings, back to the spot where they stood.

"I believe it's wisest for us to maintain a certain distance, Colonel."

"What happened to 'Stephen'? You said it readily enough a moment ago."

"In a moment of inattention."

"Is that what it was? A moment of inattention? Or was it a moment of honesty? Dammit, Suzanne—"

"And now we return to my new name."

Was it bitterness he heard in her voice? He wasn't sure. The only thing of which he could be certain was that if he permitted this scene to play itself out as she seemed to intend, he'd be farther behind than ever.

"There are certain things we need to discuss," he ground out, temper warring with frustration, neither winning as yet, and both lending his voice a deplorable harshness. "Such as events during the years '09 and '10."

"What happened, happened. I married Sir John. There's no changing that or anything else, and so there's nothing to discuss. You'll find the path that way is by far the more pleasant," she said pointing toward the stream.

She turned her back on him, started off in the opposite direction.

"Dammit, Suzanne!" he roared, seizing her arm and slinging her around to face him, "I refuse to accept any more of this!"

She dropped her eyes to his hand, gripping her so tightly it must have been painful. Then she raised them. They were expressionless, as if she saw neither him nor the woods surrounding them. Slowly he released her.

"Suzanne, please," he said more gently. "We can't continue like this. At least I know I can't. There's rough ground to be gotten over. No need to make it worse."

"We're not who we were, Stephen. Perhaps we never were who we thought we were, either of us."

"What the devil d'you mean by that?" he exploded. "Of course we're not. We're both older and, I hope, somewhat wiser. Public opinion should concern neither of us anymore. Despite all that cool collectedness I still catch glimpses of the girl I knew. Have I truly changed so much that you find nothing of the old Stephen in me?"

She gave him a hard, assessing look.

"He died," she said. "Didn't you know? I killed him."

"And what in blazes d'you mean by *that*? You're talking in riddles. Makes you sound like you're trying to play Delphic Oracle, or something equally ridiculous."

"And now I'm ridiculous? I see. Thank you for informing me."

"Blast it, Suzanne, don't be so bloody impossible—please. There's no need to play the prickly hedgehog. I'm very much alive, in case you haven't noticed, and doing my damnedest to tell you I know all about—"

"Good day, Colonel."

She stepped around him and started back the way they had come. After a moment he followed, this time well behind, watching the stiff set of her shoulders, the determined carriage of her head. He'd done it again, dammit! Or she had.

Cassie and Willie joined him as he emerged from the little wilderness. They, too, were watching Suzanne as she strode toward the house.

"Have you quarreled?" the girl asked.

"In a manner of speaking. How d'you know about that?"

"I'm not deaf, Colonel, nor am I blind. You're a fool if you can't manage my sister better than that. I'm beginning to believe there's only one hope for either of you."

"Mister?"

Gracechurch glanced down at the little stews scrap tugging on his coattail, his brows rising. "Yes, imp?" he said.

"If'n yer tells me how it was in Spain, I'll tell yer what t'do about the pretty lady. An' I won't charge yer even a penny, neither. All I arsk is y'take me on. Don't warnt ter be a page, and I don't warnt t'go live with that Emmie-worman. I warnts ter be wiv a cove what has horses, not a lady, an' you're the sort'd have some gooduns."

Chapter Fifteen

Suzanne retreated to her bedchamber as soon as she reached the house, the headache she'd fought since her father's announcement regarding Cassie's future that morning now full-blown. Lavender water, vinegar-soaked paper, powders, nothing touched it. She chased away her self-important abigail after the woman attempted to force laudanum on her insisting it was the favored remedy of the previous Lady Phelpses, choked down a few swallows of the broth Cassie brought her in lieu of the dinner tray she'd refused, indulged in a fit of rearranging drawers that left gloves, reticules, shawls, undergarments and handkerchiefs in hopeless disarray, then paced the floor in an agony of confused emotions that left her drained and trembling.

Finally she sought her bed, turned her face to the wall and did her best to ignore the soft summer sounds filtering through the drawn curtains as sunset faded into welcome darkness. Not thinking, not considering Stephen Gracechurch's words, the expression in his eyes during their bitter exchange, was infinitely difficult. This quarrel had had a finality to it there was no escaping.

He'd changed. Perhaps not in the manner she'd at first thought, but there was no way she could contend with the cold, hard-visaged stranger who'd plagued her in the little wilderness, or by the Weeping Sisters when she came to warn him of Oren's clumsy plots against his reputation. Life was too short for that, no reward or joy sweet enough.

In the drawing room that afternoon, giving Delphine such a set-down the girl was still screaming the house down when Suzanne sought her bed, he was that same hard-visaged stranger, with not an ounce of charity or kindness to him. Not a scrap of understanding for a willful child who'd been encouraged to think herself above her company when in leading strings, and still considered herself so no matter what she or Mother India said regarding the matter.

Yes, she'd giggled at that set-down. She'd even thanked him. She shouldn't have—not given the results of his cutting words. They'd all suffer for them for days if not weeks, given Delphine's ungovernable temper when roused. Instead she should have cautioned him regarding taking a hand in affairs that were none of his concern.

And the man who'd brought a kite to the vicarage children despite his own poverty, knowing only too well such luxuries didn't go with the living? Better he'd brought a few much-needed pounds to his mother instead. Far better.

True, his experiences had not been universally pleasant on the Continent. She knew a little about those years—that same little he'd permitted his parents and Mother India to learn. Given many of the duke's tales, Stephen's sudden silences and cautioning frowns, in truth none of them knew much about where he'd been or what he'd done.

Oh, there'd been countless details in his letters, some humorous, some touching: a fellow officer named Harry Smith hunting hares on horseback for sport and to fill the stew pot, his descriptions of the hey-go-mad chase sending her into peals of laughter; that same officer's marriage to a Spanish señorita barely out of the schoolroom, but wise beyond her years in the ways of war and men; a careless reference to asking a *ton* beauty for her hand in marriage while on special duty in London. That it had come to naught had not been for his lack of courting her, for all Mrs. Gracechurch had glossed over much of that particular letter and mentioned none of it to others.

No, nothing explained the hard, bitter man Stephen Gracechurch had become—unless it were she herself who was to blame. That she refused to accept despite what she'd said earlier. One had choices. Certainly hers had been bitter, but they hadn't embittered her. There was a difference. She'd selected one road, he another. The more time passed, the more greatly those roads diverged.

She rose wearily from her bed, went to the window and pushed aside the curtains. The new moon hung over the wilderness, a delicate sliver of silver light surrounded by stars, the old moon glowing faintly in its arms. How apt. Like good Sir Patrick Spens to his lady, Stephen was lost to her. And, given the moon, it would come on to storm by tomorrow evening just as it had half way to Aberdeen in the old Scots ballad, for all there wasn't a cloud in the sky as yet.

From below the sound of muffled voices broke the stillness of the night. Suzanne leaned forward, curious despite herself. People knew better than to call at Rose Cottage so late, especially the family. They retired early, keeping country hours. Emeline Dight's good-natured laugh had been clear, the tones of what appeared to be two gentlemen and at least two other women less distinct. Of course, with things as they were at Placidia it was no wonder Emeline and Roger sought refuge with Mother India, if only for a bit.

The murmur resumed after a moment, words indiscernible. She considered donning a gown, combing her hair and joining them. Certainly she was poor company for herself, unable to sleep, unable to cease an endless round of thinking that led nowhere but to another round of thinking. And, with a band about her forehead like a vise.

She pulled a chair over and sat by the window—not so she could tell what was being said, for there was no hope of that, and attempting to follow a conversation when her ability to overhear it was unknown to the participants would have been the height of impropriety in any case—but for the sense of comfort it gave her to know there were others whose lives continued in their customary fashion when her own was in shambles.

Still watching the moon, she leaned her forehead on her hand, massaging the temples.

There would be changes at Rose Cottage, she decided. A governess of the strictest sort would be hired for Aurelia and Delphine, or else a school selected where their fellow students, if not the mistresses, might teach them a little humility and decorum. A school where the other children were the daughters of barons, say, or even viscounts and earls, and who would sneer at country misses so foolish as to believe being the daughters of a knight counted for something in the world. There had to be such places. The lesson might be cruel in the beginning, but it would serve them well in the end. Best of all, when the prospect of elevated acquaintances was extended the girls would leap at the opportunity to quit Rose Cottage, little realizing the change would not be all joy and delight.

And a school for Cassie as well, perhaps—a very different one to get her safely away from their father so she'd have the opportunity to be a child while that was still possible rather than becoming a pawn in another of his self-serving schemes. There might be no need to teach Cassie her place in the world, but there was every need to extend the child's horizons.

Did she dare cut all acquaintance with her father and stepson? What a delightful possibility.

But no, she couldn't even if she had the courage. A distancing was definitely in order, however, combined with consultations with a man of business and perhaps a solicitor. She'd considered it before. Now she'd take the step. Mother India wanted Rose Cottage to herself. With the girls and Cassie provided for and her purse once more firmly in her own hands, she could consider her desire for a separate establishment, perhaps in one of the more respectable watering spots—Tunbridge Wells, say, or even Bath. She'd hire a companion. Cassie would join her on holidays. Perhaps they'd even travel a bit, in England if not on the Continent. Cassie would wed, and she'd become everyone's favorite Aunt Suzanne. The years would pass peacefully, even enjoyably. She'd fade quietly into the sunset of her life, unlamented in Chipham Common or anywhere else.

That the prospect had a bleakness to it she refused to consider. That she loved Chipham Common, if not all its residents, would have to be ignored. Stephen Gracechurch would be residing in the vicinity. Where else could he go, penniless as he was? There was no way she could endure constantly encountering him. Neither was she willing to remain immured at Rose Cottage to avoid him. Far better to find a safe harbor elsewhere. That he might eventually marry, perhaps even one of the Scowden girls, made decamping all the more desirable.

She sighed.

The murmur continued to rise from below, occasionally broken by laughter. She wasn't missed in the drawing room. Once she abandoned Chipham Common she wouldn't be missed in its slightly larger world, either.

She stood, leaving the curtains open, and returned to her bed. Just as she was sinking into sleep at last voices woke her: Cassie saying, "She won't like it, you know. In fact, she may

:ause dreadful difficulties," and Mother India responding, 'She won't have much choice," and then chuckling.

Suzanne stumbled to her bedchamber door and opened t.

"Who won't like what?" she called softly after them.

Mother India turned, peering back at her in the darkness, ace eerily lit from below by her candle.

"You're still awake? Sophia won't," she whispered. "We'll :ell you about it tomorrow. Now return to your bed. You ieed your rest, and certainly we don't want to wake the girls. They've subsided at last."

Mother India, Suzanne, and Cassie were still at the breakfast :able the next morning, Aurelia and Delphine yet to make an appearance, when Emeline Dight arrived at Rose Cottage sans bonnet, shawl or mitts, much winded, totally disheveled, and great with news. Sophia, after creating a Cheltenham :ragedy of their defection the evening before, had ordered :he Dights to depart that very day.

"Will you credit it?" she demanded, arms akimbo, hands on hips. "Sophia said as Oren is no longer welcome at Placidia, neither are we. The home where I passed my girlhood! There are still some rides I wanted to take about the place, and now I won't be able to." She accepted the chair Charles held out, staring from one to the other. "Had a dreadful quarrel about :hat, but she wouldn't listen to reason. Such a contrary, selfish woman!

"So Roger is seeing to sending our mounts ahead and arranging for changes of teams, and his man and my abigail are packing with particular care, for if we forget something you may be sure Sophia won't forward it to us, the witch. Being great with child and insulted by one's husband doesn't call for cavalier treatment of one's sister-in-law. I'm not responsible for Oren's peccadilloes."

"Sophia's showing her true colors at last," Mother India grinned. "There've been hints for years. Could've told you it would happen one of these days, Emmie. In fact, I believe I have repeatedly whenever you desired to bring her up short, as you call it. Patience yields better revenge than action every time."

Suzanne gave the old lady a sharp look, then turned to Cassie. "Is this what you both meant about Sophia causing dreadful difficulties last night?" she asked.

Cassie seemed to consider the matter.

"Yes," she said at last, "I believe it was. Something of the sort at least."

"And the worst of it, Grandmama," Emeline forged on with a quick frown for Cassie, "and this you will *not* credit, Roger was having some improvements made to our traveling carriage? Springing's always been a bit stiff, you know. It's in Little Stoking all in pieces, and Sophia won't permit us to wait long enough to have it put back together. We're having to *hire* a carriage. Ours'll have to follow later, or else Roger'll have to return to collect it. Have you ever heard of such nonsense? What's more, she's ordered the servants not to feed us—not even if we pay for what we consume. Roger is breakfasting at the inn, and I've had not so much as a crust of bread or a drop of tea."

She gazed expectantly from Mother India to Suzanne. "I'm hungry," she said with an attempt at pathos that didn't sit well on the sturdy frame of a raw-boned, independent-minded horsewoman of thirty-five, well though it might once have done for a winsome child of five.

Mother India chuckled and turned to Charles, who was now lurking by the sideboard. "You heard," she said. "Breakfast for my starving granddaughter, if you please. Best bring everything Cook has to hand. Mrs. Dight on the verge of starvation presents a severe threat to the safety of the nation, not to mention that of my household."

"Eggs and gammon, Charles," Emeline called after the departing footman's back. "That, and a slab of sirloin chased past the fire, and I shall do. Oh—and muffins, if you please, with cheese melted on 'em, and some of last night's rabbit pudding if there's any left, and fresh coffee. That'll do as there's already fruit on the table."

She selected a peach, took an enormous bite, chewed and swallowed, sighed, then whirled on Suzanne. "There, that's better! Roger and I've had the most splendid idea," she enthused, taking another bite and brushing absently at the juice dribbling down her chin. "We want you to come with us for an extended visit. What d'you think?"

"How simply super," Cassie burbled.

Suzanne sent her sister a quelling glance, then turned back to Emeline. "I don't believe—I mean, there are the girls, and—"

"With you not here to see to 'em, it's the perfect opportunity for me to send 'em to Sophia," Mother India said quickly. "Always told Oren I wouldn't house 'em forever. Time he learns I meant what I said."

"But Sophia will—"

"Forget Sophia. I intend to."

"But what of Cassie? I couldn't possibly—"

"Oh, Cassie's included in the invitation, of course," Emeline broke in. "Wouldn't think of leaving her behind. Time she saw something of the world. Time you did too, for that matter. Why, I don't believe you've ever been beyond Little Stoking or Timsborough."

"I haven't, but what of—"

"Intend to take Willie, too. Perfect opportunity for me to see if we'll suit. Wouldn't do for a page, Grandmama's already admitted that. Fool notion anyway—turning a perfectly normal boy into a painted doll. Should be a law against it."

Suzanne looked from her sister to the two ladies, head spinning.

"Oh, Suzanne, *please?*" Cassie breathed. "Just think: No Delphine and Aurelia for heaven knows how long, and no Sophia either! What bliss." She turned back to Emeline. "D'you think we could take Duro? He's mine, and he'd miss me."

"Your horse? Tie him on behind the carriage if we're not in time to include him with our string," Emeline said with a twinkle, "or else send him on with your groom. Y'have a groom, don't you? That might be best."

"But," Suzanne protested helplessly, shaking her head, "but this is so sudden."

"No other way it could be, given Sophia. Insisting on invitations issued months in advance won't do when dealing with her. Y'want fun or y'want punctilious: take your choice. I'm offering you fun."

The notion of fleeing Chipham Common and Stephen Gracechurch was infinitely appealing. No more uncomfortable encounters, no more quarrels, no more bitterness or accusations, no more misery—or if there were, it would be misery of a different sort: dull and bearable rather than sharp and unendurable. When she returned—and return she would have to for at least a bit, if only to consult a solicitor and see to finding the girls a school—he would doubtless have grown impatient with her absence, then bored with it and her, and have sought companionship, or whatever it was he desired, elsewhere.

She sensed their eyes on her as she stared at her plate in a dither of indecision, the half-eaten muffin bearing mute testimony to the state of her appetite following another sleepless night. Actually, it was worse than that. What wasn't whole was in crumbs rather than doing her some good. This endless round of anguish and despair had to come to an end. Emeline, bluff and kind and good-hearted, had offered her a way to end it. She'd be a fool not to seize the opportunity. It was what she'd decided she wanted last night, wasn't it? Now running away seemed a cowardly sort of thing to do. Not like her at all, for she'd never run away from anything, not in all her life.

No, that wasn't quite true. She'd attempted it once. And been caught, and brought back in disgrace to be chained to her bed. Running away hadn't helped then. It probably wouldn't help this time, either. Stephen Gracechurch, drat him, had haunted her life since the day they first met. Leaving Chipham Common wouldn't change that, much as she'd like to believe it would.

And yet—

She glanced up. Yes, they were watching her—almost as if what she decided regarding what was after all only a simple invitation to spend some time at her stepdaughter's home were a matter of earth-shaking importance.

"But, I don't see how we can be ready in—" she began.

"Don't babble, Suzanne," Mother India said, a martial gleam in her eyes. "You're going."

"But there'd be so—"

"And there's an end to it. We've only to pack up a trunk for you and another for Cassie, and perhaps some bandboxes, and you're on your way."

Suzanne chewed her lower lip, trying to discern a flaw in the plan. Beyond its unexpectedness, there was none she could see. Cassie would escape their father and his plans. She'd escape Stephen Gracechurch. That was what counted. They'd both escape. For Cassie the escape would be genuine. For her? It would be what it would be.

At last she nodded. "All right," she said, dredging up a smile from heaven knew where, and only hoping it expressed the proper degree of delight and gratitude, "and thank you so much for inviting us, Emeline."

"Think nothing of it, 'Mama,'" Emeline grinned. "Delighted to have you. Not as if we ain't asked you before, but this seems the perfect time to force the issue. Was Roger thought of it, y'know, giving credit where credit's due. Feed you up a bit while you're with us. Y've become decidedly thin and unhealthy-looking.

"Ah," she beamed, turning as Charles reentered the room, "here's my breakfast at last. Now *this* is something like. Just set it all in front of me, Charles. No need to do the pretty. I'll help myself."

Suzanne gave an answering smile that she could tell held more of genuine pleasure and less of artifice than the first. There was no way one could dislike Emeline Dight or take offense at anything she said, any more than one could take offense at a large and rather awkward dog who greeted one with muddy paws and wagging tail.

Then she turned back to her mother-in-law. "You're certain you'll be all right alone?"

"I? Don't be more foolish than you can help."

"I shouldn't like to think of you moping about the place."

"Not a moper, as well you know. Stop fussing. You'll have a wonderful time with Emmie and Roger, both of you. Willie too, I don't doubt."

"There's just one problem." At Mother India's irritated sigh, Suzanne rushed on, "I'd rather not take my abigail with me. I know it's not the thing, but—"

"And still more 'buts'? In this case, my girl, not taking the old besom is most definitely 'the thing.' Don't know how you've endured her all these years. Should've sent her packing—with an excellent reference, of course—the moment John cocked up his toes. Never understood why you didn't. Forever bearing tales to Oren and Sophia, and that's the least of her disloyalties."

In the event the packing, overseen by Mother India's abigail rather than Suzanne's—who declared she suffered from the toothache and took to her bed in a fit of the sulks because she wasn't to form one of the party—was simple enough. Suzanne hadn't that many ensembles to her credit even if one counted her discarded half-mourning gowns, and Cassie only a schoolgirl's essentials.

Suzanne's single attempt at practicality—with so little to bring why not put everything in one trunk, thus being less of a burden to the Dights—met with intransigence on all fronts. Recognizing when she was *de trop*, especially when repressive frowns met every suggestion or attempt to assist, Suzanne gave it up. What, after all, did she—who had never been anywhere—know of packing?

She hurriedly completed the accounts begun the day before and went over them with Mother India. She placated Aurelia and Delphine as best she could when they quitted their bed-chamber well past noon, learned of the treat in store for Cassie and herself, and demanded either to be permitted to join the party or that the visit be canceled on the instant. Nothing could convince them it was proper for Suzanne and Cassie, who bore no blood relation to Emeline, to be offered such a visit when they, who were her half-sisters, weren't.

Mother India, having far less patience with their vapors, finally sent the girls back to their bedchamber with orders not to show themselves until the following morning. Their storm-cloud faces rivaled the sky as they climbed the stairs, threatening to bring retribution down on their grandmother's head as surely as rain would come that afternoon if she didn't treat them with the respect that was their due. The old lady shrugged.

"A firm hand, that's what's needed," she declared as their grumblings faded, "and far less coddling—not that I'm blaming you for their deplorable characters, Suzanne. The damage was done years before you appeared on the scene. Were I ten years younger, I might be cajoled into attempting to regularize 'em. As it is, in the morning I'll have the pleasure of sending 'em to Sophia, bag and baggage, temper and tantrum."

The storm predicted by the moon the night before broke,

complete with gusting winds and driving rain. Infinitely depressed, putting on a cheerful face so no one would wonder what ailed her, Suzanne bustled from room to room, giving the same orders thrice over to the servants and generally making a nuisance of herself. Upon her fourth reminder to Cassie that their father's crop must be returned to him, Mother India handed her the latest London journals and told her to amuse herself with them, whether by reading or transforming them into dolls with scissors and glue pot and paints. When Suzanne realized she'd read the same shipping announcement a dozen times, even she lost patience with herself.

No one knew she was quitting the neighborhood but the Dights, Cassie and Mother India. Certainly Delphine and Aurelia and the servants didn't count. Gazing out the rain-streaked windows in the direction of Chipham Common wouldn't bring anyone to bid her farewell or wish her God speed. Why should she long for such attention in any case? It was the desire to escape it that led her to agree to this mad escapade, wasn't it?

They picked at a hurried late nuncheon, pushing the food around their plates and speaking in distracted half-sentences, and then suddenly it was time to dress for the journey. A messenger from Little Stoking—where Roger Dight was seeing to hired carriage and changes of teams—had arrived with a note saying Mr. and Mrs. Dight would be at the door by dusk.

Head spinning from the day's confusions, puzzled as to why anyone would begin a journey on a stormy night rather than waiting for clearer weather the following morning— surely the Dights could have found acceptable accommodations in Little Stoking as they refused to discommode Mother India by staying at Rose Cottage, but no, given Sophia's insults nothing would do but that they be on their way that very day no matter what the hour of departure—Suzanne climbed the stairs to her bedchamber where Mother India's abigail waited. Protests that she was capable of dressing herself, and preferred to do so, met with the same silence to which she'd been treated during the process of packing.

Giving it up, Suzanne permitted the blue gown of the traveling costume she'd been presented with by Mother India at the beginning of the summer to be whisked over her head, the tapes fastened and the restrained lace stand at the neck adjusted. Next came the jacket with its darker facings and trim.

She sighed, pulling on her gloves and slipping her reticule over her wrist. Then she turned and permitted the abigail to position the stylish matching bonnet with its delicate ruching and deep blue ribbons over her curls, not even attempting to tie the bow herself. The result was entirely too flirtatious for her taste, but she could make adjustments later in the Dight's hired carriage.

As she gazed in confusion about the bedchamber, which had lost what character it possessed with the placing of her few bibelots in drawers for safekeeping until her return, wheels crunched on the gravel drive below. The next moments were a whirlwind of trunk and portmanteaux being stowed and tied down, of kisses and hugs and best wishes and even, to her infinite surprise, a few tears and a definitely tremulous smile on Mother India's part along with a reminder that she was to consider herself and no one else on this particular journey.

Then they were dashing through rain that slashed beneath useless umbrellas and clambering into the luxurious carriage Roger Dight had hired, ankles and cloaks dampened, faces streaked as if from tears, as the muffled coachman—a mere silhouette in the growing darkness—directed the positioning and tying down of the last bandboxes and the securing of a tarpaulin over the whole to keep out the wet. Willie scampered about, jumping and hallooing, but Suzanne's suggestion that the child join them in the carriage for fear he would catch his death met with ridicule on Willie's part and a grin on Emeline's.

"A lad like Willie, choose mollycoddling over riding between coachman and guard?" she hooted. "Shows how little y'know of boys, my dear 'Mama.' They'll shelter him under a scrap of canvas, and he'll have a grand time."

The carriage door was quickly closed and latched, the curtains pulled up from their slots and hooked above the windows against the night. There was the usual polite argument regarding who would face forward and who back, a bit of a fuss regarding lighting the tiny interior lamps, of ensuring the ladies had dry slippers to exchange for their damp boots, and then they were settled with Suzanne and Emeline facing forward, Cassie and Roger Dight across from them.

"How did you find such an elegant rig in a country town?" Cassie demanded as Roger rapped on the roof at last with his walking stick, signaling the coachman that they were ready to be off. "And the team appears to be the very finest in horseflesh, too."

"Isn't Roger a marvel?" Emeline burbled, gazing about her in delight. "So resourceful! He inquired in Little Stoking as to who might be willing to lease a decent equipage for a handsome sum on a moment's notice. The gentleman who owns it was pointed out to him, and as Mr.—Soldiers, didn't you say my dear?—yes, that's it, Mr. Soldiers hasn't the slightest need of it at the moment, he was only too glad to permit us to hire it. Of course this is much better than decent. It's positively sybaritic—far better sprung and more cleverly appointed than ours. Did you get the name of Mr. Soldiers's carriage maker, Roger?"

"I did indeed," Dight assured his wife with a grin. "It'll necessitate a trip to London, but I believe we must commission one from the man."

"Soldiers?" Suzanne said. "I don't believe I recognize the name."

"Y'wouldn't. Same fellow as has bought Stormridge, you see. Doesn't plan to gad about for a bit, being just arrived."

Cassie's sudden coughing fit turned the subject.

Then, though they were barely beyond Chipham Common, Emeline declared herself to be famished. Suzanne and Cassie were hungry as well, weren't they? The wink she gave them indicated they'd best be.

Cubbies beneath the opposing banquettes yielded a pair of well-packed hampers containing all the essentials for a superior meal from soup in a heated earthenware jug to cold chicken, fruits, bread and cheese, and even cream-filled pastries and a tin of French chocolates. Cleverly wrought tables whose presence was masked by exquisite cabinet-work were extended from the carriage doors, covers set, with the Dights facing each other across one, Cassie and Suzanne across the other. Claret in collapsible cups of interlocking silver rings made the meal all the merrier. Five miles' progress saw the travelers somnolent, the remains tucked back in the cubbies, the clever tables once more masquerading as part of the doors.

"How far're we going tonight, Mr. Dight?" Cassie asked, as she knelt to fasten the cubby latches.

"The inn where we always stop when coming to Placidia," he said, flushing slightly. "It's not so grand as a true posting house, but the rooms're clean, the beds warmed, the sheets spotless, and the board excellent."

"Almost as excellent as mine host's cellars," Emeline grinned. "Roger discovered the place when he was courting me. It's where we spent the first night of our married lives—not in the cellars, of course."

"The accommodations are truly excellent," Dight said, then joined his wife in a peal of comradely laughter. "Such a deal of excellence! We should reach the Pompous Ploughman—yes, Cassie, that's truly its name; there's no need to stifle your giggles, for everyone knows it's a ridiculous thing to call an inn—about midnight."

"Roger's sent ahead, so all's arranged," Emeline added. "Punch for him, tea for us, and warmed beds for us all. Tomorrow's will be an easy stage, the next day's easier yet. The trip could be done in two days if we wished, but we're never in that great a hurry no matter which direction we're going. Comes of never taking abigail or man with us. It's servants constrain one to behave with unwanted reasonableness, don't you see, for their convenience. Neither Placidia nor home will disappear because we please ourselves rather than behave as convention dictates."

She had, Suzanne decided as Roger Dight distributed carriage robes to ward off the increasing chill brought on by the storm and sunset, made possibly the best decision of her life when she accepted Emeline's kind invitation that morning. A change of location and companions would surely encourage a change of perspective. Why, she might even return to Chipham Common so altered she'd experience no pangs when she encountered Stephen Gracechurch or his mother in the village. It was clear those who claimed one's troubles followed one no matter where one went had never traveled with the Dights. True good-humored laughter was a sound heard all too infrequently at Rose Cottage. As for Placidia, it might not've existed at all.

At Emeline's urging she and Cassie removed their bonnets and leaned their heads against the soft squabs. Lulled by the carriage's gentle sway as they came upon a smoother stretch of road, by the singing of the rain against the windows, by a feeling of contentment as rare as it was welcome combined with an inexplicable anticipation regarding what the next days and weeks would bring, Suzanne hid a yawn behind her hand, smiled ruefully at her hostess, blamed her sleepiness on the unaccustomed consumption of so much wine, and closed her eyes. Mother India was right, she'd led far too restricted a life to date.

How many hours had passed or miles fled beneath their wheels Suzanne had no notion when she roused to the sound of hurried whispers. The carriage no longer rocked, the interior lamps had been extinguished, the wheels fallen silent.

"We're at the Pompous Ploughman?" she murmured muzzily, shivering and attempting to pull herself erect.

"No, Roger and I are answering calls of nature," Emeline's voice came in the darkness. "Too much soup and wine. We never learn, no matter how much we gad about. You were wise to partake lightly and caution Cassie to do the same. Fortunately, there're some convenient bushes and the rain has stopped for the moment. Go back to sleep, 'Mama.' We've a distance to go yet."

Suzanne sank against the squabs, pulling the carriage robe more tightly around her at the sudden draft when the door was opened. The carriage rocked slightly as a pair of dark forms descended and the door was closed. The barely discernible shape that was Cassie stirred, then stilled. As her lids sank over her eyes the door opened once more, there was some exchanging of places, the door was closed, Roger rapped against the roof with his walking stick, and they were off. She woke with a start some time later as the team was being changed. The only response she received to her question of when they'd reach the inn was a grunt from Roger. She sighed, closed her eyes once more, and drifted off.

When next Suzanne roused gray light filtered around the

curtains. She blinked and yawned, froze, and gazed about her a second time. The speeding carriage held only one other passenger.

"What—What—Why—Where are we!" she babbled.

Across from her Stephen Gracechurch smiled slightly as he unwound the scarf that had hidden most of his face during the long hours of the night and glanced ruefully at the jumble of greatcoats and carriage robes that had passed for other passengers in the darkness.

"About three hours from York," he said, anxious eyes belying his breezy tone. "I should've done this the first time, but callow youths never have the needed disregard for the gabble-mongers of this world if they've the slightest ounce of compunction, and I possessed a heavy load of the stuff. I do apologize for the nine years' inconvenience."

"York?" she breathed, half rising from the banquette, then falling forward at a sudden lurch.

"Your choice," he said, regarding her quizzically as he reached out a hand to steady her. She jerked back, shrinking into the corner and eyeing the carriage door with longing as they rocketed on. "By special license in York, or over the anvil in Gretna Green. And those are the *only* choices I'll permit you."

For all his eyes, smoky in the thin dawn light streaming past the stiff curtains, held a definite twinkle, behind the twinkle lurked what in any other she would've labeled a combination of determination and desperation. Shivering uncontrollably, she lowered the curtains into their slots and stared out first one window and then the other. Moorland rolled as far as the eye could see, stark rock outcroppings silhouetted against a sky that threatened more rain. The prospect was as bleak as she felt.

"You've abducted me," she said.

"You might call it that."

"With the connivance of my mother-in-law, my sister, and my stepdaughter."

"And your stepdaughter's husband—yes."

"They know where I am."

"Not precisely, but in a general manner of speaking, yes."

"And what you intend."

He was leaning back with every semblance of ease now,

egs extended comfortably, arms crossed, head pillowed
gainst the squabs—if one didn't know him well. Only the
light narrowing of his eyes, the thinning of his lips betrayed
aim, and a fist so tightly clenched the knuckles showed white.

"It was Willie first suggested the notion after you left me
o follow you from the wilderness or go to perdition two days
go—or perhaps drown myself in the stream, a possibility
hat held distinct appeal at that particular moment—which-
ver path I chose. I thought Willie's suggestion had a certain
nerit given you and I can't seem to meet these days without
ombing each other's hair. Oh, we start off well enough—
nd with the best of intentions, at least on my part—but that's
ot how we end up."

"The best of intentions? That's what you had by the Weep-
ng Sisters? Then heaven preserve me if you ever take the
lotion to be cruel and spiteful."

"Cassie believed it to be the most splendid idea anyone
ad ever had," he continued, ignoring her.

"Cassie would. I should've realized this madness sprang
rom childish minds."

"Your mother-in-law concurred most heartily with the idea,
xpanding and embellishing it until she considered it perfec-
ion itself. The goal, to put it simply, was to get you in a place
vhere you couldn't turn tail and run away from me again."

She stared at him, caught between the desire to laugh and
he desire to rage at him until her voice gave out.

"Then there was no quarrel with Sophia," she managed.
'It was all a hum."

"Oh, there was a quarrel, all right—a jolly good brawl, as
Roger put it. Things were said that a month of Sundays won't
out right, nor all the apologies in the universe—things Eme-
ine claims needed saying for years. There's considerable justi-
ication for her point of view. She saw to it Mrs. Phelps's fit
of pique became far more than that, as she's finally lost all
patience with her brother and his wife."

"You don't say," Suzanne murmured, intrigued by images
he abbreviated tale created despite herself.

"I do say. Emeline's found a fine husband in Roger Dight,
oy the bye—probably one of the few men in England who
could appreciate and enjoy her for what she is. I despaired
of that happening when I first joined the army, and feared

she'd be cursed with remaining in that household as he brother's despised pensioner the rest of her life. Even offere to marry her. She refused of course, and encouraged me t go, even attempted to cajole Sir John into purchasing me pair of colors knowing how much I desired it and how littl love I had for the tedious round of village life. He refused also of course. In the end, she turned to your mother-in-lav so I wouldn't have to take the king's shilling. Emeline Digh is one woman without an ounce of selfishness to her.

"We're rather like brother and sister, you understand Emmie and I," he grinned at her narrowed look. "The scrape I led her into when we were children were only exceeded b the mischief in which she played tutor."

"And so she's led you into another scrape," Suzann sighed. "This won't do in the least, you know."

"It won't? I don't consider it a scrape at all. I consider i the only reasonable solution to a problem that's been becom ing more insurmountable by the day. I hope you're genuinel fond of both of them, as you can expect to be entertainin, Roger and Emeline constantly, and for the rest of your life.'

"I can? Why?"

"Because I've already issued them an open invitation t come see us whenever they wish, and for as long as they wish We may live on cheese rinds the rest of the time, but wher they visit it'll be buttered crab and pheasant wrapped in grap leaves every night." He scowled then, regarding her narrowl "I'll see to paying our way, my dear," he said after a momen "Able to do that, if not luxuriously—that I promise you. I'v no desire to become your pensioner, nor any willingness t either."

He was still sprawled in his corner, but his eyes had los their twinkle.

"You'll note," he said finally, "that we've just managed t exchange far more than two sentences without brangling. credit it to distancing ourselves from Chipham Common, an the absence of others to play the conniving marplot."

"I also note we're speaking as if to strangers," she snapped "I'd like you to turn the carriage around, if you please, a I've not the slightest interest in either York or Scotland. A for marrying you, heaven deliver me."

"Prefer to live with me without benefit of bell, book an

candle, do you?'' he said with a grin that didn't quite reach his eyes. ''How wonderfully unconventional. Wish I'd realized that years ago. Would've saved us all a deal of trouble.''

''I prefer not to live with you at all.''

''Told you that wasn't one of your choices.'' He leaned forward then, seizing her hands and retaining them firmly when she attempted to pull away.

''And I've never run away from you, not once!''

''Oh no? Let me count the times: by the lily pond, for which there was some excuse; by the Weeping Sisters, again with considerable justification; the day I arrived, and again you had the right. I was a blasted idiot—I've already admitted that. The first Sunday of my return, in the wilderness. Again in the wilderness, just two days ago. Every time I've been reasonable, you've run. Every time I've been unreasonable, you've run. Look at me Suzanne. I said look at me, dammit!''

Reluctantly, and totally against any sense of self-preservation, she raised her eyes.

''Are we back to Dammitsuzanne, now?'' she said, but her voice trembled rather than holding the fire of insult.

''Perhaps, if you force it.''

''Why am I always the one at fault, Stephen? Have you never made an error in your life?''

''Quite a few. Not marrying you out of hand before returning to the Continent was the first and greatest, and to blazes with my father's position as vicar or your father's threats and gratuitous insults. Trying to convince myself I hated you when you married Sir John was another. Not picking up on the multitude of hints in my mother's letters regarding what your life became following that marriage, or the pressures brought on you to get you to the altar, is still another. I've made a plethora of 'em, Suzanne. Why don't we admit that, and then forget them?''

''How comfortable for you. Sweep everything under the carpet, and pretend it never happened? I thank you, no.''

''Better to let the past poison your life? I've tried that road. It's a miserable existence,'' he said bitterly, releasing her hands, jaws clenched. ''I can offer you quite a bit now, you now, if that's what concerns you.''

''There is one thing, and one thing only, that you might offer which I might find of the slightest interest. *Might*, you'll notice—not necessarily would. As you haven't seen fit to offer it—"

"My love? Dammit, Suzanne, is that what you're asking for? My God, woman, you've had it from the moment I first saw you in the churchyard nine years ago! Surely you realize that? Despite myself, despite every dictate of what I considered reason, I loved you, blast it! The entire time. Can you appreciate what it was like, imagining you in that antiquated lecher's bed? I still love you—more than you'll ever appreciate. A supposedly rational man of thirty-six, abduct a staid widow of twenty-eight? With the connivance of such an unlikely cast of assistants, including a daughter who's seven years older than her mother, that even Sheridan wouldn't've dared contrive the farce? Tell me what, besides love, could drive any man to such lengths?"

"Madness?"

"Well, they do claim love is a form of madness," he said shakily. "I'll turn the carriage around if you truly wish it. We'd already provided for that. We all know you quite well, you see. I'll take you to the Dights with no one but Roger and Emeline and Cassie and your mother-in-law the wiser, and court you there properly if that's what you really want, but haven't we wasted enough time already? Nine years, dammit, Suzanne! And these last weeks into the bargain."

And then he was beside her, pulling her into his arms. "Blast it, you little fool, I love you to distraction. Is that the problem? That I haven't said it?"

Her heart in her throat—and perhaps in her eyes as well—she pulled slightly away and gazed at him, their eyes as always almost on a level.

"I find the words difficult," he said, flushing furiously, "but if you need to hear them I'll say them every hour of every day for the rest of my life—I swear it. Only say you still love me and will marry me, and to blazes with the world and its expectations!"

And then somehow she was cradled against him, with one of his hands tangled in her hair and the other gripping her so tightly it was almost painful. "I'm sorry, Suzanne," he murmured, "but I swear I'll do better in the future. Say you'll marry me. Please—I can't stand this."

"York is closer?"

He nodded.

"York, then," she sighed, blushing furiously.

"You're certain?"

"About York, or about marrying you?"

"Both, I suppose."

"Then I'm certain about both. I was never more certain of anything in my life, Stephen." She smiled at him tremulously. "You're absolutely right: we've wasted far too much time as is. And, you may call me Dammitsuzanne whenever you wish, if I may call you Dratyoustephen. We'll even make it part of our marriage vows, if you wish."

"I believe I prefer 'Circe,'" he whispered hoarsely.

He tilted her face by the chin then to kiss her, and it was the same as by the lily pond. This time he understood her closed lips, and was infinitely patient.

"I can see," he chuckled, when finally he released her, pulling her comfortably against his side and wiping away the tears that sparkled on her lashes, "that there's a deal I'm going to have to teach you about men and women and kissing, and quite a few other things as well, I expect. I only hope you'll derive as much pleasure from the learning as I will from the teaching."

And so, nine years later than would have been the case in a rational world, the squire's daughter and the vicar's son were married at last. Suzanne's shock when they pulled up before Stormridge and she learned of Stephen's great wealth and that the luxurious carriage in which they'd traveled was his rather than hired can be imagined. Her disgust at the games he'd played upon his return to Chipham Common was exceeded only by Scully's, though her disgust was tempered by a clear understanding of what her new husband had been about. There'd been scores to settle. She was secretly delighted he'd settled them in both their names, no matter how great her protests, but their happiness, delayed though it was, in the end became the sweetest revenge of all.

Cassie joined them a week following their return, at last and permanently beyond the reach of her conniving father.

The Dights became frequent visitors at the gracious old manor house, and if Suzanne and Stephen's two sons and

single daughter never did understand the precise relationshi
that pair of generous gift-givers and treat-bestowers bore t
their parents, that never troubled them. "Uncle" and "Aunt"
sufficed where explanations failed.

India Phelps banished Aurelia and Delphine to Placidi
the morning following Suzanne's departure, just as she'
threatened. Then, desiring congenial companionship, sh
invited Matilda Gracechurch to join her at Rose Cottage fo
as long as she wished. The two widows, after finding on
house and two ladies accustomed to managing things in thei
own ways not quite as harmonious as they'd anticipate
parted company with the best of good will after a few week
calling on each other daily and at Stormridge almost as fre
quently.

Sophia and Oren's fifth child, when it finally arrived, prove
to be yet another girl. Denied the fortune they considere
rightfully theirs, infuriated to find the despised Stephe
Gracechurch more respected in the neighborhood than the
far wealthier, and with entries into the *beau monde* of whic
they could only dream, they survived bitterly at arm's lengt
under the same roof, each blaming the other for Suzanne'
remarriage and their own diminished prospects. When, man
years later, India Phelps died and it was discovered Cassie wa
her sole heir, an echo of that doughty old lady's triumphan
laughter sounded in their ears for days.

And the squire? He made the best of it, boasting of hi
new son-in-law's wealth and elevated friends, even if that sor
in-law had, as he constantly reminded everyone, married th
wrong daughter. After two untoward incidents, he becam
most circumspect regarding calling at Stormridge, realizin
his welcome there was tenuous at best and that half a loa
was better than none.

Nathan Rothschild, whose sense of obligation and devote
friendship were responsible for Stephen Gracechurch'
wealth? He picked up on the former colonel's pointe
reminders regarding his consols manipulation followin
Waterloo and played the same trick in France, though th
time secretly, debasing the value of the first French nation
loan so greatly that the French, terrified of his ability to affe
their personal fortunes, granted the Rothschild family th
opportunity to float the second. Over the years the two famili

exchanged frequent visits, though Hannah's insistence on calling her "Circe" puzzled Suzanne greatly—a pet name neither Stephen nor Hannah would ever explain.

To say Suzanne and Stephen Gracechurch lived happily ever after, with never a disagreement or dispute, would be false. The appellations "Dammitsuzanne" and "Dratyou-stephen" were not unheard at Stormridge over the years. They were human after all, not figments of a writer's imagination, and continued to have their differences, but as Stephen said at the altar after slipping his ring on her finger, "We'll do better together, Suzanne, than ever we could do apart. You'll see." And, he was right: do far better they did.

Monique Ellis lives in Arizona with her husband of thirty-six years, Jim, a gifted artist and popular watercolor instructor. She is the author of four other Zebra Regency romances: *The Fortescue Diamond, DeLacey's Angel, The Lady And The Spy,* and *The Marquess Lends a Hand* as well as three anthologized novellas: "Lady Charlotte Contrives" (in *A Mother's Delight*), "The Schooling of a Rake" (in *Rogues and Rakes*), and "The DeVille Inheritance" (in *Lords Of The Night*). She is currently working on her next novella, which will appear in the Zebra *Winter Weddings* anthology in January of 1998. Monique loves to hear from readers, and can be reached at P.O. Box 24398, Tempe, AZ 85285-4398. Please include a stamped, self-addressed envelope if you wish a response.

ROMANCE FROM FERN MICHAELS

DEAR EMILY   (0-8217-4952-8, $5.99)

WISH LIST   (0-8217-5228-6, $6.99)

AND IN HARDCOVER:

VEGAS RICH   (1-57566-057-1, $25.00)

DANGEROUS GAMES   (0-7860-0270-0, $4.99)
by Amanda Scott

When Nicholas Barrington, eldest son of the Earl of Ul-
combe, first met Melissa Seacort, the desperation he
sensed beneath her well-bred beauty haunted him. He
didn't realize how desperate Melissa really was . . . until
he found her again at a Newmarket gambling club—being auctioned off by her father to the highest bidder. So,
Nick bought himself a wife. With a villain hot on their
heels, and a fortune and their lives at stake, they would
gamble everything on the most dangerous game of all:
love.

A TOUCH OF PARADISE   (0-7860-0271-9, $4.99)
by Alexa Smart

As a confidence man and scam runner in 1880s America,
Malcolm Northrup has amassed a fortune. Now, posing
as the eminent Sir John Abbot—scholar, and possible
discoverer of the lost continent of Atlantis—he's taking
his act on the road with a lecture tour, seeking funds for
a scientific experiment he has no intention of making.
But scholar Halia Davenport is determined to accompany
Malcolm on his "expedition" . . . even if she must kidnap
him!

ROMANCE FROM JO BEVERLY

DANGEROUS JOY   (0-8217-5129-8, $5.99)

FORBIDDEN   (0-8217-4488-7, $4.99)

THE SHATTERED ROSE   (0-8217-5310-X, $5.99)

TEMPTING FORTUNE   (0-8217-4858-0, $4.99)